# TOWN OF SHADOWS

### SLANTED LONDON, BOOK 1

# JESSICA SCARLETT

*For anyone who's always wished they had a little magic inside
them.
You do.*

# 1

## London, England, 1889
## The Rook

It was said in every parlor room around London that if you stared at the shadows long enough, you might see him move. The phantom haunting the night itself.

Cheapside or West End, lord or peasant—nobody was safe from his thieving grasp. And in the deep of the morning, when the lights sparked in the upper houses and the bystreets filled with the commonfolk, his name leapt to every frightened tongue.

*The Rook, the Rook, the Rook.* Their whispers gathered in the dark until all of London pulsed in terror, a pounding that eased with the eking of dawn.

Tonight, the terror was waning, letting the Rook know he was running out of time.

In bleak moonlight, he searched every surface in the house, his movements no louder than the brush of a finger on a polished banister. Behind paintings, under rugs, in the hidden compartments of every desk. His search always led him to strange objects, relics of the past whose hidden treasures were forgotten to time. Some had been easy to find.

This one was not.

Knowing he wouldn't get to delve deeper into his search until next month, when the daughter was finally gone again, he suppressed a curse. London would never be safe until he found it.

Safe from him.

Footsteps sounded on the street, making him pad toward the study's open window. A muggy blossom scent drifted inside, faintly traced with exhaust from the steel factory to the north.

Outside, two figures walked down the lane, one of them wearing a silver cape that shone under a gas lamp. Brown curls crept from beneath the hood. The daughter. Next to her, an old man hunched, cane tapping rhythmically against the granite paving stones.

The Rook narrowed his eyes, studying the man. It was dark—too dark to see his features but not his spectacles. The owner of the house. His next target.

The Rook frowned, turning his heart to stone. He couldn't wait another month. It was time to resort to more drastic measures.

He slid back from the window, becoming shadows once again.

# 2

## Earlier that day
## Dorothy

I slammed my front door shut and collapsed against it, clutching the new glass burette so tightly I risked shattering it in my hands. A bead of sweat trickled down my temple. *Too close, too close.* I rushed down the hall and into Father's lab, heels clicking on the checkered tile.

Overhead, a web of glass and metal ballooned toward the sky, as if the room were filling with gas, and I set the burette on the worktable on my way to the window. I stood to the side of it and, with a shaky hand, swung the curtain aside, peeking onto the rain-slicked street with one eye.

He was still there. A blueduster in his crisp, navy-blue uniform, standing under a tree. My throat tightened, gaze gluing to his hip where he holstered a slant gun—an enlarged magnifying glass with a trigger. To the naked eye, magic was invisible, but through the lens of a slant gun, he'd be able to see the film of blue dust that clung to a person's hands up to an hour after using magic. The incriminating residue only receded once all the magic particles burrowed back under the skin.

I shuddered. Then—

My blood slowed to a crawl, seizing up in a cold flux that only ever meant one thing. Someone had just used magic—their *slant*.

The tug of magic drew my gaze down the road to a young man hovering his hand over the locked luggage on the back of a carriage. Metal bent under his fingers. Tattered clothes hung on his gaunt frame. He couldn't be older than eighteen—my age.

My stomach churned with panic. He hadn't seen the blueduster. My fingers spidered on the chilled glass, quickened breaths fogging the window. As if I could stop it. As if it weren't already too late.

The blueduster unfastened the slant gun, pointed, and squeezed.

The lens clouded with a chemical, then cleared, and the blueduster blew his shrill whistle. I flinched. He stalked up and clamped his nippers around the young man's wrists before the whistle sounded a second time.

The window muffled the young man's screams, but they vibrated in my bones. Sour bile inched up my throat. Tomorrow, he'd face the gallows. Anyone could possess magic, but the Crown didn't tolerate *using* it.

My attention fell to my curly brown-haired reflection in the window, and then to my hand, fingers still outstretched. I snatched it away, palms caving in as if empty, but I knew the secret they hid. If someone used their magic within my radius, like the young man had, I had no control over the way my own magic reacted by sensing it. Which meant that, if I'd rushed home one minute later and the blueduster had viewed *my* hands through the slant gun first, I'd be the one swinging by my neck tomorrow.

And that was why I shouldn't have gone out to replace the burette, regardless of being on the verge of a breakthrough.

That was why I'd barely left this house for the last three years.

I slowly exhaled. I was safe now. Back among the lonely, choking silence. Stuffing down my frazzled nerves, I turned to what I'd been working on before the first burette had broken this morning and halted my progress. On the worktable, at the top of an open manual read, *Magic and its Chemical Makeup*.

Highly illegal.

The wooden lab door burst open, and my father scurried through, gray hair stringing across his forehead toward his lopsided spectacles. "So sorry I'm late, Dorothy, dear." A few papers wriggled free from under his arm while he tossed the rest onto a counter near the stove. Almost reverently, I picked up the stragglers and joined them with the others before scooting the whole stack away from the burner. The papers contained months —years—of important research.

"I hope you didn't worry," Father went on. After setting his worn leather bag on the table, he cracked it open and started assembling the ring stand to hold the vials.

I cleared my throat and tucked a few wayward curly, brown strands behind my ear. "Not at all." Shoulders setting, I closed the drapes, overlapping them, then locked the door. The servants knew nothing of my magic and knew not to disturb us, but with the image of handcuffs still fresh, I refused to take any chances.

Father filled the burette with five milliliters of lumagenic acid —the same chemical released into the hollow pocket of a slant gun lens once the trigger was pulled, thereby illuminating magic —then fastened it to the top of the ring stand while I readied the flask.

"It's the Science Society dinner tonight," I said. Even though the steam yacht dinners took place on the same day every month, I knew he'd forgotten. Because it was a group of dusty chemists and their families, no bluedusters ever came aboard, and because it was only once a month, the dinners had been deemed safe enough for me to attend. I clung to them like hydrogen to oxygen, despite the danger.

Besides the huge risk I'd taken today with the burette, they were the only connection I had with the outside world. Two excursions in a month was unheard of, much less two in the same day. My heart twisted with longing, but I ignored it. I was used to it.

"Is it?" Father said, shrugging out of his coat. "Well, I'll need my suit pressed—"

"I've already seen to it. And they sent a note, asking for a donation for their auction next month. I gave them a vase."

He sighed distractedly, patting down his plum, ribbed waistcoat. "Whatever would I do without you? Do you remember where I put my—"

I slid his watch down the worktable, and when his wrinkled hands caught it, he chuckled. "Dear me, have I always been this bad?" His brown eyes met mine for the first time since stumbling in.

I kissed his warm, whiskered cheek on my way to the corner stove. "Always." I tossed some twigs into the stove's belly. Once we'd successfully captured the magic and mixed it with the solution, we'd need to heat it quickly to form a few crystals. Then we'd be able to decode it.

I'd just struck a match when Father said, "Mr. Hart will be there tonight, I believe."

My cheeks warmed, and my fingers burned from the flame crawling up the matchstick. I tossed it in. "I believe so."

"Though he isn't a scientist, I've caught you staring at him several times since he began attending the dinners. Him at you too. Is there, uh …," he glanced at me above his spectacles mid-pour, "is there something between you?"

"No," I said quickly, fingers slipping on the handle of the stove as I closed it. Father couldn't remember what type of egg he'd had for breakfast and yet noticed little things like who I preferred to stare at, at dinner. It warmed my heart, even if the reminder stung.

Because it was true. Nothing had transpired between Mr. Hart and me, beyond a few stolen glances and my daydream involving the little freckle above his lip—and nothing more ever could. With anyone. Not until I fixed my situation. I couldn't sieve the magic out of my blood or control all aspects of my slant, but I *could* change the way people saw it. If magic could be used for good—by tracking down the Rook, the dreaded phantom haunting London—maybe everyone would stop fearing it. Eyes would open. Laws would change. I could finally step onto the streets and stop living in terror.

My mouth set. That was why I'd been so desperate to replace the burette—we were so close to a breakthrough. If this experiment went according to plan, my future started today.

"He seems like a nice chap." Father plucked an opaque gem from his waistcoat pocket and turned to me. "Ready when you are, dear."

I nodded and after one last glance toward the locked door, closed my eyes and focused.

In my mind's eye I saw my magic source, glowing, blue, needlepoint pricks of light inside my body. I followed the ever-present impulse and summoned them to my hands, sending them rushing through my blood and leaving it chilled in their wake. One by one, the cold sparks leapt to my palms, condensing into raw magic the size of two drops of water.

Even limited as it was, my head swam with possibilities for the power at my fingertips. As always, the rush was cold and addictive, euphoric and frightening. Maybe that was why they called those who possessed magic *slanted*. There was something not quite straight about it, something a little twisted, a little wrong.

For all the tingling sensations, gathering my magic had only taken a second, and now I was ready. My magic had to do with time. Visions of the future or sensing magic in the present only ever happened *to* me—but seeing into the past, that part of it I could control. I moved my hands in a circular motion until they hit an invisible wall, like a key that couldn't turn anymore in the lock. My magic was spent.

I'd only "rewound" time by five minutes, the most I could ever do. As I let my hands drop, a vision of the past sprang to life around the room. A hollow version of my father bustled through the door, apologizing for being late and dropping blanched papers that fluttered to the floor.

My real father tracked the vision for a moment, muttering, "Oh dear, I hope I haven't looked like that all day." He turned to me, commanding, "Your hands, Dory."

As my past-self closed the drapes, Father rolled the special gem on my palms that acted like a magnet to the magical particles, then dropped it in the pungent ammonia flask and adjusted the burette's flow. The liquids collided, producing a white smoke, and when Father swirled the flask, it illuminated what the blue-duster had seen through the lens. Glowing magic danced in the liquid like a map of tiny, neon-blue stars. Thousands. Millions. Not for the first time, I held my breath in awe.

It was so beautiful. Power in its raw form.

Gently, Father carried the flask to the warm stove and set it there for ninety seconds. When it was finished, he poured a drop and set it between two pieces of glass, then slotted the glass into a metallic device not unlike a slant gun. This one was wider and rectangular, designed by Father specifically for fingerprinting magic.

He fiddled with the toggles, then cried, "I think it's working!"

Over his shoulder, I watched magic and science converge.

The particles transformed into tiny, pulsing symbols; intricate figure eights dissected with a vertical line. The code for magic.

No—*my* magic. No two slants were identical, and as such, everyone's code was different.

Which meant the Rook had one too.

I squeezed his shoulder. "It's working!" A thrill bubbled through my sternum as I turned to Father's papers before penciling in our discovery.

"What *is* that?" Father mumbled.

Something crackled. Father jumped. The device slipped from his fingers and glass splintered on the floor. I stared at him open-mouthed before diving to clean up the pieces. Magic still coated a few of the shards, but it was ... green, now. I blinked at the glass in my hands, eyebrows sewing together.

What the ...

A sharp, burnt smell filled my nostrils, and my head whipped up to find Father's stack of papers going up in flames. But I'd just barely moved them—

"No!" I lunged for Father's coat on the table and batted at the flames. They sputtered and dodged, licking at my hands like they were toying with me. I batted faster.

Finally, they died, and my hold on the coat loosened until it sank to the floor. When I picked up the first research note, it crumbled to ash. *No, no.*

I clawed the blackened pages, heart sinking. We were so close. Now, months of testing and tweaking to find the right balance, the perfect formula for fingerprinting magic and tracking the Rook—gone. The freedom I'd tasted on my tongue receded to the pit of my belly.

Father stood white and shaken.

"What is it?" My voice wobbled as I touched his arm.

His wide eyes turned on me, and my pulse stopped cold at

the fear swirling in their depths. "Before I dropped the device, the magic—it had become contaminated ... It—it—"

"It what?"

"It broke the glass because it *mutated*, Dory."

I frowned. That wasn't ... that wasn't possible.

Magic only mutated when it was crammed into a confined place—like the glass—and bonded with other magical particles that didn't share the same genetic code. Essentially, when two magics converged, because they had nowhere else to go. For it to mutate was so rare, I only knew of one case, and that had ended in hundreds of people dying centuries ago ...

But if this magic had mutated, that would mean—

A trapdoor opened beneath my stomach.

I cast Father a sharp glance, but he had already turned to the blackened remains, muttering something indecipherable. He was too busy working through what went wrong to grasp the most important thing the experiment had told us.

Within the last hour, someone besides me had used magic in this room.

# 3

## Dorothy

"What has Geoffrey been researching, Miss St. James?" Mr. Vernon, the founder of the London Science Society, smiled through his neat white beard. Men in black waistcoats and women in trimmed silk sat around the large table, oil steaming from their plates of fish.

I blinked quickly. Since Father had accidentally burned the findings, there was no proof of illegal activity—but I still couldn't admit the truth. By fingerprinting magic, we could provide the science for following the Rook's magical trail, showing the world that science—and magic—could be used for good. But it was the kind of progress that would change the way London operated, and not everyone was an advocate.

Glasses of water, burgundy, white wine, and champagne lined the top of my plate, selected to complement the diversity of ten courses. Still fighting the burn of disappointment from this morning, I sipped my water glass, buying myself a little time. The course before this one, Father had stepped out of the dining room for some fresh air, so he couldn't answer the question himself. And I ...

I was more used to watching the conversation than participating in it.

"Father's been researching the compounds of lumagenic acid," I said finally, setting my glass down. Maybe it was because of my absence in society that I was unskilled in thinking up lies.

Mr. Vernon hummed in his throat and turned to the man seated at his left. "Isn't that one of the chemicals used in slant guns, Mr. Lennox?"

I ran one hand down the napkin in my lap, using the other to jab a bite of salmon drenched in Dutch sauce as I grappled for nonchalance.

Mr. Lennox laughed then sniffed through his mustache. "Pardon, sir, but I shouldn't know the smarts of it. I only pull the trigger!"

My fork paused halfway to my mouth even as tight chuckles rumbled around the table. Mr. Lennox looked like part of the *ton*, but his dialect betrayed him as a working man. Mr. Vernon had invited a blueduster.

And I was seated at the same table as him.

The salmon squirmed in my stomach like it was still trying to swim upstream, not helped by the light rocking of the steam yacht as it pumped down the Thames. I set my fork down and shrank against my chair, wishing I'd worn something more nondescript than my mother's scarlet silk dress; that I was safe at home among my books. Even off-duty, bluedusters never went anywhere without their slant guns. It was part of their code.

Mr. Vernon nodded magnanimously, stroking his white beard. "Rightly so. But lumagenic acid, it's such an interesting compound ..." The upper half of the table continued on the thread of chemistry, while the lower half moved on to talk of the London Science Society's annual benefit auction, which was only a month away.

My gaze flew to Father's seat down the table, where I

should've found an ally. Still gone. Sweat prickled my neck. Around silver epergnes and fern centerpieces, I spied the door beyond Mr. Lennox's shiny head. *No good.* There was no way off this boat until it docked at St. Katherine's. Hand trembling on the glass, I swallowed more water.

I slammed to the present when I noticed Mr. Hart to the right of Mr. Vernon, his gray eyes pinning me from beneath sweeping brown hair.

*Is there something between you?*

I batted my gaze away.

"I heard the most astonishing news today," declared Lady Faline across from me, the craggy column of her throat bobbing. "The *Rook* has kidnapped another victim, this one a young woman from Kensington. Kensington!" A loud murmur of surprise rippled around the table. "He grows far too bold. The streets are no longer safe!"

"Perhaps you are safer than you might think," Mr. Lennox said with an amused smile, swiping his mustache with his napkin. "It's Yard business. Not even the police got their hands on what us 'dusters know, but I'm not s'posed to talk about it, of course."

Everyone leaned forward in their seats.

"Come, Mr. Lennox," Mr. Vernon coaxed. "We are the souls of discretion, I assure you."

"In that case." Mr. Lennox straightened, delighted to be the important one in the room. He beamed around the table like a king surveying his subjects. "The girl was returned unharmed last night by a ... certain do-gooder."

Excitement charged in the hasty glances between the women. Amid clinking porcelain as the servants swapped out plates, the girl to my left turned to me. Though I'd never seen her at the dinners before, the way half her hair was pinned up told me she wasn't much younger than me. "Can you imagine?" she whispered. "Being kidnapped by the Rook only to be rescued by *him*?"

I blinked. "Who?"

An incredulous chuckle dribbled over her rouge-lined lips. "Why, the Samaritan, of course. The masked man. The hero of London. The Rook's antithesis—surely you have heard of him. He has been bravely returning some the Rook kidnaps."

Father didn't subscribe to the *Times* or the *Post*, but I had picked up enough through the servants to make my brow furrow. "I thought the Rook only stole items. Strange, often useless items. That's what he's been doing for the past three years—"

The girl leaned so close I smelled the salmon on her breath. "That used to be the case, yes, but the switch happened quite suddenly, several months ago. He kidnapped five people last month in the upper classes alone."

My skin tingled.

Lady Faline continued in a louder voice, "Do-gooder or not, I pity the girl—and every other victim! One minute they're there, and the next, vanished, a black rook feather where they were standing only moments before. One must wonder who is next." She eyed the group.

I focused on my plate, nausea worsening.

"I wouldn't mind if it were me," the girl beside me announced boldly with a grin. "Then I might get to meet this Samaritan when he rescues me."

"For shame!" Mr. Lennox gasped, and at his mortification, I realized why I'd never seen the girl before. A blueduster, Mr. Lennox was enjoying his first society dinner too; he must be her father. "Think of your reputation, Sophia."

But his outburst was lost within the others' swirling gossip.

"The Samaritan has hair like smoke and the eyes of a cat."

"A tiger, if he is as strong as they say."

"No—not smoke. My Aunt Aggy says he's more like the *fire*."
The women giggled.

A dry male voice said, "Your Aunt Aggy would know."

I dutifully scooped a bite of glazed mash into my mouth, but my attention was far away. I wanted to dismiss the Samaritan as typical sensationalism, but maybe he really existed.

The Rook, however, had emerged three years ago—around the same time my slant had matured with puberty—and I'd long pieced together a picture of him. He was everywhere and nowhere; a man but a shadow, said to have gotten his name from the rookeries in the East End where the houses were blackened by soot, where the women wore shapeless rags, and open sewage ran through the streets. He'd scratched, spit, and clawed his way out of that hellhole by stealing one artifact at a time.

And he was slanted. No one disputed it. How else could he slip away so quickly, so silently, that no one ever saw a trace of him? Nothing except a black feather. Now, not only was he kidnapping people, there was also someone to challenge him?

*The Samaritan.* A thrill ran down my spine.

One of the women said, "He must be young. And he only rescues members of the *ton*, so clearly, he is one of us."

"And slanted," Sophia muttered. No one else had overheard, but it made me freeze and cast a wary glance toward Mr. Lennox. It made sense. If the bluedusters had superseded the police on this newest case, it meant magic was involved.

Mr. Vernon held up a hand, silencing everyone. "They're not the same, the people that the Samaritan returns." His usually kind eyes held a rigidity that cast a chill down my spine. "There are tales of those rescued, their souls never returned with them. Whole neighborhoods come knocking from the sounds of their unnatural screams. Many of them are forced into St. Bethlem's—and if the madness doesn't get them there ..."

A gloomy silence settled in the room.

Mr. Vernon paused for effect before continuing, "Whatever the Rook is doing to his victims, it's making them deranged. The smallest thing sets them off. Letter openers, thimbles, inkwells. It is more a kindness to the *family*, what the Samaritan does, bringing the shells back for their loved ones to say farewell."

I frowned, not sure I'd prefer that at all.

Sophia raised her chin so high the line of her jaw caught the light. "*I* still say it is a romantic notion. What real harm is the Rook causing if his targets are still alive? They are never physically injured. And if it gives me the opportunity to be saved by the handsome, mysterious Samaritan, I will beg London's phantom to take me." She flung herself back dramatically, bumping a blonde serving girl and sending a wave of orange soup from the dish in her hands toward my dress.

Ice jolted through my veins, a sensation as familiar as the beat of my heart—which stopped cold.

Someone at this dinner table had used magic.

I gasped—too loudly.

Mr. Lennox's attention shifted from his daughter to me. The matrons near me sniffed, and then the stares of the entire table pivoted toward me. Dread made my tongue prickle with heat. My guilty hands fisted my dress, and I ducked my head, gulping in air.

Only to find a large, perfectly circular hole in the hem of my dress, through which the soup had spilled. My mind stuttered on the sight. The serving girl set her dish on the table and hunched over it, emitting a string of anxious apologies.

"It's quite all right," I muttered to her. "The dress isn't—"

Another wave of ice coursed through my blood.

She reared back, revealing what, exactly, she had been fussing over. Which was ... nothing. My lips parted as I pulled the fabric between my fingers.

The hole was gone. Put there and then mended. I glanced at

where my dress had been—where the girl was currently wiping up soup with a napkin. The soup had fallen through the hole and hit the floor, missing my dress entirely.

Magic.

As if she heard the thought, the girl glanced up and we locked eyes, hers widening like a rabbit in a den of wolves. One pull of a trigger, and they would rip both our throats out.

"Is something the matter, Miss St. James?" Mr. Vernon called, eyeing the bowl with orange drips still running down its sides.

*Please*, the girl mouthed from the floor. I knew from her shaking head that using magic had been an accident; the reflex of a girl accustomed to punishment.

I flinched at the sound of Mr. Lennox setting his fork down. Squinting, he drew his hand beneath the tablecloth, and I imagined it reaching for his slant gun. I needed to stop acting so suspiciously.

Turning to Mr. Vernon, I forced a smile even though I wanted to hurl myself overboard. "No," I said in my warmest tone, which wasn't warm at all. I couldn't lie worth my salt, and I was sure it showed all over my face. "I am a bit clumsy this evening. Your staff here was just helping me clean up the mess I inadvertently caused. Please forgive me."

Mr. Vernon's attention shifted between me and the serving girl who slowly climbed to her feet, eyes lowered. "But of course," he said at length.

My limbs shook.

I stood suddenly, and the room filled with the sound of a dozen scraping chairs as the gentlemen rose with me. Including Mr. Hart. I tried to avoid looking at Mr. Lennox altogether. "Please excuse me while I attempt to clean off the spill."

Mr. Hart blinked, lips parting like he wanted to say something. Raising my skirts, I brushed eyes with the servant girl one last time before edging out into the hall and breathing a sigh in the darkness.

I didn't think anyone else saw the serving girl use magic, but maybe some suspected. Hopefully she had enough sense to leave too. Hopefully my departure was all the convincing they needed that the soup had actually ruined my dress. Mr. Lennox might come looking for me. Though my breath tightened at the thought, all I had to do was evade him until we docked. One hour.

I followed the hall toward an alcove on the far end of the yacht, where a thin panel of light slunk under one of the doors.

"No one should have that much power in their hands!"

I froze. Muffled or not, I knew my father's voice—a voice he never raised. I inched my ear nearer; the prickle of curiosity was too strong to stifle.

"That wasn't our agreement," said a deep voice I didn't recognize.

My brow furrowed. He'd slipped away from the dinner for a secret meeting?

"I made that deal before I knew the science," Father hissed. "And look how it's been used. Against my own family! I won't do it again." Something wooden cracked and boots thudded near the door.

I sucked in a breath and pulled back in time for the door to swing open and hide me against the wall. Father stormed out, followed by a young figure I didn't recognize. He turned to the side, the shadows intensifying the scar that dripped over one eye and down the length of his face like a tear trail. Fists locking at his sides, he marched in the opposite direction.

I crept out from behind the door and stared into the empty room, then at my palms. What was used against our family?

*You could use your slant.*

*Turn back time.*

*Find out why that man was threatening Father.*

*Your hands already have magic on them. What's a little more?*

Though I'd used it this morning, enough time had passed that my magic would be replenished by now, incident at the dinner table notwithstanding. I placed one foot in the billiard's room. But then I heard more footsteps coming, and my mind flashed back to a pair of silver handcuffs sealing a young man's fate, and I turned and scurried to the empty foredeck.

The moon was a pale lantern lighting our path. Somehow, our carriage broke an axle a few blocks from home, and Father insisted on traversing the rest on foot, saying the walk would be good for his health even though it was the opposite. His lungs could only handle so much outdoor air before devolving into wheezing, scraping fits.

Chilly air seeped through my silver cloak as I gripped his good arm. The eerie quiet deepened, raising the hairs on the back of my neck.

Breaths labored, Father said, "You didn't return to the table for the rest of dinner. Were you not feeling well?"

I shook off the feeling we were being watched to say, "The salmon didn't agree with me." I didn't want to tell him about my sensing magic and staying away to be safe, both because the streets had ears, and because he already worried himself sick about me leaving the house. As it was, I was rethinking the dinners altogether. The idea of not having one place to associate with other people made it difficult to breathe, but ... it wasn't worth the risk.

"Are you all right, Father?" I asked quietly. "I saw you leave the billiards room with a man earlier. You were both so angry."

Father's cane grated the cobblestones as he turned abruptly. "You must never speak to that man, Dorothy. He is dangerous."

"Then why were you speaking to him?"

"Because he—" With a rasp, his lungs gave out. His inhale was like glass grinding together, each cough churning the pit in my stomach. I stroked his back and the feather-fine hair peeking out from his top hat as I waited for his puffing to subside.

When it finally did, Father patted my hand and trudged on to the deep chimes of Big Ben a few blocks away. Two in the morning.

Not wanting to re-aggravate his cough, I decided not to press the matter, at least for tonight. Dark circles rimmed his eyes, which were already foggy and slow to blink. Once he'd rested, I'd probe further and help him.

I thought of the man with the scar. If I hadn't heard it with my own ears, I'd think it impossible to anger Father. He was the kindest, most-generous man on earth. He wouldn't wish a bad cup of tea on his worst enemy.

When we finally stood outside the cast-iron fence of our townhome, Father turned to me again, his usually calm expression troubled. "I hope I haven't inadvertently pulled you into everything." He sighed, and it sounded more from his heart than his throat.

I took in his clouded gray eyes. Not understanding. "Did he threaten you? Take something from you?"

"Take," he said, almost to himself. His features tightened, voice dipping to a despairing pitch. "They are all takers, Dorothy. Every one of them. They'll steal your mind, your magic, your heart, your soul. It is what they *do*. But it is only a good man who will give them back to you, and until he does, don't believe that he's good at all."

My mouth parted, not recognizing this version of my father and wanting to ask who *they* were, but he turned and hobbled up the steps, leaving me to watch his retreat with concern. Something more had happened that he wasn't telling me. I followed him into the house and helped him out of his overcoat in the entry.

"I am miserable company tonight, I'm afraid." He unfastened his cufflinks, mumbling, "Now where did I put my—"

I extricated a scientific journal—his nightly reading material —from the pocket of another coat hanging from the wood-paneled rack and handed it to him.

He breathed an amused sigh as he took it. "How I love you, Dory, dear." His wrinkled hands cupped my jaw as he kissed my forehead, adding, "Goodnight," before shambling up the second set of stairs leading to his rooms.

I stared into the darkness, thinking for a moment. Then, instead of taking me to my own bed, my feet led me to the great hall and stopped in front of my grandfather's statue; a lonely clay figure in a marble-cased room. The moonlight peering through the drapes lit up half his face.

Bad men, good men. I didn't understand and felt instinctively like I should. It felt like a puzzle Father wanted me to solve.

Grandfather would've understood. Perhaps that was why he hid the dangerous, magical object inside his likeness, away from a world filled with power-hungry men. Perhaps that was why he'd entrusted that secret to me instead of my father, who would sacrifice almost anything in pursuit of science.

Skittering in the hall drew my attention. Beatrice, clad in her white gown and cap, held a candle.

"Beatrice, why aren't you abed?" Only after I asked the question did I notice the teacup in her other hand.

She halted. "'e asked me to bring him some buttermilk, to 'elp 'im sleep, miss."

I must've been wrapped in contemplation longer than I thought. I smiled and took the cup from her. "I shall take it to him, thank you."

She dipped a curtsy and retreated. On weary feet, I climbed

the stairs. Under his door, a panel of light flickered from the candle within. I gave three soft knocks. "Papa? I have your buttermilk."

When there was no answer, I twisted the knob anyway. He must've fallen asleep.

But the room was empty. I checked his favorite chair, behind his dressing screen, inside the adjoining bathroom, but he was nowhere. "Papa?" I called again, louder. No clothes littered the floor, or shoes, and his books remained untouched on the shelf. Nothing was out of place, and yet a candle burned on the stand and his blankets were rumpled from where he'd sat on the bed, scientific journal lying next to it. And ...

Something rested on his pillow. Something I hadn't noticed when I walked in. Something black.

I stared at it, limbs numbing, vision clouding with disbelief. I set the cup of buttermilk on the desk and forced my feet to move, forced my hand to pick it up. The moment I did, my thoughts clicked into place, and I let go as if it had scalded my skin.

The rook feather fluttered back to the bed.

I panted, shaking my head. I didn't realize I was backing up until I bumped into something wooden and my bracing hand knocked the buttermilk to the floor with a smash. Milky liquid oozed into the cracks between floorboards.

My hands trembled from gripping the desk, but it felt like they were around my own throat. I couldn't let go. I couldn't breathe. What if tonight was the last time—

Time.

He couldn't have been kidnapped more than a few minutes ago.

I couldn't change the events of the past, but I could *watch* it. *Listen* to it.

Rotating my hands in a circle, I sprinted to the foot of the bed, a choked plea at the root of my tongue. Magic spent, I dropped my hands.

The candle flickered, but the room looked the same.

When I spun wildly around, my toe hit something loose, kicking it away until it reflected the light. The steel button was solid when I picked it up and thumbed over its depiction of a roaring lion, so it couldn't be part of my vision.

And it wasn't one of Father's.

A flicker of movement at the window caught my eye. Someone's breath bloomed on the glass, obscuring their face. Gooseflesh raised the hairs on the back of my neck. A card slid between the window slats and arced downward, flipping the locking mechanism back into place.

I gasped a quiet, broken breath. I flew to the window and threw it open. But my vision sputtered out and when I glanced at the ground, the shadow was gone.

# 4
## Ashley

The only thing stopping me from jumping for joy was the fact that I was currently manacled to a wall. I tried to sit up straighter, pulling on the chain which anchored our wrists to the slab of stone above our heads. My elbow knocked into Miles, making him eye me with a frown I pointedly ignored.

Four pairs of footsteps passed our cell and the adjacent door groaned on its hinges, admitting what I assumed was its doomed occupant. Then came the sound of jangling metal, an authoritative voice giving orders, and another sound not quite as distinguishable:

The hushed babbling of a lunatic.

I grinned. Finally.

"You know, the smell down here really isn't that bad," I said around the pin in my mouth, in perfect synchronization with the water drips echoing from the corner.

Miles coughed. "Not bad? I can barely breathe."

"I rather like it. Who would've thought molding wood, rotting apples, and decaying flesh would combine so nicely? And the rat droppings give the air a certain" —I breathed deeply to prove how little it affected me, but then choked— "unforgettable quality," I wheezed.

"No kidding."

A guard's boil-ridden face pressed against the bars in our door. "You boys keep it down! Or I'll fetch the warden!"

Twenty-three hardly warranted the term *boy*, but as I was still chained, I decided to let it slide. After a glare-filled moment, the guard returned to his duties.

I leaned back, peeking around my arm at Miles. It was difficult to tell with his head hung low and brown hair obscuring his eyes, but something in his shoulders told me he was in a foul mood. "They should bottle it," I continued. "Make a fortune. I happen to know four ladies who would drop a guinea for *parfum de rat*."

"They wouldn't buy it for its smell, but rather for seeing the flash of one of your stupid smiles."

"You mean this one?"

Without looking at me, Miles said, "Yes, that one. And stop it. It's annoying even when I don't have to look at it."

"I don't understand what's got you hot under the collar. It's not like we've been here a week or can't move our legs. And we did *just* eat, a day and a half ago—"

"You know, the worst thing about this situation isn't the smell" —Miles raised his head, eyes closed in forced patience— "or my chafing wrists or even being chained up for the better part of two days. It's being forced to sit here and listen to the blathering of an idiot."

"If your own blathering annoys you so much—"

"Black fog, Ashley!" Miles rattled his chain, teeth gritting. "You drag me down to St. Bethlem's, steal the warden's keys, somehow manage to *lose* said keys by dropping them in a boiler which *tipped over* from you jumping after the keys, setting fire to a patient's room and getting us committed in one fell swoop.

If it weren't for you, I'd be in a soft bed enjoying a nap or a warm cup of tea, so the least you could do right now is shut. Up."

I settled back against the stone, unfazed.

The mysterious dripping continued, now joined by nonsensical muttering leaking through the stone. Somewhere in the hospital an ululation scaled to an ear-ringing pitch and broke off on a discordant, choking sound, raising the hairs on my neck. The torch on the far wall shivered and the shadows grew darker.

"You'd rather listen to *that* than my voice?"

Miles glared. "I'd say the sounds are pretty interchangeable."

In the room next door, a key ground into the lock and the voices and footsteps retreated. "Finally," I muttered.

"You're still talking. You never listen to anything I ..." Miles drifted off as my manacles clanged to the ground and I got to my feet, dusting off my trousers. The wet mud that layered the ground had glued tiny rocks, bits of straw, and other unmentionable things to the fabric. At the thought, I examined my hands, a grimace tightening my face. My wrists were red and swollen, but those I ignored.

"I don't believe it," Miles said in a slow voice. "You picked the lock."

"I picked the lock." I twisted to the side, stretching out my cramped muscles. Bloody silt, I was sore.

Miles was a difficult person to read, but I didn't need to. I'd acquired the ability to sense the shifts in his mood, almost like it was my slant. And now, even though his face was blank and his tone even, I could tell he was annoyed.

"You could've freed us the minute these were slapped around our wrists, yet we've been strung up like a pair of fools."

"Who do you take me for—the Samaritan?" Since I had been waiting for the madman next door to return, I couldn't free us until this moment, but I didn't bother mentioning that. Miles had probably already deduced it. Alternating my stretches, I instead said, "And *you* were the only one who looked like a fool."

Miles knocked his head against the stone, hard. Twice. A plea to a higher power to grant him patience. "I should've known. I should've *known* you did this on purpose—"

"When are you ever going to learn?" I kept my tone dry as I got to work on his manacles. Though I didn't look at him, I could feel his stare as the metal clicked open and fell away. Despite his anger, Miles grunted in thanks and rubbed his wrists.

By the time he'd hobbled to his feet, I was at the northern wall. The passages in this basement were as twisted as their patients' minds, and after the *key* incident, we'd been shoved below the hospital's pristine façade and into this glorified receptacle reserved for especially troublesome occupants. But I knew the way out.

The illusion I'd been holding flickered and died, exposing a hole in the stone big enough for a man to climb through—a present from the girl occupying the cell before us, so we might question the madman next door. She'd provided the hole; I'd provided her freedom.

My magic seemed to breathe a sigh of relief, sluggish in the way it returned to me, like the last drop trickling out of a large pitcher. Another few minutes and it would've been spent, which surprised me. I couldn't remember running out of magic before. I'd never cast an illusion for two days straight, either.

Miles didn't react and simply followed me through the hole. The torch beyond our grated door hadn't been bright, but at least we'd had one, whereas this cell had no light, probably to hide the hideous smears on the wall.

But it couldn't hide the worsened smell. Rank, sour, and thick enough to burn your nostrils. Miles gagged beside me.

Unlike us, the man in the corner was bound by his ankles. A

filthy pair of wool trousers frayed above his knees, his bare chest streaked with sweat and dirt, his sunken eyes glowing in the darkness. A graying beard stroked his collarbone with every shake of his head. He didn't seem to register our presence. And he was muttering.

"Filo ... lock me up ... what a shocking bad hat ... filo ... can't get the tea ... filo, filo ... doesn't matter for the children ..."

A lump formed in my throat as I took in his long, thin limbs, feeling a sliver of anger toward the guards for their neglect. Then I moved toward him.

"Ashley ...," Miles called in warning, but he didn't stop me. He never stopped me.

Up closer, I saw that the charred stone behind the man bore thousands of scrapes, his chipped nails stained dark with dried blood. Repressing a shudder, I crouched in front of him.

The man's muttering paused, and he looked up. "Samuel." His head tilted with a misshapen smile. "You're all grown."

"I am not Samuel," I replied kindly, "but I am here to ask you a few questions."

"Always with the questions. Always knowing, never guessing."

My eyebrows twitched down. Miles drew up behind me, and I could feel his wariness, his hands itching to reach for his slant. He didn't like this.

I didn't like it either, but I refused to show it.

"Do you remember how you got here?"

He shook his head, but it seemed unnatural; all stiff and shaking, like he was flinching from my question rather than answering it.

I leaned forward. "Who made you like this?"

"No," he croaked, eye slamming closed, open, closed. "No, no, no, filo, no, no."

I slipped two fingers into the neckline of my loose linen shirt, pulling it aside to reveal the brand beneath my collarbone. "Have you seen this before?"

His gaze shot to me. "Seen it, seen it, what a shame, what a nice bit of skin. Never touched it, seen it, never touched me ..."

I stood and sighed. It was impossible to tell how much he understood, and how much he was revealing. Maybe this had been a fool's errand after all.

I held in indecision. I only had a few drops of magic left, drops I'd been saving for our escape, until the madman's arrival had taken longer than I'd accounted for. With the guards checking on us so frequently and lingering for varying lengths, I'd been forced to use my slant to cover the hole constantly. It would be foolish to waste the rest of my magic in the hopes that this man might tell me something. He clearly didn't even know what he was saying.

Then again, I didn't need much. All I needed was *something*.

"One more question." My hands twitched and with the dregs of my magic, the illusion sprang to life, changing my appearance to look like someone else. To look like the man I had seen a week ago.

The man screamed and recoiled, heaving against the stones. "No, I'm sorry! I told you I was sorry! The north cliff, the north cliff, don't go back—*can't* go back. No Edmond, no help. Please, no fire!"

The illusion sputtered out, my magic completely spent. My gamble had paid off; he'd seen the shadow too, and even though my chest twinged at the raw fear in his eyes, it had been worth it. I straightened in satisfaction.

Through the man's shrieks, Miles said, "We need to get out of here. Someone will have heard him."

"You think they pay attention to outbursts here?" Joints stiff, I examined the keyhole in the tepid light. It was pickable, but it would take a few minutes. I set to work, doing my best to ignore the wailing from the corner. My heart gave an annoying little tug, but there was nothing we could do. He'd already lost his mind. His very presence here meant his family had abandoned him, which meant the only merciful thing would be to put him out of his misery. I couldn't do that.

"Save me, save me twice—never him. Couldn't take it. Edmond. No fire. Take it all ..."

Miles stilled. "Who is Edmond?"

I knew Miles was asking me, not the lunatic. In the lock, I twisted the pin, driving it left, right, deeper. Just like the truth. "A son. Or a brother. A stranger he owed money to. What difference does it make?"

Miles's breathing shifted, telling me he was dissatisfied with that answer, probably because he sensed more that I wasn't telling him.

It didn't matter. That wasn't why I was here.

The crazed man's ranting grew louder, his movements turning wild and vicious. "It's the fire. You can have it! You can take it, Edmond. Take it all!" I glanced in time to see his fingers extend as a burst of fire shot from his palms and struck Miles in the chest.

Ah. That explained the charred stone.

Knowing my friend was more than capable, I resumed picking the lock. Miles swore and patted at the flames. It wasn't enough. He dropped down, rolling on a ground that was more excrement than mud. When he had successfully suppressed the fire, he staggered to his feet and gagged again.

In our line of work, it happened more often than either of us preferred.

Voices drifted through the corridor, the low timbre of the warden and his guards. Through his gagging, Miles managed, *"Ashley."*

"I know. Just a few more—" The lock clicked. I smiled and the door swung open.

The madman screamed, fingers extending again, but he must've exhausted his slant, like me. Miles ducked into the dark corridor, but I hesitated, studying the man's sickly pallor once more.

"No time," Miles urged.

I ignored him. Miles's groan followed me into our old cell where I retrieved our bowl of gruel. It looked disgusting—why we hadn't touched it—but it was all I had. Before I could set it down, the madman grabbed it from my hands and gumped it down.

"I'll bring a roast next time," I quipped, but something warmed in my core, knowing it had been worth the delay.

When I joined Miles's antsy form in the hallway, the warden emerged on the other end, flanked by three guards. They sprang into a sprint. "Oy!"

"Run or fight?" I muttered to Miles.

"You dullards—!"

"Your call," Miles muttered back.

"What are you doing in that cell? What are you doing *out*?"

I smirked. "Fight."

# 5

## Miles

I sighed, every muscle knackered from disuse. Just once, I wanted Ashley to say *Run.*

When the warden swung, Ashley ducked and slipped to the side like a cat, slamming the warden into the stone floor and spinning toward the next target.

I struck half a beat after, stopping a burly guard's downward swing by smashing his arm into the wall with my shoulder. Crying out, he dropped his truncheon. The arm was broken.

"No need to save your strength, Miles," Ashley joked as the guard fell.

"I don't see you holding back either." Tired or no, breaking bones was only a piece of what we'd been trained to do.

I nabbed a taller guard's wrist and twisted it behind him, then kneed him so hard he dove headfirst to the ground. Ashley met the last guard with a blow to his stomach while I took care of the crumpled forms who considered rising.

Adrenaline heightened my senses, the brackish taste of glory on my tongue. Fighting alongside Ashley was like breathing. Easy. Reflexive.

The second the last guard hit the stone, we ran down the corridor and up some stairs, me following the blur of Ashley's wavy, black hair as he navigated the tunnels.

I didn't *think* he knew the way, I *knew* he did. If he'd planned this, he knew every entrance, every window, every doctor, the names of every cell and occupant. I wouldn't be surprised if he knew how many rats lived here, or the number of shadows.

And it meant he'd sprung someone out of this place, so we could occupy their cell. I was annoyed, yes. He had a habit of mapping out twelve steps ahead of me. I'd long given up trying to anticipate him and simply learned how to adapt to the situations he thrust me in, because his forethought had saved us more times than I could count. With Ashley, there was *always* a reason.

Maybe I'd sensed the asylum was part of Ashley's plan—but hadn't asked because I knew I wouldn't like the answer.

The constant danger thrilled me, but after two years, I couldn't deny it was also starting to wear.

We breezed past a lonely torch, making it flicker. Moaning came from above and below, the very walls bleeding with their cries and eerie laughter. I shuddered and ran faster. Ashley twisted up more stairs where a hint of sunlight peeked at the top. But once we reached the landing, Ashley continued the ascent.

"Isn't the exit—"

"Guards," was all he said. As if on cue, more shouting rang behind us, sentries pushing past nurses in hats that looked like wide, folded napkins. Boots pounded. Shrill whistles pierced the air.

My muscles cramped. Ashley didn't stop at the next level, or the next. He went up, up, up, up, and suddenly I knew why he'd brought me along; why he'd asked me to store the glider in my coat three days ago. A hard knot of dread formed in my gut.

A staircase spiraled into a vaulted ceiling, and after taking the stairs two at a time for what felt like an eternity, we reached a trapdoor. Ashley banged it open, leading us onto a very small, very high columned platform.

Below us, atop three stories filled with patients, soaring pillars formed a circle the width of the hospital, supporting a copper dome. And on top of *that* dome were the pillars I was currently gripping for dear life.

The ground rushed up at me, and I started sweating in the cool breeze. Ashley looked at me expectantly, at the pockets of my coat. When we were "admitted," the guards had stripped me down, searched my clothes, then gave them back, because my coat was empty.

They were wrong.

Or rather, wrong that it was empty for *me*.

I braced a shaking hand against a pillar.

When I still didn't reach into my pocket, Ashley prompted, "There's no time to think about it."

"Says the man who never thinks about anything," I fairly spat. It wasn't true, but it felt good to say.

"Pull it out."

My breath hardened in my chest. "Pull what out?"

"I know you have it in there."

"Let's just use the rope." My slant also hid a thick coil in this coat that had gotten us out of many scrapes in the past. And it was significantly safer than *that*.

"You know the rope won't reach," he said. "They'll lock us up here forever."

I blinked at the little dots of people walking into the entrance. "Sounds like the lesser of two evils."

"If you think I'm going to spend another minute rotting in that cell next to your smelly—"

"So now you hate the smell. Now that it's *convenient* for you."

The din of guards grew louder. They were climbing the spiral staircase. We only had seconds.

I swallowed. "Can't you illusion us invisible?"

He puffed an exasperated breath. "I'm out of magic."

"As in, *out*-out, or—"

Ashley extended his palms as if I could see his depleted stores. "I'm *out*, Miles."

Blimey.

I spun around. Two heads emerged from the trapdoor. More bobbed behind them. I jammed my hand into my coat and closed it around the glider.

Magic vibrated through my blood, and when I extended my hand and opened my fist, the glider sprang into being. As large as a bed, it dove off the edge. Together we jumped on, narrowly missing the guards grasping for our legs.

The glider wobbled and pitched left, circling around the dome and the confused, raging men on the platform. A draft of wind blew us up, and I clung to the edge of the craft with white fingers as we soared high above the trees of St. Bethlem's and the surrounding streets. Tiny drops of condensation pelted my face.

Taut strings connected the wings to form a massive spade, which attached to the platform base below with poles. The base was barely long enough for me to sit in front of Ashley comfortably, though there was nothing *comfortable* about the way I crouched in terror. Another pole finned in the back, acting as a rudder.

Ashley whooped and got to his feet. "Now this!" he said over the roar of the wind. "This is the way to get around London!" While we glided through peaks of smoke rising from blackened chimneys, I trained my eyes on the clouds.

"West," he yelled, altering my hold on the rudder, and the glider veered right.

My gaze flicked to the horizon. "Black fog," I quietly swore, blood draining from my face, "not the Thames."

But Ashley heard me. I knew he did because he smiled that confounded smile.

Over the side, the traffic of Lambeth Road rushed up at me, making my hands sweat. Far below, people stopped, pointed, yelled, causing carts and carriages to collide in the streets. There were no open fields to land in this close to the heart of London. Our best bet was to drop in the river and hope that the people on the far shore hadn't noticed our strange contraption—and who knew how long it would be before Ashley could disguise our faces.

I hated swimming. I hated mud, and filth, and lunatics, and heights, and nearly everything about the last hour.

And Ashley. I hated Ashley most of all.

"I need information on someone," he said, and I knew he was mapping out his next four moves. "Sir Geoffrey St. James's daughter."

"As long as it doesn't require any wooing."

Ashley laughed and despite my airsickness, I felt a corner of my lips tug too.

"Would that really be so bad?"

"Thanks to my mother's wish to see me married, I have more than enough seducing in my future, thank you very much."

"Poor Miles. Forced to seduce a woman to satisfy his relatives. I bet you even make eye contact with her too."

"If I'm feeling especially amorous."

The Thames loomed before us, a winding stretch of brown amid the smoky landscape. We lost the air currents, and the glider angled down, picking up speed. Then we dove toward the water and Ashley shouted something. I wrenched the glider back into my coat. And then we plummeted.

We hit the water, and it bit into my skin, making me puff in a few breaths when I broke the surface. The river was murky, but after the refuse of the hospital, I was grateful for the rudimentary bath.

We swam ashore and collapsed on the muddy banks, out of breath, rolling onto our backs while the water lapped our feet. Back on the river, a penny steamer pumped its way across. Birds scavenged the ground, one of them pecking at the hem of my trousers.

"If I had sixpence for every time you've risked my life," I breathed, shivering in the cold breeze.

Without turning to me, Ashley reached over and patted my chest. "Don't spend it all in one place."

Mud wet my cheek as I glared at him. I was furious, for the last two days. For the last fourteen years, far more exciting than the ten I had before we met. But I'd made a dying man a promise to stick by Ashley's side, and I would, always; until we brought justice to the city, and I could finally return to the sea, the only place that had ever felt like home. "I'm assuming there was a point to all that."

"Yes." Ashley chuckled. "Oh, yes." His chest was still heaving, but his unsettlingly green eyes met mine. "I know who he is."

# 6

## Dorothy

"Come on," I muttered, emotion fogging my vocal cords as I studied the magical particles rippling under the glass. I waited a full minute. Two. No magical code appeared.

Spills from dozens of solutions puddled the worktable, the heat from the stove in the corner forcing me to mop my forehead with my sleeve. I'd used my magic sparingly all morning, only replaying the past a few seconds at a time so I had enough to experiment with, but it had yielded no success.

Eyes prickling, I set the glass on the worktable and fished the button from my pocket, studying the glistening steel lion for the millionth time. It was all that was left of Father—that, and a black feather.

My meeting with a blueduster in the parlor yesterday had been a disaster; the officer had taken no notes, rambled about a case list that "stretched from here to Manchester," and implied it might take weeks until they could begin an investigation.

*Weeks.*

The quickest way to find Father was to find the Rook—and to track him, I needed to recreate the formula that could fingerprint his magic. I couldn't hire a private investigator without word reaching my uncle. I was not a blueduster. I didn't know the first thing about finding and following a magical trail.

I was just a girl with a flask who couldn't go outside.

And who, apparently, couldn't recreate an experiment if her father's life depended on it.

I returned the button to my pocket and consulted my breakthrough chapter again. I'd followed everything perfectly. Father must've done something more while I wasn't watching, which told me I needed to do more research.

But obtaining books meant going ... out.

My stomach clenched in dread, before a vision of the future seized me—the third leg of my slant.

*"Beatrice?" my uncle's chilling voice called while my aunt and two cousins shucked their things in the foyer. Uncle Benedick wandered down the hall, stopping at the door to the lab before turning the knob. His dark eyes flickered in mounting rage as he took in the apparitions from my magic, then the blue particles floating in the flask.*

The vision closed, there and gone in the span of a few seconds.

I could rewind time, see the future, or sense magic in the present—but only the first could I control, and a rush of pumping dread shot me forward. Uncle couldn't see me using magic, but, perhaps more importantly, couldn't discover Father was missing.

I locked the lab and rushed to the mahogany mirror hanging in the parlor. My eyes were puffy and red, but I anxiously smoothed my hair and pinched my cheeks to the sound of the front door admitting the chatter of my relatives, neatly avoiding the more disastrous turn of events.

The visions occurred infrequently, but they tended to happen whenever I most needed them. Magic was strange that way: living, breathing. Helpful one moment and elusive the next —but always, *always* loyal.

I'd seen it inching back to me plenty of times under a microscope, like it *knew* me. It was just a theory of mine—there was still much about slants that we didn't understand—that magic seemed to be an extension of one's subconscious. An omniscient presence that willed the best for its host.

That was what made magic so dangerous once it mutated; it became not just alive, but sentient, willing to sacrifice anything to make its host's deepest desires a reality. Even if it killed him. And, as it mutated, it became increasingly difficult to control. That was Father's theory, anyway.

Uncle called my name. I squared my shoulders and entered the foyer.

Uncle Benedick loomed over Beatrice, ordering which rooms to prepare and what to serve for dinner. My cousins, Emmeline and young Clarence removed their coats. I avoided looking at Aunt Marie altogether, whose resemblance to my father was uncanny.

"Uncle." My low-heeled suede shoes clicked against the tile as I approached. "We were not expecting you." Behind my back, my nails dug into my palms, but I forced my lips to smile.

"We had some shopping to do before the official start of the season." Smoothing back his thick, dark hair, he turned to me, and his piercing gaze narrowed. "Why is Geoffrey not here to greet us?"

I cleared my throat in preparation for the lie. "He's gone to the house at Brighton, for his health. I'm sure he would have delayed his trip had he known of your arrival."

"Given how you look, perhaps you should've joined him."

Knowing he held the mortgage to the house, I fought the urge to retort. In the past, he'd threatened, in not so many words, to repossess it. It was my mother's house, and it'd pained Father to consider losing it. We'd all settled into a strained, unspoken agreement: we could keep the house so long as we didn't upset Uncle too much. How he liked appearing the benevolent relative.

"Forgive my appearance," I said. "I've a headache and haven't been sleeping well." At least it was the truth. But with him here, everything was bound to get so much worse.

He strode up the stairs without another word, and I relaxed, marginally. Aunt Marie offered me a weak smile in the way of greeting before following her husband. Its sweetness was so like my father that I had to swallow.

Clarence stepped forward, swiping strawberry-blond curls out of his eyes on a head that barely reached my chin. "Where's the potassium nitrate?" He pulled out a corked glass of a grainy, white substance.

Sugar. Potassium nitrate. Sugar bomb?

Father kept some on a low shelf in his lab, but no one was allowed inside except him and me. "Why don't you check with Cook?" I said at last. As he scurried down the hall, I called after him, "And don't let that off in the house."

Emmeline sauntered forward, calling my attention back to her. We shared a look, and she seemed to sense there was more to the story. At last, she said blandly, "You do look terrible."

I sighed, grateful to be alone with my cousin. A year younger than me, she was the only one of her family I could trust not to report back to my controlling uncle. "It can't be that bad."

She raised her eyebrows. My blood chilled, and Emme's brown eyes grew dark circles underneath them. Her strawberry-blonde hair frizzed, and her skin paled to a ghostly white, making the dusting of freckles across the bridge of her nose stand out.

"I get your point, I look grizzly. Now stop before a servant sees."

Emme's slant granted her the ability to change her features. Just as all magic was limited, though, she could only perform the smallest tweaks—a squarer jaw, darker eyes, a few moles—whereas mine seemed to be under the umbrella of *time* and had a lot more applications.

Still, Emme used her slant often enough, though only when she was fairly certain she wouldn't be going out soon. It was still reckless, and always for her own enjoyment. Always out of sight from her father.

Emme dropped the magic, expression opening in amused concern. "Oh, Dory, why are you so glum? Whatever has happened?"

I bit my lip, aching to tell Emme everything, but ...

But she was so impetuous; she'd drawn a blueduster's attention the same night Father fell ill two years ago, preventing me from fetching a doctor. He'd almost died and so had she. The minute she learned of the kidnapping, she would charge into the streets and earn herself a noose in a matter of hours. I had to protect her from that fate. And him.

Bluedusters couldn't help me, and neither could my relatives. The first step was finding the Rook, which meant perfecting the formula, and then ... Then I would figure out what came next. For now, I needed some new books.

There was nothing for it. I'd have to go outside.

Uncle appeared at the top of the steps like a premonition, saving me from answering. "Change your dress, Dorothy," he said in a flat, authoritative tone that made my stomach drop. "We are going out."

# 7

## Ashley

Destiny was pulling all the right strings, and how I loved it when she did that. It felt like a puzzle masterminded only for me—a trail of clues no one else could follow.

Gigs, dogcarts, and glass carriages slapped against stone, a cacophony of metal and wood ringing through Paternoster Row. To the south, pigeons circled St. Paul's spire. A doughy smell drifted to my nose as I passed a bakery, making my stomach grumble, but I pushed forward.

At my side, Miles put a hand on my shoulder in warning, but because of the noise, he merely knocked his head toward something down the street.

Near the entrance of the bookshop—our destination—a blueduster perused the crowd, lips pinched, fingers brushing his slant gun. He was the fourth one we'd seen that day—double what was normal—ready to pounce on anyone seemingly moving their hands at nothing.

I sighed. After nicking a newspaper from under the arm of a well-dressed man, I reclined against a shop, pretending to read until the blueduster moved on. Because only three cartridges fit in a slant gun's chambers and they were expensive to produce, a blueduster usually waited until he had reason to suspect magical activity before triggering a cartridge. Once fired, the chemical reaction in the lens's hollow pocket would wear off after a few minutes.

Casting an illusion to make oneself invisible had its uses, but I tried to avoid bluedusters altogether.

I always had magic on my hands.

Four bluedusters in two streets, though ...

Considering the Rook's recent attacks, Victoria must be facing increased pressure to crack down on magic, using her bluedusters to do it. Even half a century after the assassination of her predecessor, she couldn't afford to appear weak.

Back then, an organized society of slanted aristocrats—*The Order of the Worthy*, they called themselves—infiltrated King William IV's court. A few months later, one of them used their magic to stop his heart, opening the floodgates to the Gloaming Trials, the bloodiest months in England's history. Anarchy reigned in the streets: looting, rioting, magic abundant and untethered.

Those who feared magic banded together and hung anyone outside the palace who was suspect, guilty and innocent alike.

Victoria, young and untried, rallied troops with the help of her surviving uncles and stormed Windsor, regaining the castle and eventually executing all involved in the coup. To establish order, she formed the blueduster division and decreed a new law: The slanted could only be hanged for *using* magic, thus tamping the people's fear. It was a necessary compromise, we'd been told. The only *peaceful* way.

I'd always hated the name. The Gloaming—like the last light of magic winking out in the dusk. Gallows were such an *English* way of dealing with a problem.

At least they weren't as messy as the French.

When the blueduster finally moved on, Miles told me he'd wait in the street, and I darted into the bookshop. Inside, the air smelled like dust and glue. I navigated through the maze of organized, towering shelves.

In the back corner, in front of where the book with Y422 on its spine was supposed to be, a girl devoured the pages of a book. A long braid of curly brown hair wrapped over her shoulder, tendrils escaping the loose bind and obscuring her face except the tip of her nose.

Subtly, I passed behind her, stealing a glance at the top shelf as I did. I kept moving, mentally sifting through the books in that one impression.

It wasn't there.

I frowned. Odd. Tanner had never been late with an update before.

By now, I'd reached the end of the aisle. I pivoted left to exit the shop and make inquiries through another channel, when my sight snagged on the spine in the girl's hands.

Y422.

She had my blasted book.

This had never happened before. For a few hours every day, a coded message sat inside a new book, containing the information needed to find the next message. The selection changed every time, and given the title of this one, *The Study of Chemistry Within the Atomic Theory*, Tanner had indeed been following my orders to only use obscure titles. It just so happened that the one person in London who was interested in advanced chemistry had wandered into this little-used bookshop.

A stab of panic hit my gut before I smoothed it over and retraced my steps, pretending to be preoccupied with scanning the shelves until my back connected with the girl's in a hard bump.

As the book tumbled to the ground, I twitched my fingers,

making it invisible, then grasped her elbows to steady her. "I beg your pardon, miss. I did not see you."

Her head whipped up and what I saw made me pause. Round face, large eyes, small nose, pointed chin; and lower down, the curves of a blossomed woman.

Not a girl.

My focus wavered, and the illusion camouflaging the book sputtered out. Before I could cast it again, she'd spotted the book and swiped it up.

Blast. Holding an illusion steady was nearly as easy to me as breathing, and I couldn't remember the last time I'd tripped up. As she rubbed the book's cover, I took her in again, slower. She was petite, but definitely not a *girl*. Despite my failed plan, I couldn't ignore the pull on one side of my mouth.

"It's quite all right," she said quietly, surprising me with very proper English. A *débutante*, then. A blush dusted her cheeks, and she pointedly avoided eye contact. When she resumed thumbing through the pages to find her original spot, I panicked again and slipped a finger inside to halt her progress.

She couldn't stumble upon the page with my message.

"Interested in science?" I said nonchalantly, like it was perfectly normal to stick one's finger in someone else's book. "I am as well. I happen to be a private tutor, employed in Berkley Square." Not exactly the truth.

She said nothing, shrinking back.

"I've done a lot of research into Faraday's findings about electrochemistry," I tried again. "Specifically electrolysis."

Her brows scrunched but her eyes darted around the floor. She was either shy, embarrassed, or both. "In fact, I'm developing my own theory about the relationship between electrochemistry and the interconversion of" —I leaned in and whispered— "*magic.*"

She blinked. "That's very—" She glanced up with excitement

that died upon finding my face so near her own. "Very interesting," she finished a little breathlessly.

Noticing the rapid pulse in her throat, I smiled smugly. "You do seem interested."

The rapture fled her face, and she snapped the book shut. "I beg your pardon?"

I raised my eyebrows. "In interconversion, that is."

She blinked again. Paused. "Is that a euphemism, sir?"

A soft chuckle burst out of me, but before I could tell her I hadn't intended it as one, she went on.

"The study of science as it relates to magic is illegal, as I'm sure you are well aware."

I shrugged one shoulder. "A minor setback on the road to serving the greater good."

"A permanent setback, if I were to report you to the authorities."

"And who would you be reporting, exactly? The man who dazzled you in a bookshop?"

"I believe the report would read, 'The man who *irritated* me in a bookshop,' actually."

"An unnecessarily long description."

"Conversing with strange men tends to make me ramble."

At least I'd managed to get her to close the book. Now to wrest it from her hands. I affected a careless expression. "Strange?" I folded my arms. "Do explain."

"This is a very empty bookshop."

"Yes."

"In fact, I believe you and I are the only customers here."

"I believe so."

"And yet you seem to be more interested in reading me than all the books at your disposal. Forgive me if I find that both unnerving and a bit strange."

"You are forgiven."

Judging by her pinking cheeks, that answer had exasperated her further. She'd expected me to deny it, or perhaps, tout how diverting she was—that was what a gentleman usually did. Instead, I'd agreed with her, and she seemed at a loss. I repressed a smile.

She licked her lower lip, drawing my eye to her mouth for the smallest moment. "I am sorry, I do not know your name—"

"Everett." Another lie, but it hardly mattered. Regardless of how much I wanted to, I wasn't going to see this girl again. "And I do hope you won't use that information to report me now." I leaned against the bookcase so that only half a dozen books lay between my mouth and hers.

She straightened. "Well, Mr. Everett—"

"You misunderstand. Everett is my first name."

Her blush deepened, uncomfortable with knowing the intimate information. She gave me a quick once-over, no doubt noting my fraying frockcoat and black vest. Clothes of someone respectable, but not well-to-do. "I beg your pardon. I had assumed you would give me your surname."

"Why would you assume that?"

She shook her head. "Because you are a gentleman—"

"Why would you assume *that?*"

Her head froze mid-shake. This time I couldn't help but grin at her horror.

I put one arm on the shelf and leaned in, making a point to capture her eyes. While blue-gray, they sparkled with an intelligence that seemed hungry, and I tilted my head, more intrigued by that hungriness than I cared to admit. "I have been called a lot of things in my life," I whispered. Her lips parted, and I felt my magic tiptoe in a circle around her, all on its own. "Man, thief, terror, saint, devil, and most recently, strange—but *never* a gentleman. I would beg you not to break that record."

Even while lost in my eyes, she must've felt my fingers

tugging on the book, because she frowned, shook off the magic, and hugged the book to her chest. "And I would beg you to give me a reason to."

The magic recoiled.

Hm. That had never happened. The magical *pull* drew women in and—without my consent—cast a spell over them. I didn't know why. And I'd never seen someone evade it before.

Her grip tightened, but everything else about her seemed to relax when I pinched the top of the spine and rotated the book toward me. "This happens to be the only copy in London."

Her face was a mockery of pity. "My condolences."

"You see, I have a student who is dumb as tacks. He needs to read this if he ever has any hope of becoming the brilliant scientist his parents wish him to be."

She patted the cover. "If he's dumb as tacks, I daresay he's not advanced enough to grasp the high-end concepts in here."

"And you are? Advanced enough?"

"I like to think so."

I grinned. "A girl who is interested in science. I can respect that."

A begrudging smile lifted one corner of her lips. "You have an odd way of showing respect when you try to steal a book from me."

"Well, respect is a high-end concept. Perhaps you are not advanced enough to grasp it."

Her eyes narrowed. She was amused and hated that she was. "You are charming," she said, "Mr. Everett With-The-Mystery-Surname. But not charming enough for me to relinquish this book to you, and I'm afraid nothing you say shall change my mind."

I emitted a slow sigh and let my hand, still on the shelf, drift to her hair. She froze, sucking in a breath when my fingers slowly trailed down the curls of her braid. When I reached the tip, I locked eyes with her, letting her swim in them, letting her drown, making myself watch and do nothing. "That is a shame," I murmured. I lingered an extra beat longer than necessary, then walked off.

It was three full seconds of her staring at my back before she noticed her empty hands. "Mr. Ev—*sir*, my book!"

I tossed the book over my shoulder before spinning around and catching it in my hands. Walking backwards, I smirked at her. "Still think I'm a gentleman?" I slipped around the corner, flipped a half-crown to the owner, and exited the shop.

The blueduster crossed toward Miles who waited in the street, staring through the grubby window with worried eyes. The girl must've followed me as far as the door because Miles said, "That girl—"

"She happens to be upset at me." I hurried past him, making him follow me into the noise of London, down the roads that navigated away from the blueduster.

Three blocks later, we came to an alley where I could hear him above the noise. "That girl you were speaking to, in the bookshop—"

"Yes," I said, knowing he was about to reprimand me for stealing from her, "but she had the note from Tanner—"

"That was Dorothy St. James. The girl you asked me to investigate. Geoffrey St. James's daughter."

I halted.

Wagons thundered past, people bumping into me without so much as a sorry governor in the swarming streets.

I rolled the name over in my mind.

Dorothy. She looked like a Dorothy.

Miles frowned. "What are we going to do now?" He saw my interaction with our target as a bad turn of events. But no.

I smiled. No, this was better.

# 8

## Dorothy

Aunt Marie prattled when she was nervous, but she tended to do it quietly enough that her husband never heard her— or at least, never bothered to acknowledge it. Silver scratched porcelain, knives cut chicken, crystal clinked, footmen sniffed, and Aunt Marie's voice fluttered like a moth around the dining room.

"Before you went missing," she said breathily, "we found the prettiest hat, with orange ribbons cascading off the back and a little yellow bird placed just so. Looked like a finch, perhaps, with a pearl for an eye—so quaint ..."

Clarence blew blond curls away from his forehead and frowned at his vegetables. Across from me, Emme enlarged her eyes—literally, sending a chill of magic through my veins—then rolled them.

Uncle's open palm slapped the table, making the porcelain clatter. "Emmeline!" His eyes widened with rage. "We've discussed this!"

Emme dropped her slant and downed the glass in front of her, all but ignoring her father's outburst.

Uncle Benedick blinked angrily before returning to eating, jaw tight. "Only *peasants* need resort to *magic*. And the noose they earn for it is well deserved. Do not disgrace me again." A pause. "Nor you," he added, and I knew he addressed me. "Scampering about the streets without a chaperone is beneath us."

The ensuing silence was broken only by hesitant forks scraping. I pushed the chicken around my plate, trying to bite back my frustration.

I'd risked angering my uncle and passed more than one blue-duster to steal away to the bookshop. After finding the right section, heart pounding, I'd speed-read several paragraphs of the cellular makeup of magic—only to have a man steal the very book I needed to complete the experiment.

And then there was the note. It was a gibberish string of letters, haphazardly tucked into the book like it had been left there by mistake. On a whim, I'd copied it onto the forearm of my dress, knowing it must mean something. But then *Everett* kept insisting I give the book to him, and I couldn't help but wonder ...

The conversation that followed was the strangest I'd had, and not exactly because of the words we exchanged.

His face was ... otherworldly. Poetry. Sculpted cheeks and soft lips, and an acute magnetism that made it daunting to look away. I'd never seen a face like it.

And his eyes were so *green*. The way he'd stared at me, the way hot tingles had traveled to each vertebra of my spine, and his smell ... I couldn't place it, but I couldn't forget it either. Warm, spiced, fresh, like—like a field of clover sprinkled with cardamom and heated under a summer sun.

I scrunched my eyes shut to refocus my thoughts.

The book was the only copy in London, and finding the vexing owner would prove nigh impossible.

I blinked, spine straightening. Father knew a few families in

Berkeley Square where *Everett* claimed to be a tutor. Perhaps I could write them, introduce myself, make a few inquiries?

"We shall attend Lady Faline's concert after dinner," Uncle Benedick said nonchalantly, like Emme's earlier incident was a distant memory. No one expressed any hopeful plans or previous obligations. Everything bent to his will.

The idea of a concert, despite being exactly what I needed to find the book, made my nerves go on edge. Nothing had happened on the streets or in the bookshop, but it was only a matter of time before my magic manifested.

But the house. If uncle claimed it, Father and I would lose everything. I had to be careful not to refuse Uncle too much—and it was better to inquire in person anyway. I merely needed to make every outing as short and worthwhile as possible.

"When is Sir Geoffrey to return from Brighton?" Oil from the chicken pooled in the corner of Uncle Benedick's mouth.

I bunched the napkin in my lap. "He didn't say."

"It must be serious, then." Uncle wiped his mouth and rested his disquieting gaze on me. "What a shame it would be if his illness were beyond the point of recovery. We were quite fortunate last time."

With some effort, I swallowed a bite of tough chicken which turned in my stomach. He'd done everything to *prevent* my father from recovering, so Father's title would fall to Clarence.

"If he is planning a prolonged stay, perhaps we will rethink the household arrangements." Uncle Benedick rang the little gold bell near his plate. Beatrice appeared at his elbow and curtsied, waiting for his command. Aunt Marie sucked in her lips and blinked a little quicker but offered no protest. My eyes met Emme's.

"That's hardly necessary, Father," Emme said quickly.

"Dorothy needs someone to look after her, and since her father has abandoned her—"

"He did not abandon me," I said tersely.

Uncle Benedick's blue eyes cut to me. "And yet he made no arrangements for your care, or governance. It is my duty to take you under my wing."

There was something tightfisted in the way he delivered the technically kind words, almost ... possessive. He coveted Father's baronetcy, societal notoriety, and everything that came with it—including authority over me. Beatrice glanced between me and my uncle, unsure which of us to heed.

Emme's chuckle cut through the tension. "Dory isn't a child anymore, Father. Uncle Geoffrey's lack of arrangements only shows how well he knows his daughter, who needs no chaperone because she doesn't care for society."

A polite way of saying I'd imprisoned myself for three years.

She took a large bite of her croissant, chewing as she added, "And you know how randomly particular Uncle Geoffrey can be —with his tea, and his books. Best not to tamper with his systems, I think, especially as he will return soon."

Oh, Emme. I wanted to cry. I wanted to sigh my thanks and collapse on the nearest piece of furniture where I could sleep for a week. Everyone at the table was still, except for Emme who continued to devour her croissant.

"Perhaps you are right," Uncle Benedick said at last, jaw pushing out. "Perhaps we may delay."

Aunt Marie nodded, though she would have nodded whatever the outcome. Clarence plopped his head in his hand and dragged a fork across the tablecloth. Then Uncle Benedick's eyes lingered on me so long I grew cold and prickly all over. "Of course, if I ever take possession of this house, it'll not be run in such a slipshod manner." He sipped his wine, staining his lips red. "Take Dorothy's plate away, Beatrice. She is quite full."

"I wasn't finished—"

"I fear any more food will unsettle your stomach." His

eyebrows lifted a fraction. "Best to take things slowly as your health improves. Perhaps no dessert, either."

Beatrice removed my plate. I stared at the empty scrap of tablecloth before me—the only empty spot on a table bedecked with candles, decanters, glass budvases, salt cellars, and silverware. The cloth was white, empty. Like the undershirt my father wore to sleep. Like the pillow resting on his bed. The one that had cradled a feather as black as a moonless night.

"Excuse me," I muttered, throwing my napkin to the table harder than necessary as I stood. "I must change for the concert."

# 9

## Dorothy

I swiped a shaky hand over my forehead when I saw the blueduster down the street from the concert hall. The society dinners consisted of a small group of trusted associates, and the bookshop had been nearly empty; a concert brimming with nobility and guarded by bluedusters was an entirely different matter. I felt exposed. Anxious and on edge.

After changing, I'd written Mr. Vernon, requesting the guest list from the society dinner, hoping I might find the man with the scar to ask him what he knew of my father's disappearance. I wanted to pursue every avenue open to me.

"Dorothy." Uncle Benedick waited at the entrance, frown deepening.

I tore my gaze from the blueduster, picked up my emerald skirts, and scurried inside. If someone used their slant, or one of my visions struck, I'd keep my head down and dart for the carriage as soon as possible. That plan in place, I relaxed my shoulders. In the meantime, I would look for the families that lived in Berkeley Square and discover which of them employed a tutor.

The foyer opened to a grand hall whose deep-set stairs descended into an amphitheater strewn with yellow rose petals. In the center, a grand piano spun octaves into a light, suspenseful march. Each stair level curved with red chairs that surrounded the stage, the hue matching the brick and terracotta walls. Three layers of balconies wound around the room, rising to a ring of alabaster columns that supported the glass dome.

Uncle navigated Aunt Marie, Emme, and me to the front row. Bodies poured through the doors, the black glacé silk, sloped necklines, and faint perfumes blooming and multiplying like algae in a petri dish.

"So many people," Emme said, seated beside me.

I kept a steady eye on the entrance, mentally listing the introductions I needed. It looked like the entire *ton* had turned out for this concert. Musicians filed onstage carrying caramel violins and basses, sleek oboes and clarinets, silver flutes and bells, and lastly, a harp with a cupid on its bow.

All thought petered out as a tall man stepped through the entrance. Someone I had never expected to see again, and certainly never here. Confident smile intact, he handed his top hat to the man inside the door, followed by a double-breasted coat with topstitching. Far more expensive than what he'd been wearing in the bookshop.

He crossed into the hall until a cluster of people blocked his path, then smiled and shook a few men's hands, saying something that made the women beside them laugh.

Emme stared at him with a wide, dazed look—a look I recognized because I'd made it earlier today when I first saw him too. "Who is *he?*"

Uncle overheard her and seemed to know exactly who she meant. And the name he provided didn't have a single Everett in it, surname or otherwise. He sniffed. "Mr. Ashley Gardner."

I fisted the emerald silk of my lap, not knowing what to make of the name, the man, or the way my eyes glued to him.

"He is moderately outfitted," Uncle went on, "and moderately charming, but everyone knows he's a social climber. You girls would do well to stay away from him."

When her father's attention was called away by an approaching lord, Emme turned to me and murmured, "I wouldn't mind if he wasn't outfitted at *all*, if you know what I—"

"I know him," I whispered back. "I met him earlier today." Mr. Gardner was now occupied with a matron and her three daughters, his smile drawing a reaction from more than those adjacent to him. *Stop it*, I told my speeding heart, my squeezing stomach. He'd humiliated me then stolen my chance to find my father.

And yet, I couldn't look away.

"You met him?" Emme's tone was riddled with disbelief. She blinked rapidly. "Sorry, let us rewind a bit? To be fair, I don't pay much attention when you start rambling about algebra and kintenetic particles or whatever it is, but I think I would've remembered you mentioning that you'd" —she dug a knuckle into my arm— "met a *deity* on the streets."

"I *didn't*." I wasn't sure which part I was denying—that I met him on the street. Probably. His voice echoed in my mind, clearer than when the words first passed his lips. *I've been called a lot of things in my life. Man, thief, terror, saint, devil ...*

"He lied about his name," I admitted.

*... But* never *a gentleman.*

She lowered her voice into a fierce whisper. "As if his name bears some importance! Did you see his face when you met him? Are you looking at it now?"

I'd had the same reaction when I first saw him. His face was so perfect that it was almost ... unsettling, and yet I ... *couldn't look away.*

Violins tuned their strings, and it was like a mallet splintering the spell he had held over me. Mr. Gardner finished his conversation and, followed by another man I didn't recognize, shuffled through the crowd. They sat across from us on the ground floor, giving me a better vantage of him than I would've liked, as I was now tempted to watch his performance instead of the vocalist's.

Mr. Gardner stared at the floor. A slow smile spread over his lips like he knew an impossible secret, then his green eyes ticked up to me.

I sucked in a breath. No hesitation. No wandering, searching for a face he recognized. He'd known I was here the whole time. Watching him. But from the moment he stepped in the room, he'd never glanced my way.

How had he known I'd be here at all?

Unnerved, I broke eye contact.

In a sweep of shimmery orange skirts, Lady Faline took to the stage, eliciting a round of applause.

Through luck, I'd found the man again; now, somehow, I needed to convince him to give me back my chemistry book. During the second performance, my eyes wandered back to him, taking in his well-formed shoulders. One moment Mr. Gardner was watching the flute players trill an introduction, and the next, our gazes connected. Electricity shot to my toes. For the second time, I ripped my gaze away.

Vocals, rich as velvet, punctured the air. One piece ended. Then another, and another. The last song was from Verdi's *Luisa Miller*. A few minutes in, the strings dipped and quivered on a low note. The alto's voice pitched lower too, then scaled high, spitting words in Italian.

*To save my innocent father from death* ... she sang.

My hands started to sweat inside my gloves. He wasn't dead. I would know if he were dead.

*I tremble to say it ...*

I needed more time. Just a little more time and I'd find a way to—

*I must sacrifice my honor …*

The vocalist jumped to a forte, and the note was dazzlingly lurid. Exquisite. A scream.

The scream I wished I could make.

With a shudder, the music ended. Thunderous applause erupted, and I joined in, blinking away the threat of tears by the time Lady Faline announced the concert's conclusion.

Some rushed the door to avoid the congestion that bottle-necked at the coat-checkers, but more lingered behind to rave about the glittering performances. Laughter floated on the humid air, faintly laced with rose and perspiration. Emme and I conversed quietly for several minutes, debating which number was our favorite.

"… and this is my niece, Miss Dorothy St. James."

I turned to find my uncle introducing me to—

"Dorothy, Emmeline," Uncle Benedick said, "this is Mr. Ashley Gardner, and his associate, Mr. Miles Kelly." He subtly glanced around, frowning, obviously displeased but more concerned with keeping up appearances.

Mr. Kelly was a nice-looking man with warm brown hair that matched his eyes, and a height and build that nearly mirrored Mr. Gardner's. The way he didn't speak as he inclined his head put me in mind of a sage—someone who valued caution and pensiveness and could fill a well with his wisdom if you dug deep enough.

Mr. Gardner smiled. "A pleasure to meet you, Miss St. James." He turned to Emme. "Miss Morgan. Lovely names for your lovely faces."

Emme laughed. "What a shame it would be if we'd been named something else, then."

"Something like Everett," I said innocently.

Emme frowned and looked at me askance.

Mr. Gardner's tone remained blithe, like we were discussing the light used in a particular painting. "I quite agree. It's a frightful name and yet London is crawling with Everetts." He leaned in and whispered to Emme, "Can't be too careful who you bump into."

*But* never *a gentleman.*

His gaze slid to me again.

"Did you enjoy the concert, Mr. Gardner?" Emme asked, eyes sparkling. Then, remembering the man behind him, corrected her manners. "And you, Mr. Kelly?"

Before Mr. Kelly could respond, Uncle cut into our circle, features tight while herding Aunt Marie and beckoning to me and Emme. "If you will excuse us, sirs, I see Mr. Riley over there, and I should like to introduce my family to him. Good evening to you both. Dorothy," he commanded sternly, indicating I was to follow, before the three of them headed for the other side of the room. I turned to do the same.

"Miss St. James," Mr. Gardner began before I could, "I was hoping I might speak to you alone."

Noticing that Mr. Kelly had mysteriously disappeared, I shot a glance toward my relatives. Their progress was slow. I had a few minutes before Uncle detected my absence—and in that time, needed to convince Mr. Gardner to give me back the book.

I planted my feet. "Yes?"

Mr. Gardner's broad frame loomed closer, and there was that scent again. Cardamom warmed in butter. "I wanted to apologize for what happened in the bookshop."

It was a sweet gesture for him to make. Sweet, or conniving. "You will return my book to me?"

Clucking his tongue, he said, "Ah, it's technically *my* book, as I'm the one who purchased it, and as for giving it to you" —his eyes narrowed as he sucked in through his teeth, a mockingly evaluating look— "I don't know that I'm *that* sorry."

My shoulders fell. "So, your apology isn't an apology after all."

"Not a very heartfelt one, but I feel compelled to make it all the same." His mouth indented from holding back a smile. "The book is a reminder of the time I met an intriguing woman, so it's sentimental to me now. You understand."

I made a noncommittal sound in my throat. "And is that the only regret you wished to express? No repentance for blatant lies?"

His eyebrows shot up and grazed the black hair swooping his forehead. "When did I lie?"

He wasn't serious? "You said you were interested in science."

"And I am."

"You said you were developing a theory with interconversion."

"Who doesn't have theories?"

"You said you've studied electrolysis."

His face pinched. "An unhealthy amount of attention you seem to have paid my words—"

"Perhaps you shouldn't use them so flippantly." I folded my arms. "Everett."

He didn't appear the least bit penitent. If anything, the depressions near his mouth deepened. "... Middle name?"

I wasn't going to fall for his lies again. "You claimed to be a tutor who has a student."

"I do. I'm the tutor. And the student." He shrugged loosely. "Always in pursuit of knowledge, that's me."

I raised an eyebrow. "A student who is dumb as tacks, as I recall you said."

"All right, that one was a blatant lie. I am sorry for that one."

I tried to ignore the tug on my lips, but I couldn't, because my uncle had been wrong. Mr. Ashley Gardner was not moderately charming. There was nothing moderate about him.

I peeked over my shoulder. They'd reached Mr. Riley, but Uncle had yet to introduce the women behind him. Emme was gesturing for me to hurry. "I need the book," I said, turning back. "And I will give you anything for it."

His expression opened, putting all pretense aside. "As tempting as that offer sounds, I'm afraid it's impossible. I no longer have it."

My heart sank. "Have you sold it?"

"Not exactly."

"If it is money you need—"

He smiled. "I don't."

Exasperated, I blurted, "Then why were you dressed poorly in the bookshop?"

"Do you suspect me of something, Miss St. James?"

I opened my mouth to say yes but faltered. Technically, he'd done nothing unlawful, it was just that ... there was *something* off about him.

"I am only curious," I finally conceded.

He studied me for a moment, and his eyes seemed to pierce right through me. "There is no such thing as 'only curious.' Not in London, where royalty comes knocking and the masses clamber for a better view. Where libelous whispers scatter like rats in the morning and the social ladders we're climbing reach up to St. Paul's. Here, the meal of the day is the murder of the hackneyman down the street, or the stunning Croesus who's taking society by storm. We live in an age of extremes. You are either too low in the dust to be noticed or inspire a burning obsession not easily ignored. I know which one I feel for you. Which do you feel for me?"

My face heated, and I had no reply. Which was answer enough, I supposed.

Mr. Gardner bowed. "Good evening, Miss St. James. I expect we will see each other again soon."

I inhaled to stop him, but he was gone too quickly, along with my hopes of regaining the chemistry book. I swallowed past the lump in my throat. Trying not to think of the exchange, I turned and scurried to my uncle just as he finished introducing Emme to Mr. Riley.

"To answer your question, Mr. Morgan," Mr. Riley said once I'd been introduced as well, "I foresee a dip in steel prices some-time next month. You should all tour the factory before produc-tion ramps back up again." His copper hair fell to his chin, framing a thin mouth that always looked pleasantly interested.

Aunt Marie clasped her hands. "That sounds lovely. Success-ful, refined; how are you unmarried, Mr. Riley?"

Mr. Riley blushed.

"How did you enjoy the concert?" Emme asked.

Mr. Riley beamed. "It was splendid. I loved the last perfor-mance particularly. It was a favorite of my departed parents."

"Oh yes, that actress did a magnificent job!" Aunt Marie said, glancing around. "I simply must congratulate her." After spotting the girl, she took a step but was stopped by Uncle Benedick's fingers curling around her arm.

Tone clipped, he said, "Don't degrade our name by associ-ating with their ilk."

Aunt Marie's face fell.

Emme and I exchanged nervous glances.

Looking between us, Mr. Riley stepped forward. "I assure you, Benedick, she is very respectable. Why, she attends church with the Lemmings. You should let your wife commend her."

The last sentence sent a cold, magical rush through my veins, making my head snap over.

Mr. Riley's smile was pleasant, easy, without a trace of guile for the magic he'd used. "There is no harm in it, and I'm sure the actress would be humbled to have drawn the notice of a distinguished family like yours."

My breath tightened. His voice could persuade; that was his slant.

Uncle's jaw loosened. After a long pause, he gave a curt nod and released Aunt Marie who swept away. Emme's mouth dropped open. My gaze darted between Mr. Riley, his palms, and my own hands, concealed by elbow-length evening gloves.

Fabric couldn't obstruct the magic on a slant gun's radar, though.

Mr. Riley brightened. "Now, Benedick, when would you like to take that tour?"

"Excuse me, I don't feel well." I backed away and dashed—I hoped not too quickly—toward the carriage.

# 10

## Dorothy

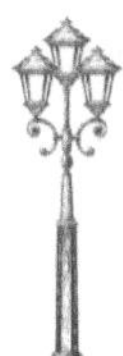

"A package was delivered for you while you were out, miss," Beatrice said in the dark foyer after everyone else headed for their beds. "I've put it in your room."

I thanked her absently and trudged up the stairs, mind still racing with the night's events. If Mr. Gardner couldn't give me the book—or wouldn't, as I believed—then I'd focus on my other leads. The steel button was both unique and expensive enough that someone was bound to recognize it. I could start by combing through the dress shops, but ...

Danger was everywhere.

Mr. Riley's slant was subtle enough—and he was charming enough—that no one had suspected magic was involved, but *I'd* known. I'd made it safely to the carriage, but if Mr. Riley had risked slanting, there were bound to be more willing to do the same. All it would take was one moment of being in the wrong place at the wrong time, and I'd swing from my neck.

I couldn't always be as lucky as I was tonight.

In my room, I disrobed and braided my hair before tying it off with a white ribbon. I slid into my desk and inked Mr. Riley's name onto a sheet of paper, followed by a question mark. After staring at it for a full minute, I underlined it twice.

My mind drifted to the memory of breath fogging Father's bedroom window, obscuring the Rook's face. The more I tried to remember details, the more muddied the picture became. I shivered.

But Mr. Riley had seemed kind when he'd used his magic to help my aunt. I couldn't reconcile the two men as being the same person.

After retrieving the lion button from the drawer I'd stashed it in earlier, I turned it over in my fingers. Even if—through sheer luck—I managed to fix my formula, I couldn't follow a magic trail without stumbling upon it first.

But how did one predict a shadow?

A knock sounded on the door, prompting me to shove the button back into the drawer. To my surprise, Emme entered a moment later, garbed in curling rags and a white nightgown which flowed over her toes as she slipped across the wood floor. She crushed me in a swift embrace that toppled me out of my chair and sent us both careening.

A Persian rug caught our fall, but Emme still squeezed my neck, refusing to let go. "Who do you think you are, deserting me with my parents like that?"

I smiled but said, "Emme, I can't breathe."

"Serves you right. The evening was onerous." She moaned, long and dramatic. "I'd rather be sent to the workhouse than endure another hour discussing tariff prices."

"I'm sorry," I chuckle-wheezed. "Never again."

She released me and jumped to her feet, then sat in the chair of my vanity. "The Rook stole another person last night."

Rubbing my trachea, I sat up, digesting the information.

She rested her chin on the back of the chair. "Apparently it was the third son of some cantankerous old baron. Nathaniel Finch or Field or something—"

"Findley?"

"Yes! Nathaniel Findley." She fished through her nightgown and produced a newspaper clipping, then shoved it at me. "Not a sign of him, his family says—only a black feather and an enraged father who is pushing for stricter legislation in the House of Lords."

Confused that her bedtime routine included newspaper clippings, I stood and drew my curtains closed without reading it. "Legislation about what?"

"Magic. Harsher punishments."

I spun back. "Harsher than *death*?"

She consulted the column. "New parameters on what qualifies as 'using magic.' Higher incentives for the bluedusters. And for citizens to rat out their neighbors. Funding for research and technology that will better equip the Crown to deal with magic."

She grinned, glancing up as she stuffed the newspaper back into her nightgown. "It'll never pass. Half the lords are slanted themselves, and the other half have children who are. They all like using it behind closed doors."

Mr. Riley had proven that tonight.

"What has any of this to do with the Rook?" I asked. "They don't know he's using magic to kidnap people." Though, given how quickly Father had been spirited away, it made sense the Rook would be slanted. His power could be masking sounds, or walking through walls, or perhaps even hiding in shadows. That last thought sent a chill down my spine.

"The whispers are everywhere," Emme continued. "Everyone hopes the Samaritan will stage a daring rescue soon."

I stopped short. The Samaritan, more than anyone, knew

something about tracking the Rook. Maybe if I gave the formula to him, along with father's prototype tracker, we could team up—

But I didn't have the formula. And the Samaritan's identity was as mysterious as the Rook's.

Emme stood and wrapped a hand around the poster of my bed, swinging herself around. "The Samaritan has been mentioned daily in the papers for a good six weeks."

I said nothing, sinking into the chair she'd vacated.

"The masked altruist of London." She rested the back of her hand on her forehead. "Sworn enemy of the Rook. Do you know the number of penny dreadfuls that have been written about him alone? Hm?"

"No."

She stopped swinging. "Thirty-four. *Stories*, not serials."

"That's quite a specific number."

The swinging started again, more vigorous this time. "Well, *forgive me* if I spend most of my allowance having them delivered poste-haste from London and then proceed to devour them until the pages are either too worn to read or destroyed by spills from my daily cups of hot chocolate that I drink to distract myself from the doldrum life I lead. And if you are going to ask me why hot chocolate, it is only because it is unseemly for a lady to consume copious amounts of brandy."

She hugged the poster against her face. "One time, I accidentally threw myself at our carrier, because I was dying to find out if the Samaritan would escape the fire the Rook had set for him. Now he won't approach our house without first poking his head through the lilacs to ensure I am not planning another ambush. The carrier, that is."

Despite myself, I chuckled. "'Accidentally'?"

"You don't know what it's like." She flopped onto the bed, belly first. "There is little else to do in Shropshire except wish you were in London. The days pass like a bloated tortoise."

Rolling her eyes back, she buried her face in the blanket. Voice muffled by the covers, she added, "Nothing exciting *ever* happens."

Inside, I grimaced. I'd had enough excitement to last a lifetime.

She lifted her head, puffing a few wayward strawberry-blonde hairs away from her eye. "We should visit the carnival by the dress shops. Do you know of any disreputable rum-holes nearby?"

I fixed her with a hard look. "What exactly do you plan to do with such information? Stop in for a beer?"

"I've been meaning to do some gambling, actually." She noticed my look, and her face didn't alter a smidge when she said, "Joking."

Shaking my head, I slipped a shawl around my shoulders and hugged it tight. "By the way, I wanted to thank you for what you did at dinner."

Emme frowned. "I'm sorry." I knew she was referring to her father's behavior. Sorry that she couldn't do more.

I gave her a wan smile. "It isn't your fault."

"You're right. I shouldn't be the one apologizing. But Mother has no spine, and Clarence is too young to understand, and Father—" Her sigh was stunted. "Father is how he is. It's the money's fault. Ever since making his fortune, he can't let go of a single penny and has to control everything. To him, the family name is the only thing worthwhile; worth spending money on." She grew quieter. "Sometimes I think he doesn't even notice us."

We sat for a moment, both suspended in contemplation.

"How is your father doing, Dory?" she whispered like the question was forbidden. Her big brown eyes watered at the corners. "Really."

I bit my lip to keep it from trembling. Maybe I could tell her? But she'd already used her slant twice and had just gotten through venting to me about not having enough excitement. She was too reckless. It was one thing to risk my own neck, but if Emme started slanting on the streets to go undercover, she'd get herself killed. And it would be my fault.

I shrugged and tried to smile. "He's getting better. He just needs some time away."

Emme nodded. "I hope he makes a full recovery. And that he returns before—" She glanced at me, and again, I knew what she meant to say: *Before my father takes over completely.* Once Uncle Benedick realized my father was officially out of the way and it was *socially acceptable* to claim the house, my possessions, and all my autonomy with it, he'd do it. Appearances were all that stood between my freedom and imprisonment.

She yawned suddenly. "Well, it is late, and I should be in bed if I want to get my beauty sleep." Without waiting for a response, she slinked off the bed and disappeared through the door.

Only then did I notice the forgotten package on top of my bookcase. It was heavy, and the brown paper ripped easily when I tore it open to reveal the book beneath.

*The Study of Chemistry Within the Atomic Theory.* The only copy in London. A rush of bewilderment and relief washed over me. There was no note attached to the package, but the inside flap bore an inscription.



A blush rose to my cheeks. My smile bloomed and then slowly wilted, moving through four seasons in four seconds.

Beatrice said the package arrived after I left for the evening and before I'd been introduced to Mr. Gardner or learned his real name. Not only had he known who I was but also where to send the book.

Which meant he'd sent it before I'd told him how suspicious he was. Which only made him ...

... More suspicious.

I flipped through the pages, searching for the loose piece of paper with gibberish on it, but it was gone. Mr. Gardner had found it then. And he'd been so obstinate about obtaining a book, only to give it to me in the end.

When I'd stumbled upon the jumble of letters, I'd impulsively penciled it onto the cream fabric of my forearm, thinking it might prove a diverting puzzle to solve since I couldn't solve the other ones in my life. I knew it meant something. The conversation that followed with Mr. Gardner had swept it from my mind, but now ...

Now I wondered if it perhaps meant something more. Something to him. Something important. Something he didn't want anyone—not even a harmless girl in a bookshop—to see.

A quick search in the soiled-linen closet near the washhouse found my dress from yesterday, the pencil faded but still readable. I copied the sequence onto some paper before heading back upstairs.

At my desk, I stared at what I'd copied, trying to make sense of it.

*Weambg pgbaao aaa Ejohkpujp aawf cjl bjztgliad KLT gaqmu ah*
*xq ycpw N231*

Having read a book or two on ciphers, I started with a Caesar cipher, shifting the first five letters once, then twice, checking to see if any of them aligned to make a word, or the beginnings of one. A quick run-through of the alphabet proved useless, although that didn't surprise me. If someone like Mr. Gardner were trying to hide something, he wouldn't pick something so simple to crack.

I moved on to a Monoalphabetic cipher, using letter-frequency analysis to check for common words or letter combinations. Because no word repeated a letter three times and yet 'aaa' was part of the text, I tried different words that ended with double consonants and began a new word with the same letter, plugging in S, L, F, then T. None of the frequencies made sense or seemed to follow any kind of rules. The code must be even more complicated. I scanned the text. There were no repeating digraphs, either, which meant square ciphers were off the table.

The candle flickered in the corner of my eye, as if to remind me I'd been about to put it out and go to bed. But I knew I'd no longer be sleeping tonight. Not until I figured this out.

The Playfair cipher was a substitution cipher. It was time-consuming to figure out the patterns but still possible.

I jotted the alphabet into a five-by-five grid, omitting the letter J. Then again. Then again and again—categorically rearranging the alphabet until my hand was cramping and I had pages and pages of possible keys. Ink splotched the tips of my fingers and sides of my hands. The candle was swimming in its own wax.

Only when I'd created the six-hundred-and-twenty-fifth graph did I straighten from my hunched position over the desk and stretch the muscles in my back and hands. Some of the papers had smear marks from another paper being shuffled on top while the ink was still wet. After a moment, I dove back in, starting with the first graph on the first page.

Hours ticked by. The candle's wax overfilled the tin holder and ran in rivulets over my desk. I flipped through the pages, crumpling and tossing one when none of its graphs proved useful until paper balls littered the floor of my room. When I finished with the last graph on the last page—still to no success—I sighed and swiped the hair out of my eyes with the back of my wrist.

It was hopeless. The stupid man *really* didn't want anyone reading whatever had been written. And that only made me want to read it more.

I glanced at the window. The charcoal sky had lightened to a heather gray. In the street, a watchman passed with his rattler, calling out the half hour and tapping the doors he'd been paid to act as an alarm for. I heard his faint cry through the closed window. Five-thirty.

I'd worked all night.

And I still wasn't any closer to knowing what the note said.

I chewed the inside of my lip, re-reading the code, trying to look at it with different eyes. There was one more cipher to try, but ... the Vigenère cipher needed a keyword, and I doubted that I'd magically stumble upon the secret word.

But blind hope, or despair, or stubbornness, or acceptance compelled me to pull out one more fresh piece of paper and begin writing out the alphabet twenty-six times and in twenty-six orders, cyclically shifting them to create my graph. My hand burned and shook when I finally finished.

I could do this. All I needed was a word. One word.

The right word.

What would a man like Ashley Gardner use?

I tried *Everett*, then *science*, then *man, thief, terror, saint, devil*, and then out of desperation, *gentleman*. The code remained gibberish.

I sighed and glanced at the book, rereading its title. The study of chemistry within the atomic theory.

*In fact, I'm developing my own theory ... A theory about ...*

Had he given me the answer without meaning to?

I plugged in T-H-E-O-R-Y above the letters and started decoding.

P ... L ...

My heart leapt at the promising start, but I knew it wasn't likely. Why would the answer be in the title of the book?

E ... A ...

Unless this wasn't the first secret message. Unless the key changed every time, and the words just happened to align.

S ...

Unless Ashley Gardner had the word *theory* on his mind, and in his haste to distract me had accidentally let the word slip. Because even though he'd flustered me, underneath that smooth exterior I had flustered him just as much.

... E

*Please.*

I gasped but didn't stop. It had worked. It was working. My eyes flew over the chart, my fingers quickening. Letters crammed together on the page, blurring and bent but no longer nonsense.

And I knew—if this wasn't the first of Mr. Gardner's messages, then it also wasn't the last.

Finished, I set my pencil down and sat back, staring at the paper and the message I'd decoded, mentally separating the words from each other. I knew the last phrase, "R231" was probably referring to a book—where to find the next secret missive. But that wasn't what made me freeze or made my heart pound against my nightgown with silly, silly hope.

*Please inform the Samaritan that the innkeeper needs to be paid. R231*

A breath eased out of me—perhaps the first one I'd taken since Father had gone missing. I felt a spark of life flicker inside. My path, blocked by a wall too tall to scale, tore itself down, brick by brick.

All I needed to do was fix the formula and enlist the Samaritan's help. He'd know where to find the Rook, and by extension, my father.

There were yet many unknowns. I didn't know what the letter meant. I didn't know who the innkeeper was. Like the rest of London, I still didn't know the Samaritan's identity.

But.

Unlike the rest of London, now I knew someone who did.

# 11

## Ashley

Thick morning rain cleared away lingering fog. I illusioned myself as a patch of sky, a plume of smoke, anything other than a man leaping over chimneys and alleyways. The moss-freckled beams beneath me sagged, and my stomach swooped from each moment of temporary weightlessness. The slick rooftops slowed my pace considerably, but it was still far faster than trekking through streets overcrowded with donkey hooves and axle trees.

Like every day, I was headed for the bookshop, but this time without Miles in tow. He hated the rooftops—anything to do with heights—which meant I only used them when he wasn't with me. A few minutes later, the buildings changed to stone and plaster as I moved into a better part of town.

Miles was currently visiting his mother and aunts for the sole purpose of listening to their complaints on his perpetual bachelorhood. He'd grumbled about going all morning, even though he'd had several weeks to prepare for their monthly brunch.

I never got used to the stab of jealousy I felt, watching him walk out the door. I never stopped wondering if he'd come back.

Unlike me, he had relatives who cared whether he ate, slept, shaved, married.

I swung onto a window ledge a story below. Using slats of rock that bordered the corner of the building, I climbed down another story, not bothering with the last one before jumping. I landed in a shallow puddle, spraying the hem of a woman's dress. She stopped to inspect it, but I was off before I saw her eyebrows fully scrunch.

I usually took greater care while holding an illusion that made me invisible, but the morning had made me sloppy, and I was ready for it to be over. I ducked into a hollow alleyway and emerged on the other end as a solid figure.

A dark part of me wished Miles didn't have a life outside—that he needed me in the same way I needed him. But he didn't, and it was a royally selfish wish, so I'd banished those thoughts to the far reaches of my mind. I only fed them once a month, when I walked the streets alone and they came prowling back like dogs, nipping at the bleeding hole in my chest.

I paused by a cold gas lamp to allow a thick group of workers past, ignoring that hole and the pain searing out. I could let it bleed. Everyone who ever cared about me had been ripped away, and Miles's absence forced me to acknowledge that he might share the same fate.

He was all I had, and I knew it was pathetic.

He knew it too, which was why every month he offered to blow off the meeting with his mother. And then he'd look at me with that perceptive, concerned look in his eye—the one that made me ache, and burn, and wish and wish—and I would flash him that smirk he hated and tell him *I'll always manage fine without you.*

An exit. A way out of our spinning, tangled web.

He never took it. He always came back.

And though each time I was relieved, I also couldn't help feeling angry that he pitied me enough to.

The congestion cleared, and I pushed forward, stepping over a mystery vegetable that had fallen from a cart on its way to Covent Gardens, now trodden to a pulp and staining the cobblestones green.

Though the gutter that ran the length of the street was full of old leaves and slow, milky water, Paternoster Row was unusually empty. Maybe because of the weather. Or maybe they'd all decided to take brunch with their families.

*Gads, will you just stop it.*

A lamp hung near the bricked entrance of the bookshop, iron cast and glowing faintly from the last dregs of gas. The bell tinkled when I opened the door.

As I crossed the threshold, a memory tapped me on the shoulder. I halted, exhaling deeply through my nose. When I didn't respond, the tapping grew harder, quicker, more insistent. The magic didn't like being ignored. And today of all days, I didn't have the energy to fight it.

My mental wall crumbled, and I gave in to the familiar tug, letting my mind sweep me back to yesterday when I'd met Dorothy St. James in this very shop. Flashes played before my eyes, the magic tweaking little details from the encounter. Her eyes were too big, and they blinked slower. She stood an inch closer. The air was sweeter than it had been.

"Oy, sir!" A muffled cry from somewhere far away. "Let in a draft, will you?"

Only when the encounter finished did the memory loosen its grip. I mentally batted it away and closed the door, now grateful that Miles wasn't with me. He'd only look at me with fearful questions in his eyes. The ones he'd let go unasked for years.

Because people weren't born with two slants. People were

barely born with one. I was an anomaly. A creature. And my second slant ...

While often useful, it was by no means a gift.

Despite the unpleasantness of having my mind subjugated for a few moments, I didn't mind reliving my meeting with Miss St. James. I'd been too busy to think of her much since the concert last night, but now I wondered if she'd gotten my book, if she'd liked it.

I allowed a small smile to pull at my lips. Perhaps I'd pay her a visit to find out. I had mountains of things to do, but a conversation with her sounded infinitely more fun; a breath of fresh air in this putrid city.

I turned down the aisle to my left, passing books in palettes of deep brown, wine red, and forest green, scanning the shelves until I found what I was looking for. R231. No girl with unusually pretty hair to steal it from.

My smile widened. Yes, I would definitely call on her today.

I flipped through the pages to ensure the message was there, exhaling in relief when I found a paper tucked into the spine.

An exhale that was cut short when I saw a different message. It wasn't coded, nor was it in Tanner's handwriting.

My smile slipped, and I threw up an illusion to keep it in place; to make it look like I was fascinated by what I was reading and not reeling with dread. The new note wasn't long. Only five simple words that made me want to break something.

*Come to the back corner*

I crumpled it in my fist. Whoever had written the threat knew I was in communication with someone and was probably watching me right now. They had my message from Tanner, and that could only mean one thing.

Blackmail.

I sighed. Bloody *lovely* way to start my week.

Leaving a magical apparition of myself reading behind me, I blended into the shelves, the illusion warm and glossy on my skin as I stuck my head around the corner to spy on the man I was dealing with.

But it wasn't a man that casually perused the shelves at the back of the shop. It was a girl with unusually pretty hair, as if my greedy thoughts had conjured her there. I glanced around. No one else was near—certainly nowhere that could be interpreted as "the back corner."

I let the illusion behind me drift into smoke, holding the other one steady until I stood directly behind her. "Miss St. James."

She whirled around, her cheeks turning the same shade as her plaid, rose dress. "Mr. Gardner—"

"I trust your family is in good health?"

She blinked at me, confused by the question. "Indeed."

"And you as well?"

Another pause. Another bout of blinking. "Yes. Very well."

I cocked my head, tucking my hands in my pockets. "Receive any packages recently?"

Just as I felt the *pull* softly close around her, against my will trying to influence her, she snapped out of her daze and cleared her throat. "None worth mentioning."

The mutated magic drifted back, curious at this new animal that didn't bend to its pleasure. Then I registered what she said.

Hm. That hadn't gone as planned.

But the blackmailer couldn't be her. There was a possibility she'd seen the coded message yesterday, but *débutantes* weren't exactly prime perpetrators of extortion. Nor were they versed in the science of cryptanalysis.

"I am sorry to hear that. Good day to you." I pushed past, catching a whiff of her violet-scented perfume. As much as I'd like to stay and chat, I needed to find the real culprit before he gleaned more fodder for his threat.

"I believe I have something you want?"

I froze, shoulders tensing.

Blast. It *was* her.

I swiveled and knocked my head back to stare at her through lazy, hooded eyes that belied the panic running rampant in my stomach. "You're going to have to be more specific."

She rolled her lips together. "The note left in R231. I believe it was intended for you—only it is now in my possession."

My mind raced. Her being the one to find two notes in as many days was too much of a coincidence. If she had *decoded* the first message, it would've led her straight to the second, but that would mean—

I stepped closer to her.

She raised her chin. "I don't have it on me."

"You expect me to believe that?"

"What kind of a fool would I be to put it in your reach, after the way you handled me yesterday?"

My boots brushed the edge of her dress, tone pitching lower. "I have many ways of handling a woman, Miss St. James. Yesterday was only one of them."

Her nostrils flared, like she needed more air than my proximity allowed. But her voice was smooth when she said, "I am happy to return your note to you, Mr. Gardner, as soon as you give me the information I need."

I decided to play along. "Which is?"

"The Samaritan's identity."

Only through years of practice was I able to keep my face blank. The *Samaritan?* Bloody silt, what trouble was the girl up to?

"And what gave you the impression that I know the answer to the question of the century?" I said blandly. "Until he wants to be known, I doubt any of us shall find it out. You'd do better among the gossip circles of the Strand."

In response, she opened a scrap of paper and held it out for me to read. Two words in, I knew it was Tanner's message from yesterday, rewritten.

She had to have penned the code somewhere before I arrived or memorized it. And then to decode it, a task few would've undertaken—who knew how many hours she'd spent? Or maybe she'd noticed my slip of the tongue and guessed it right off. Either way, it was clever.

Either way, I had to admire her ability to so thoroughly mangle my plans. It was a talent few possessed.

Ignoring the determination in her eyes, I shrugged and said, "So you found a piece of paper with the Samaritan's name on it. Sounds more like a youthful prank than a coordinated operation. I think you read too many novels."

"Except that you're here too, looking for the next clue."

"To the contrary, I'm here to learn about" —I plucked the first book my hand touched from the shelf and read its title, cursing my luck— "*Embroidery: A Stitching Guide to Doilies and Handkerchiefs.*"

While a couple wandered past us and around the corner, Miss St. James stared me down, but the effect wasn't intimidating. Her face was too open, too *innocent*. Her shoulders bunched as she inhaled a deep breath. "So, this information isn't a secret?"

"Not mine."

"That's a relief to hear." She flipped the paper around to read it, raising her voice. "Please inform the Samaritan that the innkeep—"

My hand shot over her mouth, and I pushed her back against the bookcase. Her eyes went wide above my little finger.

"Ah, *that* secret," I whispered, hoping no one had heard. "I would rather you keep that one between us."

The more I used my second slant, the more volatile it seemed to become. But now, short of giving her what she wanted, she left me little choice. I repressed a grimace, bracing myself for the phrenic battle.

With a delicate touch, I reached into her mind, shuffling through her memories like a deck of cards. One of them seemed to whisper *Over here, over here.* I ignored it and pulled out the one I wanted—the one of her finding Tanner's new note early this morning.

My control slipped and I plummeted. My insides jerked like I'd physically fallen. Here, in the new memory, the light was dim, she wore a nightdress, and a paper bearing the underlined name of Mr. Riley sat on the desk before her.

*That's not what I want.*

I tried again, reshuffling the deck. *This one, this one,* the magic whispered. Again, I ignored it and went straight to the one with Tanner's note. Before I could draw it out, my grip slipped again, harder, faster, down a slick ice wall and slamming into granite.

I grappled with the magic, pushing, twisting toward the card but getting thrown against the ice over and over. Sweat rolled down my temple.

Finally, I held the memory long enough to see her tucking it into her purse and rushing it home. Without opening it.

Exhausted, I pulled out of her mind completely—to find her still trapped against the bookcase, studying me with a furrow in her brow even though no more than a few seconds had passed. Tanner had set sail last night. The note now in Miss St. James's possession contained the critical information that had forced him to go abroad. *All* of my plans hinged on my obtaining it.

But ... I could afford to delay those plans for a week.

I cursed, and her eyes widened even more. And though I was

the one who had her pinned, I could see no way out. No way to get the crucial communique without bargaining with her.

Within reason.

"All right, it's true," I murmured, and she melted with relief. "I know who he is." She tried to speak but her muffled words cut off when I tightened my grip over her mouth. "But the thing is, I risked my neck on more than one occasion for that information. It is not information anyone should know unless they are willing to do the same."

I felt her swallow and noticed the warm brush of her lips against my palm.

"Now I am going to release you, but this bookshop—empty as it is—still has ears, so you must promise not to use your words so carelessly."

She blinked, then nodded slowly.

I lowered my hand but didn't step away. "You don't know what a dangerous game you are playing."

"Believe me, Mr. Gardner," she said, and her voice had a grittiness to it that I couldn't interpret, "I know." As I retreated, she pushed strings of hair that had been caught under my hand away from her face.

"There must be something else you want," I said.

Miss St. James shook her head.

"Money, perhaps? Or ... a favor, of some kind?" The words tasted bitter on my tongue, because I wasn't sure how far, exactly, I was willing to go.

I prayed she wouldn't force me to find out.

But she shook her head again. "This is the only thing I want." Her lips pressed into a firm line. "Unless you give it to me, you can say goodbye to your new message."

I licked my teeth, annoyed but begrudgingly impressed too. "If the Samaritan's identity were brought to light, it could pitch society into another Gloaming," I said lightly. "Blood. Gore.

Death. Hardly a fair exchange for a piece of paper with a few scribbles on it."

"That risk is entirely yours to take, Mr. Gardner."

"Just as you can risk me tattling to your uncle that you're looking into the Samaritan."

She froze, mouth slightly ajar.

I smiled, whispering, "Wouldn't want him hindering your plans, would you?"

"He's not my keeper." But she blinked nervously, like that wasn't exactly true.

"Perhaps," I said, crossing my arms, "in exchange for the note, I will give you a clue as to his identity, to aid you in your search. As a favor to you, of course."

She considered me a moment. And maybe I'd scared her enough, or maybe she detected something unyielding in my face, because she said, "Three."

My chuckle was hollow. "That would practically give him away."

"Three clues," she insisted.

"Two."

"*Three*."

I sighed again. I'd done a lot of sighing this morning. But I didn't have much choice. "Three clues, then." I looked her up and down, noting the way she seemed to step toward me then away in the same thought, gaze guiltily flitting like a humming-bird. Maybe she could decode a message, but she wasn't the type of girl who liked taking risks.

I could work with that.

The closer she got to the knowledge of the Samaritan, the more she endangered her life. If she wasn't careful, she'd be caught in the same web I was in, a web far more tangled and perilous than she was prepared for.

"I'll warn you now," I said, "you'll have to be as resourceful as you were today to learn your three clues. I'll hide them well. You won't succeed by playing it safe, as you usually do."

Her spine stiffened, and she opened her mouth like she was about to protest—against my assessment or my counteroffer, I wasn't sure, because she snapped it shut a moment later.

Another long pause passed, and I was intrigued by her candid stare. I wasn't used to prolonged eye contact from anyone but Miles. Even then, he always looked away first. I think they sensed something in my eyes, the magic thrumming under my skin, something dark and a little bent.

"All right," she said with a slow nod. "But after I've played your game, I get a guess—three in total. One per clue." She leaned in, closer than I'd been with my hand over her mouth, closer than I thought she had the nerves for. She held most of the cards and wanted me to know it.

And I did.

But I was also good at taking things while she wasn't looking.

"If I solve the mystery," she said, eyebrows arching delicately, "you will confirm it for me."

I disliked being backed into a corner. But I couldn't stop my lips from curving, from relishing the tiny breath of space between us. "Naturally."

"And in case you consider lying to me or giving me false clues, remember, I have the ability to decipher your code at any time."

I couldn't risk that.

"No need." The ring I retrieved from my coat winked in the light; it was something I rarely used but kept on me for just such occasions. "It's a truth ring," I explained, fitting the silver band around my finger. "The gem will remain blue if you're telling the truth. Tell a lie, and it will cloud black."

Her brow furrowed. "Is it magic?"

"In a way. Definitely don't let a blueduster catch you with one. The rings are rare—usually bought with blood."

Her alarmed eyes found mine, and I could read every question in them like a book. Though it was true, I'd admitted it mostly to see her reaction. I shouldn't play with her like this. I shouldn't enjoy it. But it was part of the plan, and it was so rare that the increasingly sentient mutation inside me left a woman alone that I almost couldn't stop myself.

So much freedom came from knowing her actions were her own.

"Show me," she said.

We watched it turn black when I told her it was sunny out, and glow blue when I amended my assessment to cloudy. I gave a few more examples, then let her try a few sentences of her own.

Once satisfied, she extended her hand, the tip of her middle finger grazing my waistcoat. "To our deal."

I studied her, remembering her threat to decode my message. She could do it without my knowledge, but something—perhaps her candid, innocent face—told me that Dorothy St. James wasn't the type of person to stab you in the back.

Which, in some ways, was a shame.

"No, Miss St. James." I smirked and took her hand. "To the games ahead."

# 12

## Miles

The stairway leading to our third story flat smelled of body grease and wood rot. I trudged upwards, almost tasting the relief of falling into bed though it was still early afternoon. We'd been working far too late. Far too much.

And yet, I'd trade *that* work over the chore of this morning any day.

Over chipped teacups and watered-down tea, my mother and aunts had grilled me with question after question. *What's that spot on your shirt? Have you been seeing a nice girl? You're too thin—are you still eating? Why don't you move in with us, here, where you belong? You remember what today is, don't you? Where is that friend of yours, and why does he keep working you so hard?*

Nothing. No. Yes. No. Of course. Out. He doesn't.

A morning of one- and two-word sentences that were so hard to choke out, I would rather swallow a glass of needles. I was related to these women and could barely talk to them—what made them think I could talk to a nice girl?

Avoiding the patches of exposed wood I knew by heart, I

passed wallpaper peeling in thin strips, and a black cloth pinned over the gaping hole on the landing.

Located in the heart of London, our chosen flat for the month made us easily accessible to Ashley's extensive network, while also serving as the ideal location for muddling the lines between gentleman and working class. Renting the entire third floor helped us dodge nosy neighbors and gave us three extra rooms to store our supplies. In a month, it would all be empty. I opened the door to our flat, shrugging out of my brown trench coat, damp from a drizzle, and hanging it on the peg.

"Polina is in town," Ashley said by way of greeting. He sat at the table strewn with maps, springs, cogs, bits of silver and gold, and turning over a mysterious object in his hands as he took it apart. If I asked what he was doing, his explanation would undoubtedly make no sense, so I didn't bother.

The flat wasn't large. Just enough for a table, cupboard, sofa, a grubby window, and two small bedrooms made private by the curtains covering the empty doorways. An open bottle sat on the mantle, filling the room with the faint, fruity odor of brandy.

"I was considering paying her a visit," he went on without looking at me. "Want me to tell her you said hello?"

I frowned and shut the door with my heel. The stunning Russian ballerina had a way of getting under my skin, even though I'd never uttered a word to her. "She'll know you're lying," I grumbled and sank into the washed-out damask chair, tossing my hat at the peg, missing, and feeling too lazy to rectify it. "Is this *visit* of yours going to last all night like it did last time?"

Ashley's fingers stopped. He set the object down and leaned back, draping an elbow over the chair next to him, eyes sweeping up. Cool stubbornness glinted in them. "Nothing happened."

"Much to her disappointment, I'm sure."

We stared at each other for a long moment.

"If there is anything she's disappointed about," he muttered at last, then his tone forcibly brightened, "it's that you won't even say hello to her."

I wanted to scoff but didn't, knowing better than to push him when he was in a bad mood.

Ashley was the one the ballerina wanted. Ashley was the one *every* woman wanted. I couldn't care less but hated how religiously he insisted on pretending otherwise, born of some intrinsic need to act like he was normal. He wasn't, a fact which I tried not to focus on.

I unbuttoned my spats, sighing when my stockings practically emitted steam. "Fine. Give her my warmest greetings."

"You're right, it's not believable. No message, then." He poured an inch of liquor into a waiting glass which we both knew was for me. "Polina can be a bit handsy," he acquiesced, holding the glass out, "but she's also unignorably useful."

I grunted and took it. That was where Ashley drew the line with everybody: the useful, the potentially useful, and the ones worth ignoring. He was just ... he was just *driven*. His mind was a maze, one he was constantly testing, mapping, trying to get out, out, out of. Nothing—no one—mattered more than navigating that maze and breaking free.

I used to think I was the exception to that. But lately ...

Ashley had a nose for mysteries the way some men had a drinking problem. And for better or worse, I was the one who carried him home from his metaphorical tavern, night after night, trying to ground him back into his old self. I was the only one who could. So even though I was tired of the chase, the struggle, I wouldn't abandon him. Not while he still needed me.

I tossed the brandy back while Ashley's chunk of metal started to shape into a music box. He knocked his head to the right. "There's a crowbar in the corner. Stash it with your other things, will you?"

Code for *We'll need to hide it for later*. Exhaustion had

settled into my bones, but I retrieved my coat from the peg. When I got to the corner, I realized my mistake.

My magic was far more limited than Ashley's. Though the things I stored in my invisible arsenal could be large, and heavy, I could never exceed five. And though we used my slant on nearly every job, we'd never needed to use all five slots before.

With a brush of my fingers against the scratchy fabric, I could feel what the coat already held. I changed out the contents so regularly, sometimes I needed to be reminded. A skiff. Ashley's lock-picking set. A change of clothes. A lit lantern. And ...

"Something the matter?" Ashley said.

Picking up the crowbar, I threw a "No," over my shoulder. I waited until Ashley's attention shifted back to his music box and then wadded the crowbar in the folds of the coat. I'd figure out how to sneak it past him later.

Because the coat was the only safe place for the hairpin, and I wasn't about to replace it.

As I set the bundle on my chair, Ashley said, "How was your visit?"

Catching his carefully neutral tone, I glanced at him. Maybe he cared more than he let on. "Fine."

He gestured to a stack of letters on the edge of the table. "If you don't read those, I'm going to toss them in the fire. They're cluttering the flat."

It was a rich claim, considering I was the one who regularly tidied the paraphernalia he left scattered everywhere. But I frowned and examined the first letter, the script on the front identical to six below it. The top one had been penned this morning and sent before I'd arrived on the sender's doorstep.

We hadn't talked about the anniversary of my father's death over brunch—not explicitly, at least, since my mother couldn't confront her abandonment fourteen years ago, not to my face—

but she'd written me letters all month because she still wanted me to acknowledge his sacrifice.

No, *her* sacrifice.

I opened it, reading slowly.

*It's difficult for us all,* she wrote halfway down the page. *We all suffered back then, with so little money. At least we had each other ...*

I didn't outwardly react, but anger prickled my skin. I swallowed it down, down, because she meant well. *We had each other,* it said, pretending like she hadn't shut herself in her room for three years after her husband ran off, abandoning her young son to scrounge for every meal and making him withdraw so far into himself that he barely remembered how to speak. Roaming the seas collecting rare, foreign coins wasn't an honorable life for a father, and blowing the coins he sent home on opium wasn't an honorable life for a mum.

And yet, I still kept her letters in a little stack near the window. I kept his coin collection under my mattress, too ashamed to leave it out in the open, yet still sparing it from the garbage bin where it belonged.

Hoarding their relics wasn't an honorable life for a son.

He'd died of typhus. Then, while Bram was delivering the news to my mother, he'd spotted a ten-year-old boy peeking around the corner. His face tightened as if he were to blame for the handbills she was tossing onto a small flame, the broken chair in the corner, the dirt on my face. My mother had reneged all responsibility of me, so I didn't understand why someone as affluent as Bram Gardner stared.

From that guilt, or compassion, or whatever it was, Bram offered to take me. A week later, I was heaving my guts into the sea, a fully-fledged oceanic nomad.

Ashley stuck to me—the skinny, new boy who only waited and watched with his wide brown eyes—like glue. He tried to show me the ropes around *The Hephzibah* and amaze me with his illusions: a red tiger stalking through tall grass, a horde of crickets swarming up my legs, a charcoal dragon breathing green fire. I followed him around the ship but never joined in his fun—never responded.

Six months later, while we were pulling into Cairo's docks, a ship hand fell ill with a stomach sickness that confined us to the ship. With morbid curiosity, I remembered watching his sweat-licked face, his gaunt frame wasting away and choking on water, as I wondered if this was what my father had looked like as he died. I remembered wishing someone would tear me from the room and tell me he'd left the world with more dignity.

They didn't.

The sailor worsened in the night, and Bram contracted the same illness, and it was decided we couldn't delay any longer. At dawn, the ship readied for Crete in hopes of a cure.

And all the while, Ashley riddled me with stories of the wonders we'd never see if we left—markets brighter than a field of flowers, pyramids taller than clouds, mosques that were older than magic itself. Even then, he had a tongue as silver as a beam of moonlight. And the more I watched the sailor die my father's death, the more I craved a distraction.

"To the pyramids and then straight back," Ashley promised as we sneaked off the ship.

By the time we realized we were lost, our necks were slick from sweating under a blazing sun. We wandered all day, stumbling back to the Nile as the last splash of pink left the sky and the frogs started to sing. Up and down the banks of the shimmering water we searched, into the star-crusted morning, but *The Hephzibah* was gone.

Exhausted, we collapsed on the shore, allowing the mosquitoes to peck at every inch of exposed skin. We awoke itchy and starving and miserable and utterly alone.

"Come on," Ashley said with a knock of his chin before leading me into a mass of buildings and sands the color of molten bronze. In a market, customers bought pottery, rugs, sandals, and swaths of bright fabric. Further down the street stood stands of dates, pistachios, twisted bread, roasted goat, and peaks of aromatic spices.

Stomach growling, I followed Ashley blindly, and when we reached the end of the market, we ducked into an alleyway. He handed me a roll that he'd pilfered somewhere along the way. I was so hungry that I wolfed it down before I thought to split it with him, but he didn't comment on it, only looked at me and said, "You're going to need more."

For the next few days, we drank from the Nile. Ashley stole the things we needed for survival: food, sandals, scarves for our faces to keep them from blistering. We'd been away from England for a while, so our magic was waning, but he didn't need to cast illusions to do it. He was so quick and light that I had a hard time following his movements even when I watched for his sleight of hand.

One time while stealing an apple, he slipped up. When the vendor yanked his wrist and shouted in his face, he lobbed the apple to me behind his back. The vendor caught the flash of movement, and his anger shifted to me. He patted us both down, eventually making us undress.

No apple.

We threw on our clothes while the man barked us away. Only when we were safe did I pull the apple from my magical pocket and toss it to Ashley. He caught it with one hand and looked at it curiously. Without saying a word, he grinned and took a bite.

"You're the only friend I've ever had," I admitted one of the nights, when our bellies were finally full but the shadows were deep. It was the first time in six months that I'd spoken.

We'd found a balcony shelf no wider than we were, under a length of canvas strung across the street, and though the sandstone was hard and coarse, it was better than sleeping on the ground with the shadows and the rats.

If Ashley was surprised by the sound of my voice, he didn't react. "Didn't you have friends back in England?"

The top of my hair brushed against his as I shook my head. "Too quiet. They all thought I was a half-wit. Even my mother." I stared at a patch of starlight shining through a hole in the canvas. "It's hard to be friends with someone who thinks you're stupid."

"You and I aren't friends," he'd replied. The firmness in his voice sounded like slabs of rocks being stacked on top of each other, the beginnings of a fortress. "From now on, we are brothers."

It was twelve days before the men of *The Hephzibah* found us. And all the while, young and lost as we were, I never had a chance to panic because I had him. Leading the way.

I snapped out of my reverie to find my hand still clutching my mother's letter. Ashley's music box sat whole before him, chiming a pleasant melody as it spun around. He'd already moved on to his next task: examining the detailed maps of London beneath it.

"You can burn it," I told him at last, softly, letting the letter fall to the table. "Burn them all."

Remembering that my coat was still damp and needed to dry, I snagged it from the chair and headed for the glorified closet that barely fit my mattress. A loud clanking reverberated through the floorboards. The crowbar.

I froze, heart pounding.

"I thought you were going to put that in your coat."

I swallowed, but the lump in my throat didn't budge. "I forgot," I croaked and swiped the crowbar up and continued toward my room.

Too late. His full attention was on me now.

He pushed the maps away, his unnatural green eyes boring a hole in the side of my face. When I reached the curtain to pull it aside, he said, "What's the fifth object?"

Just like that, he'd connected all the dots. I let go of the curtain. "There's only four."

"I can count, Miles."

I turned and glared at him. "Then count to four."

"A skiff. My lock-picking set. A change of clothes. A lit lantern." He ticked them off on his fingers. Of course he kept track of the things in my coat. Of course he did. "That's four things. What's the last one?"

"A jab to the jaw if you don't drop it."

He grinned darkly. "Ah, interesting! Never seen you pull one of those before. Go on, then." He reclined in his chair. "Don't let it take up unnecessary space. Punch me already and you can make room for the crowbar."

"As tempting as that sounds, I think I'll save it for later, when you're in need of some cheering up."

"It's something from a woman, isn't it."

My stomach clenched and I went cold.

"A handkerchief embroidered with her initials? A bottle of her perfume you can take out to smell when you're in the middle of—"

Blood rushed to my face. "*Drop* it, Ash." I plunged into my room and let the curtain swing closed. Only when he couldn't see me did I let my hands shake. Let myself breathe for a moment and try not to make any sounds he could interpret. My fingers brushed the coat again, feeling the hairpin, making sure it was still there even though of course it couldn't have moved.

It was. I let out a breath.

He was such a bleeder sometimes. He pushed me in a way no one else did. I hated it. I needed it sometimes, too, even if now wasn't one of those times.

After draping the coat over the edge of my dresser and sticking the crowbar on top to keep it in place, I sank onto my mattress. I felt a lump through the feathers beneath me like a brand, so I pulled the small booklet out, opening it and staring at the silver coins that had been my father's. It was the only thing of his I owned.

Every coin had the year 1844 minted on them—the year he'd been born. They came from Spain, Brazil, China, and Sweden, formed of gold, silver, bronze, and copper, ranging in size from a pea to an egg; a collection built from a lifetime of travels. Dozens of them, and I had memorized each one.

I should throw it away. With a leg, I prodded the wastebasket out of the corner until it sat under the booklet.

Just as I was about to drop the booklet in, one of the coins sparkled from the corner of my eye. It was silver, and in a language I didn't understand but looked to be Asian. My thumb brushed over the year printed on its surface. 1844. A rare coin that hadn't been there this morning. My gaze drifted to the closed curtain again, where Ashley shuffled maps on the other side.

Who knew how long he'd harbored the coin, waiting for the anniversary of my father's death. Today was always a difficult one for me, filled with conflicting emotion; Ashley remembering that fact meant more than any coin collection.

My gaze lingered so long that after a few minutes, my throat grew thick and my view of the curtain blurred. Blinking quickly, I nudged the wastebasket back into the corner. Then I slowly closed the booklet and placed it back under the mattress.

# 13

## Dorothy

The first thing I noticed upon entering the Gaiety Theater were the chandeliers; glass diadems that sparkled like diamonds hanging from curls of gold. Then came the inverted V of stairs, gilt railings curving toward the arched entrance of the balcony. And the third thing I noticed was the figure of Ashley Gardner, which was arguably just as riveting.

He wasn't looking at me, thank goodness, allowing me to study him through the sea of evening gowns and oiled hair. I could feel his radiating charm from a distance, coaxing grins and lingering gazes from the circle around him. Since striking the deal in the bookshop yesterday, I'd waited anxiously to hear word of my first clue, but—nothing. He'd remained silent, and I couldn't help but think it was a calculated move.

Not for the first time, I wondered what my clue would be. I snapped open my purse and scanned the list I'd made earlier— qualifications the Samaritan had to meet and the reasons why. It was far from complete, but once I got my clue, it would help narrow the candidates.

- *Young and strong—to stage daring rescues*
- *Member of the ton—only rescues those in upper circles*
- *Likely lives in London—see above reason*
- *Slanted??—rumors from Emme*

"Such a grand venue," Aunt Marie commented breathlessly, making me fold the list and return it to my purse. She took everything in, from the cased ceiling to the marble tile beneath her rhinestone slippers. "Isn't it grand, Dorothy?"

Emme had insisted she wasn't feeling well, and Uncle Benedick had settled into my father's den in his smoking jacket, so it was only me and my aunt tonight. To my surprise, Uncle didn't object to us attending without him, perhaps satisfied that someone was representing the family without him having to subject himself to the ballet.

"Grand indeed," said a voice above my shoulder.

I turned to find Mr. Gardner. Was he going to slip me the code to decipher now? With my aunt looking on? Or give it to me after the performance?

"Good evening, Mrs. Morgan. Miss St. James, I hoped I'd find you here." His smile told me hope had nothing to do with it. Unlike every other male in the room, his black hair wasn't combed—although its rumpled waves still somehow lay symmetrically. He had a lofty gaze, yet nothing slipped past him, not even my arrival in a crowded hall.

An aura of chaos but cunning. Luck embodied.

I barely stopped myself from blinking with hummingbird wings. It was something I did when I was nervous, and I was positive he'd noted it in the bookshop. "Good evening—"

"Oh, Mr. Gardner," my aunt said, a swirl of color in her cheeks that hadn't been there a moment before. "How nice to see you again."

He bowed a little. "You both enjoy the ballet?"

"Yes." Aunt Marie's smile vanished as if she'd revealed something terrible. "That is, no. Not as much anymore. Not since Mr. Morgan made his dislike of it clear. I wouldn't *dream* of—but it can be nice to, every now and again ..."

Her rambling made my heart ache. My father used to regale me with stories of her mischievous nature, the pranks she'd pull on him by hiding his spectacles or slipping powder into his snuff. There'd been a time when she'd lived her life fully, unashamed. And now she couldn't admit she liked ballet without fumbling for words.

"We don't get to attend very often, is what my aunt means to say," I cut in smoothly, and Aunt Marie's shoulders lowered in relief.

"Yes," she said. "Although, Emmeline will be sorely disappointed to have missed you tonight. You must stop in for a visit sometime, Mr. Gardner. Tomorrow, perhaps?" Her eyes sparkled in a scheming way I'd never seen before.

Before I could come up with a reason to extract the offer, he gave another little bow, which only served to deepen my aunt's blush. "I'd be obliged."

Mr. Gardner and I had a business transaction. He was obviously tied to the Samaritan, and although the masked man was doing society a good turn, he was still breaking the law. But my aunt looked so genuinely happy—free of her husband's looming shadow, for once—that I didn't have the heart to discourage the visit.

Her sigh carried a little giggle. "Excellent. Well, I believe the performance is about to begin. Come, Dorothy, let us take our seats." Aunt Marie stepped forward and Mr. Gardner turned away.

But when I took a step after my aunt, I felt a finger in the hollow of my elbow and the soft brush of lips on the shell of my ear. "Don't lean too far over the balcony," he whispered. Warmth bloomed from my jaw and shot to my toes. Before I could inform him that our seats were on the main floor, he'd vanished into the crowd.

Our seats were not, in fact, on the main floor.

I settled into my balcony seat that offered a bird's-eye view of the theater, restraining myself from looking around for Mr. Gardner.

A man shuffled in front of me but stopped with a glint of recognition in his keen, hazel eyes. "Why, Miss St. James! How lovely to see you here." He smiled through his neat white beard.

"Mr. Vernon." It was an odd feeling, seeing him somewhere other than across the dinner table. My spine straightened at the opportunity that had fallen into my lap. "It's good to see you too. If I may ask, did you get my letter requesting the society dinner's guest list a few days ago? I wish to make a study of everyone's accumulated research."

His face crumpled in thought. "I can't say as I have. Must've been lost in the mail." He inhaled, expression clearing. "Well, do write me again, and I can send that along to you, dear. If you're anything like your father, the scientific community will greatly benefit from your study."

My smile was forced, but I nodded.

After introducing Mr. Vernon to Aunt Marie, he said, "Lovely to meet Geoffrey's sister. He's spoken very highly of you, Mrs. Morgan." Then he noticed the empty seat to my left. "Is he here tonight?"

"My father is currently in the country, for his health," I said, the words tasting like sandpaper.

"Ah. We shall remember him in our prayers. But where are my manners? Nicholas." He gestured for the man standing behind him to come forward. "I believe you're acquainted, but might I officially introduce my business associate, Mr. Hart."

My lips parted slightly. Now he had a first name as well.

*Nicholas Hart.*

Mr. Vernon clapped the young man on the back like he was a favored son. "He's a brilliant journalist, and I wouldn't know what to do without him. Perhaps you recognize him from our dinners."

Mr. Hart's inquisitive gray eyes quickly glazed over my aunt and landed on me, sticking there and heating with interest. "Enchanted," he said, smiling in a way that made the freckle above his lip dip. His warm brown hair no longer brushed his forehead, which meant he'd recently had it cut.

Aunt Marie leaned forward, and I could practically hear the gears whirring in her head. "There is an empty seat here, Mr. Hart, and I'm sure Dorothy is eager to pick your mind on journalism. Do you think you could part with him, Mr. Vernon?"

My face heated.

Mr. Vernon beamed, waving the head of his cane at Nicholas. "Of course, of course!"

This was the second time Aunt Marie's mischievous nature had made an appearance tonight, the thrill of matchmaking turning the most timid of women into a giggling schoolgirl.

After Mr. Vernon left, Mr. Hart seated himself on my left, then immediately hopped up and turned to me. "Would you care to switch places, Miss St. James?"

I looked between our seats. His was closer to the stage. "Do you dislike this ballet?"

"On the contrary, *Les Bois Endormis* is one of my favorites. But as I've already seen it, I thought you might appreciate the better view."

I blinked. That was very thoughtful of him. With a small smile and a murmured thanks, we switched seats.

"Are you helping with the annual London Science Society fundraiser next month?" he asked, and when I pivoted toward him, he was closer than I expected. Close enough to be conspiratorial. I noticed that freckle above his lip again, then glanced away. Until I found the Samaritan and tracked down the Rook, I couldn't afford any distractions.

"I usually do, but I've written to the society to tell them not to count on me this time. I've had a sudden—" I nearly said *emergency* but decided to rephrase to avoid questions. "I have a lot of other projects right now."

Mr. Hart nodded, his smile secretive. "I am sorry to hear that." He lowered his voice and leaned in even closer. "Wits and magic are no match for what haunts you."

My lips parted, heart stopping. "I beg your pardon?"

"*Les Bois Endormis*," he said, gesturing to the stage. "It's a line from the opera the ballet is based on. A young Russian girl uses her slant to make those around her fall asleep, but one day she wanders into the forest and accidentally puts the trees into a slumber, awakening other, darker creatures who are immune to her magic. She's forced to hide in the husk of a tree until a hunting prince helps her defeat them. It's a tragic tale of a young girl facing the constant bombardment of her demons." He offered me a half smile. "Like you."

"Ah." I relaxed, cheeks warming. "You are very cultured, Mr. Hart."

"I merely ask a lot of questions. A hard habit to break when you're a journalist."

The occupation certainly fit his inquisitive gaze.

A few minutes later, the ballerinas stepped onto the stage in their white, bell-shaped tutus, their chains and graceful lines adding a layer to the dance that went unseen by those at ground level. During the performance I felt my eyes wandering, scanning the tops of the heads below. I never found him, though it didn't surprise me. I was starting to suspect that Mr. Gardner could only be found when he wanted to be.

White wood nymphs flitted around the young girl, blessing her on her journey. *Les Bois Endormis* was a rare piece of art, considering how little magic was portrayed in other cultures—and in how little magic those countries possessed to begin with.

England was sitting on the world's only source, which had led to the rise of the British Empire around the globe. During the Renaissance, the army had recruited anyone they could find who was slanted and showered honors on their family, establishing new, noble bloodlines. Over time, those bloodlines had spread to commoners.

It was soon discovered, however, that magic could only replenish itself when it was close to the source; *the Variance*, or so my father's books had called it. Its exact location had been forgotten—or erased—several centuries ago, when a man's magic had mutated, growing so powerful and uncontrollable it had sealed the entrance. Although, the Variance was thought to be close to London. Or even *in* it.

The reverberation of timpani announced the conclusion of the second act, and the stage went dark before unobtrusive employees rekindled lamps around the theater. The rumble of conversation grew with the light.

"Oh, my." Aunt Marie sounded out of breath. Her hand flapped over her heart. "That was ... so beautiful. I think I might need to step out for some air before I'm reduced to tears."

Ever observant and gentlemanly, Mr. Hart jumped to his feet. "Shall I accompany you, ma'am?"

Aunt Marie nodded gratefully, and after linking her arm through his, they both shambled away, leaving me alone with my thoughts.

After a few minutes of ignoring the invisible tug, my gaze strayed below.

And there he was, sitting in a spot I'd checked a dozen times before. Mr. Gardner glanced up at me only long enough for a smirk to pull at his lips. Then he languidly wove toward the exit.

Why was he leaving before the second half? And what was he so smug about?

I felt his finger on my elbow again. His lips on my ear. *Don't lean too far over the balcony ...*

He'd known where I would be sitting.

With the top of his hair still in my sights, I stood and stepped toward the railing. My hands slipped along the polished wood as subtly as possible, uncertain what I was looking for but compelled by blind intuition. I checked inside, under, moving along the balcony. From the corner of my eye, my aunt and Mr. Hart moved down the row, back toward our seats.

*Hurry, hurry.* My fingers slipped over the edge, and—

There. Something smooth, dry, cool. A bit of paper taped to the far side of the balustrade.

Aunt Marie's attention was shifting.

I ripped the paper away and retreated to my seat, heart pounding.

The lights dimmed and the orchestra trumpeted the ballerinas onstage. I waited until everyone was swept back into the story before slowly unfolding the crinkled paper. It wasn't a cipher, but a riddle. I tried not to move my head as I read it in the low light, eyebrows pulling in.

ALOFT IN OAKEN SEAT
OBTAIN THE RIBBON HELD

A riddle. Why had Mr. Gardner sent me a riddle and not a cipher like we agreed?

I thought back to the exact wording of our interaction in the bookshop. He'd mentioned I'd need to be resourceful, but—I suppose he hadn't specified in what way.

So now I had to track down a ribbon somewhere in this theater.

I glanced around. The chairs were tufted with velvet, but their bones indeed appeared to be made of oak. *Aloft.* A balcony seat, then.

But there were two balcony tiers.

"Excuse me," I murmured to Mr. Hart before sliding out of my seat and toward the back of the dim balcony. I studied the chairs I passed, looking for a ribbon tied around one of them, but I could only see the back legs. As discreetly as I could, I got on all fours, trying to see farther up the rows by sifting through the limbs and skirts. Slowly, I crawled down the line, tingles traveling up my neck and across my face, praying no one was watching.

Now I knew what that smirk had been about.

Something silver caught my eye and I poked my head under one of the chairs to get a better look, but it was only a pair of opera glasses. My head bumped the edge of the wood as I backed out, drawing the notice of the woman occupying the seat. Rubbing my head, I whispered, "Beg your pardon," before clambering to my feet and rushing away.

Maybe *aloft* was referring to the top tier of the theater.

I climbed the stairs to the second balcony, wondering if I could avoid demeaning myself quite so much. Bending slightly, I walked down the rows while trying to look inconspicuous. It only served to distract more people from the performance. Heads turned. One gentleman scoffed, eyes narrowing.

The tips of my ears grew hot, making me straighten and scurry toward a shadowy corner.

I wadded my dress in fists. How did Mr. Gardner expect me to find a ribbon in *occupied* seats? Even empty, there were over a hundred chairs to check on both tiers. I'd be here all night.

The music swelled to a blare, drawing my attention to the stage. The young ballerina was being chased through the woods, darting in and out of trees. Trees that were ...

Oak.

I darted back down the stairs and after some searching, found a side entrance. Backstage smelled like powder, and smoke from low-burning tallow candles. Gold-and-silver costumes shimmered on rolling wooden stands as they were rushed to dressing rooms. I noticed a pair of pink slippers hanging on a nearby peg before turning my attention to the stage. Male ballerinas danced in its glow in front of oak trees.

No, the note said *aloft*. I craned my neck and squinted at a forest of set pieces, suspended in the air by ropes. Centered over the stage, one of them appeared to have a red strip of fabric tied around one branch. I squinted harder. Next to the ribbon, something white and square had been tacked on—my next clue. *Aloft in oaken seat, obtain the ribbon held.* I sighed a little.

My eyes fell to the scaffolding that climbed to the props, heart dropping. I wasn't afraid of heights, but that didn't mean I wanted to make a straight vertical climb forty feet in the air in a heavy evening dress, then crawl along thin boards. Every instinct recoiled at the idea.

But not climbing meant giving up the search for the Samaritan before it had even begun; if I was going to find my father, I had to exploit every available channel. With one more hesitant breath, I stepped forward, hand settling over the cool metal of the first bar.

A vision flashed before my eyes.

*My arms quivered and my hands were slick as I climbed the scaffolding. One rung at a time. My skirts dangled as I neared the top. I threw my weight up as I grabbed for the next rung. My hand slipped and my knees buckled. A scream stuck in my throat as I fell—*

I crashed back into the present and backed away from the scaffolding, breathing fast.

That wasn't an option. The future wasn't set in stone, but I wasn't going to take that risk. There *had* to be another way—one that was sure to keep me safe on solid ground. *Obtain the ribbon held.* I glanced at the ribbon on the tree prop and followed the rope down to a sandbag next to me.

Maybe I could bring the clue to me.

The curtains closed to prepare for the final scene change, and I ducked behind the excess curtain folds. The lead ballerina exited, her Russian accent snapping at her assistant to bring her new shoes, complaining about a broken ribbon. Stagehands flurried around the set.

There was so much activity that no one noticed when I worked the rope from around the sandbag and gently lowered the tree to the stage. I snagged the piece of paper near the ribbon and retreated to my hiding place, hands shaking as I read the masculine handwriting.

BEFORE THE BOUGHS MAY BREAK
OBSERVE THE POINT ENSPELLED

Before the boughs broke ... Why would a stage prop break? I tilted the paper, mumbling, "Boughs may break ..."

*Bows.*

Before the *bows* may break—the end of the ballet. I moved onto the last line, muttering it a few times before fixing on the word *Point.*

If *boughs* really meant *bows*, maybe *point* really meant *pointe.*

Ballet shoes. Of course.

Enspelled could mean an enchanting dance that the feet perform, but how was that going to deliver my clue? My thumb accidentally covered the 'en' when I read the word again, and something clicked. *Spell.* They were going to spell out a message.

My eyes shot to the stage, studying the back-up ballerinas' feet. From this angle, their movements, though uniform, looked like a jumble of limbs. If I were to decipher letters from the lead ballerina's finale solo, I'd need an aerial view—

I looked at the scaffolding again, shoulders slumping. I'd thought I'd found a workaround, but Mr. Gardner was still cleverer.

"Where are my new shoes?" a Russian voice yelled, making my gaze again shoot to the slippers hanging on the peg, then to a flickering candle ensconced in a halo of blackened wall.

An idea sparking, I nabbed the shoes and brought them to the candle. Tallow wax was softer than others due to its fatty compounds, and it spread over the soles easily. I was more than liberal with the wax. Then I returned the candle, hung the shoes back on their peg, and fled to my hiding spot where all that was left to do was wait.

And pray.

A minute later, a frazzled young woman spied the shoes and whispered thankful expletives while she rushed them to a dressing room. Five minutes later, horns trumpeted the climax, and one by one, the dark creatures onstage were slaughtered, red ribbons quivering to represent spurts of blood. The lead ballerina took to the stage, stretching her leg and spinning in meticulous circles. She swooped up and to the side, sliding across the floor in a slow solo that while beautiful, didn't fit the music.

My eyes remained glued to her shoes. "Please work," I whispered.

Applause thundered and the rest of the cast joined the balle-rina for the curtain call. The curtains closed and backstage exploded in chatter. Many wandered to dressing rooms to change, while others said their farewells and left. In a matter of minutes, the stage was dark and empty. Even still, my breaths came fast as I snagged a large jar of wig powder and slipped onto the gleaming wooden planks, knowing I didn't have much time before someone came along and asked what I was doing.

I sprinkled the powder where she'd performed her solo. Then I knelt and blew. The loose powder drifted away, revealing streaks where it had stuck to the wax. My muscles went slack with relief. It had worked. I blew and blew until my lips hurt from pinching them and I was coughing from all the white dust in the air. When I finally came to a section where no waxy residue remained, I got to my feet and stepped back, surveying the beginning.

What the powder revealed wasn't as elegant as the dance had looked, but using a combination of toe slides and chains, the ballerina had constructed a crude letter.

O.

I moved to the next letter. I had to squint at the next one, which had been smeared almost beyond all recognition.

R.

I moved down the stage, piecing the crude letters together one by one until I'd reached the end, and a thrill coursed down my spine, the word she'd spelled out pulsing in my sternum. I flicked my purse open and retrieved my list, penciling one more qualification onto the paper.

- *Orphan*

A hot sigh of relief burst between my lips. My first clue was that the Samaritan was an orphan.

Only by a miracle had I been able to outsmart Mr. Gardner, and I shuddered to think what else might be in store. Next time, I didn't think I'd be so lucky. Quickly, I dusted powder off my dress as I left in search of a broom.

# 14

## Ashley

It had been all too easy to switch the tickets.

One hand on her elbow as a distraction, the other one slipping into her purse, a whispered phrase—and it was done. A riddle. A ribbon. And a debt owed by a ballerina now paid in full.

Polina hadn't wanted to switch up her solo—something that she said would anger the ballet master—but she'd had little choice. Besides, the man had been so sozzled he didn't even notice his principal varying from her choreography.

By now, half the audience had ventured into the anteroom to mingle with the cast and congratulate them on the closing-night performance. Waiters passed tall flutes around the room on trays, while others carried light cucumber sandwiches topped with sprigs of fresh rosemary.

Polina had changed into a cascading red dress, but she hadn't bothered to wash off her stage makeup. It accentuated every change in expression, including the subtle way she licked one canine with the tip of her tongue, making her appear slightly predatory. In one hand she held a glass of sparkling champagne, while the other wrapped around my bicep.

For the past hour I'd kept a steady eye on the entrance to the balcony, just visible through the open anteroom doors. I was finally rewarded by the emergence of Miss St. James and her aunt, half a step behind.

Judging by the glow on her face, she'd solved the riddle and had her clue. My head tilted to the side. Again, I was annoyed, but there was another feeling beneath that, not altogether unpleasant. More than impressed. Bordering dangerously on fascinated.

Polina's grip on my arm tightened. "Ashley ..." She held onto the 'sh' a little too long. I knew what that tone of hers meant, and it had nothing to do with the amount of champagne she'd consumed. Then I remembered she'd been in the middle of asking me something.

"Can't, I'm afraid," I said in response. "I still need to check on an artist's progress for the painting I commissioned, and I told Miles I'd meet him for drinks afterward."

"Let him drink by himself. Maybe he'll find *tongue* in bottom of cup." Her accent made the words thicker, but her English was good for only having learned a few years ago. Better than Miles's, at least by her estimation. The only language Miles spoke around her was that of glares.

"You promised you'd come, Ashley."

"Did I?" I asked, even though I knew she was lying. I never forgot when I made a promise. I never forgot anything.

I looked back to the staircase, debating whether to claim Miss St. James's guess tonight or wait for the morning, when I was due to call. The more time that passed between clues, the more time she had to unravel the mystery and use her guess on the right man—and the more urgent Tanner's note became.

"*Da!* And what is more ..." Polina started to ask me another question but drifted off when she noticed my distraction, and her gaze landed on Dorothy gliding down the steps.

I could've illusioned my stare away, kept it trained on the ballerina if only to keep her happy—but I had a long night ahead of me and didn't want to risk expending too much magic like last time. And as it was, I didn't care who she saw me staring at.

Polina took her time studying Dorothy, head to toe. Then she checked her posture, and maybe I imagined the way more of her body pressed into my side, but I couldn't be sure.

Miss St. James was a very pretty girl, but Polina Mikhailova was a fair, classic Russian beauty. She had cliffs for cheekbones and rubies for lips, and a seductive gaze that could pull a man in by his necktie. No one gifted with such deathly graceful lines could have anything to be jealous of in Dorothy St. James.

And yet.

Ever since Dorothy beat me at my own game a few days ago, it was her I couldn't stop thinking about. Her mind was like mine —I could smell it. She saw a puzzle, and with quick fingers she twist, twist, twisted it until all the pieces clicked into place. There was something about that kind of energy that dragged my eyes to her. That made me want to solve *her*.

Maybe part of that fascination stemmed from her immunity to the *pull* in the bookshop.

Miss St. James and her aunt drifted into the room, followed by a straight-backed male companion whose ardent gray eyes missed nothing. When I saw him, I stiffened then immediately forced myself to relax. *It means nothing.*

I didn't know who, exactly, I was directing that thought at.

Polina noticed the momentary weakness. "She is ... quaint. Not very tempting, if you ask me. But if it is tempting you need —" She leaned into me until I felt a dab of her lipstick smear on my earlobe. And then she whispered something so wicked I would never repeat it, even to Miles.

All Polina saw when she looked at Dorothy was an ordinary girl. And maybe that was why she was jealous. Maybe she knew those were the kind I preferred. The understated ones, the curious, the ones who were hungry but refused to sit at the table.

"Mr. Gardner!" Mrs. Morgan spotted me, and the group made their way over. "Oh, dear me," she said when they arrived, taking stock of Polina's makeup and fierce gaze, and looking supremely uncomfortable.

"She doesn't bite," I said with a lazy smile, only half serious. Polina chuckled under her breath.

That didn't seem to ease the tension in Mrs. Morgan's brow, but she snapped out of her stupor enough to introduce me to the man standing behind them. Mr. Hart and I had met before at the club, but neither of us bothered mentioning it. After I'd introduced the ballerina too, Dorothy stepped forward.

"Your performance was flawless," she said to Polina. "I cannot imagine the rigorous study and training you've undergone." Her countenance glowed. She'd definitely solved the riddle.

Polina smiled and made a small noise in her throat, otherwise not acknowledging the compliment. She'd always been prickly when she wanted to be, but flattery usually dispelled that mood, not worsened it.

"And what of you, Mr. Hart?" I turned to the man. "I recall that your parents have a devout love of the arts, so I'd be interested to hear your opinion."

He nodded. "Indeed, they do. I am sorry Mother did not see this one, as I thought it was particularly splendid." He'd said his last words while staring at Miss St. James.

I barely refrained from tensing again.

Mrs. Morgan sighed, high and light. "It is nice to enjoy society for once, instead of sitting at home, overcome with worry that every shadow you see is a phantom. I cannot conceive how the baroness must be feeling. Her own son!"

"I imagine she is quite relieved to have him back." Polina took a sip of champagne, lips wet when she pulled away. Dorothy perked up, and I would've cursed had I not been in mixed company. "Nathaniel Findley was rescued zis afternoon. He was found in foyer of house, unharmed and an opened padlock in his pocket. Yet again, the Samaritan has come to London's aid."

"Praise be!" Mrs. Morgan gasped, a shaky hand oscillating between her open mouth and her breast.

"And what of his—mental state?" Dorothy had gone still, her skin turning to ash.

"Rumor says he has more of his wits than the others. I don't care about the identity of ze masked man, but I hope Mr. Findley sheds some light on who London's phantom is. Ze Rook took friend of mine, two years ago." Polina's teeth flashed, her accent thickening with her anger. "Annushka. Stolen from bed. Never returned. I hope he rots in hell."

Mrs. Morgan gasped again, this time at the uncouth language which was made more shocking by falling from a woman's lips.

Now was as good a time as any to leave.

I wrapped an arm around Polina's shoulders. "She appears dainty on stage, but Miss Mikhailova is, above all, Russian. Good night to you." As I steered her away, I caught Miss St. James's eye, and it was full of questions—or rather the one burning question I was doing everything in my power to prevent her from answering. I made a plan to extract her guess in the morning and headed for the exit.

Mirrors decorated the south wall, and my gut clenched. The tang of blood filled my nose, and I kept my gaze trained ahead as we walked, knowing better than to risk letting it wander to the mirror's varnished frames after what had happened last time. We reached the coat checkers, and I draped her beaver stole around her shoulders.

"Does zis mean you come to my apartment?" Polina's smile was feline.

I said nothing, meeting her eye as I tied the clasp for her. She already knew my answer, so there was no point in saying it. Miles chose that moment to appear at the doors. He gave me an almost imperceptible nod.

Finished with her coat, I stepped back. "Go to bed alone for once, Polina. You might find you actually enjoy the sleep."

She pouted, until she caught sight of Miles. Her nostrils flared, eyes sharpening into daggers. "Ah. And zere he is. Your *real* lover."

There was nothing I had to say to that either. Someone like Polina would never understand the kind of bond I had with Miles. The kind that only came with starving and sweating and suffering and sailing and grieving—together. Hitting and taking hits. It wasn't something that could be reduced to words.

In a way ... love had nothing to do with it.

I put my own coat on. "Have a safe trip back to Russia."

Her head swung back. "You mean not to see me again before I leave?"

But I had already walked off and, knowing Miles was right on my heels, stepped out of the theater and into the welcoming night.

# 15

## The Samaritan

Sometimes a man's eternal resting place lasted him only a week before his remains were dug up and sold to jelly makers to make room for the next corpse. Immigrants contracted diseases, and the city couldn't keep up. Quicklime sped the process of decay. Into the ground, out of the ground, and more coins jangling in the mortician's pocket—that was the circle of death.

The Samaritan wasn't headed for one of the poorer, teeming cemeteries though. The one he sought stood on the outskirts of Town. All but forgotten, just like the object he was hunting.

Dark clouds obstructed the sliver of moon hanging overhead. He passed under the arches of a rail line, keeping to the shadows. The air tasted of metal from the grinding brakes of locomotives, but he wouldn't be taking the train. Nor a coach. Walking briskly, he adjusted the gray mask hiding his features.

Few people ventured out this late. The night belonged to the thieves who lounged in dim public houses. To the coiners and gamblers. To the Rook.

And now, to him.

On he walked. Past errant drunks who slept against buildings, mumbling piecemealed refrains. He walked so far, no more gas lamps lit his path. When he turned the last corner, a gothic gatehouse guarded a graveyard, a broken window gaping on one side.

The spiked iron fence jutted high, the round-top gate double padlocked, but it was easy enough for him to slide inside. He hadn't managed to make a name for himself without reason.

Headstones hewn from granite and quartz, now rough from centuries of rain, sprouted from the overgrown grass like crooked teeth. Some of them bore names, others just a date, but most were blank.

He slipped past the statue of an angel whose dress was half eaten by cold, creeping moss. Past sagging trees and down a little-used path in the southeast corner, plunging into darkness so thick he could taste it in his throat. More angels lined the path, bearing cracked or missing limbs and wings. One was flying, one dancing, one held an outstretched sword, one bowed its head in prayer. But every one of their pale faces watched him in horror, crying through stony lips—*Turn back, turn back, turn back!*

He kept going.

In the farthest corner abutting the fence, nestled between two great sycamores, a simple cross sat above a slab of stone. No name etched its surface. There was nothing extraordinary about it. The Samaritan retrieved the tools planted behind one of the trunks and set to work.

The slab was heavy, but he managed to turn it over, exposing dirt clumps and wriggling worms clinging to the stone. The soil smelled rich and damp. Shovelful after shovelful he tossed to the side, until his hands bled into the wooden handle, until his ankles were beneath the ground ... his knees ... waist ...

*Thunk.*

There. He dug some more, uncovering the edges of the wood.

Flimsy roots clung to the casket, guarding the treasure within. He brushed them aside and pried it open.

Dark clouds stretched to reveal the crescent moon. It illuminated bones, half of them broken, like a man-of-war heaved against craggy rock. His treasure should have been cradled in the corpse's hands. One of the seven identical objects that everything in this magical game was staked upon, but—

The Samaritan pulled the brittle hands apart which were threatening to turn to powder. The object wasn't there.

But the hands weren't empty. No, what they held was worse than emptiness.

A shiny black feather.

He cursed profusely. He hadn't been the only one to receive the tip. That brought the number in the Rook's possession up to five—nearly *all* of them. Cursing again, he hefted himself out of the hole and slipped back into the night, not bothering to refill the grave.

# 16

## Miles

"More, sir?" The barkeeper's hand hovered above the handle of my tankard. As a riverside pub, The Dolphin was a popular establishment for dockworkers and factory men, but it was known more for its cooked eel and fresh bread than its nightlife.

Four candles lit the room, barely enough to see by. A group of men rattled dice in a corner, their gruff Yorkshire accents ordering a plate of oysters every half hour, as well as Yorkshire pudding. Its smell caused a gag to work up my throat. I'd learned enough tricks from watching Ashley's sleight of hand to know the man leaning against the window was clearly cheating.

It was late—early—but I was still waiting for the Mole, so I dug a penny out of my pocket and tossed it on the table. While the barkeeper moved to refill my mug, I thought about the sea. What it would feel like to be rid of the smoke and feel the wind on my face again. An ache filled my chest.

London wasn't home. It could never be home. It was merely the place to fulfill my oath made to Bram as he lay dying. Once I'd met that promise ... maybe I could convince

Ashley to leave it all behind: the past, the mystery, the game, in exchange for our old life. Back then, there wasn't duty to tie us down.

Maybe I was wrong for hating how it tied us now.

I couldn't leave him. And he couldn't leave … everything else.

I knew it had to do with his memories—the ones he never talked about, from before Bram adopted him. I couldn't remember the last time I'd seen him sleep.

My hand drifted to the inner pocket of my coat where I kept my most secret possession. I hesitated. Then pulled it out slowly, fingers reverent.

A filigree hairpin rested on my palm, its head a bronze network of flowers and leaves. It wasn't heavy but the tongs were wide, meant for someone with thick hair. Again, I felt the familiar tingle of awe as I stared at it. The face of its owner swam before my eyes, and I whisked the pin back into my coat, afraid to dwell on it too much.

The coat was the only safe place for it, and every time I pulled it out felt like a gamble with fate. The hairpin wasn't a secret I kept from the world—but it was a secret I kept from Ashley, and that might as well be the same thing.

The group of men in the corner grumbled about something, but their dice shaking continued, a little faster than before.

A man slid into the booth across from me, his long, crooked nose sniffing like he smelled something foul. He didn't apologize for being late. The removal of his hat revealed pale, greasy hair that had been combed to one side.

The Mole belonged to the Necropolis—an underground dwelling for the slanted. The portals to it were difficult to find, and once through, it was even more difficult to escape. Residents went by pseudonyms associated with their slants, to protect their identity. Ashley had used the Mole on several occasions as he was blessed with the ability to compel someone to answer a question

—just one, ever—which was perfect for sniffing out information if you knew enough specifics.

The Mole's black eyes shifted between me and the men playing dice. "I don't like meeting above ground."

I sat forward and threaded my hands on the table. Business outside of the Necropolis could be traced, and its slant workers incriminated. My problem was that only Ashley could sneak me in and out of the underground city—and this was the kind of business that I couldn't conduct around him.

"Did you find her?"

The barkeeper returned with my pint, which the Mole immediately helped himself to. Ale dripped down his jaw, and foam coated his upper lip when he set the mug down and released a satisfied sigh.

I forced a mask of patience, even though I wanted to swat the mug away and demand some answers.

I *needed* some answers.

"The streets are uncommonly silent," he said at last, twisting the rim of the cup with the tips of his fingers. "Can't find anyone what matches her description. And her disappearing at the 'Chapel does scupper the whole bit."

Whitechapel market was one of the busiest places in London. Seas of faces passed through it on any given day, and it was the most understandable—and inconvenient—place to lose someone. Although, if my suspicions were correct, someone had caught on to her plan to meet me and had spirited her away again.

"Did you look into the other address I gave you?" I asked.

The Mole set the mug aside, ignoring my question. "It would aid greatly, sir, if you could provide a name."

I stilled.

I knew it would—and I could give him one, technically, but it was far, far too risky. Names were power.

Especially to someone like Ashley "Gardner."

It was a delicate balance of information—too little, and I stood no chance at finding her again. Too much, and Ashley would find his sister first.

My hands sweat at the thought, remembering my promise to Bram.

After a pause, I shook my head. I tapped my forefinger against the table in thought. So many dead ends. Where else to look?

"Payment?"

I glanced at him. I knew what Ashley would say—that he could scurry back to his hole. To not expect payment unless he actually found something. Ashley's methods weren't mine though.

I slid a crown across the table. "I'd be obliged if you kept your ear to the ground."

The Mole grinned, displaying a row of yellow teeth. "Of course, Mr. Kelly. Of course." After pocketing the coin, he flipped his hat on and slid out of the booth. The men gambling shook their dice more vigorously, faces red. Someone had lost a lot of money.

I stared at the drips of ale splattering to the table. Sighing slowly, I raked a hand through my hair, not wanting to acknowledge that she was probably dead. The thought brought a sick feeling to my stomach. But if she were, I wanted to know. At least then I'd be able to move on, instead of existing in a constant state of wondering. Hoping. Dreading.

Suddenly feeling tired all over, I stood.

An outburst came from the dice players. Judging by his swarthy skin and colorful language, the man cheating earlier was a sailor. Another was covered in streaks of soot—a dust man or a chimney sweep. Both chiseled faces scowled at the table. The last one—a young lad, maybe only fifteen—grinned at their distress.

They exchanged quiet words. More dice shook, and this time I caught it.

With a move so like something Ashley would do, the boy switched the dice. His young face lit up; the numbers were to his favor. Too focused on the dice to catch his little trick, the men beat their chairs with their fists. It didn't matter.

The sailor upended the table and shot forward, dragging the boy up by his collar until his feet dangled above the ground. "Why, you little—!"

I didn't realize I'd moved until I'd twisted the sailor's forearm and yanked his head back. I thrust his wrist inward, driving him to his knees and forcing him to drop the boy. Then I held him there, bones quivering. His eyes glossed over in agony.

As I knew all too well, life as a young boy scraping a living was hard enough. The lad was far from innocent, but a swindling man deserved to be swindled in return.

"Leave the boy alone," I said calmly.

"He's been half-inching us with the tatts!" the dust man said behind me.

The boy clambered to his feet and spat, "You've no proof!"

"Give us our cash back!"

The sailor said nothing, face white, too pain stricken. I ratcheted his arm forward, shortening the awkward angle until he cried out. "Leave the boy alone," I repeated slower, so quiet it was almost a whisper.

He clenched his teeth, eyes rolling back. Sweat beaded his forehead. Finally, he managed a nod. I released him and stepped back, feeling a prick of regret that I'd hurt him—but not that I'd humiliated him in front of his friend.

The dust man, having now noticed my gentleman's clothing, righted the table and collected the scattered dice, sufficiently cowed. I glanced around for the boy—and caught sight of his cap as it slipped out onto the dark riverwalk. I swore and followed him.

The sky in the east was whitening to a pewter gray, making it easier to spot him than it had been inside The Dolphin. Beneath my brisk walk, the boards groaned. The last few lazy stars winked overhead as I passed a group of women carting their wares to the nearest market.

The boy cast a look over his shoulder and jolted into a sprint. I ran too. He twisted through alleys, coat flapping, sometimes traveling in a full circle before moving on. He couldn't outrun me so he was leading me on a merry chase.

When he darted around the corner of a warehouse, I back-tracked and sped around the other side, gut telling me he would circle around again. I was rewarded when he emitted a screech just before his little form barreled into me. I shoved his shoulders against the warehouse.

"Please don't hurt me!" he cried, eyes squeezed shut. "I have money! I—!"

"What do you think you're doing?" I didn't intend to hurt him, only scare him a little, so I pushed a little harder. Something about him had reminded me of myself, before Bram had taken me in, when finding crumbs was a struggle. Someone needed to put some sense in his head—and perhaps, like me back then, he didn't have *someone*.

"I'm sorry. I'm sorry, I can explain—!"

"Don't con a man twice your size."

He stopped struggling. Slowly, he peeked one eye open and studied my face. I knew it was too dark to read much, sandwiched as we were between two looming buildings. I could barely make out the whites of his eye.

His other eye opened and he relaxed beneath my hands. "You ... you're—!"

"Do your parents know where you are?"

He gripped my elbows and tried to force me off him, but the effort was pitiable. He gave up and huffed. "No, sir—and you can thank me for your sake that they do not!"

I tried to peer under the cap hiding half his face, scoffing softly. His voice hadn't even changed yet, but the boy was an imp. An arrogant little cove. Maybe I should've let the sailor beat him.

"What's your name?" I demanded.

He flinched. "It's Em ... E-Emerson."

"What would you have done if I hadn't saved you? Hm? What if I had called a blueduster to inspect your hands?"

He shrank against the wall, but his tone was as petulant as ever when he insisted, "I wasn't slanting! And I didn't cheat!"

Holding him with a forearm to his collarbone, I reached inside the deep pocket over his chest—to which he yelped and squirmed—and extracted the weighted dice, holding them out as proof. "Amateur." I stuffed them in my own coat—not one of the magical pockets—and fixed him with a stern eye. "At least have the honor to tell the truth when you've been caught. And if I catch you again, I'll not be so lenient."

Even though it was dark, I could still tell there was no change in his expression at the threat. To drive my point home, I extricated the coins I heard jingling in his right breast pocket and transferred them to mine.

He squealed, crossing his arms in an X over his chest. "Would you *stop* that?"

He seemed more upset over the breach of privacy than my stealing his money.

"Work for it like the rest of us." I unpinned him and knocked my chin toward the mouth of the alley. "Now get on."

He huffed again and adjusted his coat before shifting into the street where a shaft of pale sunlight shone, having only just peeked over the horizon. The extra light gave me my first clear glimpse of his features, and what I saw made me pause.

Below large brown eyes lay a dusting of freckles, a small nose, and a square jaw that didn't quite fit his face. Like manhood had been thrust upon him when he wasn't quite ready. His neck was long and slender—and it was such an odd thing to notice, but he held it stretched out in defiance, almost like a ...

I frowned. Something about him tickled the edge of a memory.

He ducked and scurried away, not looking back. I stuck my head around the corner. And I watched him until he disappeared down a street that was now filling with workers, unable to shake the feeling that I'd seen him somewhere before.

# 17

## Emmeline

W ell.

Ending the night with a man accidentally groping my chest hadn't *exactly* been the plan, but beggars couldn't be choosers.

A gas man extinguished a flame with his long pole, then climbed down his step ladder, whistling. I tipped my hat at him, and he tipped his back, lighting an inexplicable thrill in my stomach. He couldn't tell I was a girl. No one could. I'd had a hundred similar interactions before, but it never got old.

Farther down the road, my magic petered out and its dregs slithered back to my palms. Cramped and foreign after an hour of slanting, my face scrunched and I swung my jaw wide, trying to work out the sore muscles. A little girl tracked me from behind her mother's skirts, glaring. Even she could tell I looked slightly unnatural.

I gave her a wry wave and moved on. The traffic thickened and I quickened my steps, knowing I'd stayed out too late—but I couldn't return to Uncle Geoffrey's house without first making a stop.

A line of peddlers down the street hawked their wares. I perused their stands, landing on one covered in short novels and weekly serials with gruesome black-and-white pictures, ready to satisfy the hungry hands that would reach for the newest issue. Being most prominently placed, the one I was looking for was easy to find.

*The Samaritan and the Rook! Episode* 10: *The Bone-Moon Corpse.* On the cover, a twisted pile of bones sat in an open grave. I grinned, barely restraining myself from launching to the first page and devouring it on the spot.

I fetched a few shillings I'd stored in my shoe. The moment the peddler's change touched my palm, I ran home, taking short-cuts until I stood at the back of the townhouse, peering through the servant's entrance door.

Blast it. I should've left earlier. The stove was already lit and bore a pot of boiling eggs for breakfast. In a corner, the cook plucked a chicken, gray feathers and down landing everywhere but in the wastebasket beneath her.

To my luck, Beatrice joined her a moment later and their gossip was loud enough to disguise my footsteps tracking through the kitchen and up the back stairs.

Though it had been my first time at The Dolphin, it hadn't been my first time sneaking out to gamble for cash. I'd done it every time my family came to London since turning sixteen.

I wasn't given an allowance, and every farthing Mother spent was scrutinized. Father's attention to detail was how he made his wealth, after all, but that meant that if I ever wanted something— something for *me,* like a penny dreadful subscription—I had to earn my own coin. And without my parents' knowledge, which limited me to nighttime activities.

Really, I could've picked something much worse than gambling.

But it wasn't all about the money. It was also about the

freedom that came from hiding as an unsuspecting street urchin. No one's eyes widened if you forgot an acquaintance or stepped in some mud. In the thick of the city, where the rich dared not step, were the stories both bloviating and bloody, harsh insults and hearty manners.

It was wonderful.

And dangerous. And immature. And reckless. And so stupid, stupid, stupid. Pointless, too, because what was I proving by disguising myself as a boy? Absolutely nothing.

It wasn't that I didn't want to get married or even delay it. It wasn't even about sticking it to my parents in an act of petty rebellion. It was just—it was just—

I ripped my cap off and flung it on the bed, feeling suddenly stifled by the clothes that granted me independence. Waves of blonde hair tumbled free down my back. Without looking in a mirror, I knew it could use a good scrubbing—my face too.

I liked my life. It was comfortable. But maybe a part of me wanted it to be *un*comfortable; to fill it with experiences my father—and likely my future husband—would never condone, nor pay for.

That discontent had become so stifling over the past few years that I'd started to build a nest egg, without even knowing what for. Maybe I'd use it to leave. I suspected it wouldn't matter where I went. Just somewhere exciting. Somewhere *different*.

I cast off the rest of my boy clothes and stashed them at the back of my wardrobe. My weighted dice, the ones I kept in my pocket for thieves such as Mason, were lost the moment he upended the table. Fellow urchins had taught me how to use them, and after practicing in my spare time, I was adept enough to switch them out if the need arose. Then a man had ripped Mason off me, the action lightning-fast and controlled.

My face went hot at the memory, and I scrubbed a hand over it.

I hadn't realized it was Mr. Kelly that rescued me until he was pinning me against a wall in an alleyway, his strength so effortless I couldn't budge an inch even by heaving my entire weight at him.

We hadn't exchanged words at Lady Faline's concert. In fact, I'd been so focused on Mr. Gardner that night that I barely remembered meeting Mr. Kelly at all. He'd looked so stoic. So reserved. Not at all like the man who would lash into a young boy for gambling.

When I finally recognized him, I refrained from panicking only because he seemed to still believe me a boy. If he hadn't, I would've done more than slap him when his hand touched my breast pocket.

Ought I be offended he didn't notice anything strange?

No, that would be silly. I was small chested to begin with, and there were enough layers between me and his hand to disguise my real sex.

After throwing on my nightgown, I snagged the book I'd bought and settled under my covers, too disconcerted to sleep despite being up most the night. Then I consumed the pages of my penny dreadful, reading about the Samaritan rescuing a maiden from being buried alive by dueling with the Rook. Open graves, shards of moon, shadows and phantoms—those were things that were safe to ponder.

Not Mr. Kelly. Not the moment I'd stepped onto the street and saw recognition light in his eyes. And definitely not how, after this eventful morning, I hoped to high heaven I never saw the man again.

# 18

## Dorothy

I ripped open Mr. Vernon's letter in the foyer the moment it arrived. After combing through his pleasantries and the accompanying guest list, I'd deduced the name of the scarred man my father had argued with the night he was kidnapped:

Mr. Sullivan Brass.

If I could track him down and arrange a meeting, maybe he could tell me why the Rook wanted my father. Or maybe Brass was connected somehow? Answering that mystery would bring me another step closer.

Gripping the letter tightly, I searched the entry table for some paper. A loud knock rapped at the front door. As the butler moved to answer it, Aunt Marie appeared from the hall that led to the kitchens.

"Dorothy! Thank goodness. That'll be Mr. Gardner, and I wasn't expecting him so early." Her eyes volleyed between me and the front door, frantically patting the air with one hand. "Be a dear and entertain him while I arrange tea and refreshments, would you?"

My heart rate spiked. "But—"

Aunt Marie vanished.

I spun around to find Mr. Gardner had already stepped inside. He smiled a little and stared at me while slowly removing his hat and raking a hand through his thick, dark hair. No wonder it always looked so messy. "Good morning." He passed the hat to the butler.

I remembered to breathe and tucked Mr. Vernon's letter into my sleeve. All I could think to say was, "You came."

Mr. Gardner cocked his head and ambled forward, stuffing his hands in his pockets. "I *was* invited."

"You didn't have to accept my aunt's invitation."

"I'm not so ill-mannered."

"Somehow I don't believe that."

He shrugged loosely, green eyes sparkling. "Perhaps that's wise."

I gnawed the inside of my cheek. Aunt Marie had said to entertain him, but I didn't know the first thing about that, so I offered a tour of the house instead. Movement might help me avoid too much eye contact. Ten minutes later, we finished a tour of the lower level. With still no sign of Aunt Marie, I led Mr. Gardner toward the stairs to start the public rooms on the second floor.

"What's this room?" A door squeaked behind me, and I turned too late to stop him from stepping into the lab.

After pausing in confusion—I was sure I'd locked the door earlier—I swallowed and followed him in. "My father's laboratory." Spider legs crawled between my shoulder blades as I glossed over the room, trying to pick out anything that might point to illegal activity.

A bustling beehive hung next to drying bunches of foxglove and lavender. Clean syringes lined a towel. The saucer cauldron sat beside the serpentine distillery tube; a round bottom flask and beaker, purplish liquid filming the glass.

Copper pans, five-gallon barrels, mismatched bottles with cork screws that oozed with dark substances, a mortar and pestle, the wooden microscope. All understandable possessions for a scientist, but the knowledge of what we'd done with them made my heart beat in my throat.

"You help your father with his experiments?" Mr. Gardner's finger tapped an open page of Father's scientific journal.

I prayed it didn't specify too much. "Why would you say that?"

"Feminine handwriting. Doesn't match the rest of these notes." He started flipping through pages, forcing me to not-so-subtly tug the journal away and close it.

"I help him where I can." A bumblebee wandered past my ear, and the buzzing mimicked my pulse as I noticed how close we stood.

"Rather skittish this morning, Miss St. James."

I wished he would stop being so observant. It was unsettling, how little slipped past him. "It is not the morning that makes me skittish."

We held eye contact a beat too long. One side of his lips curved like I'd complimented him—and maybe I had, because my gaze dragged along the line of his jaw before I tore it away and busied my hands with pumping water into a metal can and giving the potted flowers a good soak.

I cleared my throat. "These are my favorites." I brought a lavender stalk to my nose and inhaled its calming aroma. "The flowers were my mother's idea. She specialized in herbology but she, too, had a passion for science. It brought her and my father together. After they married, she assisted him in his tinkering." In fact, hers was the magic my father had used to experiment with.

"Where is your mother?"

"She died of consumption when I was two. I don't remember her, but I do remember toddling into this room and finding my father sobbing against that table, clutching one of the lavender stalks." I didn't know why I was telling Mr. Gardner this. Maybe to distract him from my nervous energy—but it felt good to talk about my father. Some of the pressure in my chest dissipated.

"I put my hand on his leg. He composed himself. He tucked the lavender in my hair. And then he asked if I wanted to help him extract the oil from the flower." I fingered one of the fragile purple petals. "He was so passionate."

"Was?"

My hand dropped. "Is." I set the watering can down, next to my father's pocket watch that he must've left on the table when we were experimenting, before he was kidnapped. A sad smile pulled at my lips as I caressed the inset opals and filigree work.

It had always been my responsibility to keep things running smoothly. To keep his spectacles away from the edge of the counter. To tie his scarf so he wouldn't catch cold. To look in all directions before stepping out the door.

Ultimately, to keep both of us safe. With enough foresight, every disaster could be avoided, and I had avoided them—all except for his kidnapping. And I couldn't help but feel that it was because I'd overlooked something.

On an impulse, I tucked the watch into the folds of my skirt pocket, then looked up to find that Ashley had tracked the movement. Before he could ask any questions I said, "What about your parents? Are they living?"

He glanced up at the sudden shift in conversation. And he studied me like he was trying to gauge if the question was earnest. Society knew very little about him, and I wondered why. There was more than enough interest, so it could only be the result of careful deflection on his part.

I placed the watering can back on its shelf. "You could tell me something about yourself. A vote of confidence if you will. We have an arrangement, and yet I know nothing about you. No one does." I bit my lip at how that sounded—as if I'd made inquiries. When the silence stretched on, I angled my heating face away.

*Stupid, stupid. What a stupid thing to say ...*

"I knew both my parents."

I rotated back.

His voice was steady, detached. "My father was hanged. My mother—burned in a fire, a month later. I was nine. My godfather, Bram Gardner, was kind enough to take me in and raise me. He gave me his name, his life on the sea, and when he died, his fortune."

"... I'm so sor—"

"I am glad they're dead. All of them."

My lips parted. I didn't know which was more terrible—the deaths of his parents, or the cold way he spoke about them. A hanging likely pointed to an illegal use of magic. There was more to this story than he was letting on.

"You seem unsettled, Miss St. James." He eyed me, then passed me on his way to the door. "Perhaps in the future, refrain from asking questions you do not want the answers to. Because if I give you one, I promise it will be the truth."

From his story, I believed him. And there was one question I knew I wanted answered. "Why are you really here?"

In the doorway, he turned back. "To collect your first guess." He cocked his head. "Did you hope there was another reason?"

My mouth dried. "No," I said a little too quickly. After returning from the ballet last night, I'd immediately consulted my list of suspects, disheartened to find that my clue only eliminated eight of them. Without more time, any guess I made would be a stab in the dark. "It's just—I've only barely begun to investigate."

"There's always a way to win." He grinned, and a warm feeling closed over me—the same one I'd felt before, in the bookshop; a caress of air that seemed to be flavored with him. "This world is not fair. And I may know you're going to lose, but I have a sense of honor, which means I must be as fair as I can be."

Not for the first time, I wondered if he was slanted, but as I'd never felt a cold rush in his presence, discarded the thought. It was silly. I shook my head, and the sensation evaporated. Then I strode forward until I faced him in the doorway. "It's only been twelve hours. How can I make use of the information I gained if I have no time to apply it? And what kind of clue is *orphan*, anyway? Half of London is orphaned."

He shrugged. "So, I eliminated half of London for you. You're welcome."

"That still leaves me with two *million* people to sort through. I cannot be expected to, in so little time—"

"I don't think you understand the rules of this game, Miss St. James." He stepped forward and I fell back against the door-frame. Bumblebees buzzed again in my ears. "I form the clues, I hide them for you, and I collect your guesses—when and where I please. If this is too challenging for you, I suggest you surrender now because this" —he ducked his head and finished in a mocking whisper that drew my eyes to his pink lips— "was the easy one."

His breath washed over me, and it smelled like oranges and peppermint. Warm and cool. A paradox. I repressed a gulp, and the fluttering feeling in my stomach. "You've played games like this before?"

"None so entertaining."

"And do you always win?"

His gaze strayed to the side of my head, and if my hair had nerve-endings, they would be tingling. He smiled lazily. "Don't ask questions you don't want the answers to."

# 19

## Ashley

We took the back stairs to explore the second floor. Wafts of fresh-pressed linen spilled through an open door, propelled by a maid shaking and settling sheets. One cursory glance into the room revealed stacks of books and a dress airing on the bed; it didn't take much to guess who it belonged to.

We turned a corner and the hallway widened, one wall lined with high windows that were weighed down by red velvet drapes. The other bore paintings of all sizes, arranged to fit like a parallelogrammical puzzle. Display cabinets and sculpture busts, marble-top tables with porcelain urns, jewels and shiny heirlooms—all of it exhibited the family's wealth.

"This," Dorothy announced, "was my father's idea." Loose curls slipped from her high bun and cradled her cheek and neck. She swiped a glass dome and rubbed the dust between her fingers. On separate paths we wandered the hall, inspecting each item at our own pace. "What is it you do, Mr. Gardner?"

I kept walking despite the way my gut clenched. "I'm in the silk trade." It was true enough, as I'd inherited the bulk of Bram's business—though I mostly reaped the benefits of it being run by capable hands while occupying my days with more essential matters. "Mr. Kelly is my business partner." Also not a lie, since Bram had employed him.

"You are well-traveled then?"

She had no idea. "Point to any country on the globe accessible by sea, and I have stepped on its land."

She spun back. "All of them?" She held still as if mentally compiling a list, her eyes growing larger by the second. "That must've been ... wonderful."

"It was. Now, we don't have much time before your aunt comes to find us. Give me your guess, and I will tell you if he is the Samaritan."

Perhaps a whole minute passed in silence. Dorothy rubbed a smudge from a ceramic vase using the underside of her sleeve. "And how do you know the Samaritan? Are you ... Are you helping him?" Pink dusted her cheeks and another curl above her ear slipped halfway out, giving me the strongest urge to finish the job and tug it free.

*Bad idea.*

She noticed me staring at her hair and brushed the errant lock behind her ear, her inhale soft and quick.

She was stalling for time, but I didn't care. A few extra seconds to deliberate wouldn't make a difference. "The less you know, the better off you'll be."

"But you are acquaintances?"

"Of a sort."

"What color is his mask?"

My gaze narrowed. Only because it was common knowledge did I supply, "Gray."

"How did he find Nathaniel Findley?"

I lied. I did very much care. And I was out of patience. "Give me your guess, or you can consider it forfeit."

Dorothy frowned and said, "The ring."

A smirk tugged on one of my cheeks as I fished the ring out of my pocket and slipped it on my finger. She didn't trust me. Probably a good thing. But though she may think I'd do anything to cheat the system, I'd never been a double-crosser.

Her eyes fixed in contemplation but at her side, two fingers pitter-pattered against her thumb, chugging like a locomotive at break-neck speed. Faster. The train derailed and she looked up. "Stephen Locke. His parents are deceased, and he is strong enough to carry a large man like Mr. Findley. Is he the Samaritan?"

The tension bunching my core loosened, making air ease out between my lips. For a moment, I'd almost been nervous. "No. Stephen Locke is not the Samaritan."

Her gaze shot to the ring, still blue around my finger. The dejection on her face gave me an urge to put a comforting hand on her shoulder—or worse, do something *more*. I clenched my teeth and tucked the truth ring back into my coat. "Give your aunt my thanks for inviting me, and my apologies that I left before tea."

I turned away, but bright jewels on a black cloth drew my eye and made me freeze. Encased in glass, the metalwork was unique, the sapphires linked by silver lions standing over four-pointed stars. "A beautiful set," I couldn't help but say. My brows pulled together. "But it's missing a piece."

Dorothy moved to my side and craned her neck around me. "That can't be right—"

I pointed at the glass. "Necklace, earrings, and here is the place for a bracelet. What happened to it?"

Her eyes darted behind me—the light brush of a butterfly's wings—before shooting to her feet. It was so small I barely caught it—barely caught the way her skin slightly paled. She was omitting something.

"I don't think there ever was a bracelet," she said.

I mentally retraced my steps, sifting through the hall's inventory behind me. Nothing remarkable. Then without any premeditation, I took a risk and slipped into her mind. Doing it always left me with a sour taste on my tongue because it felt like a betrayal of trust, but I wanted to know why she was lying.

Her mind was a warm twilight, edged by solid walls of pale sun. Shadows that smelled of lavender hugged the crevices, concealing her most special memories. They tipped out of their hiding places and caught in an eddy.

I'd been in her mind before, but I didn't remember noticing any of this. Most people had a single deck of memories that sat on a dusty table, but this was a lot more intricate—almost like she owned several pasts that didn't belong to her.

Face-up on a center table, gold and blue and white playing cards shuffled and swirled. Her mind was clouded with strong emotion, making the current swifter and harder to navigate, but unlike in the bookshop, my second slant seemed to be behaving today.

I knew the one I wanted based on the gold sheen that pulsed brighter than the rest—the memory she was currently reliving. I picked up the card and fell inside.

The room was low-lit by a popping fire—a bedroom. A breeze blew through the open window, fluttering the gauzy white drapes. Seated at a vanity in the corner, a young girl stared at her reflection. Her earlobes glistened with sapphires, and over the collarbone of her nightgown rested their companion, a necklace. Her hands, still bearing some baby fat, swiped brown curls out of her face, causing the bracelet that dwarfed her wrist to slide to her elbow.

"Dorothy!" A couple stood in the doorway, hair graying and figures stooped. They were dressed in fine clothes from decades past, coming from a ball, most likely. The woman stepped behind

Dorothy and surveyed the twinkling gems littering her vanity. "What are you doing?"

"I wanted to be pretty just like you, grandmama."

"Oh, sweet girl," she kissed her curly head, "you already are."

Dorothy touched her grandfather and the gem around her hand gleamed.

"No!" Her grandmother rushed forward and slid the bracelet off her little wrist, then cupped it in a hand which she extended to her husband. "We must do something about this, Charles. Have Geoffrey hide it—"

"Geoffrey doesn't even know it exists." After rubbing his white mustache, he took the bracelet, and the faint blue glow vanished as he tucked it in his coat. "And given his transactions recently, I'm glad I never told him. His science grows too bold."

"He is grieving—"

"He is aiding mass slaughter, by inventing those slant guns! Soon, someone is going to notice."

"Grandmama?" Dorothy's chubby hand gripped the elder woman's skirt. "I'm thirsty. Might I have a drink of water?"

Dorothy's grandmother looked down, her features softening. "Of course, child." Her wrinkled hands slid down Dorothy's arms and she crouched in front of her. "But Dorothy. You must promise not to get into grandmother's jewelry again. Especially not *this* jewel." She slipped the earrings off and unclasped the necklace. "Do you understand?"

Dorothy blinked at her, eyes going wide. Then she nodded. The memory winked out and fluttered to the table.

I pulled out of her mind as softly as I could. Only a few seconds had passed, but Dorothy looked as if they'd aged her. A crease formed between her brows.

"Is it warm in here to you?" She fanned herself with a hand.

"I feel fine." But I didn't. Because there it was. The sour taste on my tongue. Potent and bitter. Memories made in childhood weren't always remembered clearly, so I wondered if she knew what her father's science had led to.

I should've waited. I should've asked her about the memory and let her entrust it to me instead of taking it like a thief. Or maybe she wouldn't have entrusted it to me at all. She'd lied about the bracelet's existence.

The only question left was … why?

"Thank you for the tour, Miss St. James. It was most enlightening." I'd made it all the way to the stairs—and halfway down them—before I heard her calling after me and stopped.

She appeared at the top, out of breath. "When will I have your next clue?"

I turned back. "In two days."

"But when can I *expect* it?"

I finished descending the stairs. "You won't."

# 20

## Dorothy

Early morning was the only time I could work in the lab without drawing my uncle's notice, and in the gray light, my heart fluttered at the tiny blue symbols pulsing under the glass. It'd taken two days of tweaking, but I'd *done* it, thanks in no small part to Mr. Gardner's book. Quickly, I slotted the glass into Father's prototype gun—similar to a slant gun but more sensitive —and stared in awe as it revealed the invisible, blue mist streaming toward my palms.

It could take six hours for magic to fully recharge, but a slant gun could only detect up to one hour, when the bulk of magical particles were inpouring. With mine and Father's work, we could now not only identify whose magic had been used but detect it longer—even trace it to you like a trail.

Nerves sparking, I scrawled my findings into my notebook, already mentally composing a letter to the Samaritan explaining the gun and begging for his help. Ashley had mentioned they were acquaintances, "of a sort," but what did that mean?

Suppose it was someone he only knew in passing. I could

think of no motivation he'd have for keeping him a secret, whereas someone he knew intimately ...

Maybe the Samaritan was the guarded Mr. Kelly. Did Ashley Gardner have any other close friends? Who were the other players in his inner circle?

Time to discover them was running out.

Nathaniel Findley's family had denied all visitors. Supposedly he was in good health but because he kept out of the public's eye, the whispers of him grew around the Town and everyone waited with bated breath behind locked windows for the Rook to make his next move.

When he did, the Samaritan—with the aid of this gun— needed to be there to trap him, saving London's streets and proving that magic could be a force for good.

After scrubbing the lab clean of evidence, I turned my attention to pulling at the other threads of the mystery: Mr. Brass and the steel button.

I wrote missives to a few of Father's associates asking for the address of Mr. Brass, shuddering at the memory of his tear-shaped scar. Then, after circling the most prominent tailor shops on a map, I drafted more missives describing the button and asking after its owner. It was expensive; someone had to recognize it.

After posting the letters, I joined the family for breakfast as Uncle plopped a handbill for a dress shop on the table. He'd only caught a glimpse of the words "latest" and "Paris" before snapping his fingers and ordering Aunt Marie to take Emme and I there today to be outfitted.

My pulse jumped, but I agreed. It was because I'd been too afraid to go in person that I'd written the letters, but if I had to go out anyway, instantaneous answers were better.

For having recently opened, there weren't many customers in the dress shop—although that might've had more to do with the carnival drawing in the bulk of the crowds. Through the shop's sparkling windows, one could glimpse the striped red-and-black peaks of the tents and hear the music laden with swirls of fiddles, pipes, and drums.

The dressmaker unrolled different fabrics before us: yellow silk, blue taffeta, green velvet, brocades and polka dots and plaids. Aunt Marie oohed at every option. After making selections, the dressmaker steered me and Emme into a fitting room where she measured us, then forced us to try on a sampling of pre-made dresses.

"Let's go to the carnival," Emme whispered once the dressmaker and Aunt Marie finally turned away to consult.

"Your mother would never approve."

Emme pulled the sleeves of the frilly monstrosity off until she stood only in her corset, drawers, and black stockinged boots. "Precisely why I've never been. We wouldn't be gone long. We can say we saw an old friend in the shop next door and were detained."

"Emmeline," Aunt Marie said, shuffling forward and making Emme snap up from her conspiratorial position, "would you put that striped taffeta back on, dear?"

As Emme grudgingly complied, I wandered to the dressmaker's side, careful not to draw my relative's attention. "Excuse me, I was wondering if you might help me with something?" I fished the button from my pocket and held it out in my palm. "Does your shop use these?"

The dressmaker smoothed her tight, dark hair and inspected the button. She frowned. "I'm sorry, we don't."

I tried to swallow my disappointment. "Do you know someone who might? I'm trying to find the owner of this button."

She shrugged. "I don't know who this was sold to—you'd have to find the right tailor for that—but only the button factory to the east sells buttons as intricate as this. It's something of their specialty."

My shoulders fell. It was too much to hope I'd find a lead at the first dress shop, but I'd hoped anyway.

"You could try asking them who they supply," the dressmaker continued. "Mr. Brass is very accommodating."

I blinked. "Did you ... did you say Brass?"

"Mr. Sullivan Brass is the owner of the factory and personally ensures the quality of each button by overseeing the whole process."

The connection was too coincidental. What if I'd been wrong? What if Mr. Brass was the Rook? It made sense he'd wear his own buttons. What if their disagreement was why Father had been kidnapped in the first place?

I shook my head. "Thank you." I returned to Emme's side, mind reeling. Now that I had a face to put to the shadow from my father's room, new chills scuttled down my spine. Aunt Marie finished her fussing and once again returned to the dressmaker to consult.

Emme blew a raspberry as she disrobed again. Behind her dress she bounced on her toes, widened her eyes at me, and gestured to the window with her head.

"We haven't any money," I sighed.

Emme grinned. "Oh, you needn't worry about that."

Even now, I could hear the music, the revelry. But Ashley's next clue was due today, and what if it came for me while I was gone? I couldn't risk it. Besides, running off would only get Aunt Marie into trouble, and I didn't have the heart to do that to her.

I tied my skirt, followed by my bodice. Emme did the same, and I helped her cinch it up, finishing with a bow. "We shouldn't, Emme."

She huffed and turned around. "When are you ever going to do something you want? *Just* because you want to?"

"When what I want aligns with what is right." And right now, that was to play dress-up like a good little niece and encourage my cousin to do the same. Finished clothing, the four of us stepped out of the fitting room while the dressmaker gushed about our beautiful figures, assuring us of how stunning our outfits would turn out.

The shop's bell tinkled as a broad man entered, orange hair peeking out from beneath his top hat. *Mr. Riley.*

My mind flashed to the night of the concert when he'd mentioned his late parents' favorite song. He was orphaned.

I swallowed, eyes glued.

Mr. Riley was young and obviously strong. He was unmarried, and a member of the *ton* who lived in London. Persuading people was a powerful slant to have, one that would come in handy in the Samaritan's line of work.

He fit all my qualifications. The urgency to speak with him made me step forward.

"Now," the dressmaker said while blocking my path and nudging me back, "let's move on to accessories! These fans are new in stock, and we have some nice undersleeves to protect your hems. Perhaps, Mrs. Morgan, you might ..."

Mr. Riley inspected a few trimmings, lost interest, and glided out the door before I could maneuver around the women in front of me. Through the window, he wandered down the lane, heading toward the sprawling striped tents.

A vision seized me.

*A menagerie of fire-breathers, dancing monkeys, peaked canvas, and matted grass. And me at the center, running from something. Or toward something.*

My visions weren't exact predictions of the future; I had the power to change their outcome. One thing remained unchanged though—they only ever showed me important things. Things I might regret having done ... or not doing.

The dressmaker pulled Aunt Marie around the corner while saying something about lace, leaving Emme and me alone.

Staring at Mr. Riley's fading figure, I only had a split second to decide, and knowing the carnival was probably crawling with bluedusters, I hesitated longer than I should, then felt cowardly for hesitating.

By helping Father with chemicals, I'd practiced caution all my life; I wore gloves, and masks, and goggles, and when my slant manifested, I'd stayed inside where nothing could ever touch me. But here I was venturing outdoors anyway, and for all my caution, eliminating dangerous situations had only managed to make me more terrified of them.

Father would want me to stay safe.

But he wasn't here. And I was the only one who could change that.

"All right, Emmeline," I muttered, squaring my shoulders and snagging my chatelaine bag with my father's watch inside, ignoring the pit of dread yawning open in my stomach. "Let's go to the carnival."

# 21

## Dorothy

When Emme and I reached the high gates that surrounded the carnival's impossibly large circumference, my blood turned to slush, an onslaught of arctic waves hitting me one after another as people called on their slants. Too many to distinguish where the magic was coming from.

A group of three bluedusters tracked past the entrance, making me freeze and reconsider. I caught sight of Mr. Riley's top hat again, steeled my squirming stomach, and sidetracked to the ticket booth.

A man in a carnival uniform—a red blazer and black slacks—said simply, "Admittance fee." Nailed to the wood beside him was a sign specifying the cost. More words caught my eye.

GATES OPEN AT DAWN, CLOSE AT DUSK.
NO EXCEPTIONS.

I'd heard stories of people stuck inside the carnival gates after hours, forced to wait out the night. It seemed to be the one rule that the seasonal carnival took seriously. The ghost of my running vision drifted through my mind, hands sweating at the thought of what Uncle would do if I disappeared for a whole night, but I shook the feeling off. We weren't staying very long.

Emme opened her own chatelaine, revealing wads of cash.

"Emme!" I whispered fiercely. "Where did you get all of that?"

She slid the booth operator a few coins, and he unlocked the gate for us. "I didn't steal it from my father, if that's what you're worried about. I earned it honestly."

"Doing what?" I asked.

She cleared her throat. "Weren't you looking for someone?"

I pulled on her shoulder so she faced me. "Doing what, Emme?"

She cleared her throat again, her face a tight grimace that was doing its best to smile. "Playing dice."

"*Gambling?*"

"I gambled for it *very* honestly."

"Emmeline!"

Out of the corner of my eye, Mr. Riley pushed his way toward some game booths. I turned back to Emme. "Don't think we're not going to discuss this matter further. But for now, come on." I grabbed her hand, and we dove into the carnival, immediately assaulted by flapping colors and the aroma of salted peanuts. More freezing waves crashed down my arms. At this rate, my magic would be exhausted in a matter of minutes, simply from detecting *other* people's magic.

Walls of tents—red, black, white, and any combination of the three—constructed the bones of the maze. Fires hissed at the roasting chunks of meat dripping their juices. Children squealed in delight as they danced around a maypole with their ribbons, narrowly dodging a monkey that hopped from a man's shoulder while playing light, tapping notes on a fife.

I didn't know what my plan was once I caught up to Mr.

Riley. I couldn't ask him outright if he were the Samaritan, he would only deny it. But maybe ... somehow ... I could tail him long enough to find proof.

"Emmeline, is that you?" A girl with chestnut ringlets stopped Emme by the shoulders and assessed her head to toe.

"Why, Ivy! What are you doing in here? Did you read *The Bone Moon Corpse*? Riveting, wasn't it?"

I cleared my throat, tugging her elbow a little. I didn't like being rude, but my father's *life* was at stake. "Emme ..."

"Go on, I'll catch up." Emme shooed me away, but only after discreetly slipping a few coins into my palm and saying sweetly, "My treat."

"I don't want your pawned money." But I closed my hand around the coins and dashed away.

I heard her call after me, "Money I pawned *honestly*."

For a panicked moment, I thought I'd lost Mr. Riley until I spotted his impossibly tall top hat ducking under a soothsayer's beaded tent. I approached the booth but was blocked by her assistant.

"Away!" the assistant said, shooing me with her hands.

"I just need to meet with that—"

"If you want your fortune told, you will have to wait! No eavesdropping. Away!"

Sighing, I retreated to an awning across the thoroughfare that had a good vantage of the tent, and waited.

"You playing?" a carnival worker asked, slipping out of his red blazer and hanging it on a peg behind the bottle toss. He had blond hair and a young face—maybe only sixteen.

"No, thank you."

He knocked his chin. "Stand in front of my booth, you play."

I considered moving, but with how thick the crowds were, this was the only spot that wouldn't make my spying painfully obvious. In the end, I plunked a halfpenny on the counter, thankful that I had one even if it was stolen. The worker gave me six circular rings which I tossed. One by one, the first five missed.

The last ring fell over the lip of the bottle but then bounced completely off and clattered to the table with the others. I warmed, even though I didn't know why I should be embarrassed.

The young man held out a prize, a wooden box the width of my hand.

I frowned. "But I didn't ring one."

"I was told to give this to the first woman who lost on my shift. That's you, love."

He was entirely too young to be calling me 'love,' and my pride was wounded, but I was more intrigued by the box. I took it and opened the lid. Inside rested a black-and-gold music box with the statue of a white ballerina atop. My lips parted. She looked just like ...

I set the box down and examined the girl. I gave the knob on the side a few cranks and the ballerina spun, dancing to the music of *Les Bois Endormis,* erasing all doubt from my mind.

The music box was from Ashley. My skin tingled as if it felt him watching me right now. My second clue had arrived.

# 22

## Dorothy

It was clever of him, linking the previous clue and this one together.

Ashley's face swam before me, a dark, taunting smile on his lips. I spun around, searching for that smile underneath black hair, but of course didn't find it.

I didn't know how he'd orchestrated this. How he'd known Aunt Marie would take me to the dress shop where I'd see Mr. Riley and follow him to the carnival ... and lose at this particular booth. But somehow, he had planned it.

Mr. Riley finished at the fortune teller's and swept toward a nearby tent.

I looked between the music box in my hand and his ever-retreating figure, torn. Inhaling, I stuffed the music box in my chatelaine and plunged into a massive, red-canvased tent after Mr. Riley.

In the sudden darkness, I stumbled into one of the poles, earning a bruise on my shoulder. Once my eyes adjusted, I saw crystal globes dangling from stationed poles, their white flames casting eerily long shadows. Fleetingly, I wondered what chemicals they used—magnesium sulfate mixed with methanol, perhaps?

I cut down the winding center pathway, dodging flamethrowers and a giant man with claws sprouting from his fingertips. I passed booths of poisons, luxury cigars, flintlock pistols, and one where customers chortled and threw axes at a man pinned to a spinning wheel.

I reached the back of the tent to find there was no exit—only one way in, and Mr. Riley had disappeared. My head whipped around, scanning faces, feet stumbling. For another few minutes I searched, then bit my tongue to keep from swearing.

"Playing, miss?" A carnival worker stood in front of a target, a set of knives gleaming on the table before him.

I shook my head but neared anyway. "I—I don't know how to throw knives."

"Free of charge for a pretty lady like yourself."

I cocked my head and paused. The interaction felt strangely similar to the last booth, which meant maybe it was connected to my clue. I gave a slow nod. "All right." Wary, I watched the carnival worker as he selected three knives and slid them to me before stepping to the side and out of sight. Odd.

I studied the sharp blades before me. Maybe this was a mistake. The first handle was cool in my grip, and I adjusted it, a shiver coursing over my back. It felt awkward, but maybe this was what I needed. To flirt with danger instead of always cowering, for once. Not because I had to, but because I *wanted* to, like Emme suggested. Inhaling a slow, steadying breath, I raised my arm.

A hand clamped around my wrist. "If you're going to throw a knife," Ashley murmured in my ear, black hair skimming my shoulder, "don't be prepared to miss before you even throw."

I quietly released my breath, proud when my voice didn't squeak. "Miss or not, it's just a game."

"What happens if a strange man climbs through your window one night? Will you treat it so lightly then?"

My mind flashed to my father's bedroom, a steel button on the floor.

He shifted forward, until I felt his chest burning against my back. "Manage your breathing. Your strength doesn't come from your arm. It comes from here." His fingers unfurled over my stomach while his other hand braced the small of my back. I sucked in a breath as he angled me slightly away. "Throw from here." His fingers squeezed, playing me like an accordion when all the air left my lungs.

"Now look at the target ... and imagine my face in the center."

I could hardly think *at all*. My pulse zipped to my toes and back up again, settling where the warmth from his hands seeped into my dress. But gradually, I relaxed, my focus homing in on the black-and-white rings ten feet away. I exhaled.

"Throw," he ordered, and I did. Much to my surprise, I struck the outside ring of the target. A celebratory jolt coursed through me, and Ashley passed me the next dagger. The hilt still felt foreign in my grip, but my muscles were looser from the confidence of the last throw. Ashley's hands straddled my waist again, tweaking my posture.

And because I was melting into a puddle under his touch, I said the only thing I could think to. "I received your music box."

He said nothing, but his hand on my waist curled in slightly, caging my butterflies.

"What does it mean?"

"If you are hoping for my help in solving your clues, Miss St. James, you're a fool. You're like a little ballerina in her box. You spin and you dance while trying to decide which way to go but ultimately, you go nowhere. Trapped inside your beautiful cage."

I glanced at his fingers, noting the way he slid the fabric of my dress between two of them.

"Eyes on the target," he muttered, hand repositioning my chin. But instead of a target, all I could see was that image; the caressing way he touched me. He let me go and stepped back. "Now throw."

I obeyed again, and the dagger struck a little closer to the center. A puff of surprise escaped my lips.

Ashley swept the last knife off the table and tossed the dagger up between us. It spun so fast that in the steel, I saw firelight dancing in my eyes before he caught the hilt again. "Only darkness awaits you outside your cage. Take my advice. Stop chasing the Samaritan ... and stay inside."

An invisible force pulled me toward him, but I dug my feet into the grass. The space of air between us was the only thing anchoring me to reality; the one where my father had been kidnapped, and I didn't have time for distractions. "I can't."

Ashley frowned and leaned in, his warm breath caressing my lips, chin, throat. "Then which door will the clever girl unlock with her key? You have until the carnival closes tonight before your clue disappears."

My stomach sank. That was only two hours away. "I can't stay here," I repeated. In the carnival, in the cage. Despite the danger he was warning me about. "I have to find him." The Samaritan, my father.

Ashley held the hilt of the last dagger out to me. My hand shook as I reluctantly took it, turned, and aimed for the target once more.

For the second time, he caught my wrist. "You're going to miss again."

I'd been in a constant state of cold rushes since stepping through the carnival gates, but I thawed under Ashley's touch. Even felt a little too warm. I paused, on the tip of wondering why, then blurting, "I think you're enjoying this game a little too much."

Not bothering to deny it, something flickered in his green eyes. "Are you even sure what game that is?"

Flustered by my attraction to him, I forced myself to stare back, one eyebrow cocking. "Are you?"

His answer was a quick once-over of my face. A stab of pressure from his hand opened my wrist and the knife fell. His other hand stretched between us and caught it. Still watching me, he threw the dagger at the board.

I looked. The blade had sunk into the center of the target. My lips parted, heart pounding as I wondered where he'd learnt to throw knives like that.

"Yes," he said lowly, stepping back and drifting into the crowd of revelers. "See you around, Dolly."

I hesitated for a moment, before calling after him, "My friends call me Dory."

He turned back, taking slow, backwards steps with a smirk spreading over his lips. "But I'm not your friend ... am I."

A fire-breather's flame erupted, burning so bright I had to shield my eyes. I glanced back to the spot Mr. Gardner had been standing, then around the throng, but just like Mr. Riley, he had vanished.

WHEN THE SUN WENT DOWN, my clue would be gone.

With Emme still preoccupied with her friend, I paused underneath a tree, extricated the music box from my chatelaine purse, and turned it over in my hands. On the third rotation, I noticed a groove on one side. I looked at the knob used to crank the music. It was the same shape and size as the groove.

*Which door will the clever girl unlock with her key?*

A key ...

I tugged on the oblong knob, and it came out easily, then pushed its head into the notch. Click.

A compartment on the bottom of the music box opened, so tightly sprung I hadn't detected the seams, revealing a piece of paper.

Not a piece of paper. A ticket stub.

*My* ticket stub. From the ballet.

Any spark of excitement I felt at finding the secret compartment died when I saw the writing on the back of the stub. It wasn't my clue. Of course it couldn't be that easy.

$$p = \sum_{k=0}^{\infty} \left(\frac{1}{2}\right)^k \left(\lim_{x \to 0} \frac{e^{9x} - 1}{x}\right) + \lim_{x \to \infty} x^{1/x}$$

$$y = \left(\frac{\lim_{x \to 58} \frac{x^2 - 81}{x+9}}{(\cos^2 x + \sin^2 x)}\right) - -36e^{\pi i}$$

$$r = \sqrt{\lim_{x \to 0} \frac{e^{36x} - 1}{x}}$$

Math equations.

Ashley's clues were all about testing my knowledge and my ability to think on my feet—but *math?* Who did he think I was?

That wasn't to say I couldn't solve the functions, but that would take time; a resource I was quickly running out of. I had never in my life been more grateful for my father's leaflets on the evolution of calculus.

From the corner of my eye, a blueduster whipped out his slant gun. Fear spiked my blood, and I ducked behind the tree. A whistle sounded. My heart thundered louder and louder with each of the blueduster's boot thuds, until—

A blue uniform tackled a woman a few paces to my left. I jumped in my skin, a wave of nausea making me turn my face away when he handcuffed her. In the morning, the woman would be dead. Hot with shame, I slipped behind some tents and hurried to the far side of the carnival. As terrible as the sight had been, I couldn't allow myself to be distraught if I wanted to prevent the same thing from happening to me.

After scrounging up some paper and working out the problems, I was left with the numbers -19, 13, and 6. All together they equaled zero, which coincidentally was the number of ideas I had.

For over an hour, I wandered through the carnival, trying to make sense of the answers. My feet took me through a gallery of strange paintings—broken suns, insatiable eyes, a locomotive steaming through the sky, women in corsets with melting faces. If I stared long enough, the paintings shifted, someone's slant making them move. I shivered at the ice in my veins and looked away, hating the hollow feeling that settled in my bones as the last of my magic was used up.

I didn't foresee needing to use my slant, but I felt naked without it.

When I emerged, buckets of rain wicked off the canvas tents and puddled on the grass. The man operating the wishing well still lit matches and tossed them in for good luck, the flames never sputtering; the bell juggler carried out his clunky song, the rain clinking lighter notes on their shells. I stepped into the deluge, the drops tapping hard on my face. Only another half hour until sundown.

For the thousandth time, I glanced at the numbers scrawled on my paper, now blurring from the rain.

Why did Ashley have to be so *vague*? He told me he would make my clues difficult, but I hadn't counted on him using a riotous place like the *carnival* to hide it. The numbers could mean anything. A label on a barrel, the combination to a lock.

Or perhaps the numbers meant nothing at all, and I was chasing a wild goose. All so he could watch on, amused. Short of finding my father, what I wanted most was to wipe that satisfied smile off his face.

An image of my fingers on Ashley's ripe, pink lips flitted through my mind and I was surprised when I didn't immediately scrub it away.

A differently shaped tent caught my eye and I stopped. Most were circular, some rectangular, but this behemoth was solid black and shaped like a pyramid. Sure my memory was mistaken, I dug the paper out of my chatelaine and re-read the equations, doing my best to keep it dry. The variables were p, y, and r.

Pyramid?

They weren't the standard variables—but perhaps they represented x, y, and z respectively. I eyed the tent so long my hair plastered against my face and neck, and my dress felt as heavy as an anvil from all the liquid.

Could it be the answers ... were coordinates on a graph? But why three numbers instead of two?

Unless the graph was three-dimensional.

I slogged my way to the tent, blinking against the rain in my eyes, and trudged inside. This one was almost pitch black. My cold bursts of breath stopped when my eyes adjusted. Needles of light glowed from the canvas ceiling, refracting off black and white crystals hanging on bits of string. All sizes, all shapes, all heights. Most were crude but some were carved into hazy figurines.

Stepping inside felt a bit like stepping into a cathedral. Quiet and reverent. The trajectory of thousands of falling stars strung across the tent, so thin they were like golden gossamer threads. I no longer felt cold.

Remembering the rain outside, I realized someone must've slanted the light in the right direction to refract off the crystals. But given how little magic people possessed these days, it would've taken days ... *weeks* to construct and perfect.

A little unsettled, I stepped farther into the tent, noticed only one other couple ducking around the crystals in wonder, and took in the dimensions. It looked to be about forty by forty feet. A square graph.

My pulse hummed. Using the entrance of the tent as the top of the Y axis, I navigated to the opposite end until I was only a foot away from the wall. Negative nineteen. I turned right, walking forward until I hit thirteen paces.

And then I looked up. Technically the next number was six, but was that talking about the position of my feet, or my line of sight? As gracefully as I could, I tried hopping to make up for the five inches I lacked, but in those short clips, saw nothing remarkable. The six must be referring to my feet.

I sighed. How was I supposed to get six feet into the air?

I hunted outside the tent for a ladder, and found a heavy one, but it would have to do. By then, the rain had stopped, and the sun sank dangerously low in the sky. I had maybe twenty minutes before the carnival closed and I was trapped inside for the night.

When I returned to the pyramid, the couple had left, a fact for which I was particularly grateful when I dropped the ladder several times on my trek across the tent. I was breathing hard and my dress felt cold against my skin, but I finally managed to position the ladder in the right spot.

Hiking my skirts up to an indecent height, I ascended. Six feet was a long way to fall when your limbs and dress were stiff and awkwardly heavy. I gripped the top of the ladder with pale hands.

But after looking around, I saw nothing. Was I in the wrong spot? Maybe if I used the second entrance as the top of the Y axis ... After refiguring, I placed the ladder on the new coordinate and climbed the icy metal rungs again.

Nothing noteworthy. And it was too late to find another lead.

*One more.* Using north as the baseline for the axis, my cold fingers maneuvered the ladder yet again. At the top, something at the edge of my vision looked almost like ... I repositioned the ladder slightly to the left, and—there. My breath lodged in my throat.

From any other angle, the placement of the crystals appeared random. Beautifully chaotic. But now they formed a picture so large it spanned the entire tent. Light bounced between the crystals to form golden lines, shining black wheels, and the billowing steam of a train. Now I understood why I needed the coordinates. A few inches in any direction and I wouldn't have seen it at all.

*How in the ...*

The calculations required, the dedication, the precision ... A single crystal out of place would ruin the whole effect—and yet he'd ...

Awe and fear dripped into my stomach, fighting for dominance as I began to realize for the first time who exactly Ashley Gardner was.

A man who was going to win this game.

I was a flea. An insect trying to skitter up his shiny boot. He was rotating it because for the moment it amused him, watching me crawl up, fall, crawl up, fall, but soon he'd crunch me under his heel, and my father with me.

I'd seen this picture before. Recently. After checking my father's timepiece—ten minutes before closing—I clambered down the ladder and rushed out of the tent. Flea or no, I had to *try*.

The crowds had somehow thickened, a tide of people pulling me toward the exit with prizes and candy tucked under their arms. Everyone I pushed past gave me sidelong glances, a warning bouncing on their lips. *The carnival is about to close.*

I ignored their silent warnings and pushed my way through the maze—arriving at the gallery tent where artists wrapped their paintings in oil cloth and ropes, preparing to go home. To my relief, the painting of the train in the sky still stood on an easel.

"How much for your painting?" I panted as I approached.

The artist, to his credit, didn't note my bedraggled appearance, though he didn't fare much better. His short, lean frame wore an outfit reminiscent of a train conductor, and he held his eyes in a constantly wide state, intensifying his gaze and making me shrink back a little.

"Sorry," he declared. "Just sold it."

A puff of air escaped my lips. "That can't be. I need this painting."

"A gentleman paid me handsomely not ten minutes ago and instructed me not to sell it to anyone, least of all a woman in a navy dress."

A navy—

Blast it all. Ten minutes ago I'd been lugging a ladder to the crystal tent, close to solving the clue. There was only one person in the world who'd work to stop that from happening, and he'd cheated. My teeth clamped down. The artist swung an oil cloth over the painting, and I caught his wrist. I hadn't come this far to fail now. "Name your price."

He glanced at the contact and laughed. "What a bold one you are, madam."

I let go and recoiled. Boldness was not a positive attribute. This whole adventure was making me reckless, and I needed to slow down. Think ahead, prepare, avoid the danger.

But there wasn't *time* to slow down—

The artist's intense stare flickered with a moan. "'Tisn't money I want. Besides," he added, glancing me over again, "I doubt you could top the gentleman's donation." He finished covering the painting in the cloth, then tied it with rope. "I am an artist. Offer me something fashionable, and I'll make the exchange."

My shoulders went slack. I didn't have anything that could be defined as *fashionable* on me. Or at home. I didn't own pretty things.

I snapped open my chatelaine and dug through it for every last farthing Emme had given me. "Please reconsider, sir. It is a matter of life and—"

He snagged the fob dangling out of my chatelaine and held my father's watch to the waning light. "Well, isn't this positively devious?" He spun it until the opals twinkled, illuminating the wonder in his eyes. "Look at the detail of the mosaics! And the filigree edging is one of a kind." He held it to his ear and listened to the soft ticking for several seconds, eyes rolling back in ecstasy. "Like music. Smashing." Then he tucked the watch into his waistcoat pocket.

My hand reflexively shot out. "No—"

He cocked a brow. "Did you want the painting?"

My hand fell midair, and I stared at the artist's pocket, reeling, swallowing, feeling as if my father's essence had been ripped away—again. But the painting held my next clue, and ... if this was the sacrifice I had to make to bring him back ... I would make it.

Tightly, I gave the artist a small nod.

Waxy cloth filled my outstretched hand as he handed me the eleven by fourteen-inch frame. "It's one of a kind, and still fashionable for a good while yet," the artist said with a wink.

I didn't know what he meant by that, and my throat was too thick to inform him that someone had replicated this exact picture—and constructed it far more beautifully—a mere few tents away. Nodding, I hugged the painting to my chest and dashed out of the tent, with no time to inspect it just now.

The jolly raucous of an hour ago was gone, the tents deserted. I hopped over a bucket of spilled popcorn and the painting slipped a little in my waterlogged hands. A burnt caramel smell filled my lungs.

The reds and whites of the tents deepened to eerie shades, their angles growing sharper as the shadows stretched around them, trying to avoid the last dying shaft of sunlight. Half-eaten apples sat on trays, loose ribbons and balls littered the path with not a red blazer in sight—and at each of these realizations my heart beat faster, splices of my vision flashing with each of my steps.

I had to get out. I had to make it out—

I turned a corner and wanted to sob in relief at the sight of the gates. "Dory!" Emme called, safe outside them. She was the only person in sight, gripping the bars so tightly I thought she'd wrench them apart and climb through to get me.

I pushed harder, and though I no longer had my father's watch, I felt its ticking in my chest, in my fingers curling around the painting's frame. Tick. Tock. Tick—

My fingers brushed metal. A chilly wave washed over me and the gates swung in, propelled by some form of magic.

Tock.

*Clang!*

I heaved against the bars, pushing, pulling. It was no use. Locked. I was too late. I looked back up to find that Emme was nowhere to be seen. My head spun toward the gatekeeper, a man in a little red booth whose cheek pooled in his propped hand, on the verge of falling asleep.

"Open the gates! Please!"

His eyes flicked open. "You been before, miss?"

Been? What was he talking about? "I have to get home to my family. Please—make an exception this once."

"I'd recommend a change of clothes first," he said, words slurring out of a lazy smile, but a moment later the gates swung in, and I sighed in relief. I switched the painting to my other hand and dashed through the gates back onto the streets of London—

And catapulted to the edge of some kind of plaza, circular and so vast I couldn't see the other side through the crowd of people dancing to the beat of loud drums. The reverberations from the floor up my legs made my stomach drop, and underneath that, I heard the shushing of a fast-paced river. This wasn't a vision. It was real.

Somehow, I was somewhere else.

The acrid scent of lye burned my throat, and when I checked behind me, I found the source—down the covered hallway that ringed the cavern was a laundering room piled with grungy stretches of cloth.

The drums brought my attention back to the plaza. Loose-fitting dresses with slits in the sleeves and skirts allowed the dancers the freedom of movement to hop over the puddles of liquor splashing the limestone floor. Skin flashed. Glass shattered. Laughter and moaning from all sides. My head flinched at each new sound and beat, too overwhelmed to know what to be frightened of first. My heart palpitated in stabbing tingles.

How ...? Where ...?

I glanced up. I looked to be on the inside of a colosseum. A pitted, *underground* colosseum whose ceiling curved into an enormous stalactite. A cage dangled from the chain on its tip, so high up it was only the size of my thumbnail. I squinted. Crouching inside the cage was a *man*—

I fell back a step, skin pebbling with dread when I hit into a solid body. Figures in maroon hooded vests surrounded me, one of them ripping away my painting and chatelaine while another tied my hands behind my back. A blindfold covered my disbelieving eyes, and I screamed, but the sound was lost to the deafening drums.

# 23

## Miles

I faltered in my progress across the darkening carnival grounds when I saw the bent form of a young boy, head disappearing through the flaps of the utterly stupid pyramid tent. I shook my head as I approached. Ashley was the biggest show-off I knew.

The boy popped his head out, recoiling guiltily when he spotted me. "Mister, where've the crystals gone?"

I studied the tent flaps, but said, "The carnival's about to close."

"But I was 'oping for one last peek."

I straightened his cap then leaned in so my warning would carry more weight. "Go home before you're trapped here, and your parents have to find a new son." His eyes widened. I nudged him in the direction of the gates, and he scampered off.

No one died being at the carnival after dark, but many went missing. A little fear was healthy. I couldn't help but be reminded of the boy with dice from a few days ago, only *that* one had been too stubborn to be afraid. Cocky little cove.

"Poor lad." Ashley came to a stop beside me. "I hope he makes it out."

I knocked my head toward the tent. "When did you drop the illusion?"

Ashley shrugged. "The second she left."

I eyed him. Sometimes the power of his slant scared me. The fact that he could cast such large, intricate illusions—and from a relatively great distance—wasn't normal. No one had had that much magic for centuries.

"I'm hungry," he sighed.

I withdrew a scone I'd bought earlier from one of my regular pockets and handed it to him, raspberry jam oozing down the sides. He accepted it with a "Thanks," before devouring half of it in a single bite.

"You're cleaning my coat later."

"Deal," he said, mouth still full of buttery pastry, even though we both knew he wouldn't.

Because I wouldn't let him. The brown trench coat was too valuable.

It wasn't my *coat* that was magical—I could store items in anything with a pocket, and that's where they had to be retrieved —but it was the most convenient, which was why I wore my coat everywhere. I didn't want to find myself in a dire situation but happened to put on the wrong outerwear that day. Right now, it held only my pistol and ... the hairpin.

Ashley stuffed the rest of the scone into his mouth and headed east, toward the gates. I followed him as we wound through the back alleys of the tents. "Why do we need to go to the Necropolis again? I thought Lark was still hunting you." The thought of the underground sent prickles of unease down my spine. There were only so many near-death experiences one could have before your luck ran out.

Ashley wiped jam from his fingers using a handkerchief. "I need to talk to the Artifice about a job. We'll be quick. Lark will never know we came."

I didn't ask what the job was; it was only ever about the magical artifacts anyway. I repressed a grimace, asking quietly, "Do you really think Bram would approve of your methods?"

"That's a silly question."

I suppose it was. Even with the sword fighting, target practice, and stealth training that had been drilled into us as boys, one could argue that ingenuity was the only thing Bram had insisted we learn. The ability to use our surroundings; adapt. And though Bram Gardner never would've stooped low enough to set foot in the Necropolis, he'd raised Ashley to be like him.

To win.

"Speaking of Bram," Ashley said, ducking under a streamer, "it's a curious thing. Your memories of when we stopped in London, right after he died. They're missing."

I halted. Under the ghost of his touch, my brain shuddered against my skull. My face tightened, hand involuntarily brushing against my coat and feeling the presence of the hairpin. I'd known this was a possibility and had taken the precautionary measures, but— "What are you doing in my mind, Ashley?"

He stopped too, an only-slightly guilty look flitting across his features. "You're hiding something. I can feel it."

"So, you go searching through my memories?"

"No, it was ..." He looked away, licking his lower lip. "I've known for a while. When the grief was still fresh, I wanted to relive it, all right? Feel the freedom again, just for a moment, but I stumbled on those missing memories instead. It never seemed important or connected." He frowned. "Now it does."

I couldn't say anything for a long moment, wrestling with my anger.

*Black fog, Ashley.*

"You can't help yourself, can you?" I muttered. The extravagant illusion in the tent, searching my memories; magic was always the answer, papered over the urge to sacrifice himself first.

He was sliding toward a cliff with no brakes—and he saw its approaching edge. I knew he did. He just didn't care.

He stuffed his hands in his pockets. "What's that supposed to mean?"

I glared at him. "Nothing."

"You never answered me."

Though it still stung, I couldn't claim I wouldn't search *his* memories if I had the ability. Never mind that there was something wrong about his second slant. Never mind that with the crowbar incident, I'd practically thrown this riddle into his lap and begged him to solve it because he wasn't someone who left stones unturned—or in this case, magical pockets unpicked.

I looked away and shrugged, but I knew the action didn't look genuine. "I've chosen to forget that time. We were both in a lot of pain."

"No. When made in grief, memories are distorted, like deciphering a face on a rippling surface." He shook his head. "Memories are like a deck of cards. When I've found one I want, I pull it out, examine it carefully, and then slip it back into the deck before anyone notices it's missing."

My eyes narrowed, unsure how to feel about how easily the magic came to him.

"The memory after Bram ... There were no numbers, no suit, no faces. It was blank, and yet it remained in the deck."

I met his sharp gaze, unable to hide any longer. "Objects are not the only things I can store out of sight."

His head knocked back, obviously surprised to find that my slant extended to the mind. Yet another secret I'd kept from him. He leaned back against a pole. "So, I was right. It is about a woman."

I sidestepped him and strode toward the front gates. "Not every piece of my life is yours to examine."

I hadn't always had the ability, but I'd sharpened my mind

tirelessly, so I could poke holes and store a few memories there. *Those* memories. It had taken me months to build the mental stamina. I didn't know if everyone's slant could be extended or trained that way, but Bram had seemed to think so. He'd given me the idea, after all.

A minute later Ashley caught up and grasped my shoulder. "Miles, I was wrong. I just—"

A flash of strawberry-blonde hair caught my eye, but when I looked, the girlish figure ducked behind a building outside the gate. Another woman stood inside the bars, and I studied her as she heaved against them. She argued with the gatekeeper about something, and a moment later the gates groaned open.

I frowned. "Isn't that Miss St. James?"

Ashley followed my gaze, lips parting. "Bloody silt." He exhaled just as her form disappeared through the portal to the Necropolis. "And she has my painting."

# 24

## Dorothy

They dragged me forward, and I thrashed, disoriented but alert enough to know I was in a lot of trouble. We moved into a hallway, from what I could tell, where the sounds of gaiety muffled to a thrum. A minute later, hands shoved me onto a bench and metal clanged, like someone locking me in a holding cell.

Something slimy squished under my feet. I tried not to panic, but my airways iced over. Everything was dark and strange, and smelled like damp clay. My aunt and uncle were probably frantic. Emme—oh, I hoped she made it home safely.

Splinters stabbed my legs through my dress as I settled into the bench, mind scrambling for a way out. An explanation of how I'd gotten here in the first place. I latched onto the cold flash I'd felt as the gates were closing. I'd assumed they were propelled by magic, but maybe what I'd sensed was the glowing to life of a portal that had transported me to ... to ...

Where the devil was I?

I scooted back until my bound hands brushed coarse limestone walls that quaked faintly from the drums, then followed the bench until they hit bars. Somewhere to my right a dim source of light fizzed and popped. I tested the slack in the rope around my wrists but there was none.

To be blindfolded and imprisoned in an underground cavern in the middle of the night was a terrible predicament to be in, but all I could think about was how I'd lost the painting. I never examined it, and now I'd never learn my second clue, much less find Mr. Brass's factory and discover if he was the Rook.

My throat hit a lump of rising panic. Much less find my father.

A few hours later, the fall of several pairs of boots plodded near and someone hit the floor and grunted. The cell next to me clanged closed, making me jump. "Bloody ruffians," the person muttered while the steps retreated. Then shouted, "You can bet your sorry haunches I'll be speaking to the Acherons about this!"

Something about his voice seemed familiar and when I'd placed it, everything in me stilled. "... Mr. Riley?"

Shuffling. "Who's there?" He must be blindfolded too.

My shoulders sagged in relief at finding the very man I'd followed into the carnival. I doubted he'd remember me, so I said, "I'm a friend."

He scoffed. "I don't have friends. Not in this place." More shuffling.

If I were ever freed, this turn of events might prove to be a blessing. All I needed to do was ask the right questions. "You've been here before, then?"

"Many times. But I forgot to dress as a pauper this go around and look where that's got me. Rancid Talons."

Those must be the men that had brought me here. A kind of law enforcement?

"How's your dress?" Mr. Riley asked.

"I beg your pardon?"

"Is that how they got you too?" When I didn't answer, he snickered. "They don't take kindly to the upper class down here. Not after the Gloaming. Everyone who smells of money goes through a *security check* to make sure you're not spying for Victoria or other so-called unsavories. A nice way of saying you'll be a slave on the low-level for the rest of your life. It's a lot harder to get out than to get in, see."

I stiffened at the words *slave* and *rest of your life.* It had to be hyperbole.

Before I stepped through the portal, the gatekeeper had said, *I'd recommend a change of clothes first.* Now that I thought about it, I remembered seeing a few red blazers among the dancers when I first arrived. The carnival workers knew about this place; maybe even lived here.

*Low-level.* Was that referring to all the floors I'd glimpsed, like rings stacked atop each other? Remembering the man in the cage, I shuddered. "So," I went on, voice a pitch higher, "you come here to ...?"

"A man's business down here is his own," Mr. Riley said carefully. The Samaritan wouldn't explain his methods of gleaning information. If he wasn't the Samaritan, he was probably here for seedy reasons. Other than the Talons, I hadn't witnessed a modicum of decorum or order.

"Of course," I said hastily. "It's probably a lot safer underground than above, what with all the kidnappings."

"You mean the Rook." His shoes scraped the floor, like he was straightening. "Maybe. Bluedusters don't know about this place, after all. And it's seen an influx of slanted peasants since the disappearances started, since he's only been taking the slanted ones." This information was new, and not wholly accurate since my father didn't have magic. Still, I logged it away in case it was important. "The Necropolis is bursting with business, and the Acherons couldn't be more pleased."

Necropolis. *Dead city.* I shuddered. The Acherons had to be the ones in charge.

"My brother was his first victim, you know." Mr. Riley's tone was unreadable. My ears perked up, head turning toward his voice even when the silence thickened. "By the time we finally got him back, he was already mad, like the others. My brother killed himself within the week." He added through his teeth, "The Rook will pay for what he's done."

I froze, no longer aware of my itchy blindfold or numb hands. The Rook's *first* kidnapping had been Mr. Riley's brother. The timing could be coincidence, but if anyone had true motive for becoming the Samaritan, surely—

A soft *swick* and a shift in the air had my thoughts grinding to a halt. Someone had picked the lock to my cell. My fears were confirmed when a firm grip on my upper arm hauled me to my feet and steered me forward.

"Where are you going?" Scraping against the metal bars was followed by Mr. Riley's desperate cry of, "Take me with you!"

My captor didn't pause. We walked, and the banging of the drums grew louder until the sound reverberated up my legs. "Where are you taking me?"

The stranger didn't answer, only righted me when I tripped over something. Stairs. We climbed dozens of them and turned a few corners. I knew we entered an offshoot of the colossal chamber when the roar all but vanished and the hot smell of sweetened pastry hit my nose.

I tried to push down my rising panic when I was made to sit in a chair with a plush cushion. A moment later the ropes around my wrists fell away. While I rubbed them the blindfold came off, and I blinked in the low light.

Clean, arched windows, rising dough on a counter, and a half dozen tables with napkins and quaint candlesticks. I appeared to be in some sort of bakery with gothic architecture. My jaw went slack at seeing Mr. Kelly's intimidating form a few paces away. But my surprise quickly shifted to the man who slid into the seat across from me, cool smile in place as he tossed my blindfold on the table and reclined like it was child's play to break into a cell and smuggle me out.

Mr. Ashley "Everett" Gardner.

# 25

## Dorothy

Gold teacups steaming with hot chocolate arrived a few minutes later, along with a plate of bite-sized danishes drizzled with maple syrup. The bricked limestone walls held gas lanterns that glowed white from an unseen power. The warm bakery air felt nice on my chilled skin, but my mind buzzed with so many questions, it was all I could do to keep them from spewing out at once.

Ashley thanked the waiter but didn't move to eat. Maybe he was waiting for me to take the first bite, but I felt too out of my element to do anything but stare back at him. I forced myself to relax. The bakery, while occupied by other patrons, felt secluded enough.

"Well, Miss St. James," he drawled at last, "you certainly know how to find trouble."

I folded my hands in my lap. "And you know how to find me, apparently. Which makes you ...?"

"An idiot."

A woman sauntered up to our table, the black lace of her ruffled crimson sleeves brushing my chair, and her confident stride pegging her as the owner of the establishment. A thick metal cuff with a winking emerald banded her wrist, a seam on the back from where it had been welded on. I was certain I'd seen the same cuffs on the men in the plaza, before they blindfolded me. Between her necklace and neckline lay a mile of skin.

When she only stared at me for an uncomfortable moment with her dark eyes, I said, "Beautiful pearls. I've always wanted my own."

Ashley cocked his head. "An innocuous girl like Dorothy St. James doesn't have a string of pearls. Somehow that surprises me."

Was he insinuating they were the bland—the *safe*—jewelry choice?

The woman cleared he throat. "Lark's been looking all over for you, Ashley. Not your lucky night." Her eyes flicked to me again, assessing slowly. "... Or is it?"

"Not by half." Ashley didn't spare me a glance, tone unreadable.

She leaned over the table, showing off her impressive decolletage. "What could I get for turning you in? A cuff for my son?" Only then did I notice the fine wrinkles by her eyes and time-narrowed face.

Ashley smiled lazily at her. "You'd never do it, would you, Peck?"

Her inhale was long and wistful as she ogled him head to toe. "You can stay. But if the Talons come sniffing, I'll be the first to rat you out." Ashley raised his golden teacup to her and at the call of "Madame Pecan!" across the room, she traipsed off to attend to other customers.

When I was sure she was out of earshot, I asked, "Pecan?"

Mr. Kelly showed no signs of hearing me, so Ashley supplied, "Everyone uses aliases down here. Keeps things tidy."

"Do you?"

A smile. "I'm not a tidy person," he mumbled into his cup.

Ashley Gardner had a way of speaking unlike anyone I'd met. Instead of trying to impress me with an upper-crust accent, he didn't move his lips much and couldn't be bothered to enunciate. But the effect wasn't laziness, more … conspiracy. Like everything he said had a buried secret.

Across the bakery, Madame Pecan carried a platter of bread to a table, stopping short to wave a palm over the loaves. Steam rose from them, the butter on top glistening as it melted again. I gaped as the patrons accepted the bread and disappeared through the arched doorway, trying to place what was wrong with the picture—before realizing that Madame Pecan had obviously used her slant, and yet my blood felt no colder. My magic should've recharged a bit by now, and yet I felt nothing.

Was it possible my slant couldn't detect *everyone's* magic? Not wanting to focus on the catastrophic possibility, I asked, "Where exactly am I?"

"The undercity," Ashley said. Behind his shoulder, Mr. Kelly's arms folded, and he kept a steady eye on the room around us, a wolf looking for signs of a hunter. He'd effectively separated himself from the conversation; apart, but ears attuned.

I cradled my teacup, letting its warmth seep into my fingers. "The Necropolis?"

Ashley nodded.

"How have I not heard of this place before? Why isn't it crawling with bluedusters? And how did you know they were holding me in that cell? Mr. Riley is still down there. Do you know where they are keeping my painting? I must get out as soon as—"

"Whoa," Ashley said, holding up a hand, "slow down. You have a nasty habit, Miss St. James, of claiming things that do not belong to you, when I believe the term you're looking for is *thank you*." He flashed me a wide, almost sarcastic smile as he set my oil-wrapped painting on the table between us. "And you are most wholeheartedly welcome, by the way."

I sighed in relief, fingers stretching to grab it.

His hand clamped around my wrist, making me freeze. "Though, since I did just save your life, I don't think you'll have any objections to me keeping it." With a flick of his wrist, Ashley flipped the painting to Mr. Kelly behind him, who caught it and made it disappear before I could blink.

I stared at the two of them, mouth slightly ajar. Just like that, my second clue wasn't even lost in some underground pit—it was gone. Forever.

Placing both palms on the table, I said, "I have many objections, in fact. I deciphered all your little tricks, jumped through all your hoops, and paid very handsomely for that painting."

He cocked his head. "As did I, by breaking you out of that cell. Now to answer your questions." Ashley stuffed one of the danishes into his mouth, nonchalant about the way he'd devastated my progress. I was the bug. He was the boot. "I wouldn't worry about Mr. Riley. He is a man with connections; believe me when I say he can take care of himself."

I pursed my lips. His cryptic answer only seemed to confirm my suspicions that Mr. Riley was the Samaritan, and they were all in league together. "What else do you know of him?"

"Not many people know of the Necropolis's existence," Ashley went on as if he hadn't heard me, licking syrup off one finger. "Or if they do, they don't know how to find it."

Watching him eat awakened my own hunger, so even though I still hadn't forgiven him, I pinched a pastry and popped it in my mouth, barely suppressing a moan of ecstasy. Crisp and flaky with a pool of maple glaze in the center, the danish used the crunch of a pecan to bring all the elements into harmony—and a dash of something luscious and otherworldly. Magic.

I devoured another one, pretending not to notice the glint of amusement in Ashley's eyes. After washing down my fourth danish with some hot chocolate, I finally managed to ask, "How does one keep a secret so large?"

"The only way into the Necropolis is through one of the seven portals, and each of them are guarded fiercely by the Talons—the lovely men who dumped you in that cell. They dress to blend in when they're up top. And down here ..." He surveyed the room quickly. "They're everywhere. You're lucky I was able to slip past them before you were processed. Newcomers spend a decade as slaves before working up to the second level."

In this friendly bakery it was easy to imagine I was safe, but my glimpse of the plaza below had been full of mayhem and lawlessness. Grimacing, I dusted a few crumbs off the table. "I saw no Talons guarding the portal, and the gatekeeper let me through relatively easily."

"The gatekeeper was drunk." Anger threaded Ashley's voice, but then he lowered it. "And the Talons don't exist to keep people out."

I glanced at Mr. Kelly whose expression was equally serious, and then I heard what Ashley wasn't saying.

*They keep people in.*

My heart sank into my stomach as I realized the awful scope of my predicament.

Mr. Riley had said the same thing, and I mulled over the information. With access to London above granted to so few, it had likely become its own form of commodity—the likes of which granted full power to the man controlling it.

Madame mentioned someone looking for Ashley named Lark. Maybe he was the one in charge?

"So, it's impossible to get home?"

Ashley and Mr. Kelly shared a look. "It's difficult. Not impossible. Miles and I can slip in and out easily enough, but with you

... You're bound to draw some notice. We can't take any chances. We'll have to pull a Copenhagen."

Mr. Kelly's eyelashes spasmed in irritation. "Not a Copenhagen. We're trying to be *discreet*."

"I want to send a message."

"Unless the message is 'Please come kill me, Lark, and forever spare everyone else from my stupidity,' I'm not sure it will translate. He'll be incensed. The Talons will swarm in seconds."

Ashley shrugged and grinned, unfazed by the prospect of death. Maybe even thrilled by it. "Seconds is all we need."

My focus volleyed between them, still stuck at the beginning. "What happened in Copenhagen?"

"We'll need a cuff," Ashley went on as if I hadn't spoken.

"Go for it," Mr. Kelly shot back. "Make a bloody scene. Kill us all."

I leaned forward. "Cuff?"

Ashley turned back to me, remembering my presence. "The metal bands—relics of the undercity, given only to those who've proven their loyalty. Aboveground, the cuffs are useless, but they allow people to access their slant in this black hole. Can't use magic down here without one."

So that was why I hadn't sensed Madame Pecan use her slant; she had a band, and I did not. They must hold some of the gems that magic had first bonded to when the Variance was opened. But what was it about the Necropolis that obstructed magic in the first place?

Ashley drummed his fingers on the table. "Those who wear the cuffs can use magic, but more importantly, the cuffs also grant you passage through the portal. That'll be our ticket out. Dawn is when the portal shuts down, and we'll wait until the last possible moment so the Talons can't follow us through." His fingers froze midair, and he leveled me with a serious stare. "But you'll have to do exactly as I say. And you'll have to trust me. Can you do that?"

After a moment of hesitation, I nodded. The two men were risking their necks for me, so I wasn't exactly in a position to question their methods.

"In the meantime," Ashley continued, "just relax. We've over an hour to kill."

Instead, I turned back to the million questions swirling in my head. "Can't we go through the portal we came through?"

Ashley shook his head. "Doesn't work that way. There are seven portals in—all of them through various archways on the ground floor—but only one portal out, and it's heavily guarded."

I finished the last of my hot chocolate, belly now warm and uncomfortably full. "Where are the heads of the seven portals?"

"Around London. Most people here only know the location of one. Two, if they're lucky."

I studied him a long moment. "And you've found all seven." It wasn't a question. A poker smirk grew up one side of his face, and I thought maybe he was pleased that I hadn't underestimated him. I inhaled, but much to my surprise, Mr. Kelly spoke.

"Are we to answer these trifling questions all night?" He directed it to Ashley, something in the tone passing between them. "Nothing about magic makes sense, so why waste breath trying to explain it?"

"That's not true," I found myself saying, and Mr. Kelly's eyes snapped to me, as if surprised I'd heard him. "The scientific community is making advancements all the time." Scientific community being me and my father. I heard Emme's mocking voice in my head. *Always bringing it back to science.*

"Like your father?" Ashley asked, and I caught his meaningful stare.

There was no use pretending innocence when he'd seen the notebook in Father's laboratory for himself. "And me," I added. "Our joint research has made strides. We were going to make the knowledge public, once ..." I shook my head. "I can see why stigmatism surrounding magic is perpetuated. People only fear what they don't understand."

"By all means, Miss St. James" —Ashley threaded his hands behind his head and settled back like he had all the time in the world— "enlighten us."

He seemed sincere enough, so I began with, "Well, magic is genetic. And like genetic characteristics, it tends to become diluted over time.

"When the deposit of magic was first stumbled upon by miners—the Variance, it was called, and I suspect this Necropolis is the very mine—it cracked open, and magic flooded into the world. Most of the magic found humans, but some of it found other vessels. Gems, specifically." I couldn't look at Ashley as I said the last part, remembering my lie to him about the bracelet. The cuff circling Madame Pecan's wrist held a gem, which was what must let her use her magic. The ring in Ashley's coat too. "Those relics are rare, though. Some speculate they've been destroyed."

Mr. Kelly watched me with a predatory stillness. Ashley pursed his lips in thought. "Hm."

Unable to decide if he was mocking me, I went on. "Magic needs a vessel to be useful, you see—without it, it's just raw energy drifting in the air. Once it has bonded to its vessel, it will remain loyal forever."

"Loyal," Ashley echoed hollowly, dropping his arms and leaning forward to watch his finger trace a groove in the table. His mouth cut a bitter edge.

"Magic isn't a random explosion of force that will bond with anybody. It is calculated, controlled, and *always* returns to the user.

"When your slant manifests during puberty, the particles in your blood physically change. A stamp that is unique to each person—like a snowflake, or a fingerprint. Though some slants are similar, none are identical."

I knew my eyes were lit, knew my hands were moving too animatedly, but I couldn't seem to stop. "Magic changes the matter around you to perform its specialty. Then these invisible particles slowly return to the portal they made on your palms, a process that can take up to six hours. After you use your slant, slant guns detect the high concentration of magic returning to your palms. Theoretically, if you made them sensitive enough like the prototype my father created, you could trace them much longer."

It was a lot of information to dump all at once, but although both men seemed intensely interested, neither seemed surprised. Ashley cocked his head. "What of mutated magic? Like the man who sealed the Variance—this place?"

I shuddered, remembering the mutation under the glass in the lab, right before it splintered. "Well ... there's a lot we don't know about mutated magic. There's only been the one case. But as I understand, it's when magical particles of different genetic codes are *confined* together and bond. The larger the area, the longer it takes to mutate. With the man who sealed the Variance, it was ... ten, twelve years?"

Ashley's expression darkened, and his frame seemed too taut for a simple history lesson. "Loyal indeed."

"Oh, it is, still. Strangely. The more it's used, the more mutated magic increases in sentience. All it cares about is your innermost desires, and slowly, it overtakes you to make them reality. It has your will, but its own mind. Its own dark conscience. And when it grew too large for its host, it imploded, sealing the Variance and forming a black hole in the process."

"So, when the mutation overtakes you completely, you die."

"No, that's—" I chewed my lip. "There have been no studies."

"You're the scientist. What's your educated guess?"

I looked between the two men helplessly. "... I don't know," I finally admitted. "No one's ever had two magics besides him."

"But theoretically—"

My eyebrows stitched together. "Theoretically, you die, yes." A pensiveness settled in the air, though I couldn't say why. It was all purely hypothetical.

"Not the worst way to go," Ashley said at last, and for some reason that prompted Mr. Kelly to scowl at the back of his head. Ashley leaned back in his chair to study me. "You like solving puzzles."

The sudden change in topic threw me. "What?"

"That's why science excites you. It is a puzzle."

Mr. Kelly shifted behind him, muttering, "Not everyone is like you, Ash."

"*She* is like me." Ashley never took his eyes off me, and again, his lips barely moved. Another secret. It didn't feel necessarily like a compliment. Yet, there was a hungriness in his eyes, a waning loneliness as he looked at me that made my belly spark with heat.

I quietly cleared my throat. "There is a lot we understand about magic, and that knowledge will only grow exponentially. We have no need to fear it." I chewed my lip and tucked a strand of hair behind my ear, both actions carrying the weight of Ashley's gaze and making my face feel unbearably hot. "Don't you agree, Mr. Kelly?"

Mr. Kelly started and blinked at me, looking almost affronted that I'd addressed him specifically. He uncrossed his arms. Then with a frown, he slipped away and walked out the door of the bakery.

Ashley tossed a cursory glance over his shoulder then turned back to me, raising his eyebrows. "He likes you."

A breathy laugh escaped my lips, because the only other reaction was to scoff. "He's said nothing to me all night."

"He left to make the preparations for our escape. Silence is its own language, one Miles is fluent in, as he struggles with words to the female sex. Not sure why. Just something he's always had."

"So he's your antithesis."

A pause. "I suppose you could say that." Ashley sounded a little annoyed at the comparison. Perhaps he didn't see his ability to charm as a virtue—and I found it interesting. A pair of men, one who disliked charming women and another who physically couldn't.

Fingering the handle of my shiny teacup, I ventured, "You grew up on a ship. What was it like?" He'd already been more than generous in answering my questions, but I couldn't help wanting another piece of him. Any piece.

Maybe he was right. Maybe I was like him—saw him as a puzzle worth solving.

He studied me, gauging my sincerity, and he must've found enough because at length he said, "Freedom. Like time froze and I could live forever.

"If you want an adventure, it feels like salt on your skin and tastes like potential in the air. It looks like a thousand copper sunrises on a burnished horizon that no other man will ever see. Just you and a vast, vast world. Nothing you do matters there— which is either good or bad, depending on what you're running from."

"And what were you running from?"

His lips thinned a little, and he took so long to respond that I didn't think he would. But then he finally said, "What we all are. One's destiny."

Something told me he wouldn't reveal more than that. "And Bram Gardner ...?"

"Was a father I loved more than the sea." Seeing my confusion, Ashley cocked his head, making a lock of dark wavy hair fall onto his forehead. "You misunderstood me the other day, and I admit, I intended you to. My life is unconventional and sometimes dangerous. I am therefore fortunate—glad, even—that my actions put no one at risk but myself." He added in a quieter voice, "And my silent failures are a far lighter burden than someone else's disappointment."

He stroked his wrist as if it were missing a watch, and as I wondered what memory he was reliving, I checked his person for clues. Nothing flashed or shone, not his black silk necktie, nor the silver pin ornamenting it that was so old and dull, it looked more like pewter. He wore a black vest and coat with fine stitching—but not so fine as to draw attention and not tailored enough for the clothes to have been made for him. A bit of soot clung the underside of his jaw, but nothing else seemed out of place. Everything was clean but carefully understated.

Everything, except his face.

I inspected it closer, tugging at a nagging thread until the thought unraveled. He had no dimples or random creases in his smile, and both rows of teeth were straight. His nose didn't angle slightly, and his skin was golden and smooth as cream, unmarked by moles, freckles, or even wayward eyelashes.

I'd never seen anything so ...

He looked like someone had painted half a face and placed a mirror over it. Even that wasn't accurate, because half a painting could never capture something so masculine and symmetrical. It was like looking at an angel. Or a devil. He looked like someone who wished to disappear but couldn't help but be seen.

And now, after his confession, I felt like I was seeing him for the first time.

Maybe it was that thought that drew the next words from my tongue on a whisper. "The Rook has kidnapped my father."

Ashley's eyes ticked up, but his face remained inscrutable. After a lengthy pause, so lengthy it was painful, he asked quietly, "Have you contacted the authorities? Have you—"

"Yes, I've done everything. Believe me, Mr. Gardner, I have pursued every option, even one so far-fetched as finding the Samaritan so I might enlist his help."

His lips parted. He raised his cup, but I watched his Adam's apple and he never swallowed. He set the cup back on the table, thumbing over his mouth to remove the residue. A distraction to buy him time.

Time for what?

"I cannot claim to know him well, but the masked man is not the hero you make him out to be."

I shook my head. "I cannot track down the Rook on my own, so he is my last hope."

"Perhaps you should place your hope in someone else."

"Who do you suggest?" I gave him a pointed look. "Is someone else offering?"

We stared at each other, his gaze so hooded and intense that it seared into my mind. It took all my concentration not to look away. At last, he emitted a short sigh and sat back, making me wonder if I'd imagined the moment altogether.

"Have you told anyone else?"

I shook my head again. "My cousin, the only one I'd trust, is far too reckless. Anyone else, and I'd fear the information returning to my uncle." I reflexively glanced around, but no one was listening. "Once before, my father grew gravely ill. Without a thought for his fighting for every breath, my uncle moved his family to London and started managing the house and finances. He already owned the mortgage on our house, but now he wanted the baronetcy for his son. He was cruel. *Hungry* for Father to die.

"I was denied all correspondence. When my father worsened, I told Emmeline and readied to fetch the doctor myself. She begged to come, but I refused, explaining I could make better time if I were alone. But Emme followed me onto the streets—

foolishly trying to disguise herself from me with her magic. A blueduster saw. So did Uncle Benedick.

"Uncle nabbed us both and locked us in our rooms; I never found out whether we escaped the blueduster, or Uncle offered him an exorbitant bribe. But I was trapped in my room for a full week, listening to my father's rasps down the hall and unable to do anything about it." An angry tremor slipped into my voice, and I dug my fingernails into my palms as I slowly gained control.

"I know Emme means well, but I won't risk my father's life again. My uncle is here. He craves control and exercises it fully when it is given him. I cannot root out the Rook *or* Samaritan if I am locked in my own house."

A muscle in Ashley's jaw jumped as he looked between my eyes, but his voice remained even. "Why are you entrusting this information to me?"

I wandered his face, looking for the man who loved his godfather more than the sea. After clearing away some of the smoke in his eyes, I found him, alone and staring into the expanse. "Because you gave me a piece of your trust first. A token for a token."

He blinked, breath deepening like he was gearing up to say something, but then Madame Pecan shuffled back into the room. Half a glance from Ashley was all it took for her to appear at his side.

"We need to get her out," Ashley said with a knock of his chin. "Any chance you could loan us a dress?"

She leaned on the table again, and the kohl around her eyes seemed heavier than earlier. "The portal will close soon. If she takes it, I'll never get it back."

"I'll buy you a new one."

Her face broke into a wide grin, pleased with this new prospect. She sauntered closer, one of her hands sliding up his shoulder to stroke his neck. Ashley held completely still, watching her steadily as she brushed against him, her voice turning sultry. Slow. "And will you put it on me?"

"Why do I need a new dress?" I asked, not at all sorry for interrupting.

Ashley glanced at me, but it was Madame Pecan who answered while watching her sharpened nail drag along his skin. "Buttoned up as you are, the wolves will smell that you're from above. Show a little skin and you'll be much safer, trust me."

If that comment was meant to settle my nerves, it did the opposite. I didn't have the assets Madame Pecan had, so any dress she loaned me would fall way below the maximum point of propriety. She sized me up, doubtlessly thinking the same thing. "I know just the one," she mused, and reluctantly pulled herself away.

# 26

## Ashley

Out in the arcade, the drums beat louder, screams and laughter highlighting the night's climax. Inside the bakery was dark, Peck having locked up and bid me a very physical farewell before skirting off to put her son to bed. A lone candle flickered in the open window adjoining the main area to the room Dorothy was currently using to change into her dress.

Standing in a shadowed corner, I checked the clock on the wall.

Miles would be waiting for us. When we finally got down to the plaza, he'd give me a reprimanding look, and then his gaze would settle on Dorothy with meaning. As much as I disliked that, I hated the idea of hurrying her more.

The last thing I needed right now was to walk in on her before she was done dressing.

After all that careful planning, I hadn't intended for the second clue to go so catastrophically wrong.

The plan had been easy. I'd seen her penciling Riley's name in her nightgown when I'd entered her memories. Acting on a hunch, I'd employed Mr. Riley to step into a shop and lure her to the carnival, where I could stage the second clue. As for getting her to the dress shop, it wasn't hard to draw up an enticing hand-bill and put it in the greedy uncle's path. Money couldn't buy breeding, but he seemed to think so, and that was his weakness.

The plan for getting out of here was much more complicated, mainly to avoid Dorothy discovering my slant.

My thoughts drifted to the painting, a range of emotions passing through me. Usually, they were only fleeting impressions of guilt, but these stayed, twisting my insides like a knife in the gut as I thought about how Dorothy was only trying to save her father.

She wouldn't. And finding the Samaritan would only endanger her more.

But the hope shining in her eyes ...

When another scream from the colosseum ripped the air, I straightened, nerves on edge. We couldn't delay any longer. I tapped my knuckle three times against the door.

A muffled voice said, "Come in." I turned the knob and stepped inside. Dorothy stood in the center of the room, hands behind her back.

She'd changed into an off-shoulder dress that had a ridiculous amount of purple lace but still managed to look *féminine* on her. Free of its restricting coiffure, her hair was tied in a loose side braid, generous tendrils curling against her pale neck; the same way she'd worn it when we met. I swallowed hard and dragged my eyes up before I could take her in completely. "Twenty minutes until the portal closes."

She pinked and her gaze darted away. "I usually have a maid ..."

Then I realized why her hands were behind her back, and I silently cursed Peck even as my blood pumped faster in my veins. She should've given Dorothy something that didn't require help to lace up. I fell back a step. "I could fetch someone?" There was no one to fetch, and we both knew it. Peck had already left, and we were running out of time. But for my own sake, I begged her to say a name. Any name.

Dorothy hesitated, then shook her head, coming to the same conclusion as me. "I'd rather you than a stranger."

*I am a stranger*, I wanted to say, but my tongue was a boulder in my mouth. Because—

*I don't want to be.*

There were a million reasons why I shouldn't help her, our conversation at the table being one of them. In the end, strings always had to be severed.

Her innocent eyes glanced up at me, pale in the candlelight streaking through the adjoining window. Far too wide. Far too trusting. Far too ... beautiful. "Will you help me with the back?" she asked softly.

*No.*

*Yes, yes.*

When I failed to say anything, she shrank into herself. "You wouldn't let me walk through a den of thieves so indecently dressed, would you Mr. Gardner?" I picked up on the tremulous note in her voice and, against my will, lost the battle. My feet shuffled forward.

*Traitor,* my blood sang.

She angled away as I stepped behind her and a length of creamy skin flooded my vision. The petite knobs of her spine plunged into a corset that hugged her shoulder blades. I closed my eyes and turned my head away, cursing Peck anew.

It was nothing I hadn't seen on a woman before. Seen every evening at the balls and dinner parties of the *ton*, but this somehow felt different. More delicate. Like a gift. The barest breath of a wish.

*Are you even sure what game we're playing?*

I remembered her luminous, challenging eyes glowing up at me. *Are you?*

I clenched my jaw. Better not to think at all. Better to get this over with.

I opened my eyes. My hands suddenly felt too cold, fingers stiff and fumbling as they picked up the laces and threaded them through the holes of her dress. Knowing how little time we had, I should've raced through it, but I didn't. Couldn't. I worked slowly, saying nothing. Neither did she, but the fine hairs on her neck raised, aware of every accidental caress on her back. And every one that wasn't quite an accident.

*Traitor, traitor.*

Her quiet breaths filled the small room. My own lungs felt tight. I drew the strings until they had no slack, just enough to keep the dress closed, and fastened them off. And then we both stood there, frozen, and somewhere through the fog I distantly remembered we needed to hurry, but with my fingers on the laces of her dress, it somehow didn't seem that important anymore.

A note of sweetness met my nose, something floral that reminded me of French gardens, and suddenly I was drowning in it with my lids growing heavy, leaning forward to catch another trace so I could solve what it was. A lock of hair curled over the base of her neck. I tugged it lightly until the coil straightened then let it go, watching it gently spring back into shape. With a worshipful touch, I padded a thumb over the skin exposed underneath. She shuddered.

*Stop touching her.*

*Stop wanting to touch her.*

I pulled my gaze up to find the soft edge of her profile, her head half turned toward me. There were a hundred things that sprang to my tongue, a hundred things I wanted to do in this moment. That *wish* inhaled all the air in the room and sighed faintly into my ear, making me inch closer ... just a bit closer ...

The drums changed their pitch, breaking the spell. I fisted my hand and forced it to my side, stepping back. "Time to go."

# 27

## Dorothy

Cinders fizzled in the brick oven in the corner, but that wasn't why I felt hot. My back still burned from the light brushes of Ashley's fingers, and I couldn't get the moment out of my head, nor the embers I'd seen in his eyes.

"Are you ready?" he asked, stopping before the exit to the bakery.

I nodded, but I knew he didn't see it because he'd refused to look at me since lacing up my dress, making my stomach curl in disappointment. Maybe I'd imagined the whole thing. Madame's plum garment was scratchy and a few decades old, but beautiful in the way the lace dangled from puffed sleeves and peaked across my collarbone like a wrought-iron fence.

Ashley stepped into the cacophony. The enormous cavern reeked of beer and wine. Bodies dangled from the balconies and twirled from the columns, careless of the steep fifty-foot drop. A brawl broke out down the circular arcade ringing this level, and I took note of several couples who were tangled together, hands and mouths wandering to places that made me blush.

I tried to ignore the lecherous stares of nearby men and

forced a step forward. Then another. I wasn't used to feeling air against my throat and collarbone and I had to fight the urge to cross my arms over my chest.

"They'll notice if you cower," Ashley's deep voice whispered in my ear, sensing my internal conflict.

My spine stiffened. We moved down the arcade and Ashley's hand settled on the middle of my back; warmth bloomed from the contact. I needed the anchor, and I wondered if he could sense that too.

The stairs were syncopated through the levels, forcing us to walk past most of the shops before ascending. Below us, the people on the main floor were small, like scattered beads from a broken necklace. "Why-Why are we going up?"

Ashley slowed his pace. "You're not afraid of heights, are you?"

Now my nerves jumped for a completely different reason. "I don't think so."

"Good."

Two men lounged near a pillar, and I swore one of their hands tugged the fabric near my waist as I passed. I kept walking but turned toward the sound of their snickering. "Why did those men—"

"Wait here a moment." Ashley disappeared into one of the shops built into the wall.

I swallowed and glanced around, feeling like a hen in a foxhouse. Lingering chuckles and fixed gazes propelled me backward until something sharp jabbed my arm—the head of a nail tacked onto one of the pillars—making me hiss and jerk away. A ripping sound filled my ears. The black lace of my off-shoulder sleeve dangled down my arm, and I scooped it up, trying hurriedly to pin it back on.

A body jostled into me, and my eyes flew up to find a blond man thrusting me back. I pivoted but he caught me and shoved.

"I saw that bloke you were with," he rumbled, stubble scraping my jaw and breath hot on my collarbone. His calloused touch slithered up my dress, finding my thigh. I rammed my forearms into him but was met with a slam, pinning me to the coarse balcony.

"What's he got that I haven't?"

Revulsion pitched into my throat as a wet tongue pressed against my neck. I inhaled to scream.

Someone tore the man off me, and a second later Ashley gripped the same hand that had been up my skirt. Ashley's cool eyes glittered as he stared him down. "Her," he said, the word a shaft of ice. With one swift move, he yanked a knife from his belt and sliced the man's hand off.

Emitting an ear-splitting shriek, the blond man crumpled to the ground. Even from lower levels across the circular expanse, heads turned. The drums seemed to waver on a few beats. Blood spurted from his open wound and from the severed hand, still in Ashley's grip until Ashley slipped the cuff off before tossing the appendage at him.

"A little earlier than I expected," Ashley huffed, "but I can work with it."

The drums beat faster, and I couldn't help but feel like we'd woken a slumbering dragon. I stared wide-eyed, open-mouthed at the bloody scene.

After wiping the blood off the lip of the cuff with his coat, Ashley propelled me forward at a faster pace. Relief at being saved slowly ate away my mortification.

My gaze snagged on the shiny silver band in Ashley's grip. He'd said we needed a cuff to get out, but he hadn't mentioned how he'd planned on getting one. "Please don't tell me that was the Copenhagen," I said, breath still heaving from shock and stomach pitching like a drunken sailor. If only because I didn't want to imagine he'd cut off a man's hand before.

"No."

Then I remembered something else he said. "What happened too early?"

"Your dress," he explained, nudging me faster. He still wouldn't look at me. "The farther up you go, the more entitled they are. I'd rather lop off a guilty man's hand than someone who never needed the lesson, I just didn't expect it to happen while I was retrieving the knife."

I tensed. "So you dressed me as—as—as *bait*?"

"Honor is thinner than water down here, so we can't rely on someone hiding us again." Ashley's tone sharpened when he added, "We don't get out tonight, we don't get out at all. Do you understand?"

The image of blood filled my eyes, before I remembered the feeling of the man's hand up my skirt, eliciting a shudder. After another moment, I nodded.

"The good thing is, it worked," he said. But his jaw was tight, like he wished it hadn't. And his hand inched around my waist and slowly eased me flush against his shoulder as we walked, stiffening every time someone came within arm's length.

We passed teeth gamblers and ticket porters, tea shops with periwinkle boughs, an opium den and a room of dogfighters breathing thick cigar smoke. A clock told us we only had ten more minutes until dawn. The drumbeats moved faster. So did we. My legs burned from all the stairs, my breath thin like I'd hiked a mountain when we finally reached the seventh level.

A dozen pairs of boots pounded behind us. I barely caught a glimpse of the men in the maroon hoods—Talons—barreling up the arcade before Ashley pulled me toward a metal rope anchored into one of the pillars. He attached the cuff using a chain and thrust it down the line, the other end of which was fastened to the plaza at the bottom. Mr. Kelly's doing.

Ashley snagged another chain and looped it around the

zipline. As he clambered over the balcony and stood on the lip, the hoods of the Talons bobbed up the stairs. In seconds they'd overtake us. I wordlessly copied Ashley, scooting into his side until my toes only touched air.

Opposite the dancers on the circular ground floor, a fast-moving river cut in from the left and curved back, carving out a makeshift island speckled with maroon hoods that guarded a portcullis. That must be where the exit portal was. A narrow bridge spanned the river.

"Are you ready?" Ashley asked for the second time.

*Thud, thud, thud, thud.* The Talons.

"Pull the brake when I tell you," Ashley said while squeezing me to him.

My eyes widened *"Wha—"*

We vaulted off. My scream stuck in my throat as we tore across the Necropolis and down seven stories, past columns with strange symbols, my hair trailing, feet dangling, fingernails clawing into Ashley's coat in a way I would definitely be embarrassed about later.

"Now!" Ashley shouted.

Now?

Oh, the brake!

Where was the brake? A leather strap flailed in front of us but flapped away when I reached for it. I grasped air, making my hand sweat.

"Now, Dolly!"

I closed around the strap and yanked. It jerked us into a lower speed, but the ground was still rushing toward us too fast—straight toward a pillar. Just before we collided, Ashley let go and shot us to the side, angling us so he took the brunt of the fall. We rolled, rolled to a stop.

When I could breathe again, I lifted my head and found my fingers buried in his hair, my braid grazing his neck, his arms cradling me protectively. With a soft inhale, I snatched my hand back. He let go at the same time.

I gulped down the awareness of his body beneath mine, finding his eyes instead. Which was a mistake. They were still as heated as a copper compound flame. "I should've pulled the brake sooner," I breathed.

His gaze skittered down my face, then back up. "I'm not complaining."

Mr. Kelly appeared above us and cleared his throat, knocking his head toward some Talons who were flying down the stairs toward the ground level. As Ashley and I clambered to our feet, he pulled a pistol from his coat and fired off several shots at the rope. The cord we'd zipped down went slack and fell.

Ashley rolled his shoulder out. "Six rounds for one measly rope. Losing your touch, Miles?"

Over Mr. Kelly's shoulder, a massive stalactite crashed onto the stairs, crushing one Talon and blocking the path of a dozen more in a cloud of mineral dust.

Brows inching into my hairline, I blinked at Mr. Kelly who glared at Ashley and lobbed the cuff back to him.

"No." But the ghost of a smile pulled at his mouth.

If I didn't know any better, I'd say he enjoyed these stunts as much as Ashley.

I kicked the dead cable at my feet. "Was that the Copenhagen?"

"No," they both said at the same time. That was one whole word to me from Mr. Kelly. Maybe death-defying feats endeared people to him.

"Well, what was the point of flying down here like that?"

Ashley flipped the cuff into the pocket of his coat. "Cause a scene drawing the majority of the Talons up, and then trap them there."

I looked at him with rekindled awe. It was simple but brilliant.

Then he grabbed my hand and all three of us ran across the plaza—toward the river that cut out an island on the far side. The ten Talons guarding the exit portal noticed us and cracked off their pistols. People around us screamed and dove for cover. The first hail of bullets whizzed past before the eerie, magical lights of the Necropolis flickered off. Then on.

We ran blindly. The movement of the Undercity stuttered black and white like a haunted play, marionettes that died and resurrected with the pulsing of the lights. The Talons weren't aiming at us but at something to our right. Every time I tried to find out what, the lights shut off again.

By the time we reached the bridge, the Talons were out of bullets. Mr. Kelly launched himself at the first Talon across the bridge while Ashley pulled me to the side and ducked me underneath. Six feet down, the river rushed fast enough for a spray of water to hit my face.

Ashley patted the ground under the bridge—no, not the ground. A safe built into the floor. "Five more minutes. I need you to open this," was all the explanation he gave me before edging out and joining Mr. Kelly.

For three seconds I sputtered, trying to keep up with what was happening even though everything was moving way too quickly. My attention shot down to the safe. Eight digits, and it used symbols instead of numbers—

The symbols must stand for something. Letters? Then I remembered glimpsing some of the signs on the floor and columns. A symbolic sequence?

I needed a piece of paper. Casting a hasty glance around the plaza, I spotted several symbols. I tried a few blind combinations before throwing up my hands. What did Ashley expect me to do? I might be able to solve puzzles like him, but that was where the comparison ended. I couldn't dive headfirst into chaos on whim, on a hunch.

My brand of problem solving took time—something we didn't have.

I studied the safe again whose front was made of bronze. My fingers moved over the hinges.

Aluminum.

Near a roaring river, both mediums were probably chosen based on their aversion to rust, but the hinges were *aluminum*. An idea struck me, making me clamber out from under the bridge and head back across the plaza, dodging the few people who hadn't already taken shelter in the adjacent hallways.

Shouts grew distant behind me. I hopped over a puddle of ale and snatched up two abandoned flagons. Where the stalactite had fallen, the Talons had nearly cleared away enough of the wreckage to break through. A minute later, I finally reached the corner of the Necropolis where I'd first entered—near the laundering center.

I dove into a large room equipped with vats of clothing, almost gagging on the piquant soapy smell. In a corner sat an open barrel of lye, and I filled my flagons, careful not to let it touch my hands.

Sodium hydroxide.

I ran back across the plaza, the lights still flickering occasionally. Ashley and Mr. Kelly had taken down half the men and were working on the other five. By the time I reached the bridge, the drums had stopped but my heartbeat was ample replacement, thundering in my ears as I hunkered down and poured the lye over the hinges.

Almost instantly, the sodium hydroxide reacted with the aluminum, eating it away until the hinges were small, corroded bands. I hit them with a flagon, loosening the metal until one by one they popped off. Nails scrabbling, I pried the face of the safe up, failing a few times in my attempts to get enough leverage. Then I hauled its contents up, stomach dropping.

"Dolly!"

I looked toward the island to find both men ankle deep in maroon vests. I spun the other way. The rest of the Talons had broken through the stalactite and were storming across the plaza. Suddenly both men were by my side, Ashley towing me up while Mr. Kelly unloaded the dynamite and tucked it under the bridge. Once across, Ashley let me go and held an unconscious Talon's tattooed forearm to some kind of sensor, which activated the grate covering the portal to start raising.

"How did you know I'd get the safe open?" I asked breathlessly.

He grinned and snagged a fallen pistol from the ground, checking the chamber. "Just a hunch."

Finished, Mr. Kelly flew back over the bridge and to our side, only a dozen steps ahead of the descending horde. Not a moment too soon. Not a moment too late either.

Watching the pair work together was a form of lethal precision and beauty. Faultless. I'd never seen anything like it.

"*This*," Ashley said, cocking the hammer of his pistol and aiming for the dynamite, "is a Copenhagen."

The Talons reached the bridge and Ashley fired.

The bridge exploded, shooting up a spray of gray debris just as a hand clinched my arm and dragged me through the invisible portal and back onto London's streets.

We fell to the cobblestones outside the carnival.

All three of us lay silently for a whole minute, until my blood chilled as I sensed the portal close, preventing anyone from following us. As if they could. Ashley and Mr. Kelly must've sensed it too, because we all climbed to our feet at the same time.

I took my time, hyperaware of my unpleasantly swirling stomach. I guessed magical travel didn't agree with me. A few deep breaths of the coal-dusted air and the ground no longer swayed beneath me. When I finally straightened, Mr. Kelly had already slipped away, leaving me and Ashley alone in the dawn.

"Go." Ashley knocked his chin. His voice sounded disconcertingly quiet after the blaring noises of the Necropolis. "I'll follow at a distance to ensure you make it home safely."

I nodded, grateful. He'd saved me more than once tonight. "Thank you, Mr. Gardner."

He hesitated. "One more thing." From behind his back, he pulled out my canvas painting, still wrapped in oil-cloth, and held it out to me.

I froze, mind reeling, then took it mutely, too overwhelmed for words. How had he managed to hold on to it through all that? And why would he give it up when it put him at a disadvantage?

He knew the stakes of this game for me, now. It cost him, but he'd done it. For my father, for ... me. Because—

"A token for a token," he said. When I glanced at him, his gaze was steady, tilted in a soft way that quickly disappeared after staring at me a whisper too long.

A faint rattling sounded up the street, and Ashley seamlessly slipped into a side alley. A moment later, a night watchman stepped under the warm glow of a gas lamp, tipping his slouch hat when he caught sight of me. I nodded back and, when he called out the half hour, promptly scurried away from the carnival.

I didn't see Mr. Gardner the whole way home, but I knew he was there, evading the dawn's pale rays. And for the first time, I wished the sun away, because the shadows felt more comforting.

# 28

## Emmeline

The best way to trim one's fingernails was to, in an act of self-preservation, abandon your best friend to the predations of anyone left inside a rambunctious carnival and wait for her all night at her bedroom window, gnawing at your cuticles as you hoped she hadn't been murdered. Or worse.

Stomach churning, I willed her to appear at the steps. London was waking up, a morning mist kissing the streets farewell while blossoms from an ornamental pear tree fluttered to the sidewalk. My breath fogged the glass, veiling my blubbery, red-eyed reflection. The window was my last thread of hope and walking away from it was the pair of scissors that would snip it, making me fall to the floor in useless pieces.

It was all my fault.

Dorothy had almost made it out. When Mr. Kelly came into sight, my heart had dropped to the street and I'd hopped behind a building—but when I peeked around the corner a minute later, my cousin had vanished. I should have spoken to her. Formed some kind of plan. Waited with her at the gate until morning.

Though ... it would've been worse for us both (well, maybe just me) if I hadn't returned home.

When Father found out I was alone, more than one vase shattered against the wall. I'd thought quickly and lied. He didn't look relieved—if anything, his mouth had pinched tighter—but at least he stopped breaking nearby glass. If Dory didn't arrive soon, I'd have to tell him the truth, an eventuality I was dreading.

The soft *snick* of a door closing made me whirl around.

Dorothy stood in her room, curly hair in fierce tendrils and a victorious gleam in her eye, a wild animal fresh from the kill. Compared to the shell she'd been the last few days, she looked positively *alive*. It wasn't a bad look.

I nearly crumbled with relief, but instead said, "What in George's tomb are you wearing? And your *sleeve*—"

She set a package on her desk and quickly undid her hair and re-braided it, pulling extra strands away from her face. "Never mind that. Is Uncle Benedick—?"

"I told him you're visiting a friend who was sick with pneumonia. He's been mollified. For now."

She nodded and untied the package, revealing a painting. I neared and peered over her shoulder, analyzing the detailed strokes of a locomotive. When my gaze slid to Dorothy, I saw she was doing the same, but with the intensity of a starved orphan at a banquet table.

"Is that—"

"Not now, please, Emme."

After abandoning her, I didn't deserve to feel a sting of rejection at her words, but I did.

I wasn't as smart as Dorothy, but I also wasn't an idiot. She was working on something big—something that made her forget to eat, sleep. Unlike the last time we'd visited London, her flesh revealed the sharp edges of bones, and her skin was so ashen, the dustman was beginning to look at her like she was prime real estate.

So, she was going through something. Fine. Everybody faced problems.

What bothered me was that so far, she'd told me *nothing* about it.

I'd suggested going to the carnival—to at least get her mind off whatever was clearly bothering her, and she seemed to enjoy herself. But then she'd been locked within, and I'd abandoned her, and ...

I fisted my hands.

And then she'd come back like *this*.

"What's going on?" I asked, unable to bear it any longer.

Flipping the painting over, she ignored me. I was about to repeat the question when I noticed a tiny black phrase scribbled on the back of the painting. *The pen of Zeus marks his flesh.*

Seeing it too, Dorothy gasped softly, then nibbled her lip.

My forehead scrunched. What kind of riddle was this? "Um ... whose flesh are we looking at?"

"It might not mean literally," she said, sounding more like she was talking to herself.

"But it very well *might*." When she remained frozen in contemplative silence, I bit my lip, toes tapping. I wanted to scream, if only to wake her up for a moment. I said the first shocking thing that came to mind. "I hope it's Mr. Gardner."

Her head whipped over so fast it startled me, her wild eyes sparking with heat before batting away. In that moment, I saw more than enough. Whatever was going on had to do with him. And she was *excited* about it.

Dorothy covered the back of the painting with the oil cloth. "I'll be down for breakfast as soon as I change."

She was hiding something—many somethings—and was obviously trying to get rid of me, but after a long moment of hesitation, I nodded and marched into the hall. I was glad she was back and relatively unharmed, even with the mystery of how she'd gotten a new dress. And if she wouldn't confide in me, that was fine.

I'd just have to find out for myself.

# 29

## Dorothy

It obviously meant a tattoo. And *the pen of Zeus* seemed specific enough to mean something in particular. Greek. A tattoo written in Greek. What *of* it didn't say, but it hardly mattered.

I changed out of the plum gown and flung it on my bed, already missing the smell clinging to the fabric. His cardamom smell.

*Focus.*

Kneeling in front of my bookcase, I pulled out a Latin primer which contained a small section at the back devoted to the Grecian alphabet. If I could correctly identify the symbols, I didn't need to know what the tattoo said, but it still might be helpful. My body hummed in excitement, my magic now back to full capacity.

I wish I hadn't been blindfolded in that holding cell, or I might have noticed a bit of ink on Mr. Riley's skin, peeking out from a sleeve or pant leg.

Quick raps on the door made me remember I was in my underthings. I opened the door a crack.

Beatrice stood on the other side. "I've come to 'elp you dress, miss."

Wordlessly, I let her in, and she fussed around in my wardrobe until landing on a baby blue frock with white appliques around the waist and cuffs. She made no comment on my already cinched corset as she dressed me, but through my vanity mirror, I caught her eyes narrowing at something on my bed.

*The plum dress.*

The second she finished, I said hastily, "Thank you, Beatrice, I'll manage my own hair today."

She curtsied, and her eyes flashed to the plum dress once more before she swept out.

Using the scissors I kept in one of my drawers for mending, I cut the plum dress into tiny pieces and lit a fire in the hearth. Feeding it with the scraps destroyed all evidence of the night before.

Just as the last piece went up in flames, a fist pounded the door, and I jumped to answer it. My uncle's looming figure seemed to fill the entire hallway as his gaze ticked over my wayward hair. He pushed into the room, analyzing it like he was looking for something. "Where were you last night?" he said, tone ice cold.

The memory of being locked in this room once before scuttled up my neck like a handful of beetles. I hid my soot-stained hands behind my back. "My friend was sick with pneumonia, and I was so busy tending to her I didn't realize night had fallen until it was too late to respectably call my own coach. I opted to wait until morning, rather than call our good name into question."

He raised his chin and pushed it out, giving me a generous view of his lower teeth as he said, "You called it into question the moment you left your aunt's side. Marie now knows not to let anything resembling last night be repeated."

What had he threatened her with this time?

His attention landed on the fire, and he frowned and sniffed in suspicion. "If it does ... I shall rethink my decision to allow your father government of this house when he returns. If he returns at all."

My nostrils flared on a deep inhale, rage bubbling up in my throat. How easily he commanded every facet of my life, all because my father was gone. I couldn't manage a nod if I tried.

"Now, I cannot stay to chat," Uncle Benedick continued. "I promised a group of lords a tour of the button factory I have shares in, since they've taken an interest in the working-man's plight. I am to be their personal guide, and I will not stand to be late."

The mention of a factory doused the anger simmering under my skin. "Button factory? It isn't run by a Mr. Brass, by any chance?"

"It is," Uncle said, making my chest go cold with fear.

"Might I ... Might I tag along?"

Uncle's gaze narrowed.

"To repair my reputation and show a united, familial front," I added quickly.

He tilted his head, still studying me. "I suppose you may come. As long as you behave yourself." He stormed away.

Sidling up to the man made me sick with indignation, but right now it couldn't be helped. I rubbed my temples, trying to organize my crisscrossing thoughts.

Mr. Riley had both motive and means and fit every criterion for the Samaritan—and if he knew about the Necropolis, he must be privy to many other secrets as well. Ashley had even admitted to being acquainted with him. Meanwhile Uncle Benedick was growing bolder. My aunt was being punished. Prying eyes watched my every move, and soon I wouldn't be able to make any move at all.

Mr. Riley had to be the Samaritan. And if he wasn't ...

I might not have time to find the real one.

After fetching the prototype gun from the lab, I scrawled a hasty note to Mr. Riley, asking if I could meet him in person to explain, and packaged it up. If he was really the Samaritan, he'd know about Father's kidnapping and the prototype would act as a coded message. If he wasn't the Samaritan, the gun would only appear to be a strange but useless contraption.

I sent it off with a courier, then inhaled a steadying breath. While I waited for Mr. Riley's response, I would focus on the factory.

Mr. Brass had argued with Father the night of his disappearance, then one of his buttons was found at the scene of the crime. It was too coincidental. All signs pointed to him being the Rook.

Now I just needed to confirm it.

THE BUTTON FACTORY stood on what had once been the outskirts of London, far east where the Thames widened from the chemical brews dumping into its depths. Now, the city had overtaken the smokestacks, housing units hastily built to accommodate the onslaught of workers.

Emme had tea scheduled with a well-connected duchess, so it was just the three of us crunching the gravel of the yard underfoot. Uncle's party met us there. Aunt Marie jumped at every factory whistle. After the foreman showed us the docks where they unloaded the raw ivory, horns, bones, brass, pearls, silver, and steel to prepare for button manufacture, he led us inside to breathe the filament-dusted air.

Pipes sprang from the ground and wound their way to the ceiling, engulfing boilers and suspended metal grates that passed for a second floor. The lords were accompanied by several women—their wives and daughters, who appeared more fascinated by the shirtless men operating the drills than political machinations. I kept an eye out for Mr. Brass.

As an investor, Uncle knew very little of the factory's inner workings, but with every detail the foreman described, from the repairing of equipment to the intensive process of molding the silver and steel, it didn't stop him from declaring his involvement.

Half an hour into the tour, when Uncle's attention had become more infrequent, I hung back and caught the foreman alone long enough to ask whether Mr. Brass was in.

"He's gone to lunch," the foreman said, expecting interest in the owner of the factory.

A stroke of luck. "Then I was hoping to leave a letter for him. Do you know where I might find his office?"

"Second floor, miss. The left corner at the end of the hall."

I nodded and thanked him. A minute later, my uncle was distracted by a man weaving a design out of hot steel, allowing me to slip away. After ascending the metal-grate stairs, I followed the foreman's directions until I found the room.

The open window countered the accumulating heat from the ovens below and offered a pretty view of the river. Letters poked out from a casing of thin cubbies behind a simple wooden work desk. A few chairs and an armoire were the only other pieces of furniture.

Not knowing how much time I had, I rifled through the cubbies quickly. They appeared to be notes left for different workers and associates, so I moved on, knowing I wouldn't find anything about the Rook laying in plain sight. The first two drawers of Mr. Brass's desk contained ledgers and reports from the current year. The third drawer was locked.

No time to break in.

My hands dampened with nervous sweat. *I shouldn't be here. I shouldn't be here.*

What if he really was the Rook?

What if he *caught* me?

I cast a hasty glance at the door, but I was alone. The fears nipped at me like beggars seeing silk for the first time. They climbed higher, fisting more of me between their fingers.

Hand shaking, I sifted through papers strewn atop the desk. More accounts, business transactions, and letters from officials. Then my father's name caught my eye. I sucked in a breath. Careful not to disturb the rest of the stack, I slipped the sheet out and scanned the text. It indeed appeared to be addressed to my father, from Mr. Brass although it was unsigned, and dated the day before he was kidnapped.

> Geoffrey,
> Give me the research or you will be forced. You don't

That was it. Only a handful of words for a clue. Don't what? The 'o' in the last word was almost completely filled in, like Mr. Brass had gotten distracted in the middle of the draft and had forgotten to remove his quill.

Was that why Father had been kidnapped? Because the Rook wanted his research? For what?

The day we'd made the breakthrough of fingerprinting my magic, father had accidentally burned the research. But maybe ... I glanced at the note again.

Maybe it hadn't been an accident. Maybe *that's* why Brass was angry.

Maybe it meant the Rook had taken my father for a different reason than the others—and that Father's mind was still intact because the Rook needed it. For now.

But if Mr. Brass was the Rook, why would he write a letter to him first? Why give him the option?

"You're not supposed to be up here," a voice muttered behind me.

I squeaked and jerked upright, colliding with a heathered factory coat made of solid muscle.

Ashley Gardner was in costume again today. A dark gray working cap hid all but his most stubborn locks, and it was slightly skewed to one side, like he'd tipped it to passersby one too many times. At his temple beaded a few drops of sweat, and the rugged look suited him. A little too well, I thought, catching a hint of muscled forearms diving into his pockets.

"Neither are you." I hated how breathless I sounded. A moment ago, it would've been from fear, but now it was because my blood was practically singing in excitement. "I see you have taken up factory work as well as tutoring. Still need to supplement your income?"

He patted his dirty clothes, showing me several small holes in need of patching. "Ah, no. Supplementing my humility, it would seem."

"I take it you'll be working here a long time, then."

"No, I'll make quick work of it, as I do with everything else." He flashed me an ironic, winning smile that made my heart do a little flip.

Trying my best to ignore it, I returned to sifting through papers. "How did you find me here?"

Skirting around me, he circled to the other side of the desk, gaze skimming the desk. "The rumbles of the lords at the club. Your uncle's been planning this tour for weeks. After what you revealed last night about his need for control, I made a gamble that you'd be here too."

At the mention of last night, my back prickled in awareness. I tamped the heat down. Now was *not* the time to liquify into a puddle.

If his aim was to catch me alone, he didn't need to blend in with the common working man to do it. So why not come to the factory dressed as he was? Why bother dressing down? He wasn't here for me—or at least, not *only* for me.

My curiosity built, puffing me up like a hot air balloon until I finally blurted, "Why are you really here?"

He glanced at me. "To collect your next guess."

"No—why are you *working*?"

"Heaven knows they could use the help. Ah." He held up the note addressed to my father and turned to me. "So, as well as the Samaritan, you're also hunting the Rook?"

Shadows and sunlight did not mix, and neither did Ashley Gardner and probing questions. We just shifted around each other all day, and when the day was over, he overtook everything in his path, having sacrificed nothing. I crossed my arms and shook my head. "I'm *trying* to find my father."

"But the Rook did the kidnapping."

"Revenge is overrated."

His voice seemed to soften when he said, "Sometimes justice is impossible. And then *rest* is all you can hope for."

Again, I heard what he wasn't saying. Instead of tracking my father, my time might be better spent preparing myself for the worst.

I gently took the paper from Ashley's hands. I stared at my father's name. Every sinew rejected the idea of him already being dead, but I swallowed, hard, forcing myself to contemplate it. What, then, would I want? To make his kidnapper pay for what he'd done, the lives he'd ruined?

I knew my answer and carefully slipped the note back in its place in the stack on the desk. "No. The path of revenge may lead to rest, but it never leads to victory."

A pause. Then he said, "No path does." I glanced at him, catching a strange hardness in his eyes. We weren't speaking of my father anymore. "It's a matter of choosing the one that will give you purpose."

More questions burned at the back of my tongue. The one that slipped out was, "Can you open this drawer?" I pointed to the lowest drawer on the desk, knowing from my holding cell in the Necropolis that he must have some skill with picking locks.

He didn't deny it, only took my measure. "What will you give me?"

"What do you want?"

His green eyes grew warmer, sharper. It was odd, the way they glowed, only I couldn't seem to care because his intense stare dipped to my lips before attacking the window at his right, catching himself a beat too late. Heat sparked on my skin.

"Your second guess," he said, swinging back toward me. "Forfeit it."

With rapid blinks, I stared at him, heart sinking. For some reason I'd assumed things had changed for him, now that he knew about my father, but he was still playing the game.

"But the painting ... you gave it back—"

"I shouldn't have." He dragged a hand through his hair, voice low. "I'm truly sorry about your father, Dorothy, but it changes nothing." His gaze swept up, and when it found me, it was unbreakable. "For your own good, I will still do everything in my power to prevent you from finding him."

*Him* being the Samaritan.

The answer stung. Maybe because it was wrong. Maybe because my feelings for Ashley were growing so rapidly and uncontrollably that it felt like a betrayal—but I could tell he truly believed he was doing the right thing. And did it matter? If Mr. Riley was the Samaritan as I was almost positive, I could cut Ashley out of the game altogether once I found information about the Rook.

Information that was probably inside a locked drawer.

I lifted my chin. "Done."

Ashley raised his eyebrows. It made me feel like I'd made a terrible mistake. He pulled something from his pocket and worked on the lock, sliding it open in a matter of seconds.

I peeked inside the drawer. Neat stacks of cash edged the sides, but otherwise the drawer was empty. No note, no evidence.

Shoulders sagging, I turned to Ashley who had the gall to smirk.

"Double or nothing?"

Before I'd formed a retort, the office door whined partway open, making both our heads whip over. Mr. Brass had his hand on the knob and was shouting something to someone below, oblivious to our presence for only a few more precious moments. In my peripheral, I thought I saw Ashley's form flicker like an apparition, but he was solid when he grabbed my hand, and we scrambled toward the armoire. I jumped inside. Ashley stuffed himself next to me and swung the armoire door closed just in time.

My ears drummed, fear making my feet turn to ice. *The Rook, the Rook, the Rook.*

I remembered the letter on the desk.

*Give me the research or you will be forced.*

*Forced.*

My hands turned clammy, tongue drying up.

The desk rattled from someone bumping into it. I clamped my mouth shut to keep from whimpering. Deep vibrations rumbled through the armoire, but not clear enough to tell what the man was saying.

My thoughts raced, wondering if this was to be my end. If I would be taken to where my father was being held. Or—taken to where he died.

I was going to be sick. All over Ashley's coat.

A minute passed. And another. The chair squeaked like Mr.

Brass was rocking thoughtfully. Then I remembered the armoire had been practically empty when I'd jumped in. Mr. Brass probably rarely used it, and this predicament was probably a matter of waiting until he left in a few hours.

The muscles bunching my neck gradually relaxed. Ashley and I stood chest to chest, the fit so snug there was hardly room to squirm. And with every second that we weren't discovered, my awareness shifted from outside the armoire, to within.

My eyes slowly adjusted to the faint slice of light bleeding through the crack between the armoire doors. I could make out the edges of Ashley's shoulders, the angle of his jaw, the slightly parted mouth only an inch from my forehead. A mouth whose fascinating lines I could trace until Mr. Brass left.

I felt his heartbeat pounding into me like a stone mason's mallet, chipping away at the armor around my heart. *Thump, thump, thump.*

And my heartbeat answered, making me vibrate down to my toes. *Thump-thump ... thump-thump.* Then they were one. The same beat. I watched Ashley's throat bob as he closed those lips and all the secrets that lay behind them.

The air he exhaled, I breathed in. It felt intimate in my lungs; caressed me from the inside. I found myself wanting to hold it in, a moment where a piece of him belonged to me. Then in the silence, finally, I sighed, just a little. Softly. And even though my ears were drowning in the sound of our heartbeats, I swore I heard him do the same.

The creaking stopped. The chair squealed as someone stood and thudded across the room. Toward the armoire. My eyes widened and I gasped softly. "He's coming—"

Ashley's hand braced the side of my head. "Don't speak," he whispered—practically mouthed, there was so little breath behind the words. "Don't move." I could only make out the lower rims of his irises, but they bore into me. So green, even in the darkness. So sure. "Look only at me."

And ...

We were hiding in an armoire, the possible phantom of London only a few feet away, moments away from throwing open the doors and torturing us until we went insane like the others—but standing next to Ashley like this, his hand on my cheek as I looked into his solemn, shadowed eyes, made me feel braver than I'd ever felt.

For a moment, I believed I could take on the whole world. Like he did.

A warm rush spun under my skin, something foreign and glittery. By some miracle, the opposite door to the closet swung open, keeping us mostly hidden—all but the sleeve of my dress if Mr. Brass happened to look over.

Mr. Brass shuffled through different drawers, closing them harder than necessary and making the wood at my back shake. Ashley's gaze stayed glued to me the entire time, never straying. I couldn't help but stare back.

If such a face was the last thing I beheld on this earth ... if it was *his* face ... I was glad I'd finally had the courage to step outside.

Just as fingers closed around the door hiding us, a knock sounded and a someone said, "Mr. Brass?"

The hand paused. "Yes?"

"There's been an accident, near the docks. You'll want to see it for yourself, sir."

Mr. Brass cursed and shoved another drawer shut before stalking out, the armoire door creaking open. We remained frozen for another beat. Two.

I was suddenly aware of Ashley's fingers still cupping my cheek, brushing against my hair. A few inches lower and they would touch my neck. I could practically feel them trailing down to my shoulder; feel them on my back where they'd been only a few hours before, lacing up my dress.

The places we currently touched bloomed and spread with every inhale—something I was trying very hard not to do. I couldn't take it; the in, the out, the constant touching and ... touching *more*.

"Did you find what you were looking for?" he murmured. He was still staring at me.

I swallowed. "No." Because the word sounded much too like a question for my liking, I braced a hand against the wall and wriggled free, barely catching myself from stumbling to a heap.

Ashley stepped out and stuffed his hands in his pockets. "Good."

Backing out of the office, he tipped his hat, skewing it further. "You pick up all sorts of interesting tidbits in the paper, Miss St. James. Might I suggest you continue your search there?" Before he disappeared, more of his locks peeked out to wave me good-bye, and even they seemed to smirk at me.

Too preoccupied with lauding his achievements, my uncle never noticed my absence, and I slid into the back of the group with ease. The foreman finished the tour and led us back through unctuous steam, thick in my throat. The spacious room full of boilers softening bone to make it cuttable was uncomfortably hot —as hot as I felt inside, thinking about my second guess and how I'd gambled it away.

I no longer needed Ashley's clues, and I couldn't have known the drawer would be empty, but I still felt stupid. Something was missing. Something wasn't adding up, and I was tired of taking one step forward, two steps back.

One of the lord's wives asked a question about the boilers,

making the party halt their progress out the door. And if we had not, I never would've noticed the flash of movement in the corner of my eye. I recognized the black hair instantly, but even more intriguing was that Mr. Kelly was dragging him toward the back of the factory like he was injured.

My eyes widened in alarm.

As quietly as I could, I bolted for the other end of the factory before I lost the nerve.

Halfway there, a bearded factory worker emerged from an adjacent room, glancing in the direction the other men had gone, before shuffling past me and out onto the docks. My gut told me *he* was the real reason Ashley was here.

I paused. This far behind, I couldn't catch up to Ashley and ask him what had injured him, but I *could* listen to the conversation that had led up to it. And hopefully, gain some much-needed ground.

Reminding myself that bluedusters didn't patrol this far outside the city, I twisted into the room the stranger had emerged from and locked the door behind me. Packed to the ceiling with barrels, it appeared to be some kind of storage room. I summoned magic to my palms and moved my hands in a circular motion, rewinding time. When my magic hit a wall, depleted, I let go, watching the vision spring to life around me.

"... as far as I could," the stranger said near the window, beard so thick it hid his mouth. His gaze shifted to the door.

"So you lost him, then?" That was from the apparition of Mr. Kelly standing in the opposite corner, near Ashley who reclined against a barrel.

"Yes," the stranger grunted, "though I don't rightly know how. He went round one corner, and the next he was gone." The man's gaze strayed to the door again.

Ashley noticed. "No one would see us if they walked in here, Simmons. You know that."

With effort, Simmons seemed to relax. "I know, sir. Sorry, sir. They've just probably cleaned up the mussel shells by now, and the taskmaster will be looking for me. I thought you'd be here sooner."

My lips parted. He'd spilled mussel shells? To cause a distraction?

"I would've been," Ashley said, slowly, "but I was ... delayed." Was that the slightest bit of color on his cheeks? Mr. Kelly saw it too, and frowned, and even though it was just a vision, I felt my own color rise. He'd been delayed because he'd been too busy holding my cheek and staring into my soul.

"How many blocks away from his house?" Ashley went on.

Simmons shook his head. "I'd have to retrace it—"

"Where did you end up?"

"Near the abbey, past Devil's Acre. Westminster."

Ashley and Mr. Kelly shared a look. "Not very far," Mr. Kelly murmured.

"Are you certain it was him," Ashley said, turning back, "and not a decoy?"

"No. But I've been watching the house between shifts—and while the decoys look like him, they never make his signature move."

"The card?" Mr. Kelly asked.

I shivered, remembering a card locking Father's window into place. Could they be talking about the Rook?

Simmons nodded. "Every outing, on his doorstep, he first pulls it out—just a little, just enough. Fingering it like it's his good luck charm."

Ashley sighed and pushed off the wall. "You're doing excellent work. Keep to your posts until we know more. Tell the others to do the same."

He nodded. "Yes, sir."

Turning to Mr. Kelly, Ashley said, "I have a few calls to make in the West End this morning, so I'll change and see you back at the flat. Can you style my hair for me?"

It was such an odd request that I moved around the apparition to get a glimpse of Ashley's face that had since turned away. He appeared to be serious.

"I've this," Simmons said as he stepped beside me, but he was already holding a pocket mirror out to Ashley, reflective side up.

Everything slowed as Ashley turned and saw his own face in the mirror. On an inhale, he hissed. His face went white, his frame shook, locking up like he was having a small seizure. Strangled, pained sounds passed his lips, sounds I'd never heard a man make before. And never once did he look away from his reflection, or blink. Almost like he ... couldn't.

Only two heartbeats passed before Mr. Kelly knocked the mirror out of Simmons hands, and it shattered on the floor, the ghostly shards scattering to where they lay in the present, save for a few pieces I would disturb upon my entrance in a few minutes. He was shouting something at Simmons as he dragged Ashley's half-collapsed form through the closed door. Simmons cowered back against the barrels, eyes wide.

I followed Mr. Kelly's past self out into the factory. Even with the extra weight, he moved fast, fast enough I had to hike up my skirts. I blurred past button-hole drillers, set in motion by great gears and pumps; past shoveled mounds of circular bits of bone that slowly grew toward the ceiling. And my heart pounded with worry and something much stronger that I didn't dare name. All I knew was that I needed to ensure he was safe—

Somewhere in the back of the factory, my magic flickered and the vision died, leaving me alarmed, breathless, standing alone near a hissing boiler and wondering where Ashley had gone. If he was injured. Why I'd acted so recklessly, and for *him*. And ... what exactly I had witnessed.

# 30

## Ashley

By the time we made it outside, I'd forced enough strength into my legs to shake Miles off and hobble a few steps on my own. The world tilted on its axis, spinning until my stomach roiled and my brain cleaved in two. I took great breaths, filling my lungs as deep as they could go, then deeper, deeper—

"Are you okay?"

I gripped the fence lining the boardwalk and vomited into the Thames. Then again. The water beneath churned with bile. When I finally finished, I wiped the residue off my mouth with the back of my sleeve, wishing I could as easily wipe away the memories.

Wishing I could forget.

I could still feel the memory magic emanating from my unnatural eyes, then clawing into my mind and wrenching me into my own past where it warped and mangled the bloody truth into something unspeakably perverse.

When my breathing settled and the silence started to ring with the muted grinding of metal and hissing steam, Miles said tentatively, "Ashley?"

"It's getting worse," I whispered. Raking a shaky hand through my hair, I straightened and turned to face him. I'd regained control of my stomach, but the fear lingered, and so did the pain. Tight and coiled like a snake ready to strike, only the venom was already in my system and there was no saving me now. "I can't stop it." My voice didn't sound like my own. It sounded weak and pathetic, and my hands fisted against the sound. "It's getting worse."

Miles took a small step forward, voice softening. "What did you see this time?"

My throat clogged. Every time he asked, I could never answer. It was my burden alone; too excruciating to relive.

But that burden swelled to the surface like a tidal wave, making me slump against the wall of the factory. Then crumple to the ground. My body curled inward until I was sobbing into my forearms, wishing the tears would wipe away the memory. Wishing I could forget the blood.

My sobs echoed in the air until they were the only sound in the world, a bell tolling the ruin of something that had died long ago. A moment later, Miles joined me on the ground and wrapped a hesitant arm around me like we were boys again, sharing a balcony on a purple Cairo night.

# 31

## Ashley

The flat was a mess, and as usual, it was Miles's fault. Letters from his mother and aunts spilled through the letter plate, practically snowing us in. Wads of cat fur clung to every surface, courtesy of the half-starved animal he'd found in an alleyway, which currently lapped milk from a bowl in the corner.

"You know, they come back if you feed them," I said, buttoning my waistcoat.

Miles clucked his tongue and petted the cat, letting its tail curl around his palm. "Funny, I don't remember feeding you."

I snorted and tied a black ascot around my neck before sticking the pin in the center. "You're not the biggest idiot in the world, Miles, but you better hope he doesn't die."

"Why do you think I've saved your skin so many times?" Miles finished petting the cat and tightened the laces of his low-heeled boots. On the second boot, he ventured, "This Miss St. James." The hefty pause told me I wouldn't like this conversation one bit, and during it, I built up my walls, shoving any flare of emotion down where I wouldn't feel it. "You're rather fixated on the little game you two are playing," he finally finished.

"A convenient distraction."

"I've never known you to be distracted by *anything*."

I glanced at him. Flippancy was far better than the muddy truth. "I'm distracted by your wardrobe choices all the time." I gestured to the individual pieces of his outfit. "Brown, brown, wool brown—oh, and the occasional gray to switch it up when things start to feel too drab. You look like the sewage runs of Bethnal Green on a *bad* day."

He glared at me, not fooled by my change of topic.

"I can practically smell it just looking at you," I sighed, sliding into my coat and adjusting the shoulders. "Distracting? I think so."

"At least I don't pander about in a constant state of mourning. Black isn't a color."

Sinking into a chair at the table, I shuffled an open deck of cards while Miles struggled with the buttons of his waistcoat. "Black is a perfectly respectable color. Only the important people are wearing it."

"High time you stop, then."

"I'll consider it if it means I don't have to stare at *two* chamber pots every day."

"Ashley."

I hated when he said my name like that. All short and tired. He opened his mouth. Hesitated. I ignored him, flipping the cards and making them disappear between my digits.

Finally, "Miss St. James is a very beautiful woman—"

My knuckles on the cards whitened.

"—and she comes from a very respectable family."

"You don't have to say it, Miles."

"I think I do—because she may be smart. She may be irresistible. But her father's a baronet, and her uncle is richer than most Peers, and you know as well as I we don't need those kinds of connections beating down our door and threatening the whole operation. I want to be rid of Bram's past. I want to return to the sea. But you keep wasting time by toying with her, and I don't understand it because nothing can change the fact that you are who you are—"

I shot to my feet. "I *get* it!"

Miles gave up his buttons. "Which means you *can't have her!*"

I froze. The flesh around that bleeding hole in my chest tore a little more, making me swallow down the pain.

And I ignored it. Again.

Again and again and again and as long as I bloody had to until it *stopped*.

Miles was right. I'd chosen this path, and I shouldn't feel angry at him for trying to keep me on it. Dorothy St. James was special. Intelligent, hungry, frightened, but brave. She deserved someone who could keep her that way.

I sank back into my chair, lips tight. "I know," I said quietly.

He fixed me with a hard look. "Do you? Because if you wanted to—and don't bother denying it—you could be to her house and back in an hour, Tanner's note in hand and her none the wiser. You could've stolen it anytime. It's almost like ... you *want* her to discover who the Samaritan is."

I had nothing to say to that.

I wanted to keep her safe. But I could admit to myself that as the days passed, I cared less and less. Not for her sake, but my own. Initially, I formed the game as a distraction. She intrigued me, and since she was always going to lose, why not have a little fun along the way? But she kept succeeding, and it drove me to keep upping the ante, until I found myself wanting her to outmatch me. I didn't know why.

But it terrified me—the not caring.

That darker part of me was growing. I could feel the shadows edging into my consciousness, the whispers that were too low to be heard, but whose black, oily stain I felt in my chest, urging me to let it take control. The magic was spreading like a cancer.

"Give her up, Ash," Miles said, finally finished with the buttons and shrugging his own coat on. "She's not a piece to this puzzle."

UNLIKE THE NAME SUGGESTED, the Necropolis wasn't made up of people who were dead but rather of people who all but were. Once trapped there, there was no getting out without a cuff or serious skills of misdirection. Low-level men were forced into servitude—running the gasworks, smelting shops, delivery service and other grueling work—while the women were put into more unsavory positions. Over years, both gradually proved their loyalty and earned the freedom that came from the higher levels.

"Lark will be on his guard now," Miles warned. At a brisk walk, he turned his coat inside out, the patches and dark brown shade making him *démodé*. Dusk was quickly closing in on us.

A drunk man lounged on a crate in the alley up ahead, swinging a leg and hiccupping under his slumped hat. "Oy, Charlie!" I clapped him on the arm which made him jump. I didn't know the man, but confidence was key. "Still in the bottle?"

"'ey, there's my cocker!" the man grumbled excitedly, trying to sit up but tipping sideways instead. "Eh ... How are you for soap?" He garbled more words that were accentuated by another hiccup.

"Sharp as ever, I see." With swift fingers, I swapped my hat with his. When he sobered up, he could sell it for a week's worth of wages.

Miles shook his head at my new hat. "There's no chance of

you slipping into the Necropolis again without being noticed. Not after what you did for Miss St. James."

I sighed and pushed past him. This again. "Thank you for stating the obvious, Miles. As always, it's about as useful as nipples on a breastplate."

"And while we're on the subject, you don't have to be so willing to throw your life away at every opportunity."

My ribs tightened, and I recognized it as stubbornness.

Yes, I did.

We turned a corner. Miles glanced at me from the corner of his eye. "Nervous?"

I worked my jaw but said nothing, which was probably the wrong thing. He was right that especially so soon after our last escapade, visiting the undercity was dangerous. In my pocket was the cuff I'd sliced off. If I were careful, I could slip it on and conduct my business with the Artifice without anyone being the wiser.

The only way in was through one of the seven portals, all of them opening at dusk and closing at dawn, and we were headed toward the one by the docks. No one knew how the portals were made, or by whom. Those were the kinds of secrets hoarded by the Acherons, the lords of the Necropolis. An unelected, ruthless family of syndicates that kept the crime-machine running smoothly, led by Lark Acheron himself. Their limited number of cuffs were insurance: bestowed for displays of loyalty and withdrawn just as easily—at a badly worded sentence or arriving a few minutes late. The only law was that of the Acheron's pleasure.

A law I'd broken far too many times.

Actually, not many people found themselves underground accidentally like Dorothy had. Most went willingly, unable to resist the allure of unmitigated vice, and, once a cuff was earned, unchecked magic. Temptation was a magic of its own.

We turned the corner and found a burly giant leaning against the stone wall whittling a scrap of wood. The Bear, one of Talons tasked with guarding the portals, had retractable claws on the tips of his sausage-like fingers. I once saw him shred someone to ribbons for trying to leave, and the smell of the man's mangled carcass had lingered in that alley long after the portal closed.

"Ashley Gardner," the Bear said with a slow tongue as we approached. He stuffed the wood in his coat but kept the knife out, twisting holes in the air. "Lark's been looking all over for you."

"Not very good at looking then, is he."

Bear stepped aside but put the knife to Miles's chest when he moved to follow me through the portal.

"He's with me," I told the Bear.

The Bear glowered. "Not this time."

Miles's gaze met mine—a silent question of whether to take Bear down. Even though the giant was twice his size and had magical claws, I didn't doubt Miles could do it. Which was precisely why the Acherons didn't want to allow him in.

But I gave him a slight shake of my head. If I happened to be caught, Miles didn't deserve to be a spectator to whatever followed. I didn't need him to meet with the Artifice, and I was swifter alone anyway.

One moment I was facing the inside of a bridge, hand closing over the cuff in my pocket, and the next I was in an underground cavern, taller than any building above. I flicked on an illusion to make me invisible and stepped around a group being processed by some Talons.

The limestone floor was littered with black tile mosaics of horses, chariots, nymphs, and flowers, and a Celtic braid that edged the plaza. Clues to the ancient power that had built this place.

Interlaced arcades, barrel-vaulted hallways, gothic windows

and buttresses, and stairs that circled up until they reached ominous stalactites—the Necropolis would be a work of gothic art if it wasn't home to the lowest of all life forms.

Maybe fifty people milled about the underground plaza, but tonight, most were where the shops were—where the thrum of magic beckoned.

Two men stepped in front of me. Two more locked my arms behind my back. I landed a kick and headbutted another, but more men swarmed and clamped onto my still-invisible limbs. When it was clear I wouldn't be escaping, I cursed, dropped the illusion, and inspected the men.

Their white shirts rolled to their elbows to proudly display the Acheron tattoo on their inner forearm: an upwards pointing arrow encased in a circle, its fletching replaced with bird's wings. Over the shirts, they wore hooded vests the color of dried blood. Talons. Then I noticed the residue on my shoes.

Someone had spread a thin layer of mud all around the portal, which was why Talons were processing the newcomers by making them wipe their feet off before moving on. I'd bypassed it, and my footprints had given me away.

I huffed, more than a little annoyed. I'd been captured because of *mud*. Lark had finally done something clever.

They led me up the stairs. Slant workers and customers glanced at our entourage as we passed but quickly returned to their tasks. Talons meant Acheron business. No one would interfere.

Up more stairs they marched me, higher and higher until my head was even with the massive stalactites clinging to the ceiling of the plaza, and we crossed over a narrow bridge connecting the two. I was again grateful Miles wasn't with me. He'd glance down and hyperventilate from contemplating the drop.

We plunged into the hollowed stalactite and climbed more stairs to a circular room, this one with walls bearing up maces and knives, cleavers and twisting blades, metal rods and leather whips. At the far end, a man lounged in a red chair that was too ostentatious for a room with gleaming weapons. He'd probably been waiting for me longer than expected—long enough that he'd ordered someone to bring him a more comfortable chair. The thought brought a smile to my lips.

Two men flanked him. They wore the same symbol tattooed on their necks, only their arrow pointed downward. Members of the Acheron family. It was supposed to be symbolic, I supposed: the Acherons looked down, the Talons looked up—but I nearly gagged on the overt egotism.

The redness of the chair shone starkly against Lark's ash-blond hair. On the desk before him sat a bowl with a confection inside—something dark and earthy, with tufts of whipped cream that melted under drizzled honey. When he chipped off a thin piece of the bowl, I realized it was also made of sugar.

Savoring it, he tapped one ivory, spindly finger against the arm of his chair. Still as white as the day he was born. *Gads, the man never surfaces.* He was a two-legged, emaciated maggot, sucking the flesh off anyone who wandered into his pit.

Lark grinned, snapping the sugar between his sharper-than-average canines. He held his hands out as sparkling shards hit the table. "Welcome back to hell, Ashley."

# 32

## Ashley

Fists pummeled me from every direction until the only thing keeping me upright was the lock-like grips garroting my arms. Pain radiated through my bones when their blows tore skin and stung the flesh beneath. I didn't know how long they went on. Too long to focus on something like counting. A copper tang filled my mouth.

When the maroon hooded thugs finally finished, they shoved me to my knees. Hot blood rolled from my temple to my cheek. My chest ached. Black speckled my vision. Rope wrapped around my wrists, but I barely felt it—I was too busy trying to breathe.

Sweet fire, everything hurt.

But Lark was wrong. I'd been to hell, and it felt nothing like this.

I raised my head even though my body screamed at me not to. I bit back the pain, trying to make my words sound effortless. "You always give such warm welcomes."

Lark drew in his legs off the desk, tilting his head. "Right now, I'll bet you're wishing you still had that cuff you stole.

Clever trick by the way, slicing off his hand." He spooned another rich bite into his gullet. Even his tongue looked pale, too fleshy despite the inordinate amount of time it spent outside his teeth. Most would call him handsome, but most hadn't seen him eat like this. Or incidentally, kill a man. "Oh Ashley, am I glad to see you."

My gaze drifted around the room. "Quite the assembly you've gathered here, bringing Jay and Robin into this. I'm flattered."

Robin didn't move an inch, Jay snarled, and Lark grinned again. "How long did you think you could elude me, hm?"

"Seeing as I came here willingly, as long as I wanted to, I suppose." Another fist drove into my stomach. It took me longer to recover this time. I spit on the ground, and blood tinged my saliva.

Lark sucked the last bit of sugar off his spoon before dragging it along the arm of his chair as he reclined. "You have three guesses as to why you're here before my Talons finish you off."

I glanced between Robin's steely dark eyes and Jay's red complexion, looking for any weaknesses. The brothers were all blond, though their coloring spanned several shades like they were from different fathers. Or mothers. But one thing they definitely shared was a hatred for me.

That tended to happen when you stole their most priceless object and left their leader naked in the cage dangling from the ceiling.

Everything—from the Talons to the floor levels to the cuffs—was to protect this place, and anyone who escaped threatened their livelihood. I'd destroyed their bridge, but worse, had freed Dorothy.

If I caved, Lark would find her. She'd suffer a similar line of questioning that would result in years of enslavement. A creature of his whims.

I bit down the rage and inhaled a settling breath, preparing myself for the inevitable beating. "If this is about the disappearing blood samples from your creepy cabinet—"

"No," Lark said. "That's one."

"Listen, I don't have what I stole from you"—a lie—"so if you're still looking for it—"

"As a matter of fact, I am, and we'll get to that later but"—he cracked his neck—"wrong again. That's two. Now, I'd think really, *really* hard about that last guess if I were you."

The Talons flexed, shrinking the room by a percentage. Somewhere behind me, leather twisted, sending a chill down my spine but also causing something in me to harden. He could do what he liked, but Dorothy's name would never pass my lips.

I'd die before I gave her up to him.

I clucked my tongue. "I didn't realize making you look like an absolute yokel a *second* time was a crime."

Wrath flashed in Lark's cool eyes, stealing the zest from his smile and giving me a kernel of satisfaction. His fingers snapped and the rope around my wrists yanked me backward, my chest lagging half a second behind. A dozen hands reached for me and I flinched.

Adrenaline shot through my system. My fists clenched.

Lark snapped again, and everything froze.

He cocked his head as he sauntered up to me. "I've changed my mind. After all, before me kneels the infamous Ashley Gardner, the man who could once slip away like a shadow at nightfall. So high and mighty, and above it all—now bested by me. Brought low to the earth where the rest of us live in filth."

The idea was laughable. The Necropolis was a palace and Lark was its prince, which was probably why he grinned, teeth unnaturally white. "I want to see you beg. Say please, and I'll tell you what you've done." His hands swept the air in a magnanimous gesture. "One little word to your King of the Undercity, and he'll grant you mercy."

I knew what Lark's mercy looked like. Once he got what he wanted, he'd build a cage around me—without any doors I could pick, this time—and enjoy watching me waste away to the beating of his drums.

Lark waited with a satisfied smile, and that hard knot inside me tightened even more. I'd never beg. Not to him. Not to anyone.

My frame wasted with dread, prickling in anticipation of all the new bones about to shatter. *Don't be an idiot*, they seemed to plead. I met his eyes and shrugged anyway. "I don't say please to people who refer to themselves in the third person."

An iron rod rammed into my side. I lurched and gasped. Not enough air. Not enough air.

"Where *is* she?" Lark snarled.

I writhed away, into a boot that cracked my skull against the floor. My ears rang. Everything was white and burning. Sweet fire, I needed to stop saying things that made him want to hit me.

"Lark! What are you *doing*?"

Only my roped hands and my cheek pressing into the icy floor tethered me to this dimension. But through the vapor, I heard the feminine voice—and thanked every blinking star. I had a few seconds to breathe before Lark dismissed her and the attack resumed.

"Get out of ... Wren ... belong here."

*Wren.* A bird's name. One of the Acherons.

A cold hand pressed to my other cheek and blonde hair was all I saw until a girl's face swam into view. Her lips parted, and the slightest hint of longing edged into her eyes. I recognized her. She was the girl I'd freed from the insane asylum so that Miles and I could use her cell. The girl who could burn holes through anything. And I recognized her expression because I'd seen it on dozens of women before her.

Now my stomach squirmed for an entirely different reason.

Hand still on my cheek, she turned back to her brothers—and they were her brothers, I realized dismally—and said, "You'll not touch him again."

"Family business, Wren," Robin said. He still hadn't moved from his stance with his arms folded over his chest. "We have to find the woman he freed."

She frowned. "What if he doesn't know anything?"

"Then we make an example of him, to deter future defiance," Jay said, rolling his shoulders. "Win-win."

"What about the code?"

Everyone in the still-spinning room fell silent and looked to her. The Talons shuffled back as if the word alone held power.

"He saved my life," she said. "We owe him our protection now."

Jay ground his teeth, and his eyes cut to me. "Not this steaming pile of—!"

Lark stood. "When was this?"

Her hand slipped off my cheek. "A week ago, when I—disappeared. I was facing the gallows, rotting in a cell, and this man freed me." She stood and pointed at me, repeating, "He *saved* me." She looked between her brothers. "Which means that down here, we have an oath to see that he comes to no harm."

Though I didn't look up, I felt the glare of all three brothers bearing down on me, hatred thick. When the silence stretched on, she marched angrily up to them. "Break the code, and I'll invoke the blood rite!"

Jay cursed and muttered something else far stronger. Lark frowned, and he took a long time to form his next words, spitting them out like they left a foul taste in his mouth. "The code will be honored. Mr. Gardner will come to no harm." He paused. "Down *here*."

I was aware of their little code, and thugs or not, the Acherons weren't liars. To them, the only law was that of family —so if you spat in an Acheron's face, you'd be lucky if they let you live. And if you unwittingly saved one ... whether they liked it or not, you became an ally.

A Talon pulled on my roped hands, forcing me into a kneeling position. I blinked through the dizziness and blood trickling down my face. Lark approached his sister and scowled again, deeper. He knocked his chin at me. "He is still the enemy. And I will not see you look at him that way."

Wren held her ground, not the least bit cowed by the most powerful man in the Necropolis. Her stare was fiery. "Then I won't. *Down here*."

Lark's nostrils flared.

Wren spun on her heel and left the room, but not before casting me one last lingering look. I pretended not to notice.

Lark turned his incensed gaze on me, his wrath glimmering in the air between us. Code or not, he wasn't compelled to let me go just yet. Grabbing a fistful of my hair, he knocked my head back, forcing me to stare into his eyes. "Your magic aside, I don't know how you manage to disappear so completely up top." A fleck of spittle from the vicious whisper hit my cheek, his teeth inching closer. "Or here, for that matter. But trust me when I say it won't last forever. Luck follows you like a whelp, but you won't always be its master."

My hands were tied, my body bruised, I was surrounded by guards and there were a million more between me and the only way out of here—and still, I couldn't help the smirk that played on my lips. Lark knew the threat rang empty. The Necropolis might be his playground, but London was mine, and even he wouldn't be fool enough to let me prove it to him.

I glared back at him, darkening my smile. "It's not luck."

He shoved my head away and stepped back, glowering. "Untie him. Give him a cuff. And get him out of my sight."

My legs wobbled, one eye swelled shut, and my head felt like it'd been run over by a train, but once I got a cuff locked around my wrist, it didn't matter. I threw up an illusion to make myself appear normal. I disguised my hobbling gait as a thoughtful stroll, which helped me not look like I was walking on shards of glass.

I stopped by a healer's shop where I washed the blood off and drank a glass of water. For a crown, she used all her magic to heal a few bruises and make the swelling go down. I wasn't faring much better, but it helped take the edge off, and I'd gotten into enough scrapes to know the worst would come tomorrow.

Progress down to the fourth level was slow, but I finally made my way to the Artifice's door and gave it three raps. On the third one, it swung inward, a pungent organic odor seeping out and bringing to mind a potter's shop.

Stone murals that looked like they belonged in a museum hung on the walls. Jade dragons sat on a counter, next to golden eggs and the British crown jewels. Priceless clothing predating this millennia were tossed over gilded thrones like useless rags. Everything in the shop was an immaculate replica, made from a magical, loamy clay that could only be detected if you tried to break the artifact.

In a dark room in the back with only a single kerosene lantern, hunching over some nameless matter that he stretched with nimble fingers, sat the Artifice. The man whose slant could create a perfect replica of anything in the world. Spectacles perched above a waxed mustache and chin puff, making him look more like an accountant than an artist.

I extracted the daguerreotype from my jacket pocket and tossed it on the table before him. He didn't look up from his work, but he paused, noting my presence. "Can you make this? With the dimensions on the back?"

He clucked his tongue, saying in his signature nasally voice, "I am currently very busy, Mr. Gardner. My orders are backlogged by a month."

"It would need to be heavy, to avoid detection. And I need it by the end of next week."

"You think you deserve special favors?"

I plunked both hands on the table. "I'm a returning customer. I deserve special favors."

One haughty brow cocked, before the Artifice said slowly, "I suppose if your payment is tantalizing enough ..."

I set a wad of cash on the table. He eyed it but didn't move to count it. "More when you tell me you can do it."

He bent over the table wrinkling his blue vest with gold embroidered swirls. I wondered if it was real. "You know I do not deal in money, Mr. Gardner, but information. Information is beyond price, as are my works of art."

A delicate way of putting that he was in the business of selling your darkest secrets to the highest bidder. I leaned forward too. "I don't think you understand how much money I'm offering you this time."

"I understand." He readjusted his spectacles and turned back to his clay in dismissal.

"I don't ... have any information you'd consider valuable, right now." About anyone *else*. "But I will. Very soon. My network sleeps with their ears to the ground."

"I don't appreciate people wasting my time."

"Art, please, you know I'm good for it."

"And you know where the door is. Use it, or I will." The wooden stool scraped as he stood to leave.

"Wait," I ground out, and he froze.

I needed this. I weighed the risks. The benefits. Again, I was left with one obvious choice, and many secrets, but only one I could remotely afford to tell. And *that* secret ...

It was only a matter of time before it fell into the wrong hands. Which meant I'd have to act quickly. Still doable.

"The Marquis de Avèjean ...," I started, and years of careful discipline revolted at the mention of the title. A wave of memories flooded my eyes.

The Artifice went deathly still, letting me know he'd heard the rumors. And why wouldn't he? Everyone had. "Was hanged for using magic," he finished for me, blinking behind his spectacles. "And his son died in a fire that burned their ancestral home to the ground."

I glanced at him, hands slick with sweat.

Bram had been careful; so, *so* careful. If he were alive, he'd kill me where I stand. He'd cut out my tongue before I could utter the words, and even now, the walls seemed to rumble from the sound of him turning in his grave. But for all his lectures, it wasn't his secret to keep. It had always been mine.

Slowly, I shook my head and pushed it out anyway. "The Marquis de Avèjean lives."

The Artifice blinked some more, before his eyes gleamed with a goblin's glee at the juicy morsel. "The father, or the son?"

"What I've given you is already beyond price, per your requirement. Now uphold your end of the bargain."

My scowl must've convinced him of my honesty, because he cocked his head and studied the daguerreotype for the first time, flipping it over to inspect the listed dimensions. "I can make it heavy. But a project this size will take me two days to complete."

I turned, away from the stab of guilt—and dread—that was currently smarting worse than Lark's beating. "Then I'll be back in two days."

I DUCKED into the barrel-vaulted hallway that ringed the plaza on my way to the portal, limbs stiff. It'd been a long night and my muscles were begging me to lie down, but I still had a lot of work to do at the flat.

A form stepped out of the shadows, blocking my path. "Ashley."

I halted.

Wren slipped the hood off her blonde hair. I didn't like when women used my first name. It was a mockery of intimacy that we'd never shared. Nerves suddenly on edge, I skimmed the cuff around my wrist which allowed my magic free rein.

She softly cleared her throat. "I know the portal is about to close—"

"I didn't know Lark was your brother," I admitted. It was a massive oversight on my part, not looking into her background before freeing her from that cell, one I didn't often make.

"Half-brother." She shrugged one shoulder. "No one knows. And besides the next few days, I don't spend much time down here, so I'd like to keep it that way." My wariness grew with each inch she shuffled forward, shortening the distance between us. "I have a whole life up there. Which is why I wanted to thank you for liberating me from that—that prison."

I fell back a step. Just one. "We made a deal. I did my half." I felt my magic duck around her, stalking her like prey. *This one,* it seemed to say to me. *This one is yours.*

I remembered Dorothy's words from the bakery: *All mutating magic cares about is your innermost desires, and slowly, it overtakes you to make them reality. It has your will, but its own mind. Its own dark conscience.* My hands sweated. I needed to leave.

"Nevertheless, I'm out. I'm glad I was able to return the favor. Lark can be so ..." Wren shook her head, and the word she settled on was, "petty."

I needed to take this cuff off and block my magic. *Now.* "If that was all—"

"Wait, I ..." She clutched my sleeve, and suddenly it was too late.

My magic folded around her and her jaw went slack. Her pupils dilated until her irises were thin rings, glazed and stripping me of clothes, skin, flesh, and bones, until all that lay before her was a pulsing heart. She looked drugged—and she was. On magic.

On my magic.

Her head tipped over from the weight of all the magic whispered to her. "You're lonely," she murmured, words pulled from her tongue like taffy.

She didn't know what she was saying—had no control over her body, when the influence was this intense. And it was the magic that was communicating with me, not her. Tempting me.

The *pull* was mild on Polina, and for whatever reason, didn't seem to work on Dorothy. For now. I was careful not to spend too much time with any one woman, because the more they were around me, the more influence the magic had over them. It had been a long time since I'd encountered a case this strong, though, and sweat licked the back of my neck.

Every muscle tautened with the impulse to run. But it was a wild beast, this magic. Sudden movements only made it angry, and harder to grapple with.

"I'm not lonely," I said quietly.

Wren's palms spread over my abdomen and reverently slid up to my shoulders, breaking her promise to Lark. She peered up at me, and the lust there was pleading, palpable—only they weren't her eyes anymore. They were wide, innocent, and gray-blue. Looking at me like they had right before I'd laced up her dress. My heart pounded.

"I can fix it," she whispered.

Her hair coiled into soft curls, darkening to a deep brown. Her fingers inched over to my silk necktie and extracted the silver pin in the center, dragging the tip over my lower lip.

I caught her wrist in my hand and the illusion shattered. Wren stood before me. Brown eyes. Blonde hair. Nothing like the girl she'd resembled a moment ago.

It was getting stronger. I was getting weaker. I'd searched enough minds to know that Wren wouldn't remember the specifics of this moment, only her general feeling toward me, but I—I would remember.

Wren wasn't the one I wanted. Neither was Polina. I couldn't want anyone who wasn't in their right minds—and neither could they want me. The ghost of dress laces tingled on my fingers. I curled them into my palm.

I took three deep breaths through my nostrils, regaining control. Then one by one, I peeled my fingers off Wren's wrist. "I don't want you to fix it," I muttered darkly to the magic, and I know it heard me because its own grip on her loosened, shrinking her pupils as it drifted away from her. "I want you to leave me alone."

I stepped back, and, once my cuff was removed, moved through the portal. The Bear was waiting, whittling again. Miles was nowhere, having probably returned to the flat. I should go find him and give him an update; get back to work.

Instead, I went to find better air to breathe.

I walked through a church's wooden doors, passing pews and stained-glass windows, making myself disappear whenever a priest walked by. I climbed the bell tower and stepped onto the roof, swinging myself onto a higher ledge even though my body trembled with exhaustion.

Everything still hurt from Lark's beating, but I hit the back of my head against the stony spire wall, teeth grinding and cursing until I ran out of breath. As if that would take away this face. These eyes.

Miles was the first to notice it, when we were boys docked in Greece, tasting olives and wine in the sun-warmed market. "Your face," he had said under a bright yellow canopy, eyes clouded, "it's ... it looks different."

I'd brushed his hand from my shoulder and quipped, "It's the same as it was yesterday."

But it wasn't.

I returned to my cabin on Bram's ship and stared in the mirror for a full hour, inspecting every inch. My eyes were no longer blue, but a light green. My chin was different, too; the smallest, grayest shadow at its point. The adjustments didn't stop there. Week after week, they grew more pronounced.

The features were still mine, but they were tampered with. Polished. Perfected. A nose that straightened, lips that widened, lashes that darkened, eyes that could arrest you from farther and farther away. Brows that were the same shape, that sloped at the same angle, identical in every way down to the number of hairs.

I knew because I counted them.

One night when we were alone on the deck and only the moon and the sea and the wind were watching, I caught Miles studying me suspiciously. I knew why. He'd transformed from a boy into a man; I'd transformed from a boy into a demigod.

I tried to hide it. The moment I was old enough, I attempted a beard like my father's—it never came in. I wore scarves over my nose at every port—it only drew more attention to my eyes. Once, I even slathered mud on my face, which prompted Bram to dump a bucket of seawater over my head and lecture me about remaining inconspicuous. Only when he wasn't around did I illusion someone else's face onto my own, knowing if Bram saw, it would elicit a far-longer, far-more-physical lecture about the foolishness of wasting my magic.

I had more than enough magic to spare, and that was precisely the problem. Two slants meant the magic was mixing. Mutating. Mutating *me*.

Detail by detail, I changed. And when the *perfecting* of my face was complete, something clicked into place, and I couldn't look in a mirror again without using my second slant on myself and reliving *those* memories.

I became the face of magic; of my own enemy.

I couldn't look at me, but the opposite was true of everyone else. Rome, Mumbai, Athens, Cairo, Paris—everywhere we went, the women stared, drawn to me, to the magic, to the inexplicable force that exuded from my every pore that was trying to cure my loneliness. The strength of the pull varied from woman to woman, but I knew it was there because even though I couldn't control it, I could feel it working, luring them in, making their eyes beg for me.

And it stung every time because it wasn't for me. It never would be.

Of anyone, I knew that looks were deceiving—for if appearances were true, my anger would have claws and my tongue would have horns and my heart would have fangs ready to sink into the darkest rhythm. I would look like the demon I was.

I came back to the present where I stood on the precipice of a tall church, staring out at the gray city. The sunrise streaked the sky with splatters of orange, the calls of Londoners rising from the streets in a cloud of dropped t's and h's. Wind lashed at my shirt and hair, pigeons flapping so close I could catch one if I only jumped.

For a heartbeat, I entertained it.

Instead, I propped a forearm on my knee and settled back against a spire, grunting from the protest of my injuries. Maybe I'd sit here until they healed.

I remembered the scene with Wren and the hand on my knee

fisted. It wasn't just memories now—the mutation was leaching into illusions too. Soon it would overtake me completely. For a glimmer of a moment, Wren had looked just like Dorothy. For that glimmer of a moment, I had contemplated giving in.

Which meant that ... it knew. The magic *knew*.

I hit the back of my head against the spire again. Maybe I'd sit here forever.

In the end, I didn't care what I looked like. All I cared about was righting the wrongs of the past. Getting revenge for the thing that had snapped inside me all those years ago. Revenge for the secrets, the lies. For the unhinged magic.

For what I saw in the mirror.

# 33

## Dorothy

I pushed the mixture of fish, rice, mustard, and boiled eggs around on my plate, stomach hard. Father had been missing for over a week now, and I had very little to show for it; a steel button, a hunch about Mr. Brass, and still no response from Mr. Riley. Every day that passed pushed my father closer to the brink of madness.

Maybe he was there already.

I bit down on my cheek until I tasted blood.

Increased numbers of bluedusters patrolled the streets lately, but if I didn't hear from Mr. Riley this afternoon, I resolved to wait on his doorstep until he agreed to see me.

Aunt Marie quietly sipped her tea down the table, and across from me, Clarence balanced his spoon on a tipped-back nose while stuffing a whole boiled egg in his mouth, making his cheeks bulge. Emme was nowhere to be seen, and I wondered what she'd been so preoccupied with lately. The thought sent a lonely pang through my chest. I'd been a rotten friend, and perhaps I'd misjudged her. Perhaps, if I made her promise to be careful, she could help me ...

"Hurricane over the Atlantic a few days ago." Uncle Benedick grunted from the head of the table, sipping coffee from behind his newspaper. Lips giving a satisfied smack, he set the cup down. "Mr. Riley was quite fortunate to have narrowly missed it."

I dropped my fork and blinked at my uncle. "Narrowly?"

"He's been in America these past few months and only returned the day of the concert. A day later, and his business would be sitting at the bottom of the ocean."

I froze, vision focusing out. The Samaritan had rescued someone the night of the society dinner. Which was *before* the concert. But if Mr. Riley had been in America, then ...

He was not the Samaritan.

And I had forfeited my second guess. Panicked air eased between my lips. Dead ends. Dead ends everywhere.

The prototype gun—I had to get it back.

Uncle Benedick flicked his newspaper over, and bright ink made me do a double take at the back. A red rectangle sectioned off an advertisement, a fact which I wanted to disregard since we only rented our newspaper between ten and eleven, before a newsboy delivered it to the next customer.

But I couldn't disregard it, because I didn't doubt *he* could find out which newsboy had us on his route and squeeze into the time slot before us.

*You pick up all sorts of interesting tidbits in the paper, Miss St. James.*

My senses jolted awake, an electric sensation tingling in the tips of my fingers. My third and final clue.

Uncle folded the paper in half, covering it completely. I made myself take another bite of fish. Swallow. Never letting on to the fact that my heart was racing. An agonizing half an hour passed before Uncle cleared his throat and set the newspaper down. I pinched my fork to keep myself from snatching it out of his reach.

"I have business at the bank today, so I shall be absent until supper. However, I trust you shall all be dressed for Mr. Joule's private viewing when I return. The man's paintings go for outrageous prices, and I managed to secure an invitation to his highly exclusive party tonight. And Marie." Uncle Benedick stood, tossing his napkin onto his plate. "Regardless of any headaches, Emmeline will join us."

Aunt Marie managed a wobbly nod and said, "Of course, dear," but my uncle had already walked away. I flipped the newspaper over and scanned the lines within the red rectangle.

PUBLIC SALE!—TODAY ONLY
A CHARMING VARIETY OF NOVELTIES
49 ST. PAUL'S CHURCHYARD

An auction?

"What is the matter, Dorothy?"

I snapped up. "Nothing." Slipping the newspaper off the table and gripping it behind my back, I said, "I'd like to fetch some medicine for Emmeline this morning. I know she's been feeling poorly lately."

Clarence rebalanced his spoon on his nose. "And I didn't even slip anything into her tea this time." He launched the spoon into the air where it clanged against the chandelier and bounced off a candlestick before finally clattering to Aunt Marie's plate.

She set her fork down and closed her eyes. "*Clarence.*"

He merely grinned, eyes only for his spoon. "Barmy."

Aunt Marie turned back to me, brow furrowing. "I could send a servant for the medicine. No need to bother you to do it—"

"Oh, but I'd like to," I rushed to say. "Please." Another stab of guilt pricked me. "I think if I had something to do, it might help me feel ... useful."

267

Aunt Marie nodded like she understood completely. "Very well. But do not be gone long."

"I won't," I lied again.

If Ashley Gardner was involved, this would take a very long time, indeed.

THANKS to heavy traffic along the Strand and Fleet Street, it took three hours to arrive at the churchyard. St. Paul's spire towered above the intersection, early afternoon sun winking off its great silver dome. The horses pulling my hired coach whickered to a stop before a corner shop. The front was beveled and inlaid with paned glass, the yellow 49 stark against the blue storefront, so dark it looked almost black. Two bluedusters watched the crowd from under a tree in the middle of the yard.

When I entered the shop, no bell tinkled. The walls of the rectangular room were vaulted, the air musty; spoked, wooden chairs filled with gentlemen faced a man at a podium at the far end and allowed for a small center aisle. I might've felt like I stepped inside a country church if not for the books and paintings lining every square inch of wall space.

I didn't know what I was looking for. But I had a feeling that if Ashley had sent me to an auction, he had plans for me to bid on something—and so in the pockets of my skirt, I'd brought every penny I owned. Although ... Some of these gentlemen with their gold-knobbed walking canes and starched ascots looked like their pockets were far deeper than mine. I swallowed.

The man at the podium rattled off interesting facts about the candelabra beside him to drive the price up—something about it being used to illuminate the crypts of kings. I retrieved a paddle from the man at the door whose eyebrows inched toward his receding hairline at the motion, and found a seat in the back.

Item after item was brought out. The clock ticked by, fraying my nerves as I wondered if I'd already missed my clue. More gentlemen left than came, the hall having a gradual emptying effect. And still I didn't know what I was looking for.

Until I did.

"This piece was recovered from the wreckage of *The Osprey* off the coast of India," the announcer said. "Its restoration has only served to highlight the beauty of the opals and unique mosaics, making it quite the coveted article. A stunning work of art unlike any the world has ever seen."

Lies. My heart had stopped beating the moment they brought it onto the stage, because that was my father's watch. The one I'd traded with the artist at the carnival in exchange for his painting.

"The bidding will start at fourteen pounds."

A few paddles lifted in the air, and I didn't have time to wonder at how the watch ended up here, even though of course I already knew. I raised my own paddle, and the auctioneer upped the price. Someone two rows in front of me raised their paddle, too, and when the others dropped out, a bidding war ensued.

I couldn't make out more than his top hat, but I had a gut-sinking feeling I knew who it was. When the price was driven within ten pounds of my cap, I scooted out of my seat and moved up a few rows, sliding into the seat next to him.

"Isn't a factory man too poor to be at an auction?" I murmured, raising my paddle again. I couldn't afford to go very much higher.

I also couldn't afford *not* to.

"Depends on the man, I would wager," Ashley said without looking at me. He raised his paddle.

"Why sell the watch only to bid on it now?"

"I'm a philanthropist."

"Not when it comes to me, apparently." Again, I wondered why he was working so hard to ensure I never found my father; it turned my chest into a melting pot of conflicting emotion. I raised my paddle, admitting begrudgingly, "I didn't know I'd be bidding against you."

"I expected more from you, Miss St. James."

"I would've brought more money—" Somehow.

He glanced at me for the first time, a tiny smile on his lips. "Then take comfort in the knowledge that it wouldn't have made a difference." Still looking at me, he raised his paddle, smile hardening like a runner with the finish line in his sights.

Bug. Boot.

Exactly how rich was he?

My lips pressed into a flat line. The auctioneer's price rang out, and I squeezed my paddle as hard as I could. I had enough for one more bid. There he sat in the corner of my eye, thoroughly unruffled by the price, with no signs of running out of cash. He'd predicted me perfectly until now, which meant the only way to buy a few seconds was to do something neither of us would ever expect.

Anything to distract him, just for a moment. *Something—*

I could never.

I had to.

Not allowing myself to overthink it, I raised my paddle high in the air and the auctioneer announced my number.

"Going once!" he called.

"I really am sorry, Dolly," Ashley clucked, arm already starting to lift.

"Going twice!"

My hands shook. "So am I," I whispered.

And I squished Ashley's head between my paddle and my lips, planting a hard kiss on his cheek.

He froze. But he didn't pull away. His arm went slack, and his paddle slipped from his hand, thudding to the floor. I didn't let myself notice how warm and smooth his cheek was, or how clean and glittery his skin smelled. That was strange, wasn't it? How could skin smell like stars? Almost like ... like magic—

I drew back, breathing hard, face flaming. Such a gamble I had taken, kissing him. But I always played it safe, and if Ashley was anything of the mastermind I knew him to be, he'd been counting on that.

Breath soft, Ashley remained frozen for two heartbeats before his head swiveled, and he stared me down, volleying between my eyes. He snagged my hand still around the paddle, and by the set of his lips I swore they were about to whisper *Two can play at that game.* Then, to my delight and horror, he slid a hand behind my head and pulled, inching my mouth toward his.

A swarm of emotion flooded my face in that split second, excitement zipping in my stomach. And his eyes said, *What about this? Will you take this risk too, Dorothy?*

My heart drummed two different answers.

*Pull away.*

*Kiss him.*

*He's stopping you from finding your father.*

*Don't do anything you'd regret until you know. Until you know he'd keep your heart safe.*

But Ashley's pink, tempting lips were closing in, and I wasn't jerking away.

What if I didn't want to be safe anymore? What if I wanted to be wild and adventurous like him?

*With* him.

His cool breath skimmed my upper lip, black hair brushing my eyelid and making them both shutter closed. He angled my mouth upward until it brushed—

"Sold!"

Eyes snapping open, I jumped to my feet. My entire being heated until I was molten lava. My gamble had paid off—if you could call earning this lurching, yearning ache *winning.* And because I couldn't think of anything else to say, I said, "Now we both won something."

Ashley didn't even glance at the auctioneer. He cocked his head, eyes glazed and flickering over my form. "Or *lost* something." But he wasn't smiling.

I swallowed, refusing to puzzle out his comment. I marched to the front and gave the auctioneer's assistant the agreed amount, breathing a sigh of relief as the weight of the watch settled in my palm. When I turned around, Ashley was gone, my paddle abandoned on his seat. I pretended not to feel the quick stab of disappointment.

That look in his eye, I couldn't put my finger on it. The only phrase that came to mind was *burning caution*, and yet I didn't even know what that meant. Or how it made sense. Or why it was *there*. And then he'd turned it around on me, daring me to leap before checking to see if I had wings.

I'd nearly done it.

But now wasn't the time to feel embarrassed or make sense of my jumbled emotions. Outside, to the clomping of horse hooves and chiming of bells, I inspected Father's watch. I found nothing, except ... Someone had stopped the watch at 4:25, with the second hand pointing straight up. Exactly on the minute. Another hint. Of course, the watch wouldn't be the answer; Ashley would never make my last clue so simple.

But what could it mean?

Many things took place in the late afternoon. Teatime, last minute errands—but not at *exactly* 4:25. It would have to be something that was scheduled, something—

A memory jogged loose, pieces falling into place to create my painting of a train—the same train from the hanging crystals in the tent at the carnival.

"Newsboy!" I called to a small figure kicking a pebble down the walk. I hadn't brought the newspaper with me, but I had enough change leftover from the auction. The boy halted and looked around, eyes landing on me as I approached. Pointing to the folds of paper tucked under his right arm, I said, "Can I buy that issue off of you?"

His eyes widened but he sized me up, relaxing back onto his heels. "Doubtless, miss, but I'll have to charge you thruppence. A pristine copy like this'n ain't a dime a dozen."

Newspapers this late in the day were virtually worthless, and I recognized that cunning glint in his large blue eyes. I gave a begrudging smile, though, and fished three pence from the pocket of my skirt and placed it in his palm. He walked off, stature bolstered and pebble forgotten.

I flipped through the papers. Lists of rail lines lined the page with their arrival and departure times for the entire week. I checked each one, scanning down the columns until I found it.

Victoria Station. The Brighton Line. Departing at 4:25 pm. *Today.* No other train had the same time scheduled. It had to be where my clue was.

My eyes flew to the clock tower at the corner of the street, and I puffed out air through pursed lips. 3:42. There was no way. Victoria Station was back in the West End—clear on the other side of London. There was no way I'd get there in time.

Time. *Time, time.*

Ashley would've timed it. He'd have figured out how long it took to get from St. Paul's Churchyard to Victoria Station. He'd have lined up the auction of the watch accordingly—which meant that it was at least possible to get there before the train departed.

Possible, and not a minute more.

Curse the man.

I broke into a run.

# 34

## Dorothy

I had never loathed traffic more than I did in that moment. Coaches and omnibuses were worthless when the streets congealed this much, legs and elbows a far more reliable method of transport.

The downside of declining a coach, however, was that I wasn't as familiar with London's streets as most, forcing me to stop a few times for specific directions even though I knew generally where Victoria Station was. I'd lived here my whole life, but I hadn't done a lot of exploring. I'd never gotten the chance. At first, because I wasn't old enough, and then because it wasn't safe for me.

My lungs burned, ice and fire, in and out, every breath a weight on my chest that made me want to gag. I kept running.

Past stray dogs and startled men, past glinting shop windows and women with bustles who were side eyeing me under veiled hats. Cold streetlamps, doorways papered over with the word *Rook* or *Samaritan*, wagons of baskets, iron fences, gutters, and signs.

Every clock tower I passed reminded me how little time I had.

3:54.

4:01.

4:16.

My corset, which already hindered my ability to breathe, was soaked through with sweat. The same stickiness coated my neck and forehead by the time I burst into the tubed hemisphere of the terminus, the astringent sharpness of cast iron filling my collapsing lungs.

My head whipped around. *Ticket booth, ticket booth ...*

I stopped short.

I had nowhere near enough money for a ticket.

I'd have to board, find my clue, and get off before the train departed. In four minutes. But which car? There were over two dozen to choose from. I looked up and down the train.

The bidding for the watch had started at fourteen pounds. Not having any other number to go on, I plunged inside car fourteen. Again—as always—I didn't know what I was looking for, only confident that I would know it when I saw it. When I had inspected the entire car, earning a few curious stares, I moved down the line to car fifteen. I wouldn't have time to visit the first cars, so I could only hope I was going in the right direction.

Trains always departed a few minutes late anyway. Didn't they?

In car twenty, a violinist played softly to the low chatter of upper-crust accents, the air traced faintly with garlic. Starched white tablecloths bore flashing forks and the finest china, each table partitioned off to allow privacy. Sitting at one of them was a certain Russian ballerina.

I wanted to move on; hopefully find my clue attached to a window or under a seat, but I took one look at the setting for two, and knew she was expecting me.

As if she heard that thought, Polina Mikhailova locked gazes with me, folding her head in her hands and setting her elbows on the table. The collar of her cobalt coat-basque accentuated the sharp angles of her face.

When I warily approached her, she said, "Miss St. James. What a pleasant surprise." Her ruby sharpened smile said the opposite. "Please." She gestured to the seat across the table. The table bore six shot glasses of what appeared to be water but carried a subtle tang of alcohol. Vodka? "Sit."

"Do you have something for me?"

"Sit."

I shook my head. "I don't have time for—"

"Zis is dining car, Miss St. James. Leave—" She sat back and gestured magnanimously to the spread before her. "Or dine."

I could tell by her smug smile that this was going to be another test, and my fingers went cold. I slid into the seat, positioning myself on the edge in case I felt like running.

Her smile grew, and it struck me as unnatural; a face that fierce shouldn't smile. Not like that.

"Do you have something for me?" I repeated.

"Your message from Ashley is in my left boot." She drew a dark, empty vial the size of her thumb from her jacket. "This is a sleeping draught, which I have distributed between these glasses." As she set the vial on the table, I glanced at the three shots of vodka before me, and the three set before her. She removed her white fishnet glove, showing me the silver-encrusted sapphire ring on her pointer finger. "You have seen one of these before, yes?"

I stared at the truth ring, identical to the one Ashley used when I'd given him my guess. He'd said they were rare and usually paid for in blood. A chill crept down my spine. "What does all this have to do with my message?"

"Let us play game," she said without missing a beat, cocking her head to the side. "We take turns answering questions. You either tell the truth," —she held up the back of her hand, wiggling the fingers and the ring— "or you lie, and drink. Three drinks ... and you're out."

I balled my fists in my dress to keep my nerve. "What do you mean, 'out'?"

"Winner gets off train and runs back to Mr. Gardner with his note. Loser passes out and follows the line all the way to Russia."

A shrill hoot pierced the air, and the car gave a minor jolt. The train was leaving. I was either getting off now, or I was playing this game. Possibly ending up at the coast, or farther if Polina had the connections, and was feeling spiteful enough to order them to drag me onto a boat. Which, judging by her thinly veiled glare, she was.

*Woo-oooh!* Two more pumps of the whistle.

I bit my lip.

I was virtually penniless, aboard a nonstop train to Brighton which I hadn't paid passage for, and ending up at the coast would send Uncle into another fit. If I ever managed to make it back, I'd be put under lock and key for the rest of my life.

So, I'd better make it count.

The train started to roll, inching its way out of the station. I scooted farther into the velvet booth until I was directly across from Polina, meeting her daggered eyes. "I'll go first."

# 35

## Dorothy

Vodka had a very subtle odor—some would argue none at all, but I could smell the ethanol wafting up from the shot glasses. I'd never tried it before, but my stomach turned, already anticipating the sour taste on my tongue. Without waiting for Polina to protest, I asked, "Was this game Mr. Gardner's idea, or was it yours?"

She took her time responding, red lips curling in distaste. Finally, she said, "Ashley suggested to me that I ... stall. But game was my idea." As she held up her hand again, I was able to see that the ring was still blue. Truth. She took it off and slid it over to me. The moment it was around my finger, she asked, "Are you slanted?"

I blinked, eyes darting down to the shot glasses. Much of society was slanted, but it wasn't something that was discussed—it was a personal secret that could potentially be incriminating. If someone knew to watch you.

Deciding that drinking would be an admission in and of itself, I answered, "Yes."

I passed her the ring, noticing the faintest line on one of her fingers. "Are *you* slanted?"

"No," she said easily. The ring remained blue. She passed it back. "What is your slant?"

My stomach turned again. Father had told me never to divulge it. I wasn't going to take my first drink over it, though, especially when Polina still had all of hers. "Sight. I hear the past, see the future, and can sense magic in the present. It's all part of the same gift."

Her brows raised. "Or curse."

I couldn't argue with that. We exchanged the ring, and the violinist picked up a faster tune that was both melancholy and dark.

"When will you return to England?" I asked Polina. Because it was inevitable. Not just for her career, but because she seemed to have a lot of interests here.

A slight lift of one shoulder. "When I am needed."

"That's not an answer—"

One brow cocked. "Then choose your questions more carefully. It is the only answer I have for you." I glanced at the ring. Still blue. After we passed it again, she said, "No one has seen your father out in society in quite some time ... Where is he?"

My stomach dropped. Ashley wouldn't have told her, would he? A careful study of her face suggested that she was fishing, though; only trying to find a weakness. And she had.

Sand on my tongue, I lifted my first glass and tossed it back. Once I managed to swallow, I coughed, squinching my eyes at the bitter tang. Polina's smile grew in smugness.

A peppery, vanilla aftertaste sat in my mouth. Whatever that sleeping draught was, it was strong. I already felt my muscles relaxing, enough to know this game wouldn't last long. A sense of urgency made those muscles tense again.

If I was going to win, I needed to get Polina to drink her shots, and quickly—which meant asking uncomfortable questions. Questions she didn't want to answer. My gaze traveled to her ring finger again. It was a hunch, and I didn't want to waste a question, but ...

*Take risks. Be like Ashley.*

"Who is your husband?"

Three beats passed before Polina's nostrils flared, teeth pressing tight. The utter loathing in her eyes as she plucked up her first glass and tipped it down her throat had me shaking. Seconded only by the relief that I'd found a chink in her armor. One glass down, two more to go. Equal footing again.

She ripped the ring from her finger and all but threw it at me. "Zis gift of yours ... can you control it?"

A warning flashed red in my mind. Why was she so curious about my slant? The train chugged faster, enough to make us rock a little. "I can only control my ability to view the past."

She squinted and checked the ring, ingesting the information. It made me nervous—made me feel like there was more to this game than petty jealousy.

I gave the ring back to her. She was hiding her marriage; she didn't like talking about her past. "Do you have any children?"

A vein pulsed in her forehead, face reddening to the shade of her lips. "*Khvatit!*" she seethed through her teeth. She tossed a second glass back, plunking it down so hard it made the other ones rattle. "Enough of this! You will not ask these kinds of questions—"

My voice rose. "You're the one who wanted to play this game, Mikhailova." The drug was starting to control my tongue.

"Has he kissed you yet?"

I sucked in a quiet breath, taking my time with letting it out. Our outburst had drawn attention from the adjacent booth, but I ignored them, forcing calm into my voice. "Is that your next question?"

She grabbed my hand and practically shoved the ring onto my finger, repeating, "Has Ashley kissed you?"

I hesitated, wetting my lower lip. "No."

"But he wants to?"

"No," I said again.

Polina's gaze darted to the ring, and I followed the movement. It clouded black. Panic made my heart pump faster.

"That was two questions," I whispered, only just realizing it and eyes snapping up.

"No one made you answer, *zaychik*. You lie, you drink."

"It wasn't a lie—"

She smiled bitterly. "The person we deceive most is ourselves." Ashley's face swam before me—the message in his eyes after lacing up my dress, in the armoire at the factory, and at the auction ...

Polina scooted my second glass right up to the edge. "*Drink.*"

I glanced at the clear liquid, mouth already dry, head feeling too light. She'd cheated. I'd responded without thinking. But if only to stop thinking about that lie—about the truth—I obeyed. The second shot went down easier than the first but still made me grimace.

Now the score was two to two. My head swirled, eyes watering and lids as heavy as anvils. Polina's lines started to bleed into the booth behind her, the edges of the car becoming fuzzy. I couldn't keep going like this.

As I passed the ring for what I hoped was the final time, my thoughts clumped and limped along, trying to organize. I had to find another weakness. One more thing that she cared about or didn't want me to know.

I needed to think, I needed to *think*—

There was something. Oh, my head was pounding, my eyes focusing in and out—

*Focus.*

Ashley.

She was jealous because of Ashley.

*The person we deceive most is ourselves.*

"Well?" Polina asked.

If my thoughts were this scattered, Polina couldn't be faring much better. I'd be banking on it. I inhaled a steadying breath and asked, "Has Mr. Gardner kissed *you*?"

Polina scoffed. She thought I'd wasted my question. Maybe I had. "Of course," she said.

Then, to her horror, ink spread over the surface of the ring. A lie. I blinked, making sure I was really seeing black. I'd gambled right.

"We *kissed*," she practically spat. "*We* kissed."

The ink receded to a sapphire blue. True.

I had suspected from the way she'd shot her last two questions that there was some underlying bitterness. She'd kissed him, then rewritten the history—or the sleeping draught had done it for her. I locked eyes with her. "You lie, you drink." The words were slurred, but I held her gaze, no matter how much my eyelids demanded to close.

Her jaw worked, eyes red-rimmed and glistening. Tears borne of rage. Then a deathly calm settled over her features. "Once he has solved you ... he will move on. He always does." Chin held high, she scooped up her last shot, holding it out to me. "*Za lyubov'.*"

*To love.*

She drank it slowly, letting it trickle down her throat. By the time she finished, her eyes were already closing. Her head lolled back, and she slid down her seat, crumpling her traveling jacket. After a game of questions, I felt like I knew the woman even less.

Maybe it had been cruel to bring up her past; exploit it. I swallowed back the guilt—if only because I had to retrieve my clue and find a place to hide before the conductor found his way to this car.

After wiggling her left boot off, a piece of paper fluttered to the floor. I unfolded it and was met with Ashley's familiar script.

HE'LL BE AT MR. JOULE'S VIEWING PARTY.

The Samaritan ...

But the party was *tonight*. In only a few hours! Frustrated tears that I was certain were half alcohol rose to the surface. I forced them back in, commanding my thoughts to straighten up like soldiers even though they grew floppier by the minute.

Ashley had told Polina to stall. So that I'd be stuck on the train. So that I'd never make it to the party.

He'd orchestrated it all.

I fisted the piece of paper and stood, walking—stumbling—to the back of the car. Everything above my neck was a cloud of cotton and everything below, wooden limbs. I had to get off this train. I had to make it to that party. I had to prove to Ashley that he had severely underestimated me.

I stepped out the back of the car into the fresh air. We were still in London, approaching the outskirts. Tracks rumbled beneath the wheels, the train nearly at full speed and making me feel even more weightless. I plunged into the next car, following the line all the way to the platform of the caboose.

Fresh air blasted my face, and a vision clouded my eyes.

*I gripped the rails, took deep breaths and ran ... ran off the edge of the platform ... The ground rushed up at me, just before every-thing went black—*

The vision winked out, leaving me shaky and feeling like I was going to vomit. Had I ... in my vision, had I died? As I watched the tracks speed under the train, I knew we were moving too fast now. Jumping would be suicide.

But if I missed the party ... that was it. No more clues. No more guesses. No Samaritan.

No father.

My head shook, tears filling my eyes, hands fisting. Maybe sometimes ...

Maybe the *right* path was always the dangerous one for a reason. Because it was the only one worth taking.

Maybe sometimes you had to take it anyway.

I poked my head out the edge, wind slapping my face. Up ahead, Victoria Bridge loomed. With a stroke of clarity, I knew what I had to do.

My vision played in my mind again. *Are you mad?*

*No more playing it safe.*

It was my only chance to get off. To use my third clue. To find my father. I was either jumping from this train into the Thames or I'd die trying, and I didn't know if the vodka had made the decision easier, or harder.

Probably easier.

The train chugged faster. I settled against the far end of the platform, waiting, blinking, and shaking out my muscles to try and wake them up. When the caboose ricketed over the bridge, I took one last heaping breath, hefted my skirts, and took a running leap. Someone screamed, and a second later, I realized it was me.

I barely cleared the edge. Stomach colliding with my ribcage, I fell. Down, down, until I begged for it to end, until I cursed Ashley's name repeatedly. Right before everything went black.

# 36

## Emmeline

The building was in shambles.

I frowned at Mrs. Kelly's scrawl in my notebook for the third time. And then a fourth. Barmy, if Mr. Gardner didn't get more suspicious by the hour.

No gentleman could live in this crumbling stone where clothes-pinned sheets passed for windows and the alley was so steep, one was in danger of drowning in the center gutter on a drizzly day. Warehouses and small-scale factories boxed the tall flat shares in. Definitely unfashionable. But the address was right, and Mrs. Kelly had said her son's flat was on the third floor. Perhaps the building was in better shape up there.

I took a deep breath, readjusted my cap and the collar of my urchin clothes, and dove inside.

Whatever Dory was chasing involved Ashley Gardner, so I'd checked the rumor mill and the gossip columns; next, the Royal Archives, but the birth records were empty of his name and the death records were empty of any relatives. For four days, I'd attempted to glean information, only serving to grow my frustration when none was to be had.

No one seemed to know where Mr. Gardner had come from. It was as if he'd appeared one day like a mist rolling over the city, blending in just enough as to not be noticeable, and yet subtly changing the tone in the air.

It was all monstrously suspicious.

In the end, it'd been a matter of interrogating the ticket porters that delivered to his brown-bricked townhouse and finding that Mr. Kelly was not so careful about scrubbing away his footprints, possessing a mother in Cheapside who wrote him regularly.

One cordial correspondence later, Mrs. Kelly revealed that Mr. Gardner and Mr. Kelly were "thick as thieves"—*thieves!*— and that the townhouse was rarely occupied. She gave me a new address, informing me that they were never home outside of sleeping hours.

As I treaded up the faded carpet stairs, I was grateful I'd changed into my urchin clothes before coming, even though I'd already used most of my magic at the tables. I wasn't sure what I was looking for. Stolen objects. Towers of cash. Any sign of criminal activity, really.

Nothing like reinforcing your preconceived notions.

Four doors stood at the top of the rickety third story landing, all locked. Putting my fingers under each of them, I only detected heat coming from beneath one. It was my best bet for the one most lived-in. But how to get in? A thorough search of the landing found a key under a loose floorboard, which—to my relief— unlocked the door.

Luck. Pure luck.

The room was small. A hearth, table and chairs, and a sofa was its make up, but it was cluttered and carried that undefinable odor that was decidedly masculine and only slightly pleasant. A black cat watched me from its perch in the corner. Maps and piles of letters littered the table and floor. I sifted through the ones on the table first, keeping a wary eye trained on the cat.

The maps were different districts of London and bore pencil scratches. Someone was staying up to date on the ever-evolving city. After seeing that every letter was either from Mrs. Kelly or one of her sisters, I moved on.

I explored the two closets with beds, but they were mostly bare. Just mattresses, blankets, and a few other necessary items like cufflinks, combs, and wastebaskets. And a mysterious coin collection under one of the mattresses.

When I emerged, I huffed, placing my hands on my hips. Other than the suspicious nature of the residence, I could find nothing incriminating. Nothing useful at all. A wink of metal underneath the cat caught my eye. It was half hidden, but I had no trouble recognizing it, having seen it many times before. Just never without its officer.

"Hello, you," I said, petting the cat. I tried to nudge her off gently, but she only blinked, unimpressed. "Ah. I can see you're not fooled by strange ladies trying to trick you out of your rightful possessions. Such a spirit deserves a good name. How about ... Alice?" She meowed her agreement and arched into my touch, finally freeing the slant gun. "On a completely unrelated note, you don't mind if I take a look at this, do you?" After giving her one last, loving scratch, I picked up the gun, slowly straightening as I turned it over in my hands, flicking the glass to make sure it was real.

It was, and I smiled. Slant guns were expensive, and private ownership was illegal.

*Gotcha.*

Light scuffling echoed from the stairwell, making me start and instinctively reach for my magic. I altered my features to look like the street urchin as I glanced around, cursing Mrs. Kelly who had either lied or didn't know her son as well as she claimed. I'd had enough sense to return the key under the floorboard before coming in—and to lock the door behind me—but once Mr. Gardner or Mr. Kelly stepped inside, I was trapped.

Tucking myself under the table, I took a deep breath, trying to quiet my breathing. A crocheted tablecloth covered most of me, but if someone were to look closely, they might see my blinking eyes. I made myself smaller—only just noticing that I still held the slant gun in my hands.

Too late to put it back.

A pair of boots stepped inside and shut the door with one heel. Holding my breath, I followed those boots up toned legs, a muddy trench coat, and a hand that raked through thick, brown hair. Mr. Kelly.

His brown eyes cut to the table, and I almost gasped, but he only shrugged out of his boots and tossed them onto the crocheted tablecloth, dirtying what I suspected was a gift from his mother. Each thud made me flinch.

Walking to one corner, he cranked his neck and loosened his thin, stand-up tie, the movement so *male* it reminded me of the power rippling through his forearm as he pinned me in the alleyway. When he angled toward me and I got my first real glimpse of his face, I shuddered.

Pinched mouth, a thoughtful gaze that lingered too long on nothing. I didn't know what that stare meant, but whatever it was, it looked positively *guilty*. The handle of the slant gun grew heavier in my palm.

He rubbed behind Alice's ears then turned away, reaching inside his coat. I gently lifted the tablecloth, aimed the slant gun at Mr. Kelly, counted to three, and pulled the trigger. The gun whirred softly, startling me into almost dropping it. They made *noise?* Mr. Kelly's back stiffened as he finished pulling something from his coat and set it down. Was that ... *a lit lantern?* Through the gun's lens, a dusting of neon blue particles coated his fingers.

I gasped. He was slanted. Wherever he'd come from, he'd been using magic.

The table upended and crashed to the floor, making me drop the gun and dive for the cover of the sofa. I hopped to my feet, and when I did, Mr. Kelly was waiting.

"You," he said on the other side, jaw working in anger.

I liked to think of myself as being gutsier than most, but in that moment, under Mr. Kelly's snapping gaze, I felt myself turn every shade of yellow.

The knuckles at his right side curled into a fist. "I told you to stay out of trouble."

"Don't be offended—you're not the first person I've ignored."

He darted to the left and I did the reverse, keeping the couch between us because heaven knew it was the only thing sparing my life. "So, you followed me?" he bit out. "You're here to steal back what I took from you? Or *more*? When is it going to be enough, Emerson?"

Who the devil was Emer—ah. Right, it was me.

And because I was a suicidal idiot who never turned down a ready explanation for my unpremeditated actions, I said, "Never."

I could feel my magic sapping. I had to get out and quickly.

Mr. Kelly feinted right then doubled back, arms reaching for me. I twisted away, toward the door. I was only a few steps from freedom. He kicked a chair. It skidded into my path, cutting off my advance. I only had a second to retreat behind the sofa before he was there, glaring me down again.

"Going somewhere?" he asked.

"Yes—back to the tables, so some *other* cretin can stick his nose into my business and boss me around for a change."

Like a bolt of lightning, he launched himself over the sofa. He tackled me to the floor and pinned my wrists before I could react. I yelped as my head knocked against the wood at the same moment my magic petered out, face relaxing back into its normal shape. I was in too much pain to care.

This idiot. This lumbering oaf had cracked my *skull*—

I moaned. I squeezed my eyes shut at the throbbing pulse at the back of my head. He was like a cobra—too fast, too lethal. Rocking my face I groaned, "Are you always so *aggressive*? I was just a boy! George's crypt, you're heavy—can't get a—decent—breath." I moaned again, which may have been milking a dry udder, but I didn't care. I was still traumatized.

When I finally opened my eyes, Mr. Kelly was staring at my face, frozen except his lips which parted on the slowest inhale. Then he huffed it out, right in my face, eyes widening in such abject horror I might've laughed if he wasn't so blasted *heavy*.

Though, he smelled surprisingly nice. For a criminal.

Voice soft, he said, "Y- ... Y-You ..." His gaze flashed down my face.

I was already neck deep in manure; might as well take the plunge. "Listen, I'm sorry for breaking in. Most indecent of me, I grant you. But I risked a lot to gamble for that money, so you can see why I would be upset when you took it."

His expression didn't change an inch. "... Y-You ..."

"I'm sure you've recognized me by now." Though he was still gripping my wrists, they were close enough to my head that I was able to remove my cap and shake out my strawberry-blonde curls. "I'm Miss Morgan. You met me at Lady Faline's concert? Yes, I've been posing as a street urchin when it suits me, but I saw you through that slant gun just now, so I'd remember that before you go tattling to a blueduster."

The man on top of me was completely different from the one who'd wrestled me to the ground. Sure, finding out that the boy beneath you was actually a woman was a shock, but not enough to render you speechless. I wasn't *that* beautiful.

"B-B ... But ... you're ..." His throat did a strange bobbing thing, a tiny whine eking out that didn't suit him at all. "... You're ...," he tried again. "... You're ... a ..."

I nodded, eyes wide with sarcasm. "A girl. Yes. Very astute, Mr. Kelly. I am a girl. And I was a girl that morning in the alleyway when you reached your hand down the front of my coat. Remember that? That was a fun morning."

His hands on my wrists tightened, face now flaming red. He looked like he wanted to die. "M-Miss ..."

"Miss Emmeline Morgan. The one you are currently crushing under your behemoth weight."

He swallowed, every vowel droning like it pained him. "And —you're—a ..."

Now *I* wanted to die. I hit my head against the floor again—intentionally this time. "Do you always have trouble finishing very *uncomplicated* sentences? Don't answer that." I shoved at him.

I needn't have bothered because Mr. Kelly jerked away and scrambled back, his eyes pasted to me as I gingerly sat up and stood. It reminded me of the way I watched a spider while waiting for Clarence to come squish it for me. Like the slightest movement from the furry creature would send me jumping for the nearest chair.

What an odd, scary man. Who seemed to suddenly be scared of *me*.

I looked him up and down, rubbing my wrists. "Are you all right?"

His mouth opened and closed. Twice. Three times.

I put my hands on my hips. "I don't speak fish, Mr. Kelly. I said, are you all right?"

Breathing heavily through his nose, he stared at me for another lengthy pause before finally giving a tiny nod. His face contorted like he was swallowing back bile. Maybe it was something he ate.

Or maybe I just had that kind of effect on people.

"I am sorry to shock you, but as you have pinned me with your weight twice now, I think we are even. Now, as pleasant as this has been, I really must be going—" Not wanting to be around when Mr. Gardner returned, I made for the door.

Mr. Kelly shot up and stepped in front of me, face pale and chest heaving. He looked dreadful. "Stop ..."

I halted and blinked at him.

He grimaced. I couldn't imagine the kind of pain he must be in to be pulling such faces. What on earth? "You ..." He inhaled. "Can't ..."

"Can't what?" I inched backwards.

Tiny grunts escaped his lips, sweat beading his forehead. He ripped his eyes away, and that seemed to help a bit because this time he managed three words in a row. "You can't leave ..." He licked his lips. Another grunt. "Until ..."

I sidestepped him and his arm shot out to stop me, dropping away when my waist brushed against it. I took another step, and his arm shot out again. Frustrated with this dance, I clamped a hand over his forearm, making him hiss and fall back against the doorframe. "You have very strong muscles, Mr. Kelly." I moved my hand up to his bicep. His eyes widened as he jerked to the side, tripping over the legs of a coat stand and falling to the floor. Confusion pulled at my face as I smiled at his frame, positioned like a crab. "What a shame you have suddenly forgotten how to use them."

I marched through the door. The sturdiness of the stairs was questionable, but I pounded down them as fast as I could, breaking into a run by the time I reached the ground level. I didn't look back for three blocks, on the odd chance he'd come to his senses and chase after me.

I navigated home, keeping my head down since my features were feminine again, but my thoughts raced.

Mr. Kelly had been using magic. Right before returning to his secret lair. At least I'd had the cover story of wanting my money back, because I doubted I would've gotten away so easily otherwise. Although ...

Perhaps I would've. That whole encounter after he discovered I was a woman had been strange. *He* had been strange. Mr. Kelly may just be the strangest man alive.

But one thing was for certain: Mr. Gardner (and Mr. Kelly by extension) were definitely *not* who they said they were.

# 37

## Dorothy

I floated weightlessly underwater. Cold pressure kissed my skin. Far above, someone's muffled voice called to me from the surface where a gray light rippled. I didn't want to come up. I wanted to sleep. So, I drifted down, down ...

A hand clamped around my arm and yanked. I gasped awake to see the black top of a carriage and someone gently slapping my cheek. No water remained in my lungs, but I coughed anyway, trying to sit up.

"Easy there, Miss St. James," a masculine voice said. "You've had a rough go."

I glanced around the swaying carriage; the darkening gray buildings meant we were deep in the city. My soaking dress had practically frozen to my form. At some point, I must've drifted to the muddy bank of the river, because dirt crusted my face.

I hadn't died.

Then it hit me all at once: the drinking game with Polina, finding my third clue, jumping from the train. And the party! I jerked toward the only other passenger in the carriage to ask him the time and stopped short.

Mr. Brass's teardrop scar was even deeper than I remembered, and it made his right eye look like it was glowing. "Don't be alarmed. I heard a scream and a splash, and when I looked over the rail, you can imagine my surprise at finding a young woman floating toward the bank."

My hand fisted my dress until my knuckles turned white. I shrank back. The sleeping drug was still potent in my system, his face going in and out of focus, and yet I felt wide awake. Who knew how long I'd been unconscious in a carriage with the man who'd threatened my father. He'd *touched* me. I wouldn't put myself at his mercy again.

*Keep calm. Keep calm.*

"I recognized you immediately—from Mr. Vernon's dinners, of course. Your father and I have a lot of history."

*The Rook, the Rook, the Rook.*

"If I may ask, what were you doing in the Thames?"

"I fell," I blurted quietly. Admitting I jumped would look suicidal. "I was walking along the bridge, and I fell."

Slowly, he sat back and nodded, but his expression still had questions. "Well. I've instructed my coachman to take us to your house. I believe we're nearly there."

I could practically feel a black feather scratching its way up my sternum before driving into my throat. "What were you doing near the rail line?" *Near me.* I didn't know where the sudden burst of courage came from.

Mr. Brass's forehead wrinkled. "I was retrieving a shipment. For my factory." Then he blinked at me. "I am sorry, Miss St. James."

A trapdoor opened beneath my stomach and my hands went cold. "For what?" Even I heard the accusation in my tone.

He studied me a long moment, and as the shadows of his scar darkened an all-too-familiar chill crawled through my blood.

Magic. The shadows scattered and the short space between us glowed so subtly brighter than the light outside. *Shadows.*

He offered me a mollifying smile. "For startling you."

I pressed my back flush against the curtained carriage window. Anger warmed me, but I pushed it down, along with my fears. I still had no proof Brass was the Rook, and even if I did, he'd overpower me in seconds if I tried to act on it.

I needed the Samaritan. Which meant I had somewhere to be. "Do you have the time, by chance?"

"Half past six," he answered without consulting a watch.

My palm flattened over my stomach, mouth drying in both relief and foreboding. I didn't know how it was possible, but if the maids drew a cold bath, I could be bathed and dressed in an hour —just in time for Mr. Joule's viewing party. I'd be sure to grab Ashley's note I'd stolen for blackmail, in case he planned on collecting my guess tonight.

And he would, of course he would.

The carriage rumbled to a stop, and I dashed out before Mr. Brass had a chance to open it for me. He poked his head out as I took the front steps. "Give your father my best. I always liked the man." The carriage jolted forward, eventually disappearing around the bend.

I shook off my goosebumps and turned to head into the house —before freezing with my hand on the doorknob.

He had said *liked.*

# 38

## Ashley

Hands in pockets, I stared at the painting, depicting a woman in her nightdress staring out a rain-speckled window. Brown hair cascaded down her back, one lock curling over a hint of shoulder. Her face was turned away, but the light hit her cheekbone, illuminating wet lashes and a tear that nearly blended in with the window behind her. Shades of blue and gray streaked the shadows.

The painting was more depressing than Joule's usual style, but something about it made me unable to look away. I felt like I'd seen it before, even though I knew for certain I hadn't. Though I'd only dared enter it twice, I realized the painting reminded me of Dorothy's mind. Or rather, what it would look like if it were ever broken.

I'd encountered that a time or two with my second slant, and it was an unearthly, melancholy thing to behold. Someone stuck inside. Living within their memories.

Joule clapped me on the back, the crevices in his face deeper than usual. "Well, my friend, I see you found my favorite one."

I knocked my chin at the painting. "I didn't know you could paint like this."

"You doubt my abilities?"

"Never. Or I wouldn't use you."

He chuckled and I cut a bitter smile, but it was true. A trickle of guilt slid into my belly, prompting me to say, "Thank you, by the way." He'd helped me in the carnival, too, and though he never said why, I didn't think it was only because he and Bram had been shipmates in the Royal Navy.

He shrugged. "It matters little to me who is invited to see my paintings, as long as it is exclusive enough to evoke jealousy around the *ton*."

"You can be assured of that." I glanced around, seeing that the first of the guests were arriving. I'd convinced Joule to host the party at his home which was narrow and wood paneled, a maze displaying the four dozen paintings he'd been stockpiling over the last three years. His collection ranged from a tapestry embroidered with flocks of geese, to leather binding embossed with an intricate labyrinth, to a china teacup so fine a forceful breath would chip the rim—all of it *à la mode*. Clocks decorated every inch of the walls and shelves—his newest obsession.

It was an excellent place to get lost; a public setting where one could still have a private conversation. Joule moved on, mingling with the newcomers and leaving me alone again with my thoughts.

For the thirty-seventh time in the last few hours—prompted by absolutely nothing—my awareness shifted to my cheek. I could still feel it tingling from the press of her lips, the soft graze of her eyelashes. I hadn't dared touch it. Maybe I was scared that touching it would wipe away whatever magic had prompted her to kiss me in the first place.

But ...

Even though I couldn't control the pull, I could always sense it, and there *hadn't* been any magic with Dorothy. At least not mine.

My ribs caved in. Maybe that scared me most of all. The hope.

Stuffing my hands deeper in my pockets, I rolled my shoulders back and turned away from the painting, annoyed at the constant rut of my thoughts and the way I'd done nothing in the last few hours but relive that moment and think about ...

About her.

The way her eyes scintillated when rising to a challenge. Her soft, curly hair and rosy lips. Her courage when facing down an impossible choice.

Mr. Joule's guest list had been carefully curated to include men who fit the clues. It would keep her running in circles until the end of the night when I would collect her third guess.

And she would guess incorrectly.

But the guest list had been prepared only as a precaution, due to the sense of honor Bram had drilled into me; a respect for winning the game by wits alone.

Dorothy shouldn't have noticed my marking on the newspaper. She shouldn't have managed to outbid me for the watch. There was no way she'd made it to the train in time—or if she *had,* she was nearly to Brighton by now and would disembark to find a coachman waiting to bring her back to London.

Any way you cut the deck, I won. Exactly how I needed it.

And even though it gutted me, the girl in the painting would stay trapped at the window, because that was just the rotten hand she'd been dealt.

An hour later, most of the guests had congregated in the parlor where sparkling iced oranges and jelly meringues coated in cream cheese sat on the sideboard, but I remained on the landing of the thick, wooden staircase to keep an inconspicuous eye on the front door below.

I didn't know why I was here. She wasn't coming.

My gaze drifted to the door again, and—

My heart stopped. There she was.

Mr. Morgan, his wife, and his daughter filed through the door and checked their coats with the butler. Not far behind them trailed a girl with gray-blue eyes. Her hair looked damp, and her face looked alive as she handed the man her coat, revealing a beautiful forest green dress that was utterly irrelevant because *there she was.*

Bloody silt. She'd done it. She'd jumped from Victoria Bridge —I knew it in my bones. Because that was what *I* would've done. Never in a hundred years had I thought she'd actually work up the guts to do it.

I expected to feel surprised at the sight of her. Even angry.

Instead, a crushing swell of pride overwhelmed my senses, tainted with enough possessiveness to make warning bells ring in the back of my mind. Because you could only be proud of something that was yours to claim, and Dorothy St. James was not.

*Not yours. Never yours.*

But there she stood as if she were.

Her eyes landed on me and my magic tugged me toward her. I planted my feet and gripped the banister with both hands. Her family headed for the stairs, chatting about working their way from the top down. They passed me by with a hasty greeting, but Dorothy stopped.

Shaking her head, she sighed and said, "I hate you." The tiniest smile curled the edge of her lips.

Something panged inside my chest, making it hard to breathe, and I couldn't help but ask myself why I was putting myself through this torture. I inhaled through my nose, catching that French garden scent and feeling dress laces on my fingertips, making that ache flare to a roar. My throat hit a lump as I stared at her. No note from Tanner could ever be worth ... this.

And it was my own bloody fault.

"So do I," I muttered.

She swept past me up the stairs, refocusing on her mission and the reason she was here: to find the Samaritan. I watched her back, a hard knot of guilt sinking into the pit of my stomach that I would do absolutely nothing about.

He was here; I'd made sure of it. But she would never find him.

I'd made sure of that too.

# 39

## Dorothy

*He'll be at Mr. Joule's viewing party.*

I replayed those words over and over in my mind as I followed my uncle's lead. A clock on the wall to my right chimed the hour, and a split second later the house shook with sounds ranging from fairy tinkles to deep gongs.

Though there were more women present, I only had eyes for the black evening wear as I scoured for the Samaritan. Mr. Riley was absent, but that no longer surprised me. I grimaced. I had to fetch my father's prototype gun from him tomorrow.

Of the men I didn't recognize, I set to work getting introductions through Aunt Marie, mentally reciting my three clues.

1. *He was an orphan*

That was an easy enough conversation piece. All one had to do was ask about their parents. *They are in good health,* or *They've passed on, I'm afraid.*

2. *He had a Greek tattoo*

This clue was harder. Tattoos were easy to hide—but I suspected more and more that if Ashley had seen it from working with this man, it was in a place that I could view it too. I'd just have to keep my eyes wide open. And—

3. *He was here tonight*

This was the greatest clue of all. I wanted to be thorough, so I discounted no one immediately. I asked how long they'd been in London. Whether they resided here. If they were married. I sped-walked through the winding house to make sure I hadn't missed anyone, finally narrowing it down to five strong candidates.

It came down to the tattoos. Asking someone if they had one was untactful, but I also wasn't above it.

An hour later, everyone migrated toward the parlor, where the mysterious Mr. Joule was to speak about the inspiration behind his paintings. I stopped outside the brimming room to study a painting I hadn't noticed before. It depicted an old woman sitting on a chaise, cane in hand, but her face had been replaced with the roman numerals of a clock.

"Hideous, isn't it?"

I turned to see brown hair and an eager gaze that I'd all but forgotten. Nicholas Hart smiled at me. "It is ... interesting," I finally said.

He knocked his head at the painting. "Can you imagine the ticking pounding in your mind? I pity the old bird. Must be horrible."

I scrutinized the woman again, only now she didn't feel like a stranger. "It is," I said quietly. The constant worry over father had definitely taken a toll. I gestured to the house around me. "Why the clocks?"

He chuckled, flashing white teeth. "Mr. Joule lives for what is fashionable, and right now he has deemed it is clocks. His obsessions rarely last more than a fortnight, and if I were you" —he leaned in and lowered his voice— "I'd be grateful I wasn't here during his English mastiff phase." He cocked one dark brow, and I mirrored his growing smile. "Bodies underfoot," he whispered, gesturing down his suit. "Slipped on the saliva. And fur. Everywhere."

I swallowed my laugh. Mr. Joule certainly sounded like an interesting character—but I found myself noticing Mr. Hart instead and his strong arms. He'd mentioned he was a journalist ...

What if Mr. Hart was the Samaritan?

My stomach fluttered, then sank. At the ballet, he'd mentioned that his father and mother both loved the theater. Just to make sure I wasn't misremembering, I asked, "How are your parents, Mr. Hart?"

He clucked his tongue and glanced around. "My Father is around here somewhere. Mother dearly wished to come but has been under the weather recently."

I nodded. "I am sorry to hear that." And not because of his mother's health, shamefully enough.

"Friends!" someone called from the parlor, quieting the chatter. A small man with a checkered waistcoat stood atop a chair near the fireplace. Gold flecks dusted his hair and triangular manacles hung on the tips of his black necktie, giving the effect of a zooming minute hand when he brought one to his eye. "Thank you, dear duplicitous patrons, for coming to see my latest work. From the subjects to mediums, it is all, I assure you, at the *peak* of fashion."

Even dressed so drastically different, I recognized that intense stare. Mr. Joule was the artist from the carnival who'd traded me the train painting for my father's pocket watch. Apparently, I'd caught him at the beginning of his "clock phase"—or had perhaps been the catalyst.

Of course Ashley knew him. Why was I still surprised?

Ten minutes into Mr. Joule's speech, I noticed Mr. Brass tucked in the corner against the window, raising a glass of sherry to his lips that obstructed his scar. My pulse jumped—until my gaze magnetized to the dark green marking on his wrist, just visible underneath the cuff riding up his arm. An O cut in half vertically, or ...

Phi.

The twenty-first letter in the Grecian alphabet.

My insides reeled, and I had to force myself to drag in a breath. Mr. Brass was slanted; he'd used it in the carriage. He had to be nearing forty, but he was strong. Most importantly, he was *here.*

*I always liked the man.*

*Liked.*

Maybe he knew that my father was missing—not because he was the Rook, but because he was the *Samaritan.*

Maybe his and Father's disagreement was why he hadn't rescued him yet—he was holding some kind of grudge.

Everything fit together perfectly. The only thing lacking was—

"Are Mr. Brass's parents living?" I whispered to Mr. Hart.

His gray eyes glanced over my shoulder. "They died nearly a decade ago."

Brass ticked all three boxes.

Mr. Joule concluded his speech to the sound of polite clapping and the crowd dispersed to find new paintings, including Mr. Hart, leaving me standing alone. I was so lost in my thoughts I didn't hear Mr. Joule approach.

"Miss St. James," he said, heels clacking when he came to a stop, "I hear from your cousin you are something of an artist yourself." I met his too-wide stare, in awe at his transformation from the carnival. And though he made no mention of our initial meeting, I could tell by the twinkle in his eye he knew exactly who I was.

Emme knew I had no skill with the brush, so in their conversation Mr. Joule had probably missed her ironic tone.

"I am not, unfortunately—though I would like to be."

Mr. Joule offered his arm. "Perhaps you would like to see my studio, then? I'm sure something up there will inspire you."

From his secretive smile, I knew who waited for me up there. And he was right; I was sure it *would*. "I'd be delighted," I forced out, because I wasn't sure if I was ready to meet with Ashley yet.

I wasn't ready to fail.

Our arms linked, he led me up the stairs, beaming and nodding to the guests we passed. The gallery only extended to the second floor, but we traveled to the third, entering a large, dark room that domed like a tunnel and held the chemical smell of paint. Masterpieces draped in white sheets leaned against the walls while others sat on easels near tubes, brushes, and color-speckled tables. Covering the entire far wall was a semi-circle window that overlooked zigzagging rooftops and a star-crusted sky.

Mr. Joule placed a board and a white sheet of paper on an easel near the gigantic window spilling bright moonlight. "This is my favorite place to paint. Looking out on the world always helps me when I'm trying to ..." He paused, hand motioning like he was looking for the right word. "*See*."

Seeing was exactly what I needed right now.

"Draw. Feel." He closed my fist around a pencil. "I will fetch you when your family is ready to leave." Then he left.

I stared at the pencil in my hand. It had been so long since I'd sketched anything; before Father had been kidnapped at least. But I knew exactly what I wanted to draw.

Using light lines that grew darker and bolder as the minutes passed, I stroked the paper with the graphite, forming each limb with care, shading and erasing. I tweaked and tweaked, trying to perfect the shapes. It wasn't good by any stretch of the imagination, but it was the best I'd ever done.

The air shifted when he entered the room. Or maybe he'd been here the whole time, watching me, and only now chose to make his presence known. "What are you drawing?" His voice sounded even deeper than usual. Tired.

I straightened and stepped back, examining my work. A father sat next to his little girl with a clay pipe to his mouth, blowing a soap bubble the size of her head as she stared up at him in wonder.

"This was the moment," I said. I waited a few beats, and when Ashley didn't respond, I went on. "I wanted to know why it worked. Why bubbles were spheres. Why they were clear but had rainbows inside them. It seemed impossible, but Father had a ready explanation for everything. The hydrophobic ends of molecules crowding to the surface, glycerin weakening the hydrogen bonds. I became fascinated with the unknown, realizing that the answers to all our questions were sitting there, just waiting for someone to come along and uncover them." I thumbed over my father's face, smudging the shading I'd done. "This was the moment I knew I wanted to be the one to do it. The impossible. So I could be like him."

Glancing over, I found Ashley emerging from the shadows. He'd lost his dinner jacket, wearing only a white dress shirt and a bow tie that had been loosened like he'd thought about taking it off. It was the first time I'd seen him wear anything but black. "My father wants to understand how magic works—because once you understand something, you can use it for good. He has such a good heart." My eyes closed against the stinging in my chest.

Ashley was quiet a long moment as he studied my sketch. Me. "If it hurts so much, why draw it?"

"Because I want to remember." My answer was immediate but not premeditated. It just flew out of me from where it had been living, dormant. "Because I want you to see what I stand to lose."

His throat bobbed, eyes soft. "I do."

Ashley's gaze brushed my drawing, then my dirty fingers still holding the pencil, and finally my face. Lingering there. His expression was so strange—the same one he'd worn after I kissed his cheek.

When I couldn't withstand the burn any longer, I murmured, "What?"

"You sketched your father and that moment. Now I'm sketching you. And this one."

*What I stand to lose.*

My heart pounded. I breathed a watery laugh. "Without a paper and pencil?"

But he didn't laugh back. His full lips set in a formal line, his eyes turning as distant and shimmery as the stars outside. "I don't need them. I'll remember."

Something sparked in my belly.

He walked to the window and, stuffing his hands in his pockets, looked out on the smokestacks. "Remembering ... it is not the prize you think it is." He shrugged. "I wish to forget it all. The faces, the pain."

"Of what?" I asked softly.

"Everything." He shook his head. "*Anything.* The nine blasts of a pistol; bodies writhing; the smell of your mother's burning flesh filling your nostrils until the smoke ekes into your soul, and you'll keep on living, but you'll never breathe again. Ice cutting into your feet, leaving a miles-long bloody trail as you run. And run. And never stop running. It's hard to live a life that should've been forgotten. It is far better to have never lived at all."

My heart gave a mournful twist, my insides watering with compassion. I couldn't even fathom such a past. But he was wrong. Utterly wrong. I moved toward him, the coolness of the window bleeding into my arm. "'Ignorance is bliss' is something that only the very ignorant say."

"No." He gave a humorless laugh. "Those ... *those* are the ones whose eyes have been opened to something truly terrible. And the bell tolls in the tower and the creatures of the night sniff you out, but everyone else is still asleep." His mouth cut a bitter slash. "Warm in their beds. And it is only because you are awake that you are being hunted at all."

Finally, he looked at me, and the starlight danced on one side of his face like it, too, was desperate to touch him. "Ignorance *is* bliss. Because once your eyes have been opened to the terrible monster, it becomes your duty to slay him."

"Who is your monster?" I asked quietly.

He pulled in a breath. Pulled it out. Pulled one in. "Me," he breathed.

I gripped his sleeve. "It doesn't have to be this way. You could *help* me—"

He stepped back, out of my reach. "You still don't understand. If your father knew what you were chasing, he would *beg* you to leave it alone."

I blinked away the sting in my eyes, not wanting to acknowledge he was right.

"Many more than just him will be lost if you continue down this road. I warned you I would try to stop you. Am I cruel, then, for keeping my word?"

He was right that I didn't understand. "How will they be lost? What exactly is the threat?"

Moments passed in silence before Ashley's features hardened, just a little. He wouldn't tell me. "Did you bring my note?"

A painful heaviness settled in my heart, caught between frustration and sympathy and the way I ached to touch him. But finally, I set it aside. This was it. The running, the puzzles, the ballet, the carnival, the Necropolis, the auction, the train—all of it had been leading up to this moment.

Ashley fished his ring from within his coat and slowly put it on his finger. Once there, he paused.

I wasn't ready.

I nodded anyway.

"Give me your final guess for the Samaritan, Miss St. James."

From the corner of my eye, a star streaked down the velvet sky, and I snatched it from the air with my inhale, clinging to it with digging fingernails and prickling eyes before breathing out my desperate wish.

*Please.*

*Please ... please ... please.*

"Mr. Brass." My voice shook only a little. It had to be him. There was no one else. "Mr. Brass is the Samaritan."

Ashley shifted toward me, only a palm's breadth between us. He frowned and took his time studying my face. He was always studying it. Perhaps trying to solve me, like Polina said. Perhaps something more. Raising the back of his hand to eye level he said, "He is not."

Three beats passed before I registered his words. My eyes snapped to the ring. Blue.

*No.*

The floorboards shook as hundreds of clocks tolled midnight. *Dong. Dong.*

"Now give me the note."

*Dong.*

*No ... no ... no.*

"Dolly."

*Dong.*

In the past week, I'd pushed myself past the breaking point. I'd barely slept. I'd taken risks and used my wits to solve every puzzle, but it had all been for—

Nothing.

My knees buckled, and I sank to the floor, fingers spreading on the wooden planks and pointing in all the directions my father could be; to all the empty avenues I'd run down. A tear hit my forefinger.

I couldn't save him. Nobody ever would.

*No,* I thought again, but I heard my voice tremble like I said it out loud. I didn't know how long I stayed there before Ashley cupped my chin and forced me to look at him. His jaw was set, the shadows and stars in his eyes making him ripple with power. I barely recognized this cold side of him, and it made me swallow.

"Give me the note, Dolly," he repeated softly.

Something about his gaze commanded my limbs to move, and the note appeared in my hands. After taking it, he rubbed the folded parchment beneath his thumb, eyebrows pulling in, but then slid it inside his coat pocket.

"Please," I said the second I saw it disappear. My last bargaining chip.

Ashley inhaled two long breaths from his nose. "I can't—"

"Please!" I grabbed his hand, not caring how pathetic it looked or how pathetic I felt. "Please give me one more chance. I have to find him!" A tear trailed down my cheek, and I swiped it away with my other hand. "I have to find him."

Ashley said nothing as he stared at me through the bottoms of his eyes, chin raised. He crouched to my level, and I drew his hand into my lap. I couldn't let go, because that meant letting go of my father. "One more," I said again. "Just one more chance. Please."

"Secrets are currency." His voice scraped a lower decibel. "The Samaritan's identity is the greatest secret in London, second only to the identity of the Rook. Your knowing it puts many lives at risk, so if you succeed, I need to know I can trust you. That level of trust ... requires a secret in return."

I shook my head. "I have no secrets."

His hand stirred beneath my own as he began to pull away. "Then I'm sorry—"

I clamped around it and pulled him back. "I'll tell you anything. I'll do *anything*."

He paused, looking between my eyes, debating something. "When I was at your home, there was a jewelry set encased in glass." My tongue ran dry as I realized where he was leading. "You said a bracelet never existed, and yet you fidgeted nervously, and your gaze traveled beyond my shoulder. You lied to me, and I want to know why. Why this bracelet is so important to you. Tell me where it is—*show* me that I can trust you—and I will grant your wish."

I'd promised my grandfather I'd never tell another soul. I hesitated ... but it couldn't be worth my father's life.

"I used to play with my grandmother's jewelry," I began, breathing the words. "She never minded—except when I would play with that set. She finally learned to hide it, but later, displayed it at my father's house. But it was missing the bracelet. Always. On his deathbed"—I squeezed Ashley's hand a little—"my grandfather told me where he'd hid it. He told no one else—not my grandmother, because she was too sentimental, nor my father, because he was too disorganized. He said he told me because ..." I shook my head, forcing myself to swallow down the prickle of shame. "Because I knew how to keep a secret."

I inhaled a quick, deep breath. "The statue of my grandfather. The bracelet is hidden inside it, in the very same hall."

Ashley's forehead slowly knotted. "Why only the bracelet?"

"I don't know. I swear I don't."

He looked between my eyes again, and after a long moment, gave a small nod. He believed me. The secret was sufficient. Ashley could trust me. He had to.

The room seemed darker now, the shadows muddying the angles of his face. "No more clues. If you want to use your guess, then you'll have to find me." His mouth set in a grim line, and he stood. "You have one more chance, Miss St. James. And I hope to the stars you waste it."

AFTER COMPOSING myself I sneaked back downstairs, past a massive, stopped clock that loomed like a terrible omen. I was too preoccupied with my whirlwind thoughts to notice Uncle's thunderous glare until we were alone in the foyer at home, Aunt Marie and Emmeline having already fled to bed.

"Dorothy, I will speak to you in my study."

That one pronoun halted me in my tracks and sent ice down my spine: *My.*

He pivoted and stalked down the hall. I followed, bone-tired but not seeing how I could refuse.

Uncle lit a candle. Then to my astonishment, he began selecting random books and tossing them onto the desk.

They thudded and I flinched, but I watched, anger mounting. Those were my father's.

On the fifth one, I couldn't stand it any longer. "What are you doing?"

"At the party, I received a telegram."

*Thud.*

"From the house at Brighton."

*Thud.*

"And your father" —he spun, holding a copy of the very first book Father had ever bought— "was not there." He threw it to the ground. The spine cracked.

So did my control.

"You have no right to treat his things—!"

"*His* things?" The candlelight flickered on Uncle's face, a demonic gleam entering his eye. He slid into a chair. "As of tonight, legally, this house and everything in it belongs to me."

For the second time tonight, my plans crumbled into dust. This was all wrong. This was all going so horribly *wrong*.

"He is missing," I blurted, grappled for something—anything — "And has been for over a week. But I am so close to finding him. I just need—"

"It is far too late for the *truth*." He held a book over the candle until fire licked the pages.

"What are you doing!" I shot forward, but Uncle stood and lifted the book out of reach, then tossed it into the hearth behind him, where it consumed itself and shriveled. Horrified tears prickled my eyes, flashes of research going up in flames playing in my mind.

"How *dare* you!" I screeched.

"Unless you'd like to see the whole library burn, you will hold your tongue!"

My body shook with rage. And fear. Because I knew he would do it.

After a beat of silence, Uncle rested a loving hand on my shoulder, and I wanted to scream.

"With your father's death, society will have certain expectations. You will observe mourning and not step one foot out of this house for a full month. Think of your soul, Dorothy—how easily you rebuke an elder. You obviously need time to grieve. In private. I do this for your well-being."

Tears flowed down my cheek. I'd cried more tonight than I had since my father disappeared.

"And ..." Uncle leaned in, his soft voice washing over me. "One more lie, one more toe out of line, and I will burn every one of his books. I will break everything in that blasted lab. I will sell every one of his possessions and see to it your every memory of him is scrubbed away."

Uncle eyed Father's study—his study, now—with a twisted smile on his lips. "That is, after all, all that is left of him." He brushed past me and out the door.

I crumbled to the floor and sobbed.

# 40

## Dorothy

Today was cloudy. I sat by my bedroom window, heart steady, blinking slowly at the hours slipping away. Gentlemen tipped their hats. A stray dog licked from a puddle and darted around a corner.

I remember passing afternoons like this. Noting the weather. Counting raindrops. Living at the window and watching the world tilt by. After the past week, that slow, lonely existence felt like a lifetime ago.

Like a river mill, my mind churned, replaying the events of last night.

Maybe Brass was the Rook after all, but without the Samaritan or the prototype gun I'd lost, I had no way of tracking him down. And if I left this house, Uncle would take *everything*. Father's books. His glasses. His smoking jacket that still smelled like him.

Was I willing to sacrifice all those memories on the slimmest chance?

Now I was again trapped in my house, but unlike a week ago

...

Now I didn't *want* to be.

I dug the heel of my palms into my eyes. It was all my fault. I should've taken risks from the beginning; maybe then I would've solved this puzzle in time. But it all felt so—so—

*Impossible.*

"A man is here to see you."

I glanced up to find my uncle's ominous form filling the doorway. Just then, I couldn't remember a single man I was acquainted with. *You'll have to find me.* Now that our deal was concluded, Ashley had no reason to seek me out, so I snuffed the flicker of hope before it could burn any hotter.

Uncle added, "He is in the morning room. Don't embarrass me," before turning on his heel and disappearing.

True to its name, the morning room faced east, but where it normally glistened in sunlight, a dull paleness coated the furnishings on this rainy day. Nicholas Hart paced the rug—but it was thoughtful, not the frantic stride of a desperate man. When he saw me, he halted. "Please, have a seat." He gestured to the chair in front of him like this was his home and not mine.

*Uncle's.*

I frowned but complied. Every time I'd seen him before, he'd been relaxed. Personable and amiable. Now, his posture was rigid, and he sounded like he was conducting a business transaction.

"To begin, you should know I have sound-proofed this room for discretionary purposes."

Sound-proofed ... Did that mean he'd used magic? Hands suddenly slick, I wiped them down the lap of my dress.

He clasped his hands behind his back. "I do not have the skill of subtlety—nor the luxury of time, for that matter—so I shall get right to the point. I am part of the Lightfoot Agency for the Crown, a division of secret agents that carry out covert investigations, especially those involving magic. For the last several months, my objective has been caught up in a tango with the phantom colloquially referred to as the Rook. I understand you may have some information for me."

My lips parted. Those were a lot of confusing sentences crammed closely together. I'd never heard of this agency, though I'd suspected the government had covert operations. At last, I managed, "H-How did you know—?"

Mr. Hart shrugged. "I have been tracking him for the last week."

"And you know how he manages to elude the law?"

"I was referring to your father."

My spine snapped up. "I don't understand—how could you know he was missing? I've told no one." Could Uncle have spread the information so quickly?

"The case you presented to Scotland Yard was never closed. It has merely been working up the chain of command. It's a natural process for high-priority cases."

A ball of dread sank into my gut as I asked my next question, already fearing I knew the answer. "And why would my father be a high priority?"

"Because he was one of us."

The room spun, and I rubbed my forehead. Ten full seconds passed before I could formulate any words. "My father worked for the Crown?" Him? The man who could never find his spectacles and accidentally set his research aflame?

Mr. Hart nodded. "The slant guns he invented are undeniably ingenious."

My breath tightened, something hot flaring in my chest. Slant guns? The invention that had sent hundreds—thousands—of people to their deaths. The reason I'd cowered inside for two years, afraid of my own shadow.

"I work alone and deal more with logistics," Mr. Hart went on. "On-the-ground action. Your father was carrying out critical research into magical properties, under the Crown's direction—a feat which would've been impossible, as he isn't slanted, if not for someone *else* lending him their magic to study."

He gave me a knowing look, and my stomach dropped again. Me.

I felt sick. I'd assumed his research was for a good cause—helping people, our country—but what if it was just to give the government a tighter fist? So that more people could hang. More people like me.

He'd lied to me. My hands whitened from gripping my chair, chest tight. He'd let me think it was all purely a pursuit of knowledge. He'd *used* me. My magic. For years.

My entire childhood.

"In fact," Mr. Hart continued, "your father was very close to making an astounding discovery when he was taken—so close that we believe the two events to be linked."

Just like the note in the factory had said. "The Rook wanted his research?"

Mr. Hart nodded. "For what, one can only speculate. Whatever it is, it isn't good."

Pain in my throat, I gnawed my lip, head still spinning. "What about Sullivan Brass? He conversed with my father the night of his disappearance. Perhaps he is the Rook."

Before I'd finished, Mr. Hart was already shaking his head. "Brass works for us. He was tasked with collecting the research to forward to the Queen's officials—he'd been your father's go-between for many years—but Geoffrey claimed it was accidentally destroyed. The same night he was kidnapped, strangely enough."

That was what they'd been arguing about.

*I made that deal before I knew the science,* Father had said. *And look how it's been used. Against my own family! I won't do it again.*

Because of the slant guns.

"So you have found no trace of him—my father?"

"I'm looking into a promising lead as we speak and will send a message if anything turns up. I would much rather discuss *you*."

I blinked, eyes darting to Mr. Hart's waist but detected no slant gun or handcuffs. "What about me?"

Folding his arms across his chest, he said, "The Rook was stealing precious items long before he began kidnapping. These are powerful, magical objects the government has a vested interest in. We find the Rook, we expose his operation, retrieve the objects, and best of all ... no more kidnappings."

Prompted by my confused expression, Nicholas Hart stepped toward me. "We know of your abilities, which we believe would make you an invaluable spy."

"How do you know what my magic is?"

"We don't just employ factory owners—ballerinas too."

I shook my head, dumbfounded. *Polina?* A Lightfoot agent? I thought I'd outsmarted her, but she'd been working me the whole time. My head pounded.

"And," he added, "if all goes according to plan, you'd aid us in avenging your father."

Every one of my muscles locked up. Even if he'd lied to me, he was still my father. "He does not need to be avenged—he is alive—"

"Of course." He held up a hand, an apology crawling over his face. "That was distastefully put. What I meant to say is, we know what you can do, Miss St. James—and that it is a powerful gift. With some training, we could expand it; teach you to control it. And in helping you, you would help us in return."

This was the first time I'd ever heard of someone expanding their slanted abilities, but I latched onto the last sentence instead. "By helping you capture the Rook."

He nodded.

What I'd told Ashley in the factory had been true. It was one thing to make a scientific discovery that would lead to the Rook's capture; that was cause and effect. Impersonal. It was another matter to be the one actively pursuing him. Close to the action.

I didn't want revenge.

But what if this was how I found him? The Lightfoots had leads, resources; maybe this was the answer I'd been searching for all along.

Mr. Hart stepped toward me, hands outstretched. "I realize this is a lot to take in. You'd be highly compensated for your services and granted full slanting rights—no questions asked. No more being forced to remain inside."

My gaze shot to his, and I could tell he knew much more about me than he was letting on.

"But this occupation is dangerous, and you'd need to go in with your eyes wide open." His stare grew earnest, his voice grave. "You must understand, once you're in, to leave is to commit treason. I'll give you three days to consider. I would strongly urge you not to make this decision lightly."

After plucking something from his coat jacket he held it out to me—a dark-blue business card embossed with an address in gold letters. Then he left.

I angled the card down until the gold winked in the morning light. As angry as I was at the Rook for kidnapping my father, my heart wasn't in making him pay.

Even with his deceit and secrets, I just ... A tear dripped onto the blue card, and I closed my eyes against the stabbing pain in my center.

I just wanted my father back.

# 41

## The Rook

Despite the complication of the latch he was picking with a short hook, it clicked open after only a moment. He glanced around to ensure he hadn't been followed. The darkened fog coiled around him, licking smooth surfaces and smothering the streets into silence.

He slipped inside, onto the black-and-white checkered floor. Down the hall, a few candles flickered, casting a glow on the gothic arches that soared so tall they almost made him question his significance. That was what they were built to do, after all. He kept to the shadows as he passed pews and candelabras, golden statues and hanging banners. Not many had broken into West-minster Abbey.

Not many had needed to.

Opposite the nave, past the ninety-five statues of saints, lay Henry VII's chapel. A fan-vaulted ceiling curved the walls into a semi-circle. The night dulled the stained glass that surrounded the glorified tomb. He angled to the left, toward the memorial of Queen Elizabeth I who lay under a black-pillared stone canopy.

He took one look at the queen's likeness, the crown on her

head and ruff around her neck, before swinging up onto her stony midsection. On the ceiling of the canopy was a circle cut in the marble. He twisted it, meeting slight resistance before the circular stone scraped free, loosing age-old dust that almost made him cough.

The Rook felt around the hole he'd made in the canopy, but there were no more seams. Then he looked at the cylindrical stone in his hand, the top of which had been hollowed out like a bowl, obviously meant to hide something.

Empty.

Either someone had gotten here first, or he'd been given bad information. His senses kicked into a higher gear. Such things were never an accident.

A whisper of movement tugged at his ear and he paused. From under the canopy, he was concealed in shadows, so he wasn't afraid to look over his shoulder. A man in a gray mask emerged from the opposite wall of the chapel, so silently the Rook half questioned his eyes.

It was too late for him to use his slant, unless he wanted it published all over the morning papers. That would clue the blue-dusters what to look for, making his mission infinitely harder.

The Samaritan held completely still, letting the space between them pull taut before cocking his head. "I expected more caution from London's phantom."

The man was a fool to use his voice. Voices could be recognized. Maybe the Rook was a fool too, because he replied. "Aren't you the real phantom? I'm not the one hiding behind a mask."

"But you hide in the shadows. Step into the light, and we'll see which of us withers."

The Rook shook his head. "If you have any sense, you'll stand aside."

As if on cue, he heard other footsteps—dampened, but still

there. An ambush. The Samaritan shrugged lightly. "Never been good at that, I'm afraid."

The Rook vaulted off Queen Elizabeth and twisted back for the nave. Boots pounded behind him, echoing up the abbey, loud enough to wake the sleeping saints. A shadow emerged from his left and tackled him to the floor. The Rook elbowed him in the groin and rolled to his feet before the others overtook him—but they were only a few steps behind. Someone shouted. The Rook plunged into the streets, calling on his magic the moment he'd put enough distance between him and his pursuers. He couldn't see where he was going, but it didn't matter. Just away.

He ran for a minute. Two. Then tucked himself in a doorway and paused to listen to the night. All was silent.

That was close. The closest he'd ever been to being caught.

A soft whirring came from somewhere close. The Rook didn't wait. He sprinted from the alley, looping back and using every skill of misdirection he'd ever learned. His breath shortened. His blood pressure spiked. Still, the pursuer's footsteps padded nearer.

Why couldn't he lose him? He'd always been able to shake someone off his trail before. The night was dark, the fog so thick he could scarcely see the hand in front of his face. How was this man tracking him?

He wound around the alleys for another twenty minutes to be safe, then hunkered behind a tree lining the sidewalk, releasing his magic. The nearest gas lamp stood on the corner a hundred paces away. Dew pooled on his skin, chilling it. He waited in silence, barely breathing. Watching. Listening.

Nothing.

He exhaled.

This time, he didn't hear the whirring until the knife swung for him.

# 42

## The Samaritan

His prototype gun must've been too loud because the Rook's hand locked around his wrist just in time, forcing the Samaritan to twist the knife away. The Rook's elbow smashed into his head, followed by a knee to his stomach. Spots dotted his vision.

He gritted his teeth, seething through the pain.

His men had fallen behind in the fog, but he couldn't let the Rook get away. Not again. It had taken two weeks of diversions and carefully planting false information for the Rook's spy to find, all to capture him. But maybe that had been a grave error. Maybe he couldn't take the phantom down alone.

Still grappling for the knife, he yanked the Rook's arm and flipped him over onto the cobblestones, his boot narrowly missing the trunk of a tree. They were all limbs in a dark cloud, half blind, half rage. Then he charged the Rook's prostrate form, aiming for his shoulder. He needed to wound him. Just enough.

The Rook stopped the arcing knife with both hands, their arms trembling with the struggle. The Samaritan drove the knife one inch closer. Two. The Rook hooked his leg around their arms and wrenched, prying the knife away while simultaneously driving the Samaritan to his knees.

The Samaritan rolled away, stood, pivoted—just in time for the Rook to thrust the knife into his shoulder. The rough bark of the tree dug into his back, the knife grating bone and jangling his nervous system. Tugging on his waist, the Rook unholstered the Samaritan's prototype gun. Then the phantom fled, having shown only a glimpse of his face, coat tails flapping as he disappeared into the fog.

With a roar, the Samaritan ripped the knife from his flesh and threw it into the darkness. It thudded against the cobblestones a moment later.

So did he.

# 43

## Dorothy

I bolted up in bed, unsure whether the dark form climbing through my window had been a dream ... or a vision. His presence had felt so real—as tangible as the sheets wrapping my body—but the visions had never woken me from slumber before. Sweat glued the collar of my nightgown to my skin. I crept to the window and peered out, the moon a dull glow through the soupy fog. I could barely make out the railing to our steps below, much less anyone coming or going on the street, but the air thickened, an eerie hush falling over the city.

I shook the images loose. *It was just a dream.* But unable to calm my beating heart, I sneaked a knife from the kitchen and set it on my nightstand before locking the window and tucking myself back in bed.

I never quite fell back asleep, which was why I heard the click of the window unlocking a few minutes later.

I screamed, a raw, primal instinct making me hurl the knife at the dark form that had clambered over the sill. It struck the wall next to him and clanged to the floor.

"Well, that was ... pathetic."

Every panicked thought stilled. I blinked at the darkness and hurried to light the kerosene lamp on my nightstand with a match from the drawer. What it illuminated had me blinking some more. "... Mr. Gardner?"

Ashley lay on his back, one foot planted like he was mustering the strength to rise. "So that's how you attack an intruder crawling through your window? You *miss?*" He sounded insulted.

I shoved the covers away and brought the lamp nearer, noticing his sweat-plastered hair and a wet, sticky stain growing over the collarbone of his dark shirt. I couldn't speak for several moments. Then, "Y-You're ... bleeding!"

"Yes, no thanks to you. I've a—mind to be offended. I thought I taught you—better than that." He said the words lightly, but by the way they broke and gasped, I could tell they cost him. He braced a shaking arm against the wood floor and pushed himself up. "I'll have to ask you to throw the knife again—only this time, use your whole body like I bloody *taught* you—"

"Stop speaking," I said, mentally flipping through Father's medical manuals as I hoisted Ashley's good arm and began guiding him to the wall. We needed to elevate the wound.

He didn't protest, but he did say, "No one can know I'm here."

My gut lurched.

*Why?*

A noise sounded through the open window. Softened foot-steps on the street. We both froze. My heart beat faster, and I let him go long enough to close the window, drawing the curtains to block any light.

Nimble raps sounded on my door. "Dory?" Emme's voice.

My eyes flew back to Ashley, propped up on his good elbow.

He was already pale and losing a lot of blood. But his eyes were lucid enough as he stared up at me silently, every breath labored, waiting to see what I would do. If I would betray him.

He hadn't been merely nicked with a knife; he'd been stabbed. I didn't know why he'd chosen me as the one to help him. But I knew that I would never let him down.

I padded to the door and cracked it, careful to keep the hand smeared with Ashley's blood hidden. Emme stood in the hallway in her nightcap, cradling a candle that brightened the spark of concern in her eyes. "I heard a scream."

"Sorry, I had a nightmare." I started to close the door.

She wedged it open with her shoulder.

My stomach dropped.

"Are you all right, Dory? You haven't been sleeping well lately."

"I'm fine." I swallowed. I didn't like lying to Emme, but I heard Ashley's voice again in my mind. *No one can know I'm here.* As selfish as it was, I wanted to know *why* he was here. I wanted him to trust me enough to let me see the whole picture of him. I wanted it so much I could barely breathe.

Emme's gaze flicked from my face to the crack in the door, as if she might peer into the room behind me. I felt more than heard Ashley sigh in pain.

"Please, Emme, I'm really tired. Can we talk in the morning?"

After a long moment, she nodded, still dubious.

I shut the door and locked it, then rushed back to Ashley. More blood pooled the floor, and his eyes were closed, fallen unconscious. I couldn't haul him to the wall by myself, and even if I could, by the time I got him there, it might not matter.

Kneeling beside him, I unbuttoned his dark, collared shirt and slid his arms out, trying not to think about the parts of his body—the muscles—I was touching. Once I managed to get the shirt free, I wound it under his arm and around his shoulder, tugging and twisting it tighter and tighter, before tying it off. I pressed the heel of my palm into the wadded shirt, stanching the flow to an ooze. My thumb brushed his bare chest, leaving a bloody thumbprint on his skin. Skin otherwise unmarred except for ...

The silver, swollen lines of an *A* scarred his left collarbone. Air lodged in my lungs as I stared at it, mesmerized. Before I knew what I was doing, I reverently hovered one hand over the brand, fingertips extending. Heat from his skin caressed my palm. Time seemed to slow as my middle finger lightly padded over the scarred tissue, down one line.

Ashley's hand shot to my wrist and he gasped awake, half sitting up. My blood flashed hot. His eyes were wild, unfocused. Then they landed on me and he stilled. A short, relieved sigh burst through his lips and he relaxed. "Dolly," he breathed. Dragging my wrist with him, he laid back down, flattening my palm against his cheek and cradling it like a lifeline. "I'm sorry," he whispered. The tips of my fingers buried into his hot, damp hair. He felt feverish. "I'm sorry, I'm sorry."

"For what?"

He shook his head, otherwise not answering.

I swallowed from the tingles zipping over my palm. "We need to prop you against the wall. Can you help me?"

Wordlessly, he used his legs while I hefted his good arm, scooting him back the remaining three feet. Teal wallpaper swirling with white jasmine and springtime birds haloed his dark head, so at odds with his gory, shirtless presence.

Only after I propped some pillows behind him did he notice the binding over his right shoulder. "Thank you," he said, and the look in his eye made my pulse trip, the dark green of candlelight flickering in his irises.

I glanced away and busied my hands by checking his dressing again. Still bleeding. Still too much. All our movement must've irritated the wound. Climbing the vines to my window likely hadn't helped either. I didn't know how he'd managed it. "You should rest."

"Not really in the mood for a nap, but thanks for the offer."

"Then you might take another one without meaning to, Mr. Gardner." I gave him a pointed look.

"Ashley." He grimaced as I burrowed the heel of my palm into his shoulder, swallowed, and said again, "Call me Ashley."

My muscles went slack. "Ashley," I murmured, testing it on my tongue for the first time and finding I loved the taste of it. I wanted to say his name again, say it a thousand times. My eyes drifted to the *A* on his left collarbone, and my lips parted. The skin was smooth. No brand.

But I'd touched it a moment ago ...

"I think it needs to be stitched," Ashley said.

When I pulled my hand from his shoulder, slick with his blood, I agreed.

"Trouble is," he went on, "I can't see the blasted thing."

"I'll fetch a mirror—" I half rose, but for the second time he snatched my wrist.

"*No.*" His grip immediately softened, but a sliver of panic still tightened his features. "No mirrors."

The scene from the factory flashed in my mind—the ghosts haunting Ashley's eyes, and him visibly shaking as Mr. Kelly dragged him away. *No mirrors.*

"All right," I said slowly. "Then I shall have to do it."

After a moment, he gave a single nod and released my wrist. Quietly, I fetched bowls of fresh water from the kitchen. Bandages from the laboratory and a medical instruction manual from my father's bedroom were tucked under my arms. I plucked the small sewing kit from my desk drawer and arrayed everything around Ashley, then positioned the kerosene lamp so I would have enough light.

Trying to disturb the wound as little as possible, I untied the shirt. The water crinkled as I dipped a rag in one of the bowls and wrung it out. As softly as I could, I cleaned the open flesh, smelling fog and something masculine wafting off his hot skin. The water turned pink.

I kept my movements steady, but inside I was a jumble of nerves. He was *here*, in my bedroom.

Ashley watched me the whole time in that quiet, intense way of his. It brought me back to an armoire in a factory. To the darkened studio above a lively party. I kept my own gaze fixed to my work, too scared of what would happen if I let myself look at his jaw, his mouth, his eyes while I was this close—close enough to brush my lips against his and run soothing fingers through his hair.

And I wanted to.

"Are you afraid?"

The quiet question stuttered my rhythm, and my eyes grazed his long enough to touch the secrets in them.

He could've been talking about the blood, the knife wound, the task of stitching him up, the repercussions if he were discovered in my room—but I didn't think he was talking about any of them. I thought he meant him. Was I afraid of him.

I couldn't look at him as I murmured, "Perhaps I was, once. But not anymore."

"Then I'm sorry," he said softly. And he didn't clarify whether he meant sorry that I'd ever been afraid of him, or ... sorry that I no longer was.

I threaded the needle and sterilized it in the flame of the lamp, careful to maintain the pressure on his shoulder with my other hand until I was ready. "I take it you won't make it to the annual Science Society of London's fundraiser tomorrow night?"

He cocked his head ironically. "Oh, I'll be there. You under-
estimate my skills of recovery."

Just as I was about to dig the tip of the needle in for the first
time, I said, "I hope this wasn't all an elaborate way to collect my
last guess."

He breathed a laugh. "I wish it were."

I plunged in and pulled. He didn't react. Maybe the pain had
dulled, or, more likely, he'd been stitched up a few times before.
"You'd get yourself stabbed just for a guess?" Quickly, I settled
into a pattern—plunge, loop, tie off, plunge, loop, tie off.

He said nothing for so long, the silence had lost the question
in its pockets. But the whole time, his staring never let up, and I
knew it was because he wanted to ask me questions of his own.
My movements slowed as my throat tightened, suddenly finding
it difficult to breathe.

"No," he murmured. "But maybe ..." His gaze curved over my
stitching fingers, following the lines of my arm up to my neck, my
hair, and finally locking on my eyes. "... Maybe for something
else."

I inhaled, prepared to say his name and unprepared to say
whatever came after, but he went on before I could.

"You don't have to help me. I'm sorry for coming here and
begging you to. Only, I could think of no one else to turn to ... I
could think of no one *else*."

*No one else.*

I finished stitching in silence, letting the words sink in. "You
didn't beg."

"It *feels* like I am," he said in a husky voice, not missing a
beat. His jaw tightened from a different kind of pain, his gaze
leaving scorch marks on my face and refusing to look away.

I made the final loop and cut the thread. "Don't ever apologize for asking for help. It is the stronger person who does."

After I'd washed my hands in the spare bowl of water, he asked, "Then what does that make you?"

"I ..." Without the task of stitching, I had nothing to hide behind. My shoulders bunched up, thoughts flashing to Emme. "I ask for help," I finished lamely.

"Do you? Because it seems to me you've been doing everything entirely on your own." He said it like it was a bad thing, and yet I caught the quick spark of admiration in his eyes. "You decoded my note in the bookshop. You bargained with me. You deciphered each clue and sidestepped every obstacle I threw at you, all to chase down the—" His voice grew quieter. "The Samaritan." He shook his head. "I don't think anyone else could've done it. At least not alone."

"You could've."

He smiled then—all small and soft and strangely intimate. "I could've." It sounded more like a concession than a boast, and then that smile wilted. "But the difference between us, Dorothy, is that you do not *have* to do it alone."

I weighed his words and realized he was right. I had Emme. And Aunt Marie, in some regards. It was noble to carry a small burden by yourself, to be competent and confident—but when it became great, carrying that burden alone became its own form of selfishness.

"How are you going to get home before morning?" I asked. "My uncle ..."

Ashley nodded and I was glad I didn't need to explain any more. "In my pocket are two red strips of fabric. Tie the first around the gas lamp on the corner, pointing the knot toward your house. Tie the second to the gate closest to your window but tie it twice. Two knots will tell him I'm on the second story."

I didn't ask who *he* was. After hesitating, I fished through Ashley's pocket, but had to sift through the tangled mess of different colored fabric to find two red. I suspected different colors sent different messages.

"Don't look behind you out there," Ashley continued, tone carrying a warning that made me pause. "Stay out of the shadows. And whatever you do ... do not linger."

Was the man who'd stabbed him still out there?

... What had he wanted?

Ashley was still watching me, waiting for my promise, so I nodded. He sagged with relief. Eyes shuttering closed, he tipped his head back, resting it against the wallpaper as I slipped out of my room.

The house was quiet and so were the streets, and I didn't look around while I tied both pieces of fabric to cold metal. It took me all of ten minutes to finish and hurry back to my room with careful feet. "I did as you asked."

Ashley's eyes were still closed. He sighed something that sounded like, "Thank you."

I inspected his dressing again, ensuring it was still maintaining good pressure. Once satisfied, I sat back, my fingertips accidentally dragging along the skin of his chest. He didn't seem to notice but my stomach clenched in a pleasant way, and I swallowed. Now that waiting was the only thing left to do, there was nothing stopping my eyes from wandering.

And they did. Shamelessly.

I stared at the eyelashes fanning his skin. At his features that looked like a painting, unblemished, smooth, and strong. At his hair, black like the soot in the fireplace and wavy like a drift of smoke rising into the London sky. At the muscles cording his torso, too defined to belong to a gentleman. At the shadows pooling on his chest that shifted with each of his shallow breaths.

And I knew I shouldn't want it. All of it. I shouldn't crave his darkness, his secrets—his games. Shouldn't want to see him like this ever again outside of this moment. How could I want him when he had tried so hard to see me fail?

Ashley had never promised anything. He was clearly keeping secrets. And I couldn't keep from wondering ... what if he always would?

But it had cost him something, letting me come this far. And though I didn't understand it, might even be angry at him for refusing to aid me, I also trusted his heart.

*But maybe ... Maybe for something else.*

Throat thick, I scooted against the wall and lowered my head against his uninjured shoulder. The moment I did, his breath deepened, like my distance had been the real wound hurting him.

His face turned, ever so slightly, to brush the top of my hair. My hair tingled at the soft presence of his lips. At the slow, warm exhales dripping over my body like melted chocolate that gradually deepened into the cadence of sleep. Moments passed. Hours and days. When I was sure he was out, I gradually slipped away from his touch—and froze at the sound of his voice.

"Stay with me."

It was more a quiet question than a command. Slowly, I turned back. His eyes were open now, and that didn't help. They drew me in, manipulating my limbs until I knelt beside him, wanting to live in this moment forever. Just staring at him, lines of strength trapped against dark flowers.

"For how long?" I asked.

He looked between my eyes, seeming to sense that I didn't mean right now. "For as long as you will." And maybe there was a cosmic power joining our souls and this moment together, because though his voice didn't change, I sensed something in him too. A buried heartache in those words. A buried longing.

*The difference between us, Dorothy, is that you do not* have *to do it alone.*

But neither did he.

Soothingly, I sank my fingers into his hair, parting it like ships embarking on a treacherous voyage. These were uncharted waters, and yet I couldn't stop. I wanted to know what was across this sea instead of always wondering, wondering.

Ashley stopped breathing, eyes sweeping up to find me, pin me. In them, I saw a demand, a need, and an equally potent self-denial that would always keep him from satiating it. And I knew —he would never let himself blur this line first.

It made me hesitate.

But I looked at him, this man who'd been my only confidant, who'd cut off a man's hand for me and then seen me home so I could be safe, the only one who'd given me hope, however reluctantly, when I'd been about to despair—and I didn't want to hold back. My gaze flicked to the binding around his shoulder, throat clogging with sudden emotion when I realized he might've died.

I pushed my fingers deeper and slowly, gently, brought my lips to his temple, and he watched me, and his eyes fluttered closed when my lips met his fiery skin, and he released a sigh deeper than any ocean, colored with enough desperation to light a flame in my belly. I pressed a soft kiss.

Then I tipped my head down, nose grazing his cheekbone, not brave enough to draw away and meet whatever was in his eyes. But his face turned toward mine a few millimeters as he dragged in a low, ragged breath, and I could feel his gaze, tracing the curves of my lowered eyes, nose, and mouth for several excruciating moments.

His head angled back, neck extending and jaw catching the glow of the kerosene lamp as he brushed his lips against mine, just once, so lightly and hesitantly that I barely felt their presence even though they lingered, sending sparks of heat rushing under my skin.

All too soon, he broke contact, just enough for his breath to scatter around my mouth like a whispered vow.

My chest ached with a longing to be closer. To *feel* him. Something stirred within me, something that had awoken that first day when he'd stolen my book.

He'd kissed me back. On the lips. Maybe it was to say thank you for saving him, but it felt more reverent than that. More uncertain. More—*more.*

"Why ...?" I whispered.

He drew back, and this time, I dared meet his eyes, unprepared for the fealty I saw there—a thing that burned so bright and strong, it would never die. "A token for a token," he whispered back, stare never wavering and his knuckles dragging along my cheek, making me wonder how those few words and a simple touch could make me feel so ...

Safe.

Hopeful.

The back of my eyes prickled with unexplained tears. A muscle feathered in his jaw, his eyes and the brush of his thumb dropping to my lips again. In response, my body leaned toward him again, wanting—

Though I initiated, this time his mouth was more certain, his lower lip curving around mine in an agonizing journey upwards that had me begging him to never stop. Once ... twice ... kissing me like he was slowly tugging on a thread and watching me unravel.

And I unraveled.

Heat pooled in my belly. His hand slid to the back of my neck and pulled me closer, pulling us both toward a precipice that tasted so deep, it was going to swallow us whole. We were going to jump.

*Click.*

I broke away when a second form climbed through my window, his dark clothes swirling with fog. Mr. Kelly said nothing as he took in the scene; Ashley's grip on my neck and his lips that were pinker than usual. Then his attention settled squarely on the binding over Ashley's chest. "How bad?"

"I'm fine," Ashley murmured, but it was me he stared at. His hand fingered a lock of my hair before falling away.

"Not the question I asked."

"I need help standing." He still stared at me, the words slow, like he didn't want to say them. Didn't want to leave.

Mr. Kelly shifted to Ashley's other side and hefted him up. I got to my feet too. Muscles shaking, Ashley put on a clean shirt that Mr. Kelly offered him, then hunched over the floor, steadying himself.

Mr. Kelly watched, hands at the ready. "Ash—"

"I'm *fine.*" The words were quiet but hard, and this time he did look at his friend, something passing between them. After a moment, Mr. Kelly nodded, then glanced at me. He inhaled, throat working like he was trying to say something.

"You're welcome," I said with a small smile, sparing him the trouble.

Mr. Kelly remained rigid, but his face sagged in relief, and I noticed a hint of redness in the corners of his eyes. He'd been worried. He weakly nodded, and though he still hadn't spoken to me, it felt like a start. It said more than any words could.

"If you two are done communicating telepathically, I think it's time for us to leave." Ashley waited near the window, where the rising dawn evaporated the mists.

Mr. Kelly hopped over the sill.

The puddle of blood had begun drying on the edges, staining the wood a darker brown that would need to be scrubbed out before the house woke up. The bloody bandages would need to be burned. The water tossed out. Exhaustion pulled at my limbs. It had been a long night, and there was still much to be done before it was over.

But I didn't regret it. No matter what came after this, I would never regret it.

My lips burned from Ashley's sensuous kiss.

Ashley turned back, taking one last look at me, eyes glistening but not with tears. Maybe it was hope. I didn't dare believe it was love. And when he opened his mouth, I thought he might thank me again, but instead he said one last time, "I'm so sorry, Dolly." Then he followed his friend and disappeared down the vine.

# 44

## Miles

The Artifice worked his mouth in thought, making his chin puff waggle. "I was just putting the finishing touches on it now," he said. "You're welcome to wait." He disappeared into his back room, leaving Ashley and me among his priceless knockoffs.

Outside the shop, shrill laughter emerged from the cacophonous hum, and I glanced through the grubby window. A Talon in his maroon hooded vest passed by and we locked eyes. Lark's spy. He may have allowed us back in the Necropolis, but that didn't mean he wasn't watching our every move.

I hated this place. Not just because it was a fetid hellhole and the Acherons were tyrants—but because every time we came down here, it felt a lot like sneaking into the lair of a slumbering beast.

My hand drifted to my coat to check on the pistol hidden inside before realizing I couldn't use it. The Necropolis snuffed your slant like wet fingers on a flame. Ashley had the cuff, and he'd give it to me once it was time to store the heavy artifact in my coat.

*What*, he had yet to tell me.

Ashley shifted beside me, angling his left shoulder forward, then relaxing when he saw that I caught the movement. It had only been a day since the stabbing, and I knew from experience it was probably on fire right now, but still he moved like it didn't bother him. Like ignoring the pain would make it go away.

A girl with blonde hair passed the window, and I tensed. She moved on quickly, but I couldn't shake that initial reaction.

I'd never told Ashley about the boy—the girl-who-was-most-definitely-a-woman-with-a-chest—who'd infiltrated our flat. Bram had drilled us until I could navigate the stars during a storm, speak five languages, set my own bones, knock a man out with one punch, and pick off a goldcrest midflight from three hundred yards—but all of that flew out the window when she'd transformed beneath me.

Her eyes were so brown, they were almost black, her lips pink. Freckles dusted the bridge of her upturned nose. I'd taken it all in in the blink of an eye, and then all I *could* do was blink. Then she'd slipped through my fingers. Easily. All because my tongue had nailed to my jaw.

*Intense shyness* is what my mother called it. I didn't know what was wrong with me, but the description didn't seem far off.

My ears reddened just thinking about the feel of Emmeline Morgan beneath me, and I had zero plans to tell Ashley. She'd only been after money—everyone knew her father kept the purse strings cinched close. We would never see her again, so why bother bringing up the past?

Perhaps the worst part of it was that I now had *two* secrets to keep from Ashley, and statistically, those weren't good odds. The Mole was still looking into leads concerning the owner of the hairpin, and we were scheduled to meet up again in a few days.

"What's the matter?" Ashley asked, his preternatural sense telling him something was off.

Denying would do no good. "I don't like it down here."

Ashley hesitated, then nodded. "We'll be out soon enough."

As if on cue, the Artifice wheeled his masterpiece out on a dolly and set it before us. I frowned as I studied the massive clay structure, a sinking feeling settling in my gut as Ashley walked around it. He tested its weight by budging it with his good shoulder. "It's perfect," he declared after a moment.

"It's not." I couldn't sieve the anger from my voice.

Ashley's attention whipped over.

"This isn't what we agreed on." He hadn't told me *this* is what he needed me to carry in my coat.

He frowned too, before saying lightly, "It's only a precaution."

But I was tired of him using himself like a bargaining chip that could be discarded when it was no longer valuable. I crossed my arms, a wall hardening inside me that would never budge. "I won't help you. Not with this one. It's senseless and has nothing to do with getting back to the sea." The only place we belonged.

*I* belonged.

The Artifice looked between us, eyes gleaming with too much curiosity. I wanted to squish the tiny man under my boot.

Ashley was silent for a long moment while he studied me. He must've met that wall because at last, he said slowly, "All right. We'll skip this one."

# 45

## Dorothy

"I want to know what is going on. *Now.*"

I looked up from scribbling the equation in the book. Through the mess of curls around my face, I saw Emme glowering in the doorway.

She slammed the door behind her and slapped a hand on the worktable, making me jump. "Did you hear me? I want to know why you haven't been sleeping or eating; why you've been running around on useless errands and not returning until nightfall. I want to know why you're obsessed with Mr. Gardner besides the obvious reason, because I can tell it's more than that. Tell me why a *man* was in your room last night, Dory, and if you try to deny it, I swear on King George's grave, I will pluck out every one of your eyelashes."

She was pulling her punches, but real, poignant hurt shone in her eyes as she struggled to hold back tears.

I blinked at her, so overcome with fear and relief that for a few moments I couldn't say anything. Oh, Emme. "I believe you would," I said quietly. I pivoted on my stool to face the window, because I was too ashamed to face her. I was the one who'd driven this wedge between us, and my frame curled inward. "I'm sorry, Emme. I should've told you from the start, I was just ..." I sighed, slowly, wobbly. "I just didn't want to be worried about you too."

*You don't have to do it all alone.*

And then I told her everything: my father's kidnapping, the feather on his pillow, the note in the bookshop, my deal with Ashley, and the circus that had followed. She listened patiently, the anger gradually receding from her face like the tide pulling out. She still frowned, but ... maybe now she saw that I hadn't intended to hurt her.

The bees filled the silence when I finished, one of them landing on an open page of *The Study of Chemistry Within the Atomic Theory*, as if to mock me, saying, *This is the book that got you into this mess.*

Emme pursed her lips. At last, she said, "I don't understand. All this time you thought I'd be too reckless—but that's precisely what *you're* doing. And I don't hate you for it, because that's the cost of circumstances like this. I just—" She shrugged helplessly. "Why can't we *both* pay it?"

I turned back toward my cousin, throat thick. "I was afraid, Emme. I still am. Finding the Rook, the Samaritan ... my father ... it was *supposed* to be easy.

"But the minute I considered it might endanger you too ..." I shook my head. "I couldn't do it." My voice trembled, the back of my eyes scratching with tears. "I've been a coward. A rotten daughter, and a rotten friend."

"No." Emme sat on the stool beside me, hand resting on my shoulder and squeezing until I looked at her. A smile inched onto her lips. "*Just* a rotten friend." She breathed a laugh, and I did too, more grateful for her than ever.

"As for Mr. Gardner," Emme went on, "he is keeping secrets of his own, Dory. Did you know Mr. Kelly is slanted?"

My brows pulled in. "No."

"Well, he is. And he was using it. Just—" She sucked in a breath. "Just be careful."

I nibbled the inside of my lip. I hadn't expected Mr. Kelly to be slanted, but how much did I really know the man? How much did I know Ashley? And with thoughts of him came the familiar feeling that I was missing something. A key piece was being concealed, and if I could step back, it would come into focus.

"Oh!" Emme exclaimed suddenly, twisting to fish something from her skirts. "I almost forgot. This telegram is for you."

I took the piece of paper from her hands and broke the seal.

*Your father is alive. Stop. Sighted near Lincoln's Inn.*

Crushing relief made my heart pound as I staggered to my feet. "He's alive," I breathed. The suffocating weight in my chest eased. I folded the paper and gripped it until my thumbnail turned white. "My father is alive."

"Where is he?" Emme asked, eyes wide.

"Lincoln's Inn." It was kind of Mr. Hart to let me know, and now that I finally had a lead—not to the Rook, or the Samaritan, but to my *father* directly—I could track him down myself. Urgency bounced in my toes.

I remembered Uncle's warning if I dared to defy him and leave the house. There was no guarantee I'd be reunited with my father today, if I did; at most, all I could hope for was another clue that might lead me to him.

But the time for skirting risks was over. It was time to gamble it all and watch where the chips fell.

"I have to go straight—" I cut off when my eyes snagged on the open book on the table; Ashley's book from the bookshop.

The alpha particle was a new concept, not fully explored and only barely a theory—but it wasn't the theory that caught my attention. It was the graph next to it that I'd seen a dozen times, the trajectory of an alpha particle through gold foil, labeled a, for alpha.

Which was ... Greek.

My heart stopped cold.

*The pen of Zeus marks his flesh.*

A was a Greek letter too.

My mind whirled me back to last night in my room, three white lines marring Ashley's collarbone. They were gone only a minute later, but I'd felt them myself. Which could only mean—

Was Ashley slanted? Maybe with illusions, or some kind of invisibility? Had he used this slant to hide his scar? If Mr. Kelly was secretly slanted, then why not him? When we'd escaped from the Necropolis, the lights had flashed on and off—and then the Talons hadn't even been shooting at us, but at ...

An illusion he'd created. A diversion to draw their fire away.

Come to think of it, we hadn't needed the cuff to go through the portal—Ashley had used the tattoo of one of the Talons for that. He'd needed a cuff so he could use his *magic*.

But then why hadn't I sensed it? It made sense for the Necropolis, but all the other time we'd spent together, why hadn't I *ever* sensed it?

Unless ...

My eyes shot to the corner of the room where mutating magic had broken glass in my father's hands.

It was highly improbable, but *unless* ... Ashley's magic had somehow mutated, and was using that illusional capability to disguise itself. Mutated magic had a mind of its own, after all. He'd asked me about mutations in the Necropolis; what if he'd been wondering for himself?

When I thought back to the moment Ashley had gasped awake, I hadn't felt a cold rush as I usually did when someone used magic ... but I had felt a warm one. As I thought back on every one of our interactions, I realized that I'd *always* felt warm around him. The bookshop ... making my rings miss in the carnival ... camouflaging my sleeve in the armoire in the factory ... I had been sensing his magic all along, but it had been disguised as something warm. *Friendly.*

A thousand realizations bombarded me at once, making my head spin in so many circles, it felt like a perfect, dreadful story playing out before my eyes. Like stepping back and watching the picture finally become clear.

He was an orphan.

The pen of Zeus marked his flesh.

He had made his scar invisible, which meant he *had* to be slanted.

And the night of Mr. Joule's party ... *Ashley* had been there.

My lungs tightened, squeezing out every last drop of oxygen until black started to speckle my vision.

"Dory? What's wrong?" Emme ducked her head to get my attention, but I couldn't look away from the naked truth before me.

*Please inform the Samaritan that the innkeeper needs to be paid.*

I'd stupidly assumed Ashley was the messenger. I couldn't have been more wrong. More blind. I'd been so focused on finding my three clues and chasing the answers that I'd never stopped to question the clue that sparked them in the first place.

"I know who the Samaritan is," I whispered.

Ashley knew the Rook had kidnapped my father.

He'd done nothing about it.

Hot questions burned the back of my throat.

Emme pulled back. "Wait, really?"

*I take it you won't make it to the annual Science Society of London's fundraiser tomorrow night?* I'd asked.

*I'll be there,* he'd responded.

I couldn't throw away the lead Mr. Hart had given me—but if my father wasn't at Lincoln's Inn or the trail ran cold again, Ashley—

Words tumbled from my lips. "He'll be on the yacht. I have to go. I don't know when I'll get the chance to speak to the Samaritan again. I *have* to go." The telegram in my hand burned my palm. "But my father—"

Emme snatched it away. "I'll go. I'll look for your father on the streets, and you look for him on the river. One of us is bound to find him."

We shared a look, and our common purpose formed a taut string that tethered my heart to hers. I nodded, then gave her a hasty hug and dashed upstairs to change.

# 46

## Ashley

Miles left early, and after wrapping up business in the Necropolis, I headed toward the portal. The stitches on my collarbone burned, but the tightness in my chest had been a constant companion long before last night. My plans were unraveling faster than I could tangle them back together again.

I couldn't forget her gentle touch. Her fingers in my hair. Her lips at my temple. The look in her eyes that made my insides writhe with guilt.

Maybe it wouldn't be so bad telling Dorothy the truth. Maybe she would understand, and she'd forgive me for keeping secrets, and we could acknowledge the thing that was building between us. The thing that felt like a tsunami pummeling me on the beach while I merely laid there with open arms, ready to drown.

I passed the pillars of the arcade and wound down toward the last set of stairs.

"Ashley." Wren appeared before me on the stairs, out of breath, and I cursed the cuff still around my wrist. To avoid what happened last time, I charged past her, practically running to get away before my magic could influence her.

"Wait!" she called, footsteps pounding behind me.

The crowds in the plaza congealed at the bottom of the stairs, so I hopped over the banister and made a dash for the portal. *Not again. Almost there ... Not again.*

Wren was surprisingly quick, managing to push past most of the crowd, close enough to shout, "I saw you with Dorothy St. James."

That name on her lips made me crunch to a halt, and I hated that it did. I screamed at my limbs to move, but they waited, waited with prickling dread to hear that Lark had found her and was dragging her back here to lock her in chains and slave her out.

I forced my posture to lapse into carelessness even though I felt a knife burrowing under my ribcage straight toward my heart. Forced my voice to sound nonchalant. "I am sighted with many people. That does not mean I associate with them regularly."

"Good." Wren caught up and swept in front of me, the concern in her eyes genuine. "Because she's not who she seems."

The words felt wrong and instantly put my senses on alert. The tips of my fingers tingled. "What do you mean?"

She knocked her chin up. "I told you I had a life up top—as a servant on a steam-yacht. It wasn't much, but it was mine. The Science Society holds monthly dinners aboard the yacht, and they're a stiff-collared bunch. Several of my friends have been sacked from the society's complaints over the smallest mistakes.

"A while ago, I was tasked with serving the third course. But when I got to Miss St. James, I tripped, and some of the soup fell toward her. I reacted without thinking. I made a hole in her dress, and the soup hit the floor instead—but she saw. Next thing I knew, bluedusters were smashing my door in and hauling me to the asylum to await my hanging ... My *hanging.*"

My blood turned to slush and slowed my pulse to a heavy, lonely drum.

Bloody silt.

It couldn't be true. It was like trying to swallow vomit; like forcing your hand into the jaws of a bear trap; my whole being rejected the idea. And yet a tiny kernel of doubt wormed its way in, and without realizing it, I found myself reaching for my second slant.

I dove into Wren's memories, praying it would work today; praying it wouldn't. Praying she was *wrong*. If Dorothy's mind was lilacs wrapped in a misty dawn, Wren's mind was buoys near a shore, each one a pillar that guided her life. I found her deck of memories under the water, and when I touched them, they scattered, laying out on the surface like branches on a tree.

After finding the one with Dorothy at the dinner and reliving it through Wren's eyes, I pulled out of her mind, and it felt a lot like coming up for air but never reaching the surface. I was back in the plaza of the Necropolis, but I wasn't breathing.

Everything was spinning. My jaw hardened and my feet dug into the limestone floor.

"It was her," Wren insisted when I still didn't say anything. "No one else saw."

*No one else saw.*

Wren's hand settled on my arm, and I barely registered it. No longer cared. "I'm only telling you this because I want you to be careful." Wren squeezed my arm and I tensed, glancing at her. "If she catches you slanting ..."

I pulled away from her touch and stepped back. "Thank you for telling me," I managed, but it tasted like ashes in my mouth because I wasn't sure I was grateful at all. As I crossed the last few feet to the portal and stepped through, I couldn't help but remember a conversation in Joule's studio—about monsters and slaying them and how it was better ... easier ... to remain blind.

Was she a spy? Was she working for someone? Had she been playing me this whole time?

Burning, poisonous betrayal slid from the apex of my throat into the pit of my stomach. Why her? Of all people, why *her*?

# 47

## Dorothy

Steam puffed through the thick funnel in the center of the boat. The reflection of the string lights bobbed along the Thames, keeping the moon company as the yacht silently cut through the obsidian water. One of them sputtered, almost making the whole line go dark, and I prayed it wasn't an omen.

I found myself at another auction, but this one was silent, giving everyone the opportunity to enjoy the refreshments and symphony of strings wafting from the stern while they inspected the items displayed. The Science Society of London's yearly benefit auction was open to the public—mostly. You had to pass an unspoken dress code, hinting at the size of your billfold, before being admitted onto the boat.

I rolled my lips together and smoothed my dress, even though it didn't need it.

The yacht had already made four of its scheduled seven stops, gaining and losing passengers each time—none of them Ashley. By the end of the night, it would travel from St. Katherine's Docks all the way to Vauxhall, where Mr. Vernon would give a speech thanking everyone for their generous donation that would fund another year of scientific research. But Ashley wasn't the only one I was keeping an eye out for.

Uncle was here.

I'd hired a separate carriage after he and Aunt Marie departed, stealing onto the boat a few minutes after them. Emme had wriggled out of coming by pretending another headache and was currently exploring the fields at Lincoln's Inn. Worry for her safety dueled with the knowledge that if I could trust anyone with tracking down information, it was her.

When the yacht made the sixth stop with still no sign of Ashley, I clutched at my skirts. I didn't know the first thing about finding Ashley Gardner. He'd always found me. To ease my nerves, I snagged a glass of tart champagne with notes of cherry, lips puckering after I'd downed the whole thing.

I never saw him board, which was why I straightened in surprise when a few minutes later a shadow slipped into the narrow stairwell.

By the time I followed him to the deserted upper deck, Ashley was facing me, leaning with his hands braced against the far rail. He was expecting me. The river suddenly felt too quiet, the darkness more vivid than any moon or string of lights. Power rippled off him in waves, the shadows gravitating toward him like he was their architect.

I had to take a few breaths just to be able to look at him without shivering.

"I'm glad you came," I said, and my voice sounded loud and nervous. Maybe it was the champagne. He said nothing, but his hands on the rails tightened as he took me in. Slowly. Traveling from the teal folds of my skirt to my elbow-length evening gloves, my fitted lace bodice and cap sleeves, my wide V neckline, and finally, to the black velvet choker with an emerald pendant on my neck. I felt the ghost of his lips and my mind continued the scene from last night, making me feel hot all over when I imagined the kiss deepening, his mouth opening ...

I covered the distance between us. He watched my approach in silence. "How are you healing?" My fingers grazed his wounded collarbone.

He didn't pull away, but he seemed more guarded than usual, his expression hollow. Harder. "Fine," he said, still not quite meeting my eyes. I couldn't read anything in his tone, and it made my hand drop away.

The unnatural beauty of his face shone even starker when he wasn't smiling, and I wasn't used to it. Now that I knew what his magic felt like, it was hard to ignore the soft tingle of warmth tugging between my breasts, trying to draw me toward him.

Instead, I came beside him and looked out on the water, almost tasting the coal dust in the air—the last of the season as spring thawed into summer heat. "The last time I was on this boat," I said softly, "was the night my father was kidnapped. The night everything changed." I glanced at Ashley, and his head turned to the side, eyes still downcast but listening to every word.

"I feel the same as I did then," I went on. "Like I'm holding my breath before taking the plunge into an unknown abyss; I don't know how deep it goes, or how long I'll be under. But when I come up, everything will change again."

Ashley's eyes finally sliced up, both hard and sad like stones under a deep river, churning with something sparkling and dark. Tone soft but clipped he said, "It already has, I think." The air shifted with a different emotion as he stared down at me, eyes flicking over the shape of my lips before a frown darkened his forehead and he pushed off the rail, sweeping back toward the stairwell.

"My final guess," I said suddenly, making him halt as I spun around, heart pounding. "You promised me one final guess and I want to make it now." I rallied my courage. A soft breeze flew over the yacht, ruffling the back of his wavy black hair and stealing the words from my lungs on a whisper. "Is it you, Ashley?"

He went deathly still, not turning around, not even breathing. Then finally, a quiet, "I told you not to waste it."

"Are you the Samaritan?"

He took the longest moment to respond, head bending low, frame expanding on an inhale. "And if I were?"

Butterflies fluttered inside me, wings beating faster and faster, swirling in a vortex. "The Samaritan hasn't returned my father, and I want to know why. I need his help." My bones shook, wishing he would turn around. Let me see his face. "... I need *your* help."

"Can I trust you?"

My lips parted, a frantic pulse buzzing in my throat. "What?"

He glanced over his shoulder, and slowly the rest of his body rotated with him. "Can I *trust* you?" The words were so full of breath, they were barely audible, the wind snatching them away quickly and rippling them across the water.

"Of course you can," I said, exasperated. As if I hadn't proven it already. "I have given you all my secrets—"

His lips cut a bitter slash. "All of them?"

To my mortification, frustrated tears sprang to the corners of my eyes. "I never even broke the seal on your note. I told no one about your wound or your presence in my room last night—I stitched you up—I *saved your life*. What more can I do?"

"More?" His eyebrows pulled together in a gathering storm as he stepped forward. I fell back with him, heart spiking, lower back hitting the rail and bracing myself against it; his eyes guttered with a range of emotions I couldn't interpret as he towered over me. "The masked man—you know nothing about him. What all he has done. What he is willing to do. A secret like the Samaritan's identity holds the power of nations. The Gloaming, the Variance, the gems, the kidnappings, the Rook, the Samaritan, they are all linked together—and the one who unmasks it will be in the greatest danger of all. You have no idea of the onslaught that awaits."

I said nothing—I couldn't. But I leaned toward him again, fingers curling around his lapels and giving in to his familiar pull, mutely begging him to give in to mine. The yacht veered left, passing the gas lamps on the riverfront as it prepared to dock for the last time, and the extra light cast half of Ashley's face in shadow.

Shadows and sunlight.

"He is not the hero you seek." Ashley's muscles tensed in an invisible battle. His gaze never wavered as he muttered, "Ignorance is bliss."

And I remembered the rest of his words from before. *Because once your eyes have been opened to see a terrible monster, you are duty-bound to do all in your power to slay him.*

*Who is your monster?*

*Me.*

But he wasn't a monster.

I lifted a hand to his face, thumbing over one black, perfectly symmetrical eyebrow before cupping his jaw. He seemed to soften under my touch. Just a fraction. A tiny spark of melancholy hope. "I don't want bliss," I whispered back. "I want to be awake ... With you."

His nostrils flared. He swallowed. Then one by one his features blanked; brows, mouth, jaw, eyes, locking into place like a vault sealing up secrets. Each one a door with a complicated combination. "No," he said at last, and the syllable was low, even, smooth, final. "I am not the Samaritan."

Heat coiled in my stomach.

*Lie.*

"Pull out your ring," I whispered.

His jaw flexed. "You don't need the ring. I am telling you the truth."

"*Prove* it." I didn't recognize my voice. Raw, and angry, so angry that even now—when he was caught, and I desperately needed his help—he still refused to step out of the shadows. Angry that he'd played with my father's life and still wouldn't *trust* me.

Ashley frowned, a blackness flickering in his gaze as he tipped his head back, exposing a stretch of throat. A deliberate hand slid into his coat and reappeared with the small shiny object. I watched him glide it over his knuckles, my heart beating so hard it was going to break a rib, beating so loudly its roar was all I heard.

Ashley held up the back of his hand. "I am not. The Samaritan." The gem entwined in silver pulsed with a soft glow, making its color unmistakable.

Blue.

Truth.

A blooming warmth sparked in my sternum and my lips parted—

*It's an illusion.*

*He's using magic.*

*If he can make a scar disappear, he can change the color of a ring as well.*

The thought made me jolt back, farther over the rail, and then lock eyes with him—and I wondered how something so green could look so ... dead. He'd used his magic to help me, but how did I know he hadn't used it to trick me as well? How could I know it wasn't all one, elaborate lie?

*... What if it was?*

Something gave a horrible *crack,* and I thought it might be my heart—until I heard Aunt Marie scream.

# 48

## Dorothy

I left Ashley and my confusion and heartbreak behind as I dashed for the stairs. When I burst onto the foredeck and pushed through the cloister of people ringing the on-ramp, I took in everything at once: The yacht had docked. Everyone was shouting. Aunt Marie wailed from where she'd collapsed to the deck, fingernails leaving streaks in the wood. Uncle Benedick's face twisted in intense revulsion, and I followed his line of sight to where several bluedusters in their crisp, navy uniforms had boarded and now attempted to calm the crowd while two of them dragged a thrashing woman toward the ramp.

Emme.

They'd followed her onto the boat. Her hair hung in streams over her face, eyes shining with rage as she kicked and yelled, her words lost in the fray.

Adrenaline shot to my feet, and then I was by her side, pulling one of the blueduster's sleeves. "Stop! What are you doing!"

The blueduster shook me off with practiced calm and barely

spared me a glance. "This woman has been charged with the illegal use of her slant—"

Emme sighted me and her eyes widened. "Dory! Dory, I came as soon as I—"

"She no longer has the privilege of conversing with family or friends," the blueduster cut in, pulling Emme back hard enough to make her cry out. "She will be placed in a cell where she will receive no visitors. As of now, Emmeline Morgan is property of the Crown until dawn when she will be hanged for her crimes against society. Long live the Queen."

My heart dropped to my feet, and everything after that happened too quickly.

Emme shot forward. "Dory, I saw him! I *saw* him. He's—!" The rest of her words were cut off by a gag clinching over her mouth. I charged toward her but two of them shoved me back. I hit the deck. Then they dragged her down the ramp and into a windowless black carriage, there and gone like a mirage.

*No.*

"No!"

*No, no, no, please, no.*

Not Emme too.

My throat was hoarse by the time Uncle Benedick cut off my screaming by roughly hauling me to my feet.

"Get up," he bit out. "Both of you. Comport yourselves."

Everyone was staring, but I didn't care. Emme had been arrested by bluedusters—because of *me*. I'd sent her to find my father in my place, and again, it had been the wrong choice. Of course she'd used magic. I knew she would yet sent her anyway.

My insides heaved.

Uncle's ironclad grip led me off the boat and into a hired coach, but I barely registered it. Somehow, Aunt Marie had followed, and Uncle rapped the roof, making us all lurch forward.

Silence settled over us like a thick cloak. We crossed the bridge into the West End and wound through rows of dimmed, expensive shops.

It was too dark to see Uncle's palm until it belted my cheek. I gasped, stings zipping across my face.

Aunt Marie started crying.

"How dare you!" Uncle's eyes flashed. "How dare you break the mourning custom and humiliate us all."

I blinked, unable to form words for several heartbeats. His daughter had just been arrested, and he was still worried about appearances? "My father—"

"Your father is *dead*."

Aunt Marie cried louder.

"And as is my duty, I will make you respectable even if it kills me."

I inhaled quick breaths through my nose, unable to focus on my own problems right now when Emme ...

"What are we going to do," I whispered. "They're going to ..." I couldn't even say it. "In a matter of hours, Emmeline will be—"

"Using magic!" Uncle hissed through his teeth, and his tone made me flinch. "She deserves to be hanged for the shame she's brought upon us. I will not hear her name spoken again."

I balled my fists. "She's your daughter!"

Uncle raised his hand again, but Aunt Marie cried out, making him hesitate. At last, he dropped it and offered only two more words before the carriage arrived home, and he hauled me kicking and screaming to my room, locking me inside. "No longer."

Three hours remained until dawn.

The house had settled into the eerie quiet of the wee hours, I having long given up beating the door with my fists and sobs. I paced the rug in my room, wringing my hands and unable to settle while I thought of ideas. But I didn't have any. I didn't own anything heavy enough to heave against the door. Uncle had switched the locks on my window too, so it locked from the outside.

Even if I managed to break free, I didn't know where they *hung* the slanted, let alone where they kept them in the interim.

Ashley might know. He might help. But ... after our conversation, I didn't feel like I could ask. Then again, maybe I didn't have a choice.

What had she been about to tell me about my father? She'd found him—and I felt relieved, but that warred with the knowledge that my cousin and only friend was about to die. It felt like an awful trading of one life for another.

I sank onto the edge of my bed, tears streaming freely down my cheeks now. I wished I had risked it all from the beginning. Even in that worst-case scenario, it would be me in that cell awaiting death, not Emme.

Now, it was just me and my broken breaths in a dark, silent house.

I blinked and a vision unfolded—there and gone so quick, I only caught a glimpse.

*The Great Hall. A shadow, moving. A slithering sense of dread waiting for me there.*

I wasn't the only one awake.

My gaze flicked to the door. Why would my future show me something outside this room? Slowly, I padded across the room and tested the knob one more time.

The latch gave, and the door swung inward.

My eyes widened, knowing it couldn't have been my uncle who'd freed me.

My shoes rustled softly along the wooden floors as I slipped to the other end of the house. Both sets of French doors bracketing the hall hung open, like they always did, and I peeked around the corner, heart in my throat. Moonlight beamed through the wall of windows. A wisp of shadow moved at the end of the hall and then all was still. Threads of fear trailed between my shoulder blades. I quieted my breathing and listened.

Nothing.

Had I imagined it?

But I couldn't quite accept the idea, because my visions only came when my future hit a crossroads—which meant *something* had just happened in this great hall that would change my life. Heeding my hammering heart, I moved down the objects lining the hall, taking inventory to see if anything was stolen. A fine film of dust coated the cases, vases, and frames.

I circled everything twice and couldn't find anything. Not a snuffbox slightly shifted or a bit of rug askew. Everything was exactly as it had always been. I released my breath. I didn't have time to be chasing hunches. Emme only had a few hours left.

Spine snapping up, I headed for the exit—then halted. Slowly, I pivoted back, eyes going to my grandfather's statue. As I studied it, my head fell to one side. Something seemed off, but I didn't know what. He looked the same.

I swiped a finger along his coarse shoulder and inspected it in the limited light. My blood stopped cold.

No dust.

After everything I'd been through, I knew better than to believe in coincidences.

After circumventing the statue, I heaved myself against it until it fell to the floor. But it didn't crash. The moment it hit the ground, it gave a soft thud and crumbled into a strange substance I'd never seen before. Dark gray and aerated, the material had an outside crust that protected a loamy, springy center. It felt a bit like bread, and even stranger, it was no longer heavy, even though I'd had to use my entire weight to tip the statue over.

Yet, it was not the material of the statue that caught my interest most. It was what lay in the center of the carnage, moonlight glinting off its shiny surface.

A black feather.

Cold sweat pebbled on my skin. My grandmother's bracelet had vanished. Grandfather had entrusted the secret to me and no other. No one else knew. No one else ...

*I'm so sorry, Dolly.* Those were his words while he'd been bleeding out last night in my room.

A blue ring and the power of illusions.

*I am not. The Samaritan.*

*I will always tell you the truth.*

Knees buckling, I sank to the floor, but I never hit—I free fell into the center of the earth, and it swallowed me, burying me along with every tender hope. I clutched the feather in my trembling hands as my head shook, slowly at first, and then faster. This wasn't a dream. *None* of it was a dream. Then the stinging began—a prick that morphed into a knife, twisting in my chest, screwing out my heart and leaving an ugly, mangled mess in its wake.

A guttural wail scratched up my throat and flooded around the room, unleashing a darkness that had been struggling for breath but now consumed everything in its path. I inhaled it, seeing red. Seeing black. Seeing the truth. My hands clawed the fake statue remains and beat the floor with it, pulverizing all that was left of my grandfather's likeness. I threw it at the window with a scream that was sure to wake my uncle. But I suddenly didn't care.

Because someone had stolen my grandfather's statue. Someone had taken the bracelet inside. And as it turned out,

Ashley *had* been telling the truth. Ignorance *was* bliss. He was not the Samaritan, trying to rescue my father. He was the one who'd abducted him.

Ashley was the Rook.

# Epilogue
## Ashley

The floor rose toward me, making me feel like I'd shrunk several inches in the last few hours.

In a way, I had.

I took one last look at the bar of dim light under the door before forcing myself to turn the brass knob and step inside.

The air smelled slightly sour from the milk the cat was licking in a corner. A kerosene lamp burned on the table and Miles half-sat next to it, arms folded and brown eyes guarded as he watched me enter. The low light cast a weary pallor on our plans around the flat, and I couldn't help but agree with the tiredness; the longer Bram was gone, the harder it was to remember why we were doing this. I silently shut the door.

"You stole my slant." Miles's voice was gravel.

I turned to the side, making my moves deliberate, methodical, stupidly trying to stall the storm I knew was coming—the one that had been brewing since Bram's lifeless body was lowered into the sea. My gaze strayed to the bracelet on my wrist: a silver band as thick as the tip of my little finger, with two inverted lion's heads devouring a center sapphire. Few knew of its ability to temporarily steal someone else's magic by touching them while wearing it—but then, few knew the bracelets even existed.

Centuries ago, they'd been scattered and hidden among England's elite, but now I had six out of the seven. One encased in a chandelier. One twisted into a tapestry. One sewn into a wedding dress. One plucked from a grave. One stolen from Lark. And now, one stolen from Dorothy.

I'd walked her house the day before the kidnapping to hunt for the bracelet, making myself invisible when a suspicious servant had walked in on me scoping out the lab. When I couldn't find it, I'd had to form a new plan.

Tanner's note—the one Dorothy had blackmailed me with—led me to Westminster where I was supposed to gain the final bracelet, but the Samaritan had caught on to my spy and planted bad information. Then set up his ambush.

Involuntarily, I brushed a hand against my collarbone, where the wound still throbbed. Only through blind luck had the knife found me when the Samaritan threw it into the fog. He'd worn his mask through the altercation, but thanks to the crazed man's confirmation at the insane asylum, I knew the face underneath.

And I would deal with the Samaritan later.

The magic inside the sapphire strained against it, eager to return to Miles, its rightful owner. My time was almost up.

Instead of answering, I dug through the coat pocket and captured the statue in my fist, and when I extended my hand, flexed fingers open, the statue of Dorothy's grandfather sprang to life in the middle of the room. It looked larger in the cramped flat. Out of place.

I hung my coat on the peg, taking my time. Maybe if I took long enough, it would dull the self-loathing slicing my insides and I could look him in the eye again. "You refused to help me," I finally said. "And it needed to be done."

He shook his head. "You told me we'd only steal a bracelet

when it was about to fall into the wrong hands. But in Dorothy's care, this one was safe. It still *is* safe, inside this statue, because no one else knows about it. Take it back before she notices it's missing—before she discovers you're the Rook."

"She'll never know."

"She will. Take it back."

The rigid edge in his voice made it sound both like a plea and a threat. I exhaled through my nose, dreading this conversation, but knowing it was time. My face hardened, and I turned and finally locked eyes with Miles.

"No."

He flinched like I had struck him. He fell silent for a long minute, studying me, glaring. We were at an impasse. He was tired of losing. I had finally pushed him too far. He worked his jaw, seething, sparks of flint shooting from his eyes as he willed me to burst into flames.

And maybe I would catch on fire. Maybe I would burn. But I had been burning all my life and if he wanted to feel the wild anger raging under my skin, I would let him.

"You need it for something," he said at last, softly. His lips twisted in disgust. "That's why you're not content to just keep them safe. You've been planning this all along."

Instead of answering, I kicked the statue. It crashed to the floor, the head rolling away. Where it had severed from the neck, in a pile of dust and stone, a bracelet identical to the one around my wrist gleamed. With a reverent touch, I picked it up. Six out of seven. Only one more to go.

"It's a myth, Ashley. You don't even know if combining them will work. No one does. Yet you'll sacrifice everything Bram did to bring down the Order—everything he *trained* us to do—on a reckless gamble?"

I shook my head, but it wasn't a denial.

"You know what happens if we lose," he shouted. "The

Order never would've found this bracelet, but now because of your *addiction*—"

That fire erupted into an inferno and I shot to my feet. "You're not the one who has to live like this!" I jammed the bracelet into the coat, ripping a seam on the pocket. "Like you're a *thing*. Like you were *made*—meant for only one purpose, a terrible purpose, and your mortal frame is the only thing holding it at bay."

*It's going to shred me apart.*

*It already has.*

Raking a hand through my hair, I shook my head. "I'm not addicted to the magic, Miles. I want to rip it out of my blood, but I need every bracelet to do it. And unlike *you*, I'm not content to sit around waiting for a new life while the old one eats me away."

His eyes glimmered, and I rammed the guilt down.

"I'm not addicted," I repeated. "I just. Can't. Stop it."

"You can, but you don't want to." His voice was deathly quiet. I'd broken the wall of unsaid things between us, and now it was his turn to tear at the rock. "Every time you use your magic, the mutation worsens."

I gritted my teeth. "It's going to kill me anyway—!"

"No, *you* have a death wish! You live for the game, raising the stakes ever higher because it thrills you to look over the edge while the wind is pushing you, to see how far you might fall. And one of these days you won't be able to resist the temptation, and you'll jump."

"It will be better than living like this."

"You don't mean that."

I didn't used to, but now I wasn't so sure. I wasn't sure of anything.

Miles's face, usually a study of stone, contorted with so many emotions it couldn't settle on one—and I knew it was because I had fissured something fundamental inside him. "Where is her father?"

Everything in me stilled. The clock on the mantle did too, jumping forward a minute in complete silence. Now it was my turn to glare at him.

"Where is Geoffrey St. James?" Miles repeated.

"You're a real cad, you know that?" I muttered.

"Answer the question, Ashley."

"You really believe me capable of—"

"I used to believe a lot of things about you!" His face twisted bitterly and he slapped the table, narrowly missing the lamp. "With all the rumors of people disappearing, I decided the real culprit just needed a scapegoat, and black feathers were easy to come by. Kidnapping people—it didn't seem like you.

"But now ..." He shook his head again, mouth working. "Now it all makes sense. You kidnapped her father so you could get close to her and find out where the bracelet is. Even *she* was the means to an end. Turns out there is nothing you will not do—*no one* you will not disabuse yourself of—in order to escape your own mind. Even me." The last two words were quieter, said with a tremor while his eyes dropped to the bracelet around my wrist. Hot betrayal squirmed in my chest, and I knew he felt the same— just as I knew I was to blame for both. His lips flared in disgust. "I want no part of it."

"Then *leave.*"

I saw it coming. He shot forward, forearm to my collarbone, shoving me into the wall so hard it knocked the wind from my lungs and my wound blazed with agony. But I let him, because I didn't have any heart to fight back. He stared me down, jaw tight, breath hard, fist winding back.

*Do it.*

I relaxed completely to make it easier.

*Clout me.*

*I can never have peace, but maybe this will help you find some.*

His features trembled with rage, and it traveled into his arm pinning me. For a moment, I was sure he'd do it—until I glimpsed the angry tear slipping down his face, gone a moment later when he shoved off me.

In one swift move, Miles ripped his brown trench coat off the peg and slid into it. "I won't turn you in—for Bram. He wouldn't have wanted it. He always knew you were destined for greatness; though greatness and *goodness* are not the same thing." He inched forward, eyes like steel. "But if I catch one whiff of you targeting someone else—one little twitch of your devil hands—I won't hesitate."

Involuntarily, my eyes strayed to his pocket where I knew he kept his pistol loaded.

Miles tracked the movement and answered the question I didn't ask. "Whatever it takes." He stalked out, leaving behind a history so broken and convoluted I didn't know how to fix it.

And maybe I didn't want to. Maybe I'd always known it would end this way; with me staring at his back, knee-deep in a carnage of my own making. Maybe some part of me had always wanted him to break away, so he didn't have to watch me turn into this thing I was becoming.

My gaze drifted to the statue and the shambles of stone littering the floor. To the dull bracelet around my wrist, now devoid of Miles's borrowed magic. I took one last look at his hat. His cat in the corner. At myself. All things he'd left behind.

My jaw clenched. And I slammed the door.

# Nicholas

The day started typically enough. I bought a morning paper and cut across the Strand to find a cup of coffee and a sausage roll. If someone had cared, they could've followed my crumbs like Hansel and Gretel right up to the steps of the ivy-riddled government building that covered as a printing shop, its shiny plaque half hidden in leaves. Inside, I passed cold cylinder presses, drawers full of letter plates glinting from disuse, and stacks of paper that would never be passed to the masses. As usual, the rest of the Lightfoot agents wouldn't arrive for several more hours.

The only untypical thing about this morning was the bleary-eyed girl sitting in my office.

Mussed, curly hair hung in a braid over one of her shoulders, covering the top of a high-collared dress. Her eyes were puffy and red-rimmed like she'd been crying, but there was a fierce, devastated set to them, like she'd been to hell and the only way to crawl was up.

I knew the look well.

Before me sat a girl who was hungry for vengeance. That was always the best hunger to work with. Her next words confirmed my suspicion. "I accept your offer, Mr. Hart."

I cocked my head and tried not to outwardly show how pleased I was as I circled my desk and set my briefcase down. "That is excellent—"

"But I have a few conditions."

I'd expected nothing less, so I nodded for her to continue.

"My cousin is currently being held in a cell, awaiting her hanging which will take place in an hour. I want her freed. And I want a guarantee that neither of us will ever be arrested or prosecuted for using our magic."

Since I'd already been planning on allowing her slanting rights, that part wasn't an issue. I'd have to pull a few strings for allowing the same for the cousin, but it would be worth it. As for getting someone out of a hanging, we'd done it—discretionally—before.

"Done," I said.

"And I need a new residence far away from my uncle, with enough of a wage to support myself."

"Naturally. What else?"

She leaned forward in her chair. "You said you can teach me to expand my magic. What does that mean?"

I sank into my office chair. "Most people, through a series of mental exercises, can multiply the magical particles in their blood. Often this manifests in a new, tangential ability—or increases your capacity, letting you use your slant for longer. It varies person to person, and there is always a limit, but you are capable of more, Miss St. James.

"I am interested primarily in your ability to see the future. Tracking a man as slippery as the Rook has proven to be nigh impossible. London is full of shadows. But—to see where he will strike before he does ... that might finally give us an upper hand. Given you can control it."

She stared at her lap, face grave like she didn't like the path of her thoughts. She was silent for a long time. Almost long enough to be suspicious. "What do you plan to do to him ... once you catch him?"

My eyebrows raised, and after a moment she glanced at me. I thought I'd detected the thinnest thread of sympathy in her voice, but the eyes that met me were hard as granite. Imagined or not, I wouldn't sugar-coat the truth. "We'll question him. We'll seize the magical bracelets he stole. And then he'll swing by his neck until all the rooks in London have pecked at his carcass and he's nothing but a pile of bones."

She swallowed but said nothing, gaze drifting to the window behind me.

I stood again, resting the tips of my fingers on my desk. "We'll have you fill out some paperwork, sign a confidentiality agreement among other things, and then we can get to work. Our first task will be to uncover the Rook's identity, since we still don't know who, exactly, he is."

Her large eyes swept up and for a moment I couldn't help but be drawn in by their allure. Not for the first time either. But what she said next, low and thick with hatred, fascinated me far more.

"I do."


TO BE CONTINUED ...

# Acknowledgments

As a writer I grew so, so much with this book, and it was a lot of firsts for me: first time in the Victorian era, first time writing multiple POVs, first time writing from a man's POV, first time writing magic, first time banging my head on my desk and questioning whether I ever possessed the smallest scrap of talent, first time lying about it being my first time banging my head on my desk.

I'm so grateful to God for his direction and inspiration. Along the way I questioned whether this type of story was even possible to tell, and He kept guiding me through it.

It was also my first time with a whole team behind me, and I want to thank Tanya and everyone at OHB who worked on this story. Shout out to Madi who basically did all of my chemistry research and had the brains where I don't. I loathe renaming characters, so thank you to Alli Anderson for helping me with a certain surname! Thank you to all the beta readers who worked on this story, of which there are too many to name but filled in all my cracks and saw this book from the angle it needed!

Sally, you get your own paragraph, because holy cow do you know how to cheerlead. Thank you for responding enthusiastically to every one of my annoying texts, for working tirelessly on aspects you didn't have to. You championed this story and fought for it in more ways than one. I'm forever grateful.

I want to thank Alayna and her eyes' inhuman ability to say *Yes, of course I would like to spend two more hours brainstorming with you! Never mind the other hundred I've already spent! It's my favorite thing in the world!* And you claim you're no actress.

For my fans who stuck with me through a genre/publishing change: I love you, and you are the best!

For anyone in my family who was appalled and disturbed at the hand-chopping-off part: DON'T BLAME ME IT WAS DANIEL'S IDEA.

Lastly, I would like to thank Daniel, who grows less and less helpful to my writing process with each passing year. But, you have always cheered me on. I see the pride that shines in your eyes. And you will always be my inspiration. (So maybe you're helpful after all.)

# Also by Jessica Scarlett

**Slanted London**

Town of Shadows

**Wycliffe Family Series**

A Lily in Disguise

A Lord of Many Masks

A Lady on the Chase

# About the Author

Jessica Scarlett writes amazing books and lame author bios. She hates the pressure of encapsulating everything about herself in a hundred words or less, because she's too divergent, dynamic, and different for that. And simultaneously not that interesting.

She is the author of the Wycliffe Family Series, Slanted London series, and a couple plays. When not writing, she loves composing music, laughing with her four kids, or doing life on a ranch in Utah with her cinnamon-roll husband.

www.ingramcontent.com/pod-product-compliance
Lightning Source LLC
Chambersburg PA
CBHW020528110726
47899CB00004B/1291